June Barraclough is of the same generation as the children in *Family Circle*. She was born in the West Riding of Yorkshire and after attending a local grammar school studied in Paris and at Somerville College, Oxford. She has been a teacher and lecturer of various languages and literatures in schools and colleges and has published a translation, two anthologies and two fictionalized memoirs. In 1994 *Portrait of Maud* was short-listed for the Romantic Novel of the Year. *Family Circle* is her twenty-third novel. She is married to David Wedgwood Benn and they have a philosopher son, specializing in Medical Ethics, a daughter who read History at Somerville, and an extremely lively grandson.

FAMILY CIRCLE

Sally, the daughter of Sir Jack Page of Pettiwell House in Kent, Jennie, the daughter of his housekeeper, and Caroline, Sally's cousin, are all brought together at the outbreak of war in 1939. Though from very different backgrounds, they grow up together amidst international and domestic conflict. In the 1950s, they make their tentative beginnings in work and love, against the background of Pettiwell, London and Paris. But their upbringing in Pettiwell does not prepare them for the changes that come with the following decade and all of them, married or single, will have to adapt their adult lives to the New World that begins in the 1960s.

Books by June Barraclough
Published by The House of Ulverscroft:

TIME WILL TELL
FAMILY SNAPSHOTS
THE VILLA VIOLETTA
NO TIME LIKE THE PRESENT
ANOTHER SUMMER
LOVING AND LEARNING
THE FAMILY FACE
EMMA ELIZA
THE WAYS OF LOVE

JUNE BARRACLOUGH

FAMILY CIRCLE

Complete and Unabridged

ULVERSCROFT
Leicester

First published in Great Britain in 2003 by
Robert Hale Limited
London

First Large Print Edition
published 2004
by arrangement with
Robert Hale Limited
London

The moral right of the author has been asserted

British Library CIP Data

Barraclough, June
    Family Circle.—Large print ed.—
    Ulverscroft large print series: family saga
    1. Female friendship—Fiction
    2. World War, *1939 – 1945*—Fiction
    3. Large type books
    I. Title
    823.9′14 [F]

    ISBN 1–84395–672–1

Published by
F. A. Thorpe (Publishing)
Anstey, Leicestershire

Set by Words & Graphics Ltd.
Anstey, Leicestershire
Printed and bound in Great Britain by
T. J. International Ltd., Padstow, Cornwall

This book is printed on acid-free paper

Acknowledgement

The quotation on page 341 is from poem 15 in the collection *Veinte poemas de amor y una canción desesperada* by Pablo Neruda (1904 — 1973) published Santiago de Chile, 1924.

Part One

THREE VOICES

1

JENNIE

When I remember Pettiwell House there are always two pictures in my mind. One is of the highly polished table next to the front stairs in the entrance hall. It is summer and the sun is streaming through the half-open oak door of the vestibule, and through a long window. Outside I have noticed a stripy orange-and-green curtain hanging on a side door to stop the sun blistering the paint on the woodwork, but I remember going through the big front door of the house, which I am not supposed to do.

I can see a large crystal vase on the hall table in which are arranged sweetpeas of the most delicate colours imaginable — pale pink and salmon pink and dark pink, pale mauve and a darker purple, white and yellowy white. The flowers smell so wonderful I can't believe they are real. There is nobody about, so I stand on tiptoe to sniff the scent for as long as I dare. I am only small — I must be about five years old — so I can smell only the lowest blooms arranged over the side of the vase.

The hall is hot and the floor as polished as the table. It is absolutely quiet, until I hear a door open next to the passage that leads in the end to the kitchens, and so I slip back out through the vestibule and the front door, and on to the grass, and trot back under the ground-floor windows round the house to the part I live in with my mother and father.

The visual memory of the flowers is always accompanied by their scent. I used to think that these particular tints of pink and mauve possessed the 'true' pink-and-mauve smell, even when I discovered that pink roses and carnations had a different scent, and that the purple of Michaelmas daisies did not smell like mauve sweetpeas.

My other vivid early memory is of the library, also on the ground floor of Pettiwell House. I must have been helping Ethel, a housemaid at that time, to polish a long table. This time it is winter and I am looking at a painting hanging not too high up on the wall. I think at first that it might be a picture of the very room we are in, because in it there is a big low table, like a desk, rather like the table I am helping to polish. On the table in the picture there stands a brass lamp with a shade of bright green, but there is no such lamp here. The picture also has two or three girls sitting all bunched up together at one end of the table, looking at a big open book placed on what looks like a music stand. There is a man, too, seated directly behind the stand. However, it is the green lampshade that attracts me most.

'We ought to have a lamp like that,' I say to Ethel.

When I study the painting more closely I see little pictures on the wall inside the frame, but they are not like the pictures on the real walls here, so it cannot be a painting of the Pettiwell library. I remember asking myself later: what if one of the pictures on the wall in the painting was a picture of the green lamp picture, and that picture had tiny pictures on its walls? It made me feel queer. You could go on for ever. I told my father about this, and he said it was like a Chinese box. I didn't know what a Chinese box was and he didn't explain.

I would look at the lamp picture whenever I was allowed in the library, and the colour of its green shade became my favourite colour. Years later I realized that the picture was a copy of a famous one painted in 1830, twenty years after the building of the original Pettiwell House was finished.

I didn't know then about the dates of houses, but I loved everything about Petti-well. I thought it must be the biggest and most beautiful house in England. Later I realized, of course, that it was not very big or even perhaps especially beautiful, only one of the hundreds of pleasant late eighteenth century and Regency houses built for gentlemen and scattered all over England. Ours might have begun as a square brick house, but about forty years later a stone wing had been added on one side, and at the back, where our quarters were. The front of the house from the outside did not give the impression of being large. Inside our part of the house a door led to a corridor between 'home' and the main house, and at the end of this there was another door, covered in green baize. If you went through that, you arrived in yet another passage with one door leading to the housekeeper's sitting room, which had once been a servants' hall, and where Mother worked during the day. The days of sixteen servants, in the time of Sir Jack Page's grandparents, were long past. The other door opened into the big entrance hall of the main house where I had smelled the sweetpeas that summer morning.

The façade of the house was of white stucco, and there were lawns spread around, with a drive on the far side that led down in one direction to curly wrought-iron gates set in a high wall. A path wound round from this drive to the back of the house in the direction of the old stables. I was told that the fancy gates had been fashioned a long time ago by the 'Page Iron Works'. I thought they must be famous, though they were far from being as large or grand as the gates at Penshurst, a great house I had once been taken to see in Sally's father's car. I was often taken out for a treat, and to be a companion for Sally.

Father told me that the Page family firm had made their money patenting a form of wrought iron. He did not explain what exactly that meant, except to say that our Sir Jack hadn't so much to do with the firm now. I knew without anyone telling me that the Pages were no longer rich, although of course they were richer than we were.

We were only half a mile from the village of Pettiwell, even nearer than that to the church, which was at the edge of the village near some old cottages. To me, the village felt a lot further away, especially if you approached it by a roundabout path, the one I called the Secret Lane. This was an old, narrow, elm-and-blackthorn-edged lane that must once have been a bridle path and which led to a back entrance to the house on the opposite side to the stables.

This lane went by what had once been an ornamental pond, which I could see from my bedroom window at the back, but which was now a duck pond belonging to the farmer at Pettiwell Farm, our nearest neighbour. Further on, the lane widened out and reached the main road, but you could imagine the house was hidden and secret if you came home that way. Across the fields on our side of the Secret Lane you could see farm buildings. The farmer did not use that lane any more for his vehicles, and only ducks waddled along there. Sally told me that once upon a time the farm had been the Home Farm and had belonged to her great-grandfather. I knew that the family had picnicked there in summer and had enjoyed skating parties in winter, for I had seen a photograph of ladies in enormous hats lounging by a little Chinese bridge that had once arched over the pond. On another photograph, the same ladies were wearing furry hats and muffs, about to venture out on skates. The photographs were in heavy albums with gold clasps kept in a cabinet in what had been the gun room. Lady Page did not mind our looking at them.

The land and the farmhouse had been sold off by Sally's grandfather. Sally wished *she* lived on a farm. She loved animals, especially horses, but in my childhood there were only two horses in the Pettiwell stables, and later only one, and then Sally's pony, Caesar, died. Sally talked a lot about things I didn't understand at all and was just not interested in: saddles and bridles and hunting. Not that her family hunted. Her father had been a member of the harriers; it was not real hunting country, even if there was a picture in the breakfast room of a hunt, showing men in top hats, wearing what Sally taught me to call pink coats, though they were really red.

I often used to look over in the direction of the farm from my first-floor window on summer evenings, and glimpse the elms hiding the pond and the willows, and it was one of my favourite strolls at all seasons. From the window in winter I could imagine a silvery mirror of water, with the pond back as it once had been before it shrank and became shallow and muddy. Nobody ever skated there now, or even went for picnics there in the summer. Poor old pond, I thought.

When I was a little older than the self who had smelled the sweetpeas or had been ravished by the greenness of the green lamp, or had christened the Secret Lane, I tried to imagine what Pettiwell House had been like before the Great War, or further back than that. The Great War was the one the grown-ups all talked about; it had ended twelve years before I was born, but at the time those twelve years seemed to me to be as long as a century. Later on, in my history lessons at school, I found those pre-Great War years described as 'the Edwardian dusk some people had believed to be a golden dawn'. I thought that was a beautiful sentence.

My mother, Mrs Polly Wilson, housekeeper to the Pages, had never known the house at that time, but she told me that there would have been heaps of servants: a butler, one or two footmen, a cook, a kitchen-maid and a scullery-maid, a head housemaid with at least two under housemaids, and a lady's-maid. That was just for inside the house. Outside, there had been a groom and a head gardener with two under gardeners and some stable-lads. The footmen had gone first, in the Great War, and Mother had never known the butler, though his pantry was still there, now supervised by herself. For a time the family kept on a cook, and two housemaids, and I think I can remember a fourteen-year-old girl in the kitchen, but there had been five men doing what Father was doing in my childhood. I added up the number of maids doing the work my mother, with the help of Ethel and Elsie, and later just Ethel, accomplished, and I asked Mother whether Sally's grandmother, another Lady Page, thus named in the old photographs, would have had a lady's-maid to do her hair. Mother said, Yes, but our Lady Page could do her own hair. Even so, I thought my mother was more like a lady's-maid, since she had once been a sort of maid to Sally's mother before she got married. Mother told me Sally's grandmother had died when I was a baby, but by then there were no longer enough servants to look after the house properly. Somehow, money had been lost, so that when 'our' war came along the Pages were used to managing without help other than what Mother and Father and Ethel could give them.

Once upon a time it had all been very different. No empty rooms then, shut up and shuttered, swept out only twice a year, containing furniture shrouded under dust-sheets. Most of these rooms were upstairs and no longer used, including some of the rooms on the first floor of our wing next to where Elsie and Ethel slept. The top floor of the main house was shut up too and we called these rooms the attics. I liked to imagine servants who had once slept there, and was hopeful of a ghost or two. Even though my family lived prosaically on the ground floor at the back of the house, with two rooms over, I was still proud of belonging to Pettiwell House.

Mother had once been Polly Hicks. She

had begun as under housemaid to a London family, the grandparents of our Lady Page, who had once been Ruth Ogilvie. Mother called her first employers the 'Old Ogilvies'. I was interested in names and I liked their Christian names, Alexander and Christina. These maternal grandparents of Sally had lived in London in Westminster Square where Mother had started in service at the age of fifteen, in 1905, the very year Lady Page's elder sister, Clare, had been born. Clare and Sally's parents were called the 'Young Ogilvies' by my mother and others, and in 1905 they were home on leave from India.

Our Lady Page, Ruth, was born three years after her sister. By then my mother was eighteen, had been three years in the Westminster Square house, and helped to bring up Baby Ruth when the Young Ogilvies had eventually gone back East. It seemed odd to me to leave your children to be brought up by your parents and their servants, but because of this Mother had known Ruth Ogilvie and her sister very well when they were children. It had not taken long for her to stop being an under housemaid and become a general help to the Old Ogilvies when the babies' nursemaid had suddenly given in her notice, just after the Young Ogilvies left England.

Mother did not marry my father, William Wilson, until 1929. By then she was working for her old employers' younger granddaughter, Ruth, who had married Jack Page of Pettiwell. I found it odd that Sally Page's mother was so much younger than mine. Ruth had been 'out' only three years — my mother explained this peculiar expression to me — when she had agreed to marry into the Page family. My father had worked on and off for the Page household ever since the end of the Great War, in which he had been batman to Jack Page. I gathered they were both of them lucky to survive the Somme battlefield. After a shot at helping to run a chicken farm, which enterprise failed, Father had worked for Sir Jack's father as gardener and chauffeur and general factotum. He didn't know then that he was one day to marry the maid of his employer's son's fiancée, whom he met first at Pettiwell when Jack was courting her! My mother, still Polly Hicks then, had been detailed to be of use to Miss Ruth on her weekend visits over from London; or sometimes my father had driven Jack up to London and been entertained in the kitchens of the house in Westminster Square.

Polly did not waste a moment getting hitched to such an eminently responsible man, and she was married to my father even before Jack Page and Miss Ruth were wed. There was a great scarcity of young men and I don't suppose Mother had thought she'd ever find one, never mind such a one as Father. He had had a pretty terrible time in the war and needed a woman to look after him, she told me later.

'It was Fate,' Father said. 'We were destined to meet.'

In my childhood he worked both indoors, putting up curtains, shifting furniture and cleaning the silver, and also outside in the gardens. He liked garden work best, for it suited his temperament. I believe after his experience of war he always preferred plants to people. He was an intelligent man, and if at first — very occasionally — the older Pages had wanted to pretend they still had a butler he'd been happy to go along with the idea. Soon, though, he was the only male help, for Jack Page drove his own motor and could not afford an army of gardeners.

'Sir Jack had to cut his coat according to his cloth,' said Mother. He wasn't Sir Jack at first, only after his father died, not long after his son Jack's marriage. Jack's mother, Lydia Page died two or three years after her husband.

I don't think either my mother or my father thought of themselves as servants exactly.

14

Mother had been very much needed by Ruth Page after the birth of her daughter Sally Charlotte, eighteen months after my own birth. Mother had not been called the housekeeper at first, but by her early forties she was certainly in charge. The new Lady Page, apart from needing help with the baby, was not used to domestic management, and she very soon depended on Mother. Cooks came and went, and housemaids left in a sulk and went to work in the town where they could earn more as shop-girls. Kitchen help was cheap, but never stayed long either. Even in the early nineteen thirties the lowliest maid could find work in the paper factory in the nearest big town in our county. Mother was not a hard taskmistress but she was thorough, and by the time the war broke out the house, if much reduced from its former glories, was at least well run.

I always supposed Mother loved her job. I think now she was just used to hard work. I had also supposed that she must have loved Father passionately or she would never have risked giving up her post in London, deciding to marry him after, for those days, such a very brief courtship. I realize now that she wanted a child before it was too late. She had become indispensable to the Ogilvies and they would never have wanted her to leave after almost a quarter of a century in their service, if their granddaughter had not needed her more. Mother was almost forty-one when I was born. I feel I only just made it.

She wanted to name me Johanna after her own mother, a name I'd have preferred when I was a bit older, but Father didn't like it. He preferred Joy, from Joyce, a very popular name at that time, but unfortunately one Mother did not like. They came to an agreement, since she rather liked the name Jennie, and persuaded Father to like it too, so Jennie I became, with Joyce as a second name. Mother had always wanted me to have two names, in case I didn't like the first — she'd never liked her own name, Polly. She had wanted me to be called Sylvia for my second name but had given way to Father, who thought it was too 'fancy'. This was typical of their way of doing things, and J.J. Wilson I became.

At school there were heaps of girls called Joan, and some called Joyce, yet nobody except me called Jennie. Later on, people thought I had been christened Jennifer, which was of course untrue. Sally Page had two friends called Jennifer, a rather stylish name then, and one I wouldn't have minded having, so when I was at university I did not contradict people who assumed I was a

Jennifer. I was quite fond of Jennie though, sometimes shortened by my father to Jen. Mother on the other hand always kept my full name when she talked to me. I loved listening to Mother's story of my naming and all the stories of Pettiwell, and Mother's and Father's past, and even tales of my own babyhood.

★   ★   ★

The Young Ogilvies, Andrew and Laura, still away in India throughout most of their daughters' childhoods, did not return home permanently until about the time of Ruth's marriage. Once returned for good they lived at first in the Westminster Square house with Christina, old Alexander Ogilvie having died suddenly at about this time. When Andrew and Laura returned to Westminster Square my mother was relieved she was no longer to work there. She told me later that Ruth Page felt she hardly knew her own mother. Mother had loved the Old Ogilvies and been close to the girls, especially to Ruth, but I could tell she had not been very fond of the newcomers. It had been yet another reason to get married, and why she had been so happy to go along with Father and work first for Jack Page's parents at Pettiwell, and then the

17

newly married couple. When Jack became Sir Jack, Ruth, who was about thirteen years younger than her husband, became Lady Page. I had the impression from Mother that Ruth had not found her own mother of much help when Sally was born, rather the contrary. The maternity nurse was incompetent, and Ruth, whose own mother-in-law was still at Pettiwell, suffering from her last illness, was desperate. That's how my mother became once again indispensable.

Christina Ogilvie, of whom my mother was so very fond, died when I was four. I can remember Mother going off to London for the funeral dressed all in black. By that time I was the playmate of three-year-old Sally Page, soon to be regarded by me as my best friend.

Ruth Page's sister Clare had been living in France for some time. She had married a painter called Francis Fitzpatrick and had a daughter Caroline who was older than Sally and me. It was not until 1938, when the clouds of war were gathering, that we saw the Fitzpatricks at Pettiwell. About Clare Fitzpatrick and her husband and family I knew little.

The Page family had never gone back to the old pre-1914 way of life, or even the less formal life of the twenties, and when the next war came along, Pettiwell was to have under its wing not only the Pages and Sally, and her new baby brother James, and ourselves of course, but also Ruth's sister and brother-in-law and their two children Caroline and Lily. Eventually, the Fitzpatrick parents went off on war work in London and abroad, leaving Caroline and her sister with us at Pettiwell.

When Jack Page inherited the house he ought to have sold up, cut his losses, started in some new business, and left to live nearer his part-time City job, but family loyalty held him in Pettiwell. I think he must have had the idea that his father-in-law, Andrew Ogilvie, would help them financially when he inherited money after old Alexander's death. Andrew might not be able to keep up the London residence indefinitely, so perhaps they might share the expenses of Pettiwell and come to live with them there. This was not to be, and I feel sure Ruth was relieved. The Young Ogilvies were themselves in straitened circumstances. When Colonel Ogilvie retired from the Indian Army in his late fifties, he had returned home on a pension, and according to my mother, had not been left a great deal by his parents, for everyone had lost money in the depression. Mother knew pretty well what it had cost to run the Westminster Square house after the first war. Christina Ogilvie must have confided certain details to her. I realized she had been trusted far beyond the usual trust accorded to a faithful servant of twenty-five years. Mother had been sure they would not help financially with Pettiwell and was as relieved as Lady Page that they would not. The couple sometimes came over before the war, and during the war stayed with us for six months after their London house was damaged, but then they moved to Oxford where Laura had relatives.

I heard some of these items from the family's past when I eaves-dropped on my parents' conversation. Mother relished telling me family stories yet was always careful not to criticize people to me. I had sharp ears however and was perhaps preternaturally sensitive to her 'atmospheres' and opinions. I was very curious about families, and it was from listening to her over the years, that I pieced together the narrative of my parents' lives, and Sally's parents' lives, remembering and filling in details when I was older. I found it all out bit by bit, but in my childhood, as the housekeeper's child, I took all the arrangements at Pettiwell House for granted. After the war, events decided for them all, when it was found that the Westminster Square house, which had suffered from bomb damage, would have to be demolished.

Fortunately the Young Ogilvies had put all their goods in store.

In my childhood the Pages were looked up to in the village even if Sir Jack was not the sort to throw his weight around. The Great War had crushed something out of them all. Sir Jack was easy-going about everything but his family's past. He would have put up with his in-laws so long as he could keep the house going, but was probably relieved he did not have to.

You may be wondering how it was that I, the daughter of the housekeeper and the general-factotum-cum-gardener, should have a best friend who was the daughter of a baronet, even a relatively impoverished one. We had become friends when I was three and a half and Sally not quite two, since neither of us had anyone else to play with. I was an only child, and used to follow Father round the kitchen-garden where he kept an eye on me whilst Mother sorted out the errands and the cleaning and the menus. The Page nurse-maid, who had followed the unsatisfactory maternity nurse, was not to stay very long, but she used to walk her charge in a perambulator round the grounds, often ending up in 'our' part of the garden.

Eventually, when Sally graduated from the pram and ran around, we got to know each other and ran around together. I thought that Sally looked a bit like Patsy, my dolly, who had a mop of curls and big blue eyes, and I became as fond of my new little playmate as I had once been of my doll. I believe she enjoyed playing with me too. Her parents never tried to stop us becoming friends, my provenance being well known. I was an over-imaginative child and had decided that my father must have saved Sir Jack's life in the war, though nothing definite had ever been said about that to me. Mother had just said that Sally's father and mine had both survived 'only by the skin of their teeth'. She had not known Father then of course. On the other hand, she had known Sally's mother from the time she was born, even if she had only been a servant-girl of eighteen at the time of the future Lady Page's arrival in the world. Mother had already had the experience of bringing up her own sisters and brothers before she left for service in London.

When I was about thirteen, influenced by the sensational novels I read, I made up a story about an aristocratic friend of Sir Jack falling in love with my mother, the humble maid, so that my 'real' father was a lord. I never really believed it, nor did I recount this flight of fancy to anyone. A year or so later I was ashamed of my silly fantasies when I realized I looked rather like my father, whom I loved, and that you did not need to be aristocratic to be noble.

★   ★   ★

When I was five I went as a pupil to the village school. Sally wanted to go with me but had to wait, and then she would not be sent to my school — democracy had its limits, I suppose — but would begin lessons with a governess at the house of another family in the next village. Sally would be destined for boarding-school when she was twelve. On the other hand, when I was ten I'd have to try for a scholarship at the grammar school in the nearest town. This was my mother's plan, and I went along with it enthusiastically.

Both my parents were very keen on schooling. The Old Ogilvies had come originally from a successful professional family of Scottish provosts and engineers, so, unlike other employers of the time, Christina Ogilvie had encouraged my mother to believe she had a good brain and must 'improve herself'. Not that she wanted her to leave their service but she must rise in it. Just as she had. Mother would certainly make sure that I 'improved myself', but she never encouraged me to expect that it would be easy. Her addiction to hard work — I was to realize later — went with some ancestral puritanism, just as Mrs Ogilvie's attitudes probably had.

Mother was also a great respecter of authority, I suppose because in her first forty years she had been used to others wielding authority over her, however lucky she had been in her employers. She was lucky in the Pages too, who were not quite typical of their class. Sir Jack no longer hunted or went on shoots, though he did fish in Hampshire or sometimes with a relative in the highlands. Ruth Page spent a good deal of her time planning the garden, reading, and trying to improve her piano-playing. Mother of course had not much time to read, but both my parents approved of books.

Lady Page was easy-going and kind, and I confess I sometimes wished my mother were more like her. I realized when I was a little older that generations of scrimping and saving could never make for a relaxed nature. I believe though that Sally's parents and mine, from such different backgrounds, Mother coming from a poor but respectable family in an Oxfordshire hamlet, and Father from a slightly better-off rural Kentish background of small builders, were equally matched in intelligence.

There was not much to do in Pettiwell village in the nineteen thirties. It was a peaceful place, except when young men in sports cars whizzed through it. I knew some of the village children, as they were at my school, and once or twice I played football after lessons with schoolmates called Trevor and Keith and Brian. I preferred the boys, imagining most of the girls regarded me with a mixture of suspicion and slight menace. I came from the big house, but I was not 'posh' or I would not have attended their school, and that puzzled them. I wanted to be liked, and at first I could not understand why I was, as I thought, unpopular. I was very self-conscious, had the notion that people stopped talking when I went into the village shop to buy my sweets. There would be a pause and they would alter their voices and say, 'How's her ladyship then today?'

I always answered, 'Very well, thank you.'

Sometimes Lady Page asked me to buy ten Cadbury's twopenny bars for her. I could keep one and give one to Sally. She must have had a passion for chocolate. Perhaps it was around the time she was expecting James. If Sally were with me, the shop lady would never ask how her ladyship was but would be struck dumb as if my friend was a fairy or a goddess. I could see it embarrassed Sally.

25

Nobody however thought *I* was a goddess. I was just a useful person to pump for information about the doings at the big house. I had the feeling that my parents were slightly resented by some of the villagers, and I may have been right.

In the wooden shelter on the village green old men sat smoking their pipes, some of them reminiscing about 'their' war — the war in the Transvaal — and their sons' war in France or Gallipoli. They were retired now, out of the way of their wives' or daughters' housework, sharing the solidarity of old men and the smell of tobacco. In much the same way Sir Jack would retire to his library with a cigar. Mother said you could never get the smell of the cigars out of the velvet curtains there.

The quiet Pettiwell life turned any visit into an exciting event, but by the time I was old enough to notice, our employers did not entertain much. When Lady Page's parents were on a visit they liked their daughter to ask a couple called Cozens over to play bridge. Maurice and Beatrice Cozens lived on the other side of the village in a 'new' house called Stair Court. New compared with ours, I mean. I say 'ours' because, as I have explained, I always felt I belonged to Pettiwell House. I found out when I was older that

Stair Court had been designed in the early 1900s by a famous architect, or at least a pupil of his. It looked modern and was long-fronted and gabled. The Cozens had a married son who lived in London and whom I never remember seeing, but I remember being told by my mother that they had lost their elder son on the Somme.

They seemed to me to be very rich, for they had a chauffeur and a big car, in which they would come over to play bridge with Laura and Andrew Ogilvie before the war. I overheard Lady Page saying once that she detested bridge. I didn't believe she liked the Cozens very much, but then I had the impression that she didn't much like her own parents either, which I found very odd. I once said something like that to Mother and she was angry with me: where did I get that idea? Lady Page was the kindest-hearted person and it wasn't her fault if she didn't like playing bridge. Sally liked her Grandpa Ogilvie, and Sir Jack appeared to get on well with his in-laws. I noticed all these things — nothing much that went on in the house escaped me — and although Mother and Father had their own quarters I know they were well aware of everything too.

★ ★ ★

The great event in the summer of 1938, when I was seven years old, was the first visit of Lady Page's sister, Clare Fitzpatrick, and her husband and two daughters, Caroline and baby Lily, to Pettiwell. It was Caroline Fitzpatrick who made the greatest impression on both Sally and me. I remember the date because it was the year after the coronation, and Sally's mother had just had her baby, a boy they named James. Sir Jack was as pleased as Punch and we'd been ordered into the main house for a glass of champagne. I drank in all the family details from Sally along with my chilly lemonade.

We'd been playing kings and queens, and Sir Jack said,

'Are you still playing at the coronation, Sallykins? That's all old hat now!'

We ran off after our drink to continue the game. Sally told me excitedly that her Auntie Clare and Uncle Frank, and her cousin Caroline, and her new cousin Lily were to come over on a visit the following week from London. They lived a long way away, in a country called France, and they were coming in an aeroplane from Paris to Croydon airfield.

The next day Sally and I abandoned the coronation game, of which we were beginning to grow a little weary after a whole year, and sat in the shrubbery to compare notes about where babies came from.

I had often imagined 'Cousin Caroline'. Sally had met her only once before and did not remember the meeting. Caroline, as I have said, was older than both of us. I was rather hurt when Sally told me she had always wanted an elder sister. Secretly, I had always regarded myself as Sally's elder sister, but I had enough common sense not to tell her that.

'Mummy and Auntie Clare will want to introduce their babies to each other,' said Sally solemnly.

She was not too enamoured of baby James, who cried a good deal.

*　★　★*

It was a hot July morning. I was in the kitchen garden with Father picking strawberries when we heard the sound of a car's wheels scrunching the gravel round the front of the house.

'It'll be a taxi from the station,' said Father, 'Unless her husband's hired a car.' He meant Mrs Fitzpatrick and her family. They had not been sure about the train so Sir Jack had decided not to meet them himself. Mother had been talking about the visit at breakfast time and had helped the part-time cook make a salmon mousse, a dish I had never heard of. The strawberries were to be for them too. As soon as Father declared we had gathered enough, we took them in to give Mother, and I decided to have a look at the visitors for myself.

The family and their guests hadn't yet started their lunch and I saw Sally on the terrace round the front of the house — Sally and a tall dark girl. I bided my time. I wouldn't just announce myself, but would wander over to the lawn after I had had my dinner. Sally and her cousin would probably go there when they had finished their meal and it was felt they had been long enough being polite to the grown-ups.

I did just that. About two o'clock I strolled casually round to the lawn. My hunch had been correct. The two girls were sitting on the grass and Sally had her doll's pram with her. As I approached, Sally waved to me. The other girl looked up and I ran over to them.

'This is my friend Jennie,' said Sally to the other girl. She might be only six years old but she had been brought up to introduce children to each other.

The other girl extended her hand but did not get up. I advanced and shook the hand. I too knew how to behave, but I was surprised.

It must be what they did in France. Caroline said nothing but looked at me carefully. She had a pale face and long dark straight hair tied back with a scarlet bow. Sally was staring at her in fascinated sort of way.

'Where do you live?' asked Caroline.

'Over there' — I pointed to the back of the house.

'I didn't know you had another family living in your house,' said Caroline to her cousin.

'My mother and father work here,' I said. 'Did you like your meal?'

'It was lovely,' said Sally. 'I ate seven strawberries.'

'I gathered them,' I said proudly.

Caroline looked at me thoughtfully, and turned to Sally.

'Shall we play statues?' she asked her. She had a funny voice. I supposed it was that she usually spoke French. I was ready to be impressed by her, but just then a lady and a gentleman came out on the terrace and the man shouted:

'Caro! I want to take some snapshots. Can you come along?'

'That's Papa,' said Caroline. Then Lady Page's voice came over to us from the terrace like a bell.

'Sally — family pictures, darling.'

31

I was going to walk over with them but Caroline said pointedly to me: 'It'll only be the *family*.'

Sally said, 'See you later, Jennie,' and they both ran off.

I felt excluded and cross. Only the other day my father had taken a picture of Sally and me in the garden. I went in and complained to my mother.

'I told you not to tag along,' she said. 'They won't want you with them today.' She sounded cross too.

I wondered whether Mother had seen Lady Page's sister yet. I said to Father, who was sitting there with his newspaper,

'Sally liked the strawberries.'

'There are a few over for your tea,' he said.

I went into the back garden with *Little Women*, but it was almost too hot to read and I wanted to see the others. Later, I was called in to tea. Mother was not there.

'She's been called over to greet the visitors,' said Father.

As I ate my own strawberries I heard the taxi leaving, and a few moments later Mother came back in from the main house. She looked quite excited.

'They didn't keep you long,' said my father.

The day after that visit, to which I had so looked forward but which had disappointed me, I had an idea.

'Let's become blood sisters!' I suggested to Sally.

I had read in a schoolgirl annual about a girl called Ruby who made a pact with her best friend Pearl. They each pricked their finger with a needle and mingled the blood and wrote a special message in a notebook promising to stick by each other for ever, using the mixed blood to sign their names on the page. I was very keen on signatures at the time. I had learned to do copperplate writing and I described this to my friend.

'We can do it in the shrubbery,' I said.

Sally wanted to talk about her new cousins. I had brought a piece of paper and a needle and when we sat down in our favourite spot in the shrubbery I made her hold the paper and bravely pricked my own left thumb.

'Ugh,' said Sally. 'Do I have to?'

'Well, if you want us to be blood sisters you do. We have to mix the blood and swear aloud to stick by each other for ever.'

I was not sure how long it would take to write all that down so I thought saying it would do.

'You prick my finger then for me then,' said Sally, shutting her eyes and holding out her hand with her nose all screwed up.

'I think you are supposed to do it yourself,' I said.

Just then we heard her mother's voice calling her.

'Sally. Auntie Clare on the telephone. She wants to say goodbye — they're just off.'

'Sorry, I must go,' said Sally, 'but I promise — what you said — I'll prick my finger tomorrow.'

I held the paper and intoned: 'I promise to stick by Sally Page,' and had to be content with that. It was not quite right but I should have remembered that Sally hated the sight of blood.

My own blood was smearing the intended page. Never mind. I knew we were best friends anyway.

'Miss Clare seemed indifferent to the house,' Mother was saying to Father when I went in for my dinner. 'It was a shock to see her again — she's grown a bit thin. Her new baby's lovely though.'

I had wanted to see baby Lily but I had not been invited to have a look.

If Sally and I both belonged to slightly odd households, and some boundaries were not crossed, the Pages were before their time in the way they behaved to us Wilsons. That did not mean that I could be a family guest. Sally's mother might call my mother Polly, but Mother never called her Ruth or even Miss Ruth to her face, though she called her Miss Ruth when she spoke of her to Father. Mother was not obsequious but she sensibly followed the rules she had learned in her early London household. I had often thought of Mother knowing Lady Page as a baby and wondered what she and her sister Clare had been like. By now I had gathered from my reading of children's books taken out from the public library that children in the olden days were probably closer to the servants than to their own parents. Especially when parents were away in India. Mother would not like it if I said I had not liked Clare Fitzpatrick's daughter, because she had said I was not 'family'. I *knew* I was not 'family', even if people always called the families they worked for 'their' families. Some of the older village people still called Sally's father 'Our Sir Jack', and would recall Jack's parents, now deceased, and the glory days of Pettiwell House.

I thought Sally's cousin Caroline had meant to be rude. I might have been only seven but I was aware of all this.

In adolescence, the fact that Father had met Mother only because his commanding officer had married into the family Mother worked for did not embarrass me but made perfect sense. Soon my reading would also tell me that Mother was technically what used to be called an upper servant. I never denied that fact, and I was quite comfortable with it when I was a child. I had thought: Mother and Father have jobs, unlike some of the parents of pupils at school who were what was called 'unemployed'. I suppose if Sally and her mother and father had been cruel or unkind or stand-offish I'd have felt differently. When I was older, and even when I became quite 'left wing', I still did not think it was their fault that they had been born in the class they were. I never felt I wanted to be just like them, so long as they regarded me as an equal.

I had a happy infancy, which was to stand me in good stead when I met the other members of the tribe. In 1938 my only worry was that Caroline might want to be Sally's 'best friend' and thus displace me. She was her cousin though, so perhaps it didn't count. Sally and I always got on well. We both took our families for granted.

★   ★   ★

For the time being war did not come and we went on more or less as before. The following year however, when Caroline Fitzpatrick and her parents came to Pettiwell for the second time, I was to experience a new feeling, that of an uneasy dislike, about which I felt guilty.

Even a child like myself had heard rumours of war. We had been told at school the summer Caroline came that first time that we would soon be measured for rubber gas masks. That was when they began to dig up part of the park in the town; I did not understand why. The following year, when we saw sandbags piling up in odd places, we had already collected our gas masks in little square cardboard boxes that you had to carry with you wherever you went. Baby James had a different contraption. Because he was too young to put the mask over his face he had to have a sort of box over him that would have oxygen pumped into it.

I had talked about war with Mother, and what might happen. I think she didn't want to frighten me so she talked about the last war and how Ruth and her sister had been children then but had helped their aunt roll bandages and tried to knit Balaclavas for Tommies. When Mother was launched on the old days she always ended up telling me how the two sisters had 'come out' after the war in the nineteen twenties, when young ladies had been called 'Bright Young Things'. None of this really interested me then. Anyway, I could not imagine our Lady Page as a 'Bright Young Thing'. She was kind, and quiet, and a little nervous, and I believe she always wanted to believe the best of people. I heard Mother tell Father that 'Miss Clare' was quite different. After being a Bright Young Thing *she* had insisted on going to study painting in Paris.

'She takes less after her grandparents than her sister does,' said my mother. 'She was always a very different kettle of fish from our Lady Page.' She did not explain further and Father never asked the right kind of questions.

I think the coming of the Second World War must have really surprised Ruth Page. I remember overhearing her talking to her husband in the 'garden grove', where they strolled after dinner. I had gone one evening to gather some roses for Mother to put in the main house, and I heard her say:

'My sister was always tougher than me — pretended she didn't expect much from life. She must be very worried about the future now. They will have to come here, you know, and live with us.'

'Don't let's be too pessimistic,' replied her husband.

I asked Mother if Caroline and her parents really would come to stay at Pettiwell if there was a war and she said:

'They might very well,' and pursed her lips.

I reported to Father that I had heard Sir Jack say we must not be too pessimistic.

Father replied, 'When the worst happens, pessimists are often able to deal with it.'

I did not want him to think I had listened on purpose to the Pages talking because I hadn't, but it was true that I was a bit of an eaves-dropper on conversations. Father never volunteered much about war, or life in general, so that when he did I always remembered it. I suppose it might appear unusual for him and my mother to take an interest in world affairs, but they were both very concerned about war. They would listen to the wireless when they had done their day's tasks, and Mother had checked that Ethel, now the maid of all work, and Cook, who no longer lived in, had done theirs. She would sit mending Father's socks or a tear in my red-check cotton dress. I had heard about the war in Spain on the wireless. How long before one started in our own country? I knew there had been one in Abyssinia and in China because we had been told to pray for the Abyssinian children in Sunday school.

★　★　★

I was already interested in the history of our house because it had been there before the grown-ups had. We didn't do that kind of history at school. That day in the summer of 1938 when I first saw Caroline I had already been two years at the village school, and had begun to understand that the grown-ups had all had lives before I was born. Some of the parents of the children in my class had scratched their initials on the same desks at which we sat ourselves! I loved the idea of things staying the same, had not yet reached the age when one yearns for change.

It gave me a queer feeling to know I had not been there when Father and Mother and the others had lived in a country at war. Sally's father and mine had fought together in France, so *they* knew about wars. I consoled myself with thinking that girls did not have to fight. That was the only thing that reconciled me at the time to being a girl. I saw France as a place where soldiers marched up and down, alongside the trenches that I had heard those men on the green talking about, and I imagined soldiers dressed in red and wearing busbies like the new king's soldiers at Buckingham Palace. War might be quite exciting in a way.

Those summers of 1937 and 1938 and 1939 seem to me now to span long vistas of months and years, years like railway lines going on and on for ever over viaducts, my life at the time a thin straight track towards the future. Only two years spanned the last three pre-war summers, and I find that hard to believe. I remember Caroline coming on that first visit, but it seems years before she and the rest of the Fitzpatricks came for good. Time is everlasting when you are six and seven and eight. I look back and remember us as we were then, myself thin and brown and ordinary; pretty Sally with her curly dark hair, the small bundle called baby James, and the two cousins — pale Caroline, who was usually called Caro, and fat toddler Lily.

The summer before the war really did begin, I remember the superintendent at chapel Sunday School praying for people in a place with a long name. It was probably Czechoslovakia. Father said it was not as far away as China or Abyssinia. I went to chapel because Mother was chapel. Father wasn't anything. I had also attended the village church, St Barnabas, where the Pages went, for the village school was a Church of England foundation and we were sometimes taken there. It was a much older building than the chapel, and smelled more interesting. Sally said she would like to come to *my* church because we had prizes for attendance, which I had won, and shown her, but her parents did not send her to any Sunday School. At mine they went on praying that there would not be a war. I prayed along fervently, having the idea that if there were a war Caroline Fitzpatrick would come to stay at Pettiwell and I didn't want her there interfering with my life!

My prayers did not work. In 1939 war was declared. Clare Fitzpatrick and the whole Fitzpatrick family, including Lily and Caroline's 'Papa', came to live for a time at Pettiwell.

'They will all need gas masks too,' I said.

★   ★   ★

When you are a child you take everything for granted, a war, the black-out, ration books. You take yourself and your family and friends and other families for granted too, especially your mother and father. You grow up with a name, and that name is who you are: Jennie Joyce Wilson. Or Sally Charlotte Page; and Caroline Mary Fitzpatrick. I thought when I was a child that what I didn't know about our family and, a bit later, about Caroline and her family was not worth knowing.

We children of the nineteen thirties, Sally

and Caroline and I, along with toddler James Page and little Lily Fitzpatrick — friends, cousins, sisters and brothers — all grew up together, sheltered by dear Pettiwell House.

★　★　★

My life at Pettiwell was not completely bounded by the house and the family and the chapel and the school. Above all, I had books to read. I have already mentioned the public library. There was the travelling library that came to the village, and a little later I visited the public library in our nearest town, not far from my second school and reachable on the bus. I was allowed to go to school by myself on this bus by the time I was eleven, and on Saturdays I often went to the library on the same bus.

I had been given other books for birthday and Christmas presents, usually by my parents who asked me what I wanted, or I saved up to buy them with my threepence a week pocket money. There were the book prizes at Sunday School too, even in the war, and book prizes at school.

I was also allowed to borrow books from the library in Pettiwell House. Most of those did not interest me as a child, except for ancient *Little Folks* annuals that had belonged to Sir Jack's mother, and *Girls' Realms* once owned by his sister Margery, who had left them behind at Pettiwell when she got married.

At the tobacconist's and sweet-shop, which doubled as a commercial library, you could buy old paper-backed books for twopence which the shopkeeper no longer wanted to lend out. The covers, usually of blonde ladies who looked like film stars, were what Lady Page called lurid. By that time of course they were a bit dog-eared, and the stories were mostly what Sally and I learned to call 'soppy'.

You might come across another kind of storybook at my first school if you asked to be allowed to tidy dusty old cupboards. Somebody had once bought schoolgirl stories and adventure stories and forgotten about them so I read May Wynne and Ethel Talbot and Christine Chandler. Apart from reading, I don't think I learned much of interest at the village school, although I enjoyed poetry lessons, and singing, and painting. Of course we learned how to do things like plain sewing and to have neat handwriting, and to do sums, but that was not the same as having my imagination fired.

Sally had not yet done long division or fractions but Caroline had, and when she came to live with us we used to set each other sums. She was good at arithmetic. Even if she was older than me I did not like to be beaten. I wouldn't have minded if Sally had been better at sums than I was.

Books and school and the wireless were where I got most of my information. Even before I went to school or could read, the pictures, as we always called the cinema in the town, had also widened my horizons. Later, I was not allowed to go quite so often as some of my school-friends, but if she could be spared from work on a Saturday afternoon, my mother occasionally took me to a film, and now and then my father took us both for a treat. Sometimes Sally came with us, and then Sir Jack would let Father take the Morris into Oxridge. I remember many of the films we saw, films that Mother thought were 'suitable' for us. 'Suitable' was a word often on Mother's lips. Lady Page never asked what was on — she must have trusted Mother's judgement.

At school, I found children talked a lot about Hollywood film stars: Clark Gable and Robert Taylor and Cary Grant. I knew Mother liked some of those, but they were in films I had not yet been allowed to see. One Saturday Mother had dragged Father to see *Gone with the Wind*. Every grown-up had seen that film, I thought, but Mother said it was not 'suitable' for me. Father told me he preferred listening to his wireless. Mother, though, had grudgingly admitted that Shirley Temple was talented, so early on I had seen *Curly Top* and *Dimples*. I thought Sally looked a bit like Shirley Temple, except that her curls were dark. The only film I could remember later was *Poor Little Rich Girl*: that title suddenly came back to me after Caroline Fitzpatrick had come to live at Pettiwell. Caroline had of course seen *Gone with the Wind*, or said she had.

★ ★ ★

It was the October of what they later called the phoney war. There had begun to be newsreels, or perhaps I had never noticed them before. Sally and I, now accompanied by Caroline, had been taken to see *Snow White*, which we had missed first time round. We had heard about *The Wizard of Oz*.

Sally's Auntie Margery had seen it in London and told her it was wonderful, and we all looked forward to its arrival in Oxridge, but in 1939 everybody at school was talking about *Snow White*, and when we went that Saturday afternoon the cinema was full of children who made an awful din. There was a newsreel first which the boys in the audience cheered. I wondered if they would show France on it, and waited for Caroline to say she had seen it all before, but she did not. We all waited impatiently for *Snow White* and when it came there was complete silence for a time, until the witch appeared, and then some boys hissed. We had heard that many children had been frightened by the witch, though strangely enough this had not made the film 'unsuitable' in Mother's eyes. I found I was not at all frightened of the witch. I was not especially fond of witches in fairy stories, but I found real people much more frightening. At the end of the film, however, Caroline insisted that I had been scared.

'You were! You were! You had your eyes shut!' she said.

Actually, I'd thought it was Sally, as she was younger than Caroline and myself, who had been frightened. I was not going to tell Caroline that.

Sally whispered to me the next day — I remember it was a Sunday afternoon and her cousin was doing something with her mother — that Caro had had a nightmare about the witch! I was surprised. She had not appeared to be frightened of anything.

I had read the story of Snow White of

course, having been presented with fairy stories as presents, but by this time I preferred books about girls and families to Wicked Queens. I did not spend my time reading great books, for Sally and I both loved comics. I used to buy *Tiger Tim* and at first Sally had *Chicks' Own* bought for her. Caroline said *Chicks' Own* was babyish and people did not read comics in France. She must have wanted to read them though, for her mother began to buy us *Sunny Stories*. Now we had three to share each week until we found *Chicks' Own* really was too babyish even for Sally, and Caroline told her mother that *Sunny Stories* was boring too. I bought a comic called *Butterfly* for a halfpenny one Saturday and offered to lend it to her. She looked surprised.

'It's a comic for boys,' I said. 'Adventures and jokes and things — you'd like it better than *Sunny Stories*.'

'Thank you,' she said. Usually she barely tolerated me and tried her best to take Sally off to play without me. She was often rude to me. A little later I became really popular for a time, when I borrowed the *Girls' Crystal* from a girl at school to read at home, and Caroline enjoyed reading it, though she pretended she didn't. She said the drawings were not very good. I had never really studied

48

the pictures — all the girls looked alike, I thought.

Even my lending her the magazine was eventually turned against me. I can't remember exactly when I had copied out a list of schoolgirl slang, but I do remember some of the phrases. It was possibly because I knew that Sally would one day go to boarding-school, to the sort of school we read about in the stories, that I had taken such an interest in such places. Not that I wanted to go away myself but I knew I'd miss Sally. I'd practised saying some of the slang phrases for ages, and Caroline had looked at me suspiciously. Mother had told me that when Sally went away to school her cousin would most likely go with her and that prospect filled me with real sorrow.

'It isn't as if you had no other friends,' Mother said. 'You'll be off to your own new school when you're ten!'

I wasn't so sure. I had to win that 'scholarship', something that was always happening in the stories we read but which seemed to be fairly rare at our school. Perhaps I could win a scholarship to Sally's school?

'We shan't want *you* leaving home yet,' Mother said, 'Not unless bombs start dropping around here.'

* ★ ★

Sally suggested one Saturday that we explore the Secret Lane.

'That would be a *topping* idea!' I answered. I wished Caroline didn't always have to go with us but there was never anything I could do about that. I remember thinking that it was my contribution to refugees and the war effort, such was the egoism of a nine-year-old. Sally was always nice to both of us, but Caroline had to share in everything we did, even more now that her father, having volunteered his services, was at present in London doing something 'hush-hush'.

'My mother wants to go and drive ambulances,' said Caroline as we walked down the lane. It was a cold morning but we were young and didn't feel the cold outside for we ran everywhere. It was the first I had heard of the ambulance idea.

I tried out another of the phrases as nobody had said anything about 'topping'.

'They say there's a secret passage down the lane,' I rapidly invented. 'It once led to the farm when there were smugglers. There might be spies using the same passage!'

'How could there be smugglers here?' asked Caroline. 'There's no sea or boats.'

'People smuggle other things,' I said

50

hurriedly. 'Anyway, it'd be *a great stunt* if we unmasked a gang of spies!'

I was not the only person to be obsessed with spies. Rumours were rife about Germans disguised as nuns and it was true that all our sign-posts had been taken down or turned round the wrong way.

'Just you wait,' I went on. 'We'd all get medals and . . . '

Caroline who was nearly twelve looked at me with scorn.

She said, '*I'm bored stiff*!'

I recognized one of the phrases I'd copied. She knew what I was doing. Had she seen my private list? I hadn't yet been able to use all the phases I'd copied down and was looking forward to incorporating 'No end, Don't mensh, Cheerio, Jolly shame, I'm stumped, Don't boss, Botheration, What a spree, How killing, Cheer up, By Jingo, Be a sport, and Honest Injun.'

I was not sure what the last phrase meant. I had culled it from the *Butterfly* comic, which, as I had explained to Caroline, was for boys.

Sally looked puzzled. 'I'm sorry — what would you like to do?' she asked her cousin in reply to her complaint. Caroline was always 'bored'. She shrugged her shoulders in that infuriating French way she had.

'We could turn back if you want, and go to

the village and spend our Saturday money,' suggested Sally.

I had noticed Sally always tried to please Caroline. I supposed it was because Caroline had been uprooted from her house in France on account of the war. Paris was after all her home. We often heard Sally calling her to come and play. 'Carr-o! Carr-o!' would resound through the garden and the house. I wondered whether Caroline, wanting to be by herself some of the time, found Sally a bit of a bore. I hoped she did, and then I could have Sally to myself, but that made me feel disloyal to Sally, of whom I was fond.

'I don't care what we do,' Caroline said now. I wasn't going to pander to her. She both fascinated and annoyed me. I think I annoyed her but I certainly didn't fascinate her. She was always pointing out my faults or pooh-poohing my suggestions. Once she said to me after some slight disagreement, 'You don't *own* Sally, you know!'

Well of course I didn't, but I longed for the day when Caroline would go back home. This seemed unlikely unless the war ended — another reason to pray for it to finish as far as I was concerned. Mother had told me right at the beginning when they came to Pettiwell that I mustn't mind if Sally played more with her cousin than with me. I don't think my mother was all that fond of her. Sally and I had had such a good time before she came but I never went so far as to tell that to Caroline. All the books said, 'Two's company, three's a crowd,' and it seemed they had been right. Father had made me feel guilty by saying, 'How would *you* like to have to leave your home?'

'I wouldn't care if you and Mother were there,' I had replied. Secretly, I had often longed to have adventures, even go to boarding-school, or be 'evacuated' but I hadn't really thought it out properly.

We'd stopped walking and were leaning against the gate to a field.

Sally said suddenly, 'I know — let's do that blood sisterhood thing you told me about, Jennie. I never did it right, did I?'

'What's that then?' asked Caroline.

I explained.

Sally said, 'I could prick my thumb and be a blood sister to you, Jennie, like you did before and then we could both do it to you, Caroline . . . '

'I'm not your sister, I'm your cousin,' said Caroline, frowning. 'So we don't need to do it.'

'Well then, just let Jennie prick her thumb or you prick yours and then we'll all be joined up together — '

'No thank you, I don't want to be blood sister to Jennie,' said Caroline rudely. Then she added something in what I supposed was French.

'What's that in English?' I asked her.

'Oh, nothing.'

She looked as if she might tell Sally. I was sure it was about me. Sally's idea was dropped and we turned back and walked to the village where we mooned around the sweet-shop and I bought a pencil and notebook.

Later that day when Caroline had gone out with her mother to the town to buy a mackintosh, Sally and I were playing in the stable yard and I asked her if Caroline had told her what she had said in French.

Sally blushed.

'It was about me, wasn't it?' I asked.

Sally could never tell a fib so uttered an unhappy 'Yes.'

'What did she say?'

'Oh, she didn't mean it — you know she says things she doesn't mean — '

'Did she say why she didn't want us all to be blood sisters?' I pursued.

Sally whispered, 'She said you can't be her blood sister 'cos you're . . . ' she stopped.

I thought she was going to quote her cousin and say, *Because you don't belong to our family*, but it was worse.

''Cos you're only a — a — servant's daughter,' whispered Sally.

My throat went tight and my mouth dry. I knew it was a horrible thing to say. It was true, but why should it matter? I didn't think it really mattered to Caroline — it was just a way of getting at me. I knew it did not matter to Sally.

'She's jealous,' I said in retaliation. I wasn't going to show I cared.

'She's just a bit silly,' said Sally, 'She says you want to be one of her family.'

Then she appeared to put the whole thing out of her mind, which I should have done too, but couldn't, and she shook her mop of curls saying:

'Let's race to the green gate!'

I didn't tell Mother or Father what Caroline Fitzpatrick had said. They would have told me to be polite. Perhaps Sally told Lady Page though, because I noticed Caroline's father, whom I liked, and who had come back from London for a few days, was especially nice to me that week and smiled at me when he gave us all a toffee.

What I actually did was to swear I would learn to speak French too so Caroline couldn't have any secrets from me.

Just you wait! I thought.

It was soon after this, I think, that we were told something important called the War Office had asked Francis Fitzpatrick to do something secret for the war effort. It was Caroline who said it was Something Secret. She loved secrets. It turned out later that his work really was important. We didn't see her father then for months and months. He came back once and then went away again for ages.

About this time I overheard my mother say to my father, 'Miss Clare wants to work in London and learn to be an ambulance driver. Perhaps she'll be able to see her husband in London.'

I thought, but what will little Lily do?

We were very soon to discover that some of Lady Page's war work would now consist of looking after Lily and Caroline at Pettiwell as well as her own two children. She was also working for the WVS so she was very busy. We expected evacuees might be billeted at Pettiwell, or refugees, or wounded soldiers, and so we got the three remaining more or less habitable bedrooms clean and ready for them in case. Children evacuated from London at the beginning, and then later when the blitz started, and even later in 1944, usually went to Wales or the North of England, though we did have a few refugees from the Channel Islands in June 1940, though not for long. People all thought we were too near London to choose as billets.

After 1940 there were no more wounded or weary soldiers on their way home from Dunkirk. Father had seen some of them on the main road in big lorries and said people on the road had taken them out drinks of water. I knitted blanket squares and took all the kitchen left-overs to the pig bin at the front of the drive, my special job.

Father then told us that he had volunteered to be an ARP warden. Mother did not try to stop him but she was as relieved as Father was disappointed when he was told he was too old. He could however join the Local Defence Volunteers who not long afterwards were renamed as members of the Home Guard. My father joined that, and became a sergeant under Sir Jack's command. It was just like the old days, he said. I was amazed. My father hated war; he liked being peaceful, gardening, and keeping himself to himself. He'd been injured in the last war, as had Sir Jack, so why should they have to start up all over again? Mother said it was patriotism. She hated Hitler even more than Father, I think.

For the time being though, not much happened. They drilled and drilled on the village green where the men older than they, who had also served before, had used to talk about war. The blackout was pretty well total, the village had a first aid post ready in case of bombs, and people practised in groups using stirrup pumps. Buckets and sand were kept everywhere. The grown-ups were all prepared, but we children could not really do very much. Most of us, I confess, hoped something exciting would happen, and I used to make up secret codes with my friend Joan Dawson from school when we were bored in lessons.

We did not understand how close danger might be to ourselves from some lurking daylight raid, until the flying bombs arrived in 1944. Before that we had seen searchlights in the sky chasing stray German aircraft and we had got used to shelter practice, but we were not told what was really going on in London and other cities. War felt like a play that went on and on. I knew places had been bombed but they were not places I knew, only those I had heard mentioned. I remember hearing about the destruction of Coventry Cathedral, and the burning of the City of London, but I had no idea how many people, just ordinary people — and children — were being killed day after day.

The blitz had begun in earnest in September 1940 all over London and went on until the spring of 1942. Much later, when I was grown up I read about the bombs on West London and East London, over Kensington as well as the docks, over churches and famous buildings, bombs falling night after night. As a child I was not told the details, and the wireless did not tell people very much either, apart from saying: 'bombs fell last night'. From people who worked in London or who had visited it recently my parents must have heard terrible stories of destruction. Only Clare Fitzpatrick, who actually did go to drive ambulances in London that autumn *really* knew, and I don't think she went into details even to her sister, not wanting to frighten her. She might have hinted to Caro that she was doing dangerous work but she would not want to frighten her daughter either, so probably played it down. A few years later she was to edit a diary a friend had kept at the time, but of course I didn't know anything about that at the time.

Life seemed to go on much the same for me in Pettiwell apart from the blackout and the rationing, whilst over many English towns and cities and coastal resorts, after a slight lull, bombs continued to fall. All that we children heard from the adults around us was that we would win the war in the end, and we believed them implicitly. The children of

Pettiwell Village had not been evacuated, though we were within an hour or two's train journey from London. If I had known about the high explosives, and incendiaries and oil-bombs, probably the worst time for England there had ever been, I don't think I could have imagined it clearly, and I cannot begin to understand it even now. I could only have realized the feelings that must have been choking people all over London if I had imagined little children and animals being killed, or losing their parents or owners, and not knowing why. It's only when something is made personal that you really feel it, at least that is what I have found. I did not know at the time how many churches and famous buildings had been destroyed. Only very much later did I understand that the past was being demolished whilst we children meta-phorically slept. I suppose it was the second Great Fire of London, though London was not by any means the only place to suffer.

★   ★   ★

Caroline let slip to me one day that her mother had not been able to paint since she, Caroline, was born. I knew that Fitzpatrick easels and brushes and paints were up in one of our attics, where I sometimes went to be by myself. I loved the smell of linseed oil that lingered there, and wondered when they had last been used. Someone had cared enough to keep them.

This was about the time I began to learn French properly from an old book I found in another attic storeroom. Perhaps it had belonged to Caroline's mother when she first went to Paris. I hid it from the others. I thought it might come in useful if the war went on and I could be a spy in occupied France. I suspected Caroline's father was one of those.

Wealdridge Grammar School, the school Mother and Father wanted me to attend, was to have an examination in February 1941 for those scholars who aspired to be pupils there, with papers in arithmetic and English composition and an intelligence test. My major preoccupation was doing well enough to win what was called a county minor scholarship.

I managed it — and started at my new school in September 1941, having won a free place.

2

SALLY

I had a very happy childhood at Pettiwell. When we were very small, Jennie and I often played outside together with our dollies in prams, which we would walk round the paths like nannies in Kensington Gardens. I had a dolly called Rosie and she had one called Griselda. We'd make up stories about what they did every day; mostly it was what we were doing ourselves — what they had for breakfast and tea, and what they bought at the shops. Jennie had probably almost grown out of this sort of pretend game by the time the war started but she still played with me because I still loved my dolls. We used to take our 'babies' to the air-raid shelter. Mr Wilson had dug an Anderson shelter in the kitchen garden. Caro was too old for dolls when she came to live with us but she did like dressing paper ladies and she drew and painted all the clothes for them.

I've never had a very good memory for dates, so the things that happened in my childhood and the war are all mixed up in my head. I can't remember exactly how old I was when certain things happened, though I can sometimes tell when I look at the dresses I am wearing in old photos. I'm not sure exactly when we were taken to see various films at the Picture Palace in Oxridge. I do remember seeing *Pinocchio*, which was, I think, after we saw *The Thief of Baghdad*, but before we saw *The Bluebird*.

After Caro and I went away to school, dates get even more muddled in my head. School life went on much the same all the time and nothing especially different ever happened.

I think it was after the war had been going on for about a year that London had the real blitz. I remember Daddy talking about bombs that had fallen on Wimbledon and Croydon, places I knew because I had a great aunt who lived in Wimbledon, and a second cousin, who had got married before the war — I had been one of her bridesmaids — and she had gone off on her honeymoon from the airport at Croydon. Daddy said the Germans would sometimes drop bombs anywhere just to get rid of them, but they must have wanted to bomb Croydon because of the airport. Some men from the village who worked on the coast saw the 'dog-fights' over the Channel all through August that summer. We did not see any of those, and we hadn't yet had anything bad at Pettiwell, but later when I was away at school there were German planes dropping bombs over Kent and Sussex. I do remember the searchlights in 1940 that tried to track stray enemy planes, but I was not told much about the blitz whilst it was going on in London.

Caro's mother was in the thick of it when she worked for the ambulance service. I don't think she told Caro much about what she was doing. When a bomb dropped on the house next to our grandparents' house in Kensington — actually the house where Caro and Lily and their parents might easily have been living if they had not decided to come to us in Pettiwell — Granny and Grandpa Ogilvie came to stay at Pettiwell for six months. I knew from what Mummy said that they didn't much like living with us at Pettiwell, though we all *tried* to be quiet and well behaved. James wasn't quite three years old but he loved imitating aeroplanes, which made rather a lot of noise. Eventually, Granny and Grandpa went to live near Oxford. Mummy was relieved, though she didn't like to say so.

We couldn't keep ponies or horses at home in the war because there wasn't enough stuff to give them to eat. That was an awful pity. I absolutely longed for one. Caesar, my dear old pony had died the summer before the war began and I'd been promised another. The Broughton family over at Field Place had said I could have the pony that had belonged to one of their daughters, which she had become too large for, and I'd been over to see it. Horses and ponies all have different characters and I had talked to Star, the one that I was going to have. She understood me and I her. The deal was not quite sorted out when the war started. I'd spent a lot of my childhood with ponies and now I could only see Star from time to time. I read all the books about ponies and horses that I could find. I absolutely adored them.

Caro didn't like animals and never read my books at all, unless there was nothing else in the house to read. Jennie always had a book to read from the public library. She loved cats, and quite liked other animals, but not especially horses or ponies. I think some horses frightened her a bit. She had not been put on a pony when she was two the way I had. It was the one thing we'd never shared, since her parents were not keen on her riding. Anyway, a bit later on in the war we heard that horses were being given ration books! I went over to the Broughtons for ages till they sold Star to someone else, and even afterwards, and helped in the harness room cleaning and oiling saddles and reins.

★ ★ ★

When Jennie sat her exam for Wealdridge Grammar School, Caro and I were still at Miss Hodson's in Tanstead, though Caro, as she was thirteen that year, was having some extra lessons with an ancient lady to prepare her for Benton Big School. I was sure Jennie would win what she called the 'scholarship', and she did. I was jolly glad I didn't have to get one. It would be three years before I could go to Benton Big School myself, but they decided I was to attend Benton Prep when Caro began at Big School. What with the war and all, the Prep and the Big School had been put together and they had both been evacuated to Yorkshire! It was a sort of being evacuated for us too for part of the year. Lily was at Miss Hodson's now, but James was still too little to go to school. I did wish Jennie could come with me to Benton Prep. I made her promise to look after James. I knew I'd really miss him. He could talk quite well and he was so sweet. Caro said she wouldn't miss Lily, and that she was a pest! Lily sang in a very loud voice all the songs we heard on the wireless like 'Run Rabbit Run' and 'Roll out the Barrel.'

Jennie said she would be learning French at her new school, and told me secretly that she had already begun to learn it all by herself. I had already guessed what she was doing when I saw her reading a picture-book written in French about a lady mouse. She made me swear not to tell Caro because she said Caro would tease her and tell her she had not got it right. My mother spoke some French. She and Auntie Clare had had a French ma'mselle: Mummy said she'd never been any good at it, but that Auntie had always been very good at French, even before she went to study at the Beaux Arts and then live in Paris.

The summer before I went off in September to Benton Prep, Jennie told us what she and her friend Joan had been doing at the village school during her last term there. Once they knew they were going to the Grammar, they had been so bored that they begged to be allowed to make scrapbooks. Their teacher said they could, so they had done one on warships, one on lovely places in Europe with postcards that a retired teacher had given them, and one on Florence Nightingale. Jennie brought them home to show us. I decided to do a scrapbook about horses. Caro said that Jennie couldn't be as bored at school as she was, but she was quite nice about the warships book, and said she might do a scrapbook about clothes. She knew all about clothes and was awfully good at dressing up and looking grown up. She told me her ambition was to be a mannequin.

'Don't tell Jennie — it's a secret,' she said. She did love secrets.

So I had both their secrets! I don't think Jennie really enjoyed having secrets. She always liked to tell everyone all about what she had been doing. It was only Caro she didn't want to know. Caro used to tell her she was boastful.

One Saturday — I think it must have been during the summer after the summer of the Battle of Britain — we all went with my mother during the hols to see *Pride and Prejudice*, which had come round again at the town cinema. I thought it was a good film. Mummy said it was from a book and Caro should read it.

'Oh, that's a book for Jennie,' said Caro. Jennie looked surprised.

'It's too old for Jennie,' Mummy said. It must have given Jennie an idea because I remember after we had been away at school for another year she showed us a story she had written about us all as if *we* were the Bennet girls. She said she'd found a copy of *P and P* in the library. Caro did not take any interest in Jennie's writings but Jennie showed me some of it and she had written one bit specially for me. It started:

Everyone agreed that Sally Page was a very amiable young woman . . .

I was awfully flattered. It was so sweet of her. I can't remember what she said, if anything, about a character called Caroline.

Caro often said that she envied me and she said it again after I told her about Jennie's story. I was frightfully embarrassed when she said that. I explained that Jennie was just imitating the book and it was only a story. I wasn't really amiable.

Caro said, 'I didn't mean that, you ass!' She added, after a moment, 'You are just lucky to live in your own house and have both your mother and your father here.' I was surprised. I had thought that by now Caro no longer missed her parents.

'Jennie has both hers here as well,' I said.

'Oh — *Jennie*,' she said. 'I don't think I envy *her*!'

Jennie had been my best friend for ages ever since we were little and Caro knew that, but she seemed to think I ought to have a best friend from school instead. I said I could have a friend at school and a friend at home. I had thought perhaps that she might mean that *she* should be my best friend when we were both away at school, but she was too old for me to be her real best friend. Anyway, we were cousins. I had not forgotten about the blood sister thing Jennie had wanted to do with me. I was awfully fond of Jennie, and Caro could be difficult to understand. I supposed she'd thought me a bit babyish when I said *we* could be blood sisters if she wanted.

I told Mummy that Caro was sometimes hard to understand and Mummy said that she had often been upset by Auntie Clare when they were little. I was surprised. Mummy didn't usually say much about her feelings. I did like Caro but I was glad we were only cousins, not sisters. Mummy said that things were not easy for Caroline on account of her having to leave everything in France and now her father was away, as well as her mother — who had not been *obliged* to go and work in London but wanted to do her bit for the war effort.

Soon after Caro's saying she envied me, she must have been thinking about it, because she said, 'I just meant that this is your home. It's only an accident that Jennie Wilson lives here.'

Did Caro not like Jennie because Jennie didn't like *her*? I was not sure what Jennie really thought about my cousin. Caro did not care as much about being liked as I did and later on I admired her for that.

At the end of our school holidays, the day before we went back to school, Mummy always took us to the pictures. I remember a film called *The Bluebird*, which I liked even better than *Pride and Prejudice*. It was up till then the best film I'd ever seen. There were two children in it, a brother and a sister called Tytyl and Mytyl who were looking for the Bluebird of Happiness. It was a fairytale, I suppose. I thought Caro would say that it was babyish, but she said it was very well done. Jennie, who was always invited along with us, told us that her teacher at school said it was from a play written by a very good writer.

Afterwards, we all had tea for a treat at the Tea Shoppe, and Mummy said that finding happiness was not difficult if you were a happy person and there was no war going on. I couldn't believe the war would ever be over, and yet I had a very happy childhood at Pettiwell. I think I was always a lucky person and I enjoyed doing most things, except living in London — but that was later.

That afternoon, in reply to Mummy, Caro said, 'Finding happiness is not so easy if you're away at lousy school!' Jennie had often told me how she loved her own school, but she didn't contradict Caro. To me on the bus back home — we couldn't go in the car because Daddy had not enough petrol — Jennie said, 'Some people are just born happy.' I was just thinking how happy I felt in spite of going back to school, but of course I'd have been even happier if I'd had a pony. I wondered if Jennie was always happy. I didn't ask her. Caroline changed the subject and said to Jennie, 'It must be hard having an odd name like Mytyl — or Jennie.'

Jennie looked puzzled but laughed and said her other name was Joyce and anyway both were better than being called Mona. Jennie could always make you laugh, even Caro. I don't know why Caro liked to pick arguments with Jennie but it was probably because she was not happy.

Auntie Clare came over from time to time for a rest when she could be spared from her London job. She didn't show off about her work and I heard her tell Mummy that she was not brave but that driving ambulances in the blitz was less hard work than looking after Lily.

Auntie came in one day when I was with Jennie in the kitchen helping Mrs Wilson make a cake with dried eggs. Mummy must have told her about the story Jennie had written because Auntie Clare asked Jennie if she wanted to write books when she grew up.

Jennie said, 'Oh, yes, Mrs Fitzpatrick, I would, but it's easier trying to copy the *P and P* way of thinking than making it up for yourself.'

'Did you know that Jane Austen's brother lived in one of the grandest houses in the county?' Auntie asked her.

Jennie replied, No, she didn't, and Auntie said she must one day go and have a look at it.

'Then you'll know what a really grand country house is like,' she said. 'Caro, do go and find Lily,' she added.

Caro flung out of the kitchen.

Jennie had told me before that she wanted to write books. I longed at that time to be either a jockey or a ballet dancer, and I said, 'Oh, I do wish I could have ballet lessons!'

Mrs Wilson said, 'Well, if you stop growing you might be a ballerina!'

Caro overheard that remark as she came back to complain that Lily was pestering my mother.

She sat on a stool and looked at her fingernails, and said:

'Wouldn't you rather get married and have children, Sally?'

I answered that of course I would — one day — and then I went off to help play

73

with Lily. We used to cut out pictures of animals from a tattered old book and stick them into a scrapbook I made from old newspaper. I really enjoyed playing with Lil — more than I did with my brother James.

I often wondered what Auntie Clare and Mrs Wilson really thought of me. I knew I wasn't as clever as Caro or Jennie, but I didn't see why you couldn't be a ballet dancer or a jockey and then have children. I often wondered whether Mummy had ever wanted to do anything else than marry Daddy and have James and me. Caro told me her mother had always wanted to be a painter but her talent had deserted her after she had had a baby. Those were her very words. Caro could be very dramatic.

I asked Jennie the next day if she thought that having a baby would stop me being a ballerina. We were gathering windfalls for Mrs Wilson to stew, though the sugar ration was very tiny. Jennie said:

'Well, *my* mother worked all the time — and she had me! Mrs Fitzpatrick has her important war work, which she couldn't do if your mother didn't look after Lily. I suppose though that she might go back to painting after the Duration?'

Everyone called the war the Duration and

kept saying 'after the Duration', which we found funny.

'I would like to get married one day to a really nice man,' I said. I told only Jennie about my day-dreams because she never thought I was silly. That day she laughed and said:

'I'm sure you will — you deserve a Really Nice Man,' and then we both started giggling. 'You had better not marry a man like Captain Wickham, though,' she said. I could not remember at first who he was, but then I remembered the film. Caro came out of the back door and asked us what we were giggling about but we couldn't really explain. We often had fits of laughter and couldn't remember why afterwards.

I thought a lot about Jennie and Caro. Actually, they didn't seem to argue quite as much as they once had. Caro got cross with her sister more now, and argued with her mother whenever she was there. I expect that when she was twelve or thirteen she had lots of secrets we didn't know about. Jennie and I were a better age to play together. She was nearly two years older than me but Caro was two years older than Jennie and seemed always to have been too old to play the kind of games we two had enjoyed.

Caro and I now had longer holidays than

Jennie, and Jennie always had piles of prep, but they called it homework at her school. Before we went away to Benton at the beginning of our terms though, she would arrive home from school at about half past four and come over and talk to me before she got on with her work. Lily was soon old enough to play with us as well and Jennie was always nice to her. As time went on, that is what we always did after the Grammar School terms had started. Caro grumbled that her mother should be at home whenever she was still on holiday herself, never mind her 'war work', and that Lily was not *her* responsibility. I heard Mummy tell Daddy she thought Auntie Clare really enjoyed herself doing dangerous things in London!

Jennie always wrote to me at school and said it didn't matter if I didn't always write back. Mummy had told me it was rude not to reply to letters though you didn't have to answer straight away. I loved getting letters, and on Sundays, after I had replied to Mummy, if I owed her a letter I wrote to Jennie. After Sunday supper you were allowed to talk to members of your own family even if they were in a different year so Caro sometimes came over to chat to me. She often asked me if Jennie had written to me.

'*You* ought to write to her,' I said.

'I have enough to do writing to Ma,' she replied. I knew she liked to hear from her mother in London and she once had a letter from her father — posted in England, but she told me she was sure he was abroad.

The war dragged on and we had maps of battlefields at school and little flags to stick in to show where our soldiers had got to. I had been a bit too young to know what was going on earlier, when Hitler had been fighting the Russians, and before that when the Battle of Britain was happening — and even after that, when stray bombs were apparently falling all over the place, especially on the coast. I wasn't told about all that but when the fighting started and went on for ages in North Africa, I began to take more interest.

Daddy had been an officer in the Home Guard right from the beginning of the war and they were always having exercises and marching up and down in the village. After the very first siren that had gone when the war started, we in Pettiwell hadn't heard another for ages, and I could not imagine how awful it had been in the blitz in London. Granny and Grandpa just went around looking grim but saying nothing and Auntie Clare never said much about it either, not to us anyway. We children didn't know the details till we were older. Jennie said her father maintained they didn't tell you everything on the news. Mummy and Daddy always listened to the nine o'clock news bulletin.

I remember that after the bombs had stopped being dropped for quite a long time, Auntie was given the job of chauffeuring some American officers. We didn't know then of course how soon the V-1s and V-2s, flying bombs and rockets, would be arriving. The great news when I'd just had my eleventh birthday and was going back to school in two weeks was that Italy had surrendered in North Africa.

Mummy said, 'Oh, it's wonderful — it'll be over soon!'

To which my father replied, 'It'll take more than a few months to drive the Germans back up the length of Italy.'

I have just looked it up and discovered that Italy surrendered just four years after the beginning of the war, on the third of September 1943. The order of events is still all a bit of a muddle in my head. As I said, I've never been good at remembering dates or what came before what. Most of the time when I was at Pettiwell I was just getting on with ordinary things, helping with the shopping, helping Mrs Wilson around the house — I enjoyed that, more than Jennie did, I think — and knitting and reading and going to the pictures and sometimes running in the garden with our dog Bruno to get warm because there was never enough coal and it was a big house to heat. Elsie too had gone to work in munitions and so we all had to help with housework and Caroline even did a bit of gardening, growing potatoes. Wilson had turned his strawberry-beds into a vegetable patch, whenever his Home Guard duties spared him. 'Digging for Victory', they called it. We were always being told what to do and what not to do by the government. 'Make do and Mend' was always on Jennie's mother's lips and Jennie said that wouldn't be much of a change since her mother never threw anything away and mended everything. Father's favourite slogan was 'Careless Talk Costs Lives', and mine was 'Coughs and Sneezes spread Diseases'. I pointed out the poster to Lily who never had a hankie.

Lots of the village boys had been called up and were scattered all over the world. At about the time of the Italians surrendering, Caro must have been nearly fifteen and did not talk to me as much as she once had. She was very thick with a girl at school called Gwendoline but at home she seemed to disappear into herself and if Mummy asked what she was thinking she'd say she was thinking about nothing.

Jennie said you couldn't think about 'nothing' because 'nothing' was still 'something', and anyway you'd be thinking about *thinking nothing*. Caro got up — we were sitting at the nursery table at the time and Jennie was helping me do my holiday task. Caro shouted, 'You think you know everything don't you, Miss Wilson!' in a really sarcastic voice.

Jennie went quite red and said, 'No I don't, and I wasn't being nasty — it's an interesting thought, that's all.'

Caro flung out of the room, banging the door. Afterwards I said to Jennie that she was probably thinking of her father and missing her mother, and Jennie said:

'You are probably right, Sally — you always are. I talk too much.'

Actually, by this time I don't think Caro did miss her mother all that much. She'd got used to her being in London, and after all she was still doing her bit for the war effort, so Caro could be proud of her. I think she worried more about her father. We all did. We all loved my uncle Frank.

I have not said very much about Lily or my brother James. Mummy said Lily would hardly remember her father, being not quite five when he went away on official work for the War Office. Mummy had become a sort of mother to her, so that whenever Auntie Clare did come back to Pettiwell for a rest, Lily was cross. By the time he was five, James had become Lily's best friend. They went to school together and were inseparable. When she was eight and a half Lily was to go to another school, not a boarding-school, but Father wanted James to go away to prep school when he was eight. That wouldn't be for years though.

'The war will be over by then,' he said. The little private school, which Lily was about to attend, did take boys till they were eight, so Mummy said to Daddy:

'I think James could go along with Lily — he's growing out of Miss Hodson and Miss Bell!'

They were the two middle-aged ladies who owned the little school in the neighbouring town. We'd all been there, except for Jennie. They were getting old too and there was never enough fuel to keep the schoolroom warm. I agreed with Mummy. She was so sensible, and knew James would miss Lily when she left Miss Bell's. She managed to persuade Daddy, and so both Lily and James were taken to the new day school. It must have been the Christmas eighteen months before the war ended. I think it was about now that people began talking about what the Nazis called their 'secret weapon'.

I started to enjoy playing with James, although I could not interest him in horses. He was a nice little boy but it was Lily who was the more adventurous. She was a real tomboy and climbed trees I had never climbed myself though I was a good climber. Sometimes Jennie came and played with us too and when they got tired of rushing round, the little ones liked her to tell them stories. I could never invent very good stories but Jennie made up tales about two children called Jilly and Willy who had lots of adventures. She was clever at burying a moral in a story. Caro heard one or two of these stories and said Jennie should have been a preacher.

'No,' replied Jennie, 'a teacher, not a preacher.'

'Much the same thing, isn't it?' said Caro.

Jennie told me her mother wanted her to be a teacher, but she was not so keen herself. We still talked about our ambitions when we were together. Jennie said she'd considered being an actress — she had a big part in their school play — but she'd changed it to wanting to be a writer, or perhaps a librarian. Her teachers at school had told her that writing was not a very well-paid occupation unless you were someone like Dickens.

'I shall have to earn my living, you see,' she said.

I hadn't really thought seriously about a career for myself in that way. I'd wanted to be a ballet dancer or a jockey but then, as Mrs Wilson had hinted, I had soon become a bit too tall to be either. Also, I was afraid I would never pick up all my riding skills again.

Caro had slightly changed her ambitions too, no longer wanting to be a mannequin. One day she told us she had decided instead to be a fashion designer.

'I shall found a business selling the clothes I design and make,' she said.

Jennie remarked, looking up from her book, 'You'll have to go to art school to train for commercial art then.'

They had careers talks at her school so she knew a bit about it.

Caro said, Yes, she knew all about that. Strangely enough — or at least I found it strange because I was hopeless at maths — my cousin was very good at arithmetic. She would sit her school cert the following summer. Jennie pointed out that if she was going to make a profit from selling her clothes she'd have to have a business brain and maths would come in extremely useful.

We all took our ambitions seriously. I had

decided that if the war went on I'd like to be either a nurse or a pilot. It wouldn't matter how tall you were for these jobs. I wasn't sure how much pilots were paid, if at all. I knew nurses did it for love.

'Drop bombs?' enquired Jennie. 'You're far too kind-hearted.'

'I meant piloting a plane in peacetime as well,' I replied.

I'd looked forward to learning to drive a car ever since I was a little girl. Five more years till I could get a driving licence!

'Driving' an aeroplane must be a bit similar, I thought.

'It would be better to be a nurse, if the war goes on,' said Jennie.

'Then you'd be useful binding up the wounds of the people the pilots had dropped bombs on,' said Caro.

I think she was teasing me but I didn't mind.

★ ★ ★

It was next year that Wealdridge and many other places nearer London were to have experience of pilotless planes. At first some people called them robot bombs and then 'doodlebugs', and then V-1s and afterwards there were V-2s. Caro and I went back to

84

school for the summer term and Jennie wrote to me about them. It had been on the news on the wireless, which we were allowed to listen to once a day. Jennie wrote that her father called them 'flying bombs', and Mummy wrote to tell us not to worry, but we did. *She* called them doodlebugs. People in our corner of the south-east of England had realized what they were when they saw one or two in the sky, travelling towards London. I found out later that they could go at 700 miles an hour. Daddy thought that perhaps Mummy and Lily and James ought to go and stay somewhere away from Pettiwell just in case, but Mummy didn't want to.

'Most places in England are out of their range — they certainly won't fall in Yorkshire,' Daddy wrote to me. Perhaps he thought I'd be worrying about them falling on the school! I only worried about my family and wished I could be with them, flying bombs or not.

Jennie then wrote again a week later to tell me that one had crashed only a mile or two away! As far as she knew, nobody was hurt, though they had dug some people out, and her father and Daddy had gone to help. The worst thing, Jennie wrote, was when you heard the 'buzz' of the plane stop and waited to see if it was going to drop on you. They

85

were not quite like bombs. These were the V-1s, but they weren't called that until the others came over, the V-2s.

Caro and I came back home from school in July and nothing happened for some time. By August they seemed to have stopped, only to be replaced just before we went back to school by this other kind, the V-2s, rockets with no wings but much quicker than the first sort. I don't know which was worse. Apparently they were crashing all over South London. There were no further details on the wireless about them — they just went on calling them flying bombs. This time once you heard the crash and knew you were still alive you knew it wouldn't be you that was going to be killed. Jennie told me people in the village said: 'If it's got your name on it!' I thought they were very brave.

V-2s were to go on for quite some time, almost right to the end of the war, but it was only the south-east of England that was affected. Some children were evacuated again. Daddy grumbled that very little was being said on the news about them. The danger did not really stop till almost the end of the war.

Before then, Jennie wrote to tell me that a friend of her mother's had been killed by one in Lewisham. I still have that letter, so the

V-2s must have gone on for months and months.

Uncle Frank had been away for four years, but he came over on a short leave just before what we later were to call D-day! Nobody was allowed to know what he had been doing, but Caro said he had told her mother a bit about it. Caro kept saying: 'How long is this bloody war going to go on?'

The headmistress heard Mr Churchill say the war was over, on her wireless at school on 7 May 1945. It was a Monday, and on Tuesday we had all the celebrations for Victory at school. Mummy wrote to tell me how they had celebrated in the village with a party and everybody sitting at a long table. She helped with the teas. We had the jollifications again at home in August for victory over the Japanese, and we at Pettiwell made a bonfire, and found some sparklers left over from 1938! I remember all that very well. We hadn't been able to have a Guy Fawkes bonfire for seven years and we'd had the blackout for six years so you can imagine how people loved having bonfires.

Caro left school at the end of that summer term after a year in the sixth, and had her seventeenth birthday a little later. I was thirteen and I wished I could leave school too!

Jennie was worried about the atom bomb and everything, and we had all been horrified when they opened the concentration camps. Uncle Frank came back again in October but went away soon afterwards to London to stay with Auntie Clare. Mummy said he and Auntie Clare had to decide where they would live.

Caro was determined to go to art school.

I went to stay with a friend from school whose father had a big farm in north Yorkshire. It was a lovely visit — they had horses and ponies and I rode on a lovely little horse called Rosemary.

I felt really grown-up. It was a super happy time.

3

CAROLINE

I can remember hating England at first. I was eleven when we went to live at Pettiwell, leaving my home, a flat in Paris, and the Jardin du Luxembourg, which I loved, and where Papa used to take me to see the Petit Guignol, a sort of Punch and Judy show. When I was little I had played under the trees on the sandy paths and watched the fountain in the Bassin; in summer I had been bought my favourite ice cream — *plombière* it was called. The English didn't even have a name for it and called it by the Italian name, *tutti frutti*. In winter we bought roast chestnuts from the man by the gate at the Boul' Mich end.

The summer we left I'd just finished at the *petit lycée* and was looking forward to the big *lycée* in the seventh *arrondissement*. I already spoke English of course, because of my parents, but I always spoke French to my school friends. There is a picture of my class at school, all of us in our *tabliers*, a sort of smock everyone wore in French schools, with

89

the name, (surname first) embroidered on the front, so that the teachers would know who you were. I was angry with my mother because I thought Papa would have stayed in France after the war started and it was her fault for being English and wanting to help the English win the war. My father wasn't completely English but what was called Anglo-Irish, and I had decided he didn't need to leave France. I knew, though, that he had a British passport as well as an Irish one! He had been born in Ireland when it was part of Britain. Ma said that Lily and I had dual nationality because we were born in France. I was quite proud of this.

I had not enjoyed our visit to London and Pettiwell the previous year very much, except for making friends with my cousin Sally who was easy to get on with and always fell in with whatever you wanted to do. I hated English bread, and puddings, and I missed my *pain au chocolat*, as well as missing my friends and the warmth of our flat on the rue de Rennes.

At first I felt frozen with cold everywhere I went in England, especially at Pettiwell, which was freezing even in summer. I found all English houses cold. Mother's relations talked about the rector and the village and were crazy about horses and dogs. They always seemed to be making a big effort to be

90

kind. I suppose they were, but I resented them. If Mother liked England so much, why had she stayed in France up to now? I didn't think my father was as keen on fighting the war as she was. (I think I was wrong there.)

My English grandparents lived in an old house in a London square. I had the notion my mother had never got on with them and I remembered meeting them only once before, when I was about four. I remembered better a very old lady from that time, my mother's grandmother, who had brought up both *Maman* and Aunt Ruth. She gave me some chocolate and I thought she was nice, but she and her husband, my great grandfather I suppose, had both died since then. It must have been before Lily was born that my mother had taken me over to see them. My father's relations, the Fitzpatricks, all appeared to have either died or, like Papa, gone to live abroad. Not in France though, but in America. I never remember seeing them. Anyway, I didn't know many English people.

I'd screamed and cried at first when I was told that we were leaving Paris, and *Maman* was very cross with me for making a fuss. I was quite old enough to understand, she said. Lily did not cry but she was only four. I remember shouting:

'You're taking me away from my *home*. I won't go, I won't go!'

Papa understood better, I think. He had lived in London when his family had had to leave Ireland, so he knew it quite well, but I feel sure he preferred Paris. He could not take us all back to Ireland because only Northern Ireland was in the war on the side of the British. His family's house, which I thought sounded very grand, was near Cork and that was in Southern Ireland.

I know I was very sulky at Pettiwell at first and I heard my mother tell Aunt Ruth I was 'difficult'. Even my father whispered, 'Don't let your mother down — make the best of it,' which, when I come to think of it, was an odd thing to say. Aunt Ruth wasn't a bit like *Maman*, so in a way it was easier to be nice to her. I felt that in an odd way *Maman* didn't like her sister, yet I couldn't think of any particular thing she'd done or said to make me feel this. She always expressed her gratitude to Aunt Ruth for taking us in and was always reminding me to be grateful to her and Uncle Jack, but . . . I had the feeling, as I grew older, that many things were just not being said. I even told Sally that I had a secret though I didn't really have one. I used to make things up, I know, and write them in a special code to impress her. Once, I even put

92

a letter in code in a box in the attic! I wonder what became of it.

I never mentioned any of this to Jennie Wilson. She would have pounced on me and asked me what I had written. At Pettiwell I usually took my crossness out on Jennie. I had discovered the year before, when we all went there for the day, that she was the daughter of the housekeeper. She wanted to be one of a threesome with Sally and me. I felt she was an outsider and wished I had my French friends there to show her that I did have lots of friends and did not need another one. My cousin Sally was enough. I reasoned, I suppose, that *Jennie* would consider *me* as an outsider. I knew I was, and I didn't really want to belong to Pettiwell at first, but she was a different kind of outsider — and didn't even know she was. It wasn't my fault that I had been forced to go and live there.

Jennie wasn't unkind but she irritated me terribly, and it also irritated me that Sally didn't find her irritating too. Aunt Ruth said she was a clever girl, but I knew that she used to swot up things to say that would impress people. I found a notebook once where she wrote down special schoolgirl slang words that she thought I would not understand, and she pretended she understood French. Sometimes I'd answer her in French just to see her puzzled look. I imitated her saying some of the words I'd seen she'd written down, words like 'topping' and 'no end' and 'jolly decent', silly words Jennie thought English schoolgirls at boarding-schools used, but not the sort of words her friends from the elementary school knew. She guessed I'd seen her notebook and was mocking her. She was always making scrapbooks and writing stories. There was a scrapbook about women writers she was very proud of and she wrote adventure stories, which she read aloud to Sally, and to me if I could not escape.

I made a scrapbook about France, and places I'd been to in Italy with my parents, and I could see Jennie was impressed. I wanted her to realize I was exotic. Another time I started a book of fashion plates. Jennie had no idea of fashion — none of them had. Aunt Ruth used to ask me about clothes. She was so unlike my mother, and I used to tease her without meaning to. I hated being grateful to them all.

I did not show Jennie my sketchbooks, though I know she was interested. She was nearer me in age than Sally was and I suppose she was really more like me than Sally but I did resent her. She was not bad-looking, though nobody would have called her pretty. She had thick brownish hair and grey eyes and quite big ears. Her profile was good, though I would never have told her so.

Jennie once wrote a story about some girls. It was after Aunt Ruth had taken us to see *Pride and Prejudice*, and Jennie made Sally into the heroine, calling her an 'amiable girl'. Sally *was* an amiable girl, good and kind, but like her mother, my Aunt Ruth, a little naïve. Later, I wanted to discuss Aunt Ruth with *Maman*, whom I now called Ma, but by then she had gone off to her war work, after telling me to behave myself and not let *Papa* down. It struck me again as peculiar that my mother didn't want me to let down my father, and father didn't want me to let down my mother, as though they were being frightfully worried about each other, not about me.

I suppose that if Lily and I had been too difficult they would not have known what to do with us. We might then have been evacuated to strangers, unless *Maman* gave up her London job to look after us. I just knew however that she did not like Pettiwell and did not want to live with her sister. Of course my Aunt Ruth would never have let us go to strangers even if I had burned down Pettiwell! Lily was happy there. She loved her aunt and uncle and I think she forgot all about France. She loved Sally too, more than she liked me, I think.

I was furious when Jennie asked me if I was homesick. After my parents had left Pettiwell to help the war effort I was angry with them too, but I knew I had to make the best of Aunt Ruth and Sally. Uncle Jack was always nice to me. I think he was probably sorry for me and thought he ought to spoil me a little.

Jennie was very possessive about Sally. She had had a ridiculous idea she had found in some book, of making Sally her 'blood sister'. I didn't like that at all. I told Sally that *she* might have blue blood, but Jennie certainly hadn't! I thought Jennie was sometimes quite mad, or that she had a fantasy that her father was really an aristocrat — perhaps one of the family her mother had worked for, though they weren't really aristocrats, just rich, and Sally's father was just a baronet. Jennie never said anything like this but I imagined it was the sort of thing she might think. She was very romantic.

Things got a little bit better later, when we were a bit older. Jennie was clever enough to argue properly with and I didn't care if I hurt her feelings. I thought she was tough. I told Sally secrets sometimes and asked her not to tell Jennie. I don't think Jennie ever grumbled to Sally about the arguments she had with me. They were both of them really too young for me to bother with, until we were all grown up. I did always realize that Sally was that 'amiable' girl and that my victories over the two of them were too easy. Jennie would be a harder nut to crack when she grew up, I thought.

I felt useless when I was sent away to Queen Eleanor's. I just *hated* it. I'd always enjoyed drawing and painting, but the teachers there were hopeless. Apparently they had once had a drawing-master, before the war, but all the male teachers had been called up, unless they were too ancient. Our women teachers were all spinsters and middle-aged or they'd have been called up too. I was bored and angry a lot of the time, and it didn't help when Sally joined me later in Big School. She was just too young and I was lonely. I did want to be an important person for her as I imagined my mother had been for her sister Ruth, but at home Sally was still close to Jennie.

I think it must have been Sally who persuaded Jennie to write to me. One day during my School Certificate year there was a letter waiting for me in the Big Room where our letters were distributed under the eagle eye of Miss Horrocks — 'Horrible Horrocks'. The envelope was addressed in handwriting I didn't at first recognize, though I knew I'd seen it somewhere before. When I opened it I saw it was written partly in French, and not bad French either, though there were some mistakes. A letter from Jennie — well, well!

She wrote that as she couldn't have a French pen-pal because of the war, and was tired of waiting for one from Montreal, she hoped I didn't mind writing to her. I knew she loved writing letters. She said, as I was bilingual, if I had nothing better to do perhaps I would correct her mistakes? I was surprised. Right from the beginning I had never been able to praise Jennie, but she knew me better than anyone here at school, even though she was younger than me, and she'd bothered to write, even if it was with the excuse of having her French corrected. I think she was the sort of person who can't bear not to be liked.

I challenged Sally when I saw her at Sunday supper and she admitted she might have mentioned it in her letter to Jennie. After supper you were 'allowed' to talk for half an hour to your friends. Kind of them, wasn't it? Honestly, I wouldn't have sent a cat to board at QE's. The food was execrable, like everywhere you went in England. I knew it was partly the fault of the war, and the reason for my parents' absences was the same, but it was not much fun being fifteen and a fish out of water, with nothing nice to eat and most of the other girls great hulking hockey-players. So I did reply occasionally to Jennie — at least she wasn't a keen hockey-player.

I was so glad to leave that school. I'd taken my School Cert quite early, but it felt years before I left, as I just had to kick my heels in the sixth form. One teacher, Miss Arnold, who was half-French, did take an interest in my drawing and encouraged me to go to exhibitions. There was one in Leeds she took us all too. 'Fantasy of Fashion', it was called, and it was wizard. I'd taken my sketchbook and I sat and copied lots of super clothes. Though I say it myself, I guessed that a 'new look' was just around the corner and would soon burst on us. I could improve on the fashions I saw in Leeds, I thought, wonderful as they were. A year later the real New Look did arrive! By then I'd filled lots of sketchbooks with my own ideas.

My parents had agreed I could go to art school when I was eighteen. Even the headmistress later admitted that there had been no point to my staying on longer in the sixth. I think she knew my parents still had no permanent home so it had been easier for me to stay on at school. She was jolly relieved when I was off her hands. We had still not gone back to Paris to see *Papa* and it was not for another eighteen months that I did.

I had had to make a big effort over Easter '46, when *Maman* and *Papa*, now called Ma and Pa, both came over to Pettiwell, and I had had to persuade them both to let me go to art school. They had not been very keen about the idea at first, though they must have known for ages what I was really good at and wanted to do. Having once tried to live on their painting they knew how hard it was, and I suppose they wanted me to have an easier life. I'd have to follow a general course at first if I went to any good college of art. Ma hadn't painted for years and kept hinting that she had new plans for when she was free, so, all that summer, as I waited for them to come back, I drew and planned my portfolio of drawings. My father had obviously given up any idea of being a professional painter long ago. He'd had to earn his living in Paris for several years before we were all forced into exile in *Angleterre*. I knew he'd left his painting gear at Pettiwell in hopes, but I think now that the war was the making of him and it certainly changed his course.

When I got back for good that July, Pa was still in Paris and Ma in London. Although the war in the Far East had been over for a year my mother had gone on driving round VIPs, but that life would soon be over when the

Americans were all back home. My parents still had to make up their minds where we all lived. Pa had just been offered a job connected with the British Council in Paris but Ma intimated she didn't want to go back to live in France. At first I was surprised. We had found out before the war ended what my father had been doing during it, being dropped clandestinely in France from one of our planes and linking with the Resistance. He'd been back in France when de Gaulle re-entered Paris, and there had still been a lot for him to do over there for a year after the end of the war.

I was too busy thinking about my future to dwell on the past, especially the war. For four years of it I'd been in Yorkshire, or at Pettiwell. It was only later that I began to think about my childhood. I thought at the time that I'd never been really close to my parents and I was now ready to manage without them. I'd never considered either what Pa was really doing at — or for — the War Office, had vaguely thought he might be painting battlefields. I'd worried about Ma being in London when the flying bombs started, but during the blitz I hadn't known enough about what was happening to understand how dangerous her work was. It's only now I realize how tough she must have been. I remember saying when the buzz bombs started that my mother always did what she wanted, so she wouldn't want to leave her war work to come and stay with Lily and me. Aunt Ruth had looked searchingly at me when I said that and I could tell she was about to say something, but she didn't.

I didn't see much of Jennie at Pettiwell that summer. Since she'd begun to write to me and I had replied in as idiomatic French as possible, I'd thought she'd want some French conversation when we met again, after I arrived back for good from Queen Eleanor's. She had just done her own School Cert. I guessed she'd worked very hard for her exams — she was a real swot. She wasn't there when I got back: her father had taken her for a two weeks' cycling holiday, and Mrs Wilson, who hardly ever had a holiday, had gone to visit her nephew whom she hadn't seen for years. I could see Aunt Ruth expected me to help around the house when I returned, aided by Sally who actually enjoyed helping her mother and just adored country life. Then Sally went to stay with a friend for two weeks. I just got on with my own work when I thought I'd done my bit with the duster.

Once I'd been accepted at Wimbledon I would have to sort out my digs problem. I was impatient to discover what allowance my parents would give me. I'd no intention of staying in Pettiwell! I had a letter from my father a few days later, implying that he left the decision about my studies to me, so long as my mother did not object. He would see that my fees were paid and an allowance would be given to me. He was putting aside an annual sum for that express purpose and sending it to Ma to settle with me. I expect he thought she should keep an eye on me. Once I was of age, I hoped I'd have an allowance paid to me directly, though he said nothing about that.

There weren't many grants for art unless you were poor and applied to the county. You might get a special scholarship when you'd done three years. I knew that Sally's parents didn't have all that much money left after keeping the house going, and I hoped they'd been paid by Ma and Pa for having Lily and me around all through the war. I hated the idea of sponging on them, but I think I remember Pa sending bank drafts to Uncle Jack, so that must have been for our keep. When I thought about it I came to the conclusion that Pa had no intention, at present anyway, of returning to England.

I toyed with the notion of joining him in Paris and attending an art school there leaving Ma to stew in her own juice, but thought I'd better wait for my mother to come to Pettiwell and see what her plans were. I knew that she was always the one to make the big decisions, especially about anything to do with me. Strangely enough, I felt nervous about going to a college in France. In addition, if Pa had really wanted me to go to live there, he'd have said so.

In the meantime I cycled around the lanes and quite enjoyed myself sketching. If Jennie could go on bike holidays, then so could I. I reflected, though, that *my* father was not waiting on *my* every whim even as far as accompanying me on holiday! I couldn't imagine his ever doing that, and I suppose in a way it made me feel more independent and free of the family. I never felt close to *Maman* now, which was only to be expected, yet I still used to wish that we knew each other better and got on better. I seemed to remember a time when she and I had been really close, before the war, perhaps even before I had gone to the *école maternelle*. When we did see each other now I felt almost embarrassed, if that isn't a silly word for a relationship with your mother. Shy, anyway, which became reserve on my part. I knew she wished me well; she knew I was ambitious. I wondered if she had ever been as ambitious as I was. I suppose having me had put paid to that.

When I was small I vaguely thought that mothers existed to look after children. It was only much later, perhaps only after I had stopped being a student, that I realized how having children 'end-stopped' their mothers in a way it didn't inhibit their fathers. I didn't think my mother had ever had a nanny for me, as Aunt Ruth had at first for her daughter. She had looked after us all in Paris as well. It was the war that had enabled her to change her life. Why should I — who had certainly decided by the time I was fifteen never to have children — resent that she had finally chosen a different path, and no longer appeared to put her family first?

Part Two

1946–1951

4

Mrs Laura Ogilvie, wearing a grey cardigan which she kept pulling across her chest with both hands, was sitting on the rustic bench. The cardigan looked worse for wear though it had obviously been washed many times.

She's probably cold, thought Jennie Wilson, who had been skulking across the stone terrace in front of the house. Not that she was forbidden to walk there but she did not particularly want to be seen by Sally's grandmother. Mr and Mrs Ogilvie had stayed six months at Pettiwell in the war but had then departed to a boarding-house near Oxford, which they hoped would be both warmer and quieter. Jennie's own parents had been on their toes whilst the visit took place, and Jennie had gathered that her mother did not find Laura Ogilvie, her old employer's daughter-in-law, easy to please. Her mother had hinted that even Ruth Page had felt relieved, if guilty, when they had left. Now that the war was over they were back for a few weeks' holiday whilst they considered where to go next.

It might just as well have been the war still,

the old woman was thinking. Everything had changed, mainly because you could not get decent servants, or even any servants at all, unless you were much better off than Sir Jack appeared to be. Laura Ogilvie often felt angry nowadays, and although the war was over she seemed even to herself to exist in a permanent state of simmering rage and anxiety. Sometimes she woke in the night and found herself thinking she had been a failure with both her daughters. She had not brought up Clare and Ruth herself, had been grateful to her parents-in-law for taking charge of them. Sometimes she wished she had kept them in India until they were ready to go away to school, but the climate there was hazardous for children, and most of her friends had left their offspring at home in England. One's first duty had been to one's husband, and both Clare and Ruth had seemed happy enough in London when they visited on leave. Clare had had problems later, but Granny Ogilvie had dealt with them.

Now she wished she and Andrew had never come back at all from India, fifteen years ago, when he was retired from the Army, but it was no good wishing. Very soon, 'they' said that India was to be given back to the Indians. After all that had been done for them! It was all the fault of the Labour government. She doubted the English would be welcome there in future, and it just made her realize her life was nearly over and would end unhappily.

At other times, when she had got up and felt a little more cheerful, she would think the girls had not done too badly, whatever problems there had been, and the grandchildren were a sort of comfort to her. Now that England had won the war and the evacuees had returned to their slums, and the men had come back, and the bomb damage was being repaired — though 'they' were taking their time over that — surely things could get back to normal?

'It will never go back to what it was like before, Ma,' her elder daughter had insisted, but Clare had always been abrasive, liking an argument. Spoiled by her grandmother, in Laura's opinion. As for things improving, food was still in very short supply, rationing was as bad as in the 'duration', and you could still only buy your food at the shop where you were registered. It was still 'tighten your belts', and 'all pull together', and people were no longer respectful to their elders and betters. All the women cared about was getting hold of nylons and having a good time. You had to be young now to be pandered to.

She looked up, caught sight of Jennie Wilson and stared at her.

'Oh, I'm sorry, Mrs Ogilvie . . . '

Jennie began a hasty retreat, banging her ankle on a sticking-out edge of stone at the bottom of the terrace wall, which needed repair.

What made Laura say: 'No — don't go!'

Was she lonely? Did she just want someone to sympathize with her? Andrew was so deaf nowadays that it was no good trying to communicate with him. Ruth was always busy and today she was helping Polly Wilson clear out attics.

'It's Hicks's daughter, isn't it?' said Laura. She thought the girl looked blank for a moment.

As though she didn't know! thought Jennie. She must have seen her when she stayed here during the war. Then she realized that Mrs Ogilvie's sight might no longer be so good. She still had her knitting specs on.

The old lady took these off just as Jennie was thinking this.

'When your mother was my mother's parlour-maid we always called her Hicks.' Of course she'd been Wilson for ages. Why was she burbling on as though it had to be explained to her daughter who Hicks had been? Had the message of 'we're all equal now' somehow insinuated itself into her mind against her will?

'Yes, I'm Polly Hicks's daughter, Jennie Wilson,' replied Jennie in a clear civil voice. She had never yet had a proper conversation with this lady. Even Caro, who was the lady's granddaughter, tended to avoid her, and Sally found her intimidating. They all knew James was her favourite.

The girl spoke well, thought Laura, with little trace of a rustic accent.

'My eyes are bad but you don't look like your mother when she was younger,' she said, adding, 'Well of course my husband and I were away when she was about your age. She was a great help to my mother-in-law with my daughters.'

She was thinking that the child's father had been a mainstay to Sir Jack too for a very long time. A pity Sir Jack's grandparents and parents had left so much at Pettiwell that needed to be seen to. Her son-in-law's ancestors had once upon a time lived in a much grander house a few miles away, about the time this house was being built, and she had been told that the other house had since been pulled down, so she supposed they were lucky still to have this one. Even before the Great War, many families could no longer keep up a house and estate even as small as this one, and in the nineteen twenties the Wilsons must have replaced a whole army of servants.

She sighed. When Ruth had made such a good marriage she had thought their problems would be over, but now she suspected her son-in-law had always been extremely strapped for cash. The money had all come from business in the first place. Her husband had explained to her that the 1914 war had probably alleviated things for a time, since the iron their subsidiaries manufactured would go into armaments. It was tiresome having to think about these things. Her younger daughter had never intimated to her that they were in financial trouble but she knew the signs. The plight of the house made her feel useless, an encumbrance. Not that Ruth would ever have considered her one, but it added to her annoyance.

Jennie stood irresolutely now. Laura made an effort. She knew the child had always been a friend of her granddaughter Sally.

'Come and sit here next to me. Tell me, what is your Christian name.'

This must be unusual behaviour from Mrs Ogilvie, thought Jennie, who was well aware what a gloomy grandmother she was on her visits to Pettiwell.

'It's Jennie,' she said again. The lady might also be a little deaf. Her eyes were red-rimmed. From tiredness, or a cold? Or had she been crying?

Jennie remembered her own mother had never liked Ruth's mother much even when she was young. She'd liked Colonel Ogilvie better, even if he was not a patch on the 'Old 'Uns'.

Now Jennie sat down carefully at the other end of the rustic bench. Politeness was expected. However, she could not resist remarking:

'Sally's mother calls Mother her housekeeper, but my parents do all sorts of different work here, you know.'

Mrs Ogilvie looked a little surprised to hear such a frank statement from a child. How old was she? Fourteen? Fifteen?

'I expect your mother has her work cut out trying to get hold of more servants for Lady Page.'

'Neither Ethel nor Elsie wanted to come back,' said Jennie, thinking she had better put in a good word for Sally's mother. 'It was a blow for Lady Page. They are all very hard-worked. The house needs heaps of people to make it like it used to be in the olden days,' she added.

As though I didn't know that, thought Laura.

'You are interested in Pettiwell in the olden days?'

'My mother never saw it in its heyday,' said Jennie with relish. 'There would once have been scores of servants.'

'All houses need good servants,' said Laura severely. 'Those you can get now are not trained.'

Jennie was amused. It was interesting listening to a survival of days gone by. What must the old life really have been like? Sir Jack was no longer rich, but the Wilsons' lives were not unpleasant. There would not have been much chance of a long-ago Jennie being a real friend to the children of an older Pettiwell House. She realized that.

'Girls who were once servants can earn more money in offices and factories,' she added, having no intention of working in either.

She smiled at Mrs Ogilvie. It must be hard to have to live in such a different way from what you had been led to expect.

'Things have got worse, and will get even worse,' said Laura firmly. She saw the girl was listening. 'Life is impossible really — and yet the war is supposed to be over! Everything is out of kilter. It isn't the world I used to know — or even the one your parents knew! Remember that.'

Jennie tried to look sympathetic. She did wish her parents didn't have to work so hard for so little, though they loved their work and never complained. Their employers were kind ones. It was only recently that Jennie had realized that they were still, strictly speaking, servants, however well treated. Her mother though had always been loyal to the Ogilvies, even Ogilvies by marriage like this old lady. But Jennie had heard her mother talking to her father about her, saying Laura Ogilvie had never had any sympathy for her elder daughter. Jennie was unclear as to why Clare Fitzpatrick should have needed such sympathy. Perhaps she meant that Mrs Ogilvie could have had her daughter and family to live with her or near her in London, and had not offered? Caroline and her family could after all have gone there instead of Pettiwell when they had been forced to leave Paris? This had not occurred to Jennie before. Still, it had been a good thing they hadn't, what with the bombing in London, the extent of which Jennie was only just realizing.

Laura peered in Jennie's direction.

'I hear you are a clever girl,' she said feebly.

Jennie was always having her cleverness reported to her at second hand. Who had told the lady?

'Well, you see, if I win scholarships it will

not matter that my parents are not very well-paid,' she explained confidingly. 'I mean, as far as my own finances are concerned. If we were rich my father would have to pay fees for my education. I am at the Grammar School you see, and want to go to the university.'

She added the last sentence in explanation, knowing that old ladies did not expect girls to go to universities, never mind the daughters of servants. Mrs Ogilvie might think her mother had been complaining about the amount of work she had to do.

'I hear that you are a good friend to Sally,' said Laura, trying her best to sound democratic. Her mother-in-law had been very fond of Polly Hicks, and, come to that, her own daughters too, especially Ruth.

'Yes, we've always known each other.'

She wanted to add: *We were like sisters till her cousin came along,* but that would sound ignoble and perhaps boastful.

'How times have changed,' murmured Laura after a pause, 'It is all so depressing!'

She spoke without considering the effect her words might have, but Jennie, whatever her inmost thoughts, had been brought up to be both tolerant and tactful to old ladies in public. Her mother could trust her. She might even educate an old lady about a changing world?

Sally had said she didn't want to go to university. Would Mrs Ogilvie think Jennie was getting above herself to nourish such an ambition? Would she think that a housekeeper's daughter should not be aiming for higher education? Jennie was ever sensitive to other people's reactions, but for some reason she rather wanted this old lady to approve of her. Once, even Mrs Ogilvie had been young! Fancy staying most of the time in India though, and letting your mother-in-law bring up your children. Mother-in-law plus faithful servant, anyway.

Laura was now launched on to what was a familiar diatribe. Jennie had overheard the same phrases from many people who visited Pettiwell.

Food in such short supply . . . still rationed . . . punishing taxation . . . lack of proper heating . . . all the government's fault . . . scarcity of petrol . . . scarcity of servants . . . house and garden neglected . . . American influence . . .

'And now we are to give away India!' she ended.

Jennie listened, thinking, even as she listened, that she was listening respectfully. Most people she knew in the village complained of much the same things, but the shortage of servants was a problem confined to the well-off. Would she too feel one day that things had gone from bad to worse? Was it just age that made you dissatisfied? Did things always change? Or was it just the war?

'You are young,' said Laura, 'and I am glad that you are doing well — as I have been told. I'm sure *you'll* be fine in this — er — Brave New World. Now I must go in — it is cold out here.'

She put the book on her lap back into her knitting-bag. It was a Boots library novel. Had she read it?

Jennie said: 'Let me help you,' and took the bag which seemed full of lumpy knitting. 'I'll take it in for you,' she said, smiling.

Laura Ogilvie thought, I think I have made an impression on this one. She is a nice girl, if a little forward.

5

As I grew into adolescence I was irritated by Mother's always saying how wonderful Sir Jack or Lady Page were. I didn't want to hurt Mother's feelings so I tried not to show my irritation, which is not easy when you are that age. The years just before and after the end of the war were a busy time for me at school. I think I worked better then than I ever have since, in spite of the pains and perils of growing up. I was quick, and I had always enjoyed Latin, and French, and history, if not physics and chemistry. I loved writing English essays of course, and I liked the big spread of subjects we all had to study for the public examinations. I liked mastering facts I might never have found out for myself, like the American War of Independence, or how to read a map, or the imperfect subjunctive passive, or photosynthesis. It suited me to know a bit about a lot of things and juggle them all for the exams.

I knew all the time that it wasn't real learning, and I'd probably forget a lot of it later, but it kept my friends and myself busy as the war dragged on, and the peace came, which didn't change all that much in our daily lives. I knew Mother was really pleased when I did well at school though she never told me to my face that she was proud of me. Perhaps I really wanted her to say that *I* was as wonderful as the Pages!

I didn't work all the time. I read some rubbishy books and could scarcely admit to myself that for relaxation at the pictures I also enjoyed some of the terribly melodramatic British films we saw like *Madonna of the Seven Moons* or *Fanny by Gaslight*. Joan and I thought Phyllis Calvert was admirable in some of these films and there was a time when we wanted to be actresses, but it didn't last long. Provided that I had enough time to go on reading novels I was happy.

We sat School Certificate, Joan and I, in 1946. At the end of July, whilst we were awaiting the results, Dad took me on holiday. We went on our bikes to explore parts of the county I had never seen, or seen only from a train window. Nobody had been able to travel much in the war, and petrol for trips by car was still rationed, so bicycles were the perfect way of getting around. Not that my parents had ever yet had a car of their own. Dad liked driving but Sir Jack was rationed for petrol, and the Pages now used their old Morris mainly for shopping trips to Tonbridge or Sevenoaks.

We had a railway not too far away of course, and if you sat on a train as far as its final eastern destination you'd find yourself by the English Channel. The other way went to London, but since the end of the war I'd been there only a few times, either on Saturdays or during the holidays. The war and the bombing had considerably reduced Sir Jack's visits to the City. Until the war he had gone up once a week to the office of Pages Ironworks but after part of the City office was destroyed I overheard mysterious talk of a sell-out or a 'take over', which I didn't understand.

'He wants to retire,' opined Mother.

'Well he can always stay on as a non-working director,' said Dad, who seemed conversant with such things. He appeared to know quite a bit about Sir Jack's problems. Apparently there were other more distant branches of the Page family who had been actively money-making in the war when iron was used for more sinister things than gates, so the bomb might not have been the cause of the problems.

Anyway, we were to go on our bikes. I already knew there was a lot to discover even within a few square miles, and in the smallest village. I pored over maps and realized how many places quite near to Pettiwell I had never visited. I had been once or twice further west to stay with a friend whose aunt and uncle lived over the border in Surrey, and I knew our nearest castle of course, and Knole and Penshurst and Hadlow's strange folly, and one or two villages like Matfield where mother had a friend, but we decided to cycle in the genuine Weald. We'd be on roads that were not too far from a railway line so that if we got tired or the weather suddenly turned cold and rainy we could always put our bikes on a train.

I wanted to go further, as far as the coast. They said you could see France from Hythe, and France was where I longed to go. Not so long ago it had been a forbidden country and had now become for this reason very alluring. Dad had shown me a big map and sorted out for me our Weald, and the North Downs and South Downs, and all the different kinds of countryside we had, the parts where there were fields of hops, and the old wool villages.

I loved our own part of the west of the county, with its small green fields on gentle slopes, its many trees and little laneside woods.

'Ours is a county of small villages,' he had said and made me keen about exploring more of them. My friend Joan was to have gone with us but at the last moment her father came home from being rehabilitated after release the previous year from a prisoner-of-war camp in the Far East, and so it was just Dad and me. Mother took the chance to go and see her relatives, or those of them who were still alive, near Banbury. This necessitated crossing London but she said she was quite capable of travelling alone.

In the end the weather held, neither too hot nor too windy, and we took some days to cycle without any hurry. I really enjoyed that holiday. We couldn't see more than a fraction of all he wanted to show me in a fortnight, but we stayed in some Youth Hostels, or if there were no hostel we found little B-and-Bs to put us up in small villages. The hostels were quite spartan — the men's quarters even more so than mine, I guessed. Dad seemed to enjoy it all, and I certainly did, though the grey blankets were really prickly and you slept on hard bunks. I cooked whatever we had bought on the way, though in some of the hostels the wardens made good vegetable soup.

We had cycled via Paddock Wood and Marden to Staplehurst; Goudhurst and Lamberhurst we'd have to see another time, but we made a detour to Smarden and then down to Tenterden. What contrasts of countryside we saw; what woods and fields and orchards and lovely villages strung out between all these places before we came to the Marsh. We arrived in Appledore and the next day we were in New Romney.

This was almost fifteen years before the first English motorways and the artificial 'new towns'. As I remember it now, it still belonged to 'pre-war', as I probably did myself, the time that belonged to the poets we were reading at school.

I loved Romney Marsh; that seemed to be another country, and from there we got down to weird Dungeness and then up again by the coast to Dymchurch. We rode the next day by the military canal and there we were in Hythe. That day though was rather misty so I did not see France.

'One day we'll take the train to Folkestone from home and then cycle up to Canterbury,' said Dad. He was full of plans. 'You've never been yet to the greatest city in Kent — or to Thanet — or to Dickens's country!'

'Have you been to all those places?' I asked him.

'Oh yes, all of them — before you were born or I even met your mother. I tried to farm south of Canterbury and I looked for work in Rochester and Chatham — after my war, you know. I roamed a bit round everywhere till I got tired of it and Sir Jack tempted me back. I decided to stay in Pettiwell then — the heart of Kent, I thought . . . ' His voice trailed away.

I realized that not all his post-war memories were pleasant, but he was still as enthusiastic as a boy about cycling. His father had introduced him to it, he said, when he was a little lad — there'd been cycling clubs in the nineties and his father had belonged to one in Maidstone.

We put our bikes on the train at Folkestone and went back home through Ashford and Headcorn and Marden, not far from the lovely places we'd seen from the saddle.

I felt very healthy after all that exercise and I knew Dad had thoroughly enjoyed himself. He'd lived in the heart of Kent and he was himself at heart a man of Kent. Unlike Mother, who still had her slight Oxfordshire accent.

I really got to know Dad on that holiday. I had the feeling though that if I went youth hostelling again it would be with a friend, and so I had the fancy that this holiday had been for him a sort of farewell to my childhood. He had wanted to show me some of the places that interested him and had wished to indicate how to do things properly. Had he once wished I had been born a boy?

Mother had returned just before us and was ready with tea and cake, saying she'd missed us both.

She was overjoyed when my School Cert results came through, even more relieved than I was. They were as good as the school had hoped for, except in biology, which I had never liked.

We seemed to have been away for months, not two weeks, and I felt I was looking at Sally and Caro with new eyes. I had seen so much of the 'Garden of England' — but even then only a tiny fraction. There was the whole of England, and then Europe, to explore . . .

In the autumn, with the release from the grind of public exams that year, there began, I believe, the years when I began to think more about life in general. My horizons were beginning to extend beyond reading and studying, even if reading was still my favourite occupation. I read a lot of poetry, and wrote some of my own, but I was never satisfied that I had conveyed my true perceptions. I had a miscellaneous bunch of feelings running around my head, and whole hosts of words, but they did not always connect. I needed time to live and record my living, but there appeared to be a gulf between just 'living' — noticing the weather and skies and flowers and trees and people — and getting on with ordinary life.

I was torn between nature — the country landscape with its woods and fields and villages, and the feelings it aroused in me — which made me want to create something myself. The essence of all the places and feelings, expressed in words or pictures or music that might last for ever, was art, wasn't it?

I suspected that I would never be a genuine artist: a real writer, or a real painter, and certainly not a composer, though I enjoyed dabbling in all these, and more than dabbling as far as writing was concerned. I was not original enough, had not the courage of my inner convictions — or rather 'the world was too much with me' — as the poet had almost said. You had to choose.

Now Caro was a really creative person and had apparently already chosen her way of life, and Sally was good at just being alive, lived without too much introspection.

My existence was always going to be different from Sally's. It had to be filled with academic work, and exams, and striving, if I were to do well. I could not help striving. Sally used to tell me I worked too hard, but I didn't. I just liked learning new things, each day realizing the increasing depths of my ignorance. I became annoyed when school-work got in the way of my thinking my own thoughts. Work and self did not always match. I could not think of anything I wanted to do, or be. I wished I were like Caro who knew what she wanted to do. Even so, I believe I was happy and I was certainly busy. I had two years before me in the sixth form. We were treated more like adults by the teachers now as there were no 'teenagers' for us to be at that time.

The following summer I did not go cycling with Dad, who had not been well, but went for the first time to Paris, with a small party from school. I had been with school on day trips to Penshurst and Knole, but the fortnight I spent with two friends in a French hostel under the not so beady eye of our French teacher, Miss Rose, and the following two weeks all by myself in a French family, found for me by the school, was the longest I'd been away from my parents. I didn't think any the less of home when I saw another country, or any the less of France when I returned; the countries were so near and yet so different. You have to belong somewhere, and I began to think about England's past, all its churches and villages with their own special magic, and thought perhaps I ought to be studying history instead of French. Then I read French novels and felt released from English puritanism. I began to understand why Caro was so different from Sally, and Aunt Clare so different from her sister.

Caro, on holiday after her first year at art school, and her father, Francis Fitzpatrick, were at Pettiwell in the early autumn when I returned from France. Mr Fitzpatrick, or Mr Fitz as I thought of him privately, wanted to hear my impressions of Paris. I felt a little less forthcoming when Caro was present, a bit shy of saying things in front of her, as if it might look as if I was showing off. This time I might appear to be currying favour with her father. Mr Fitz spoke to me in French and she listened to me doing my best in that language. I had at least acquired the beginnings of a good French accent.

I was to be torn not only between life and work, between my own home and my parents' place in it, but also between Pettiwell and another part of England. After Higher School Certificate I was to study for three years in the north of England, having been offered a place at Manchester University. I went off in 1948 to study English and French, the only university then that offered both subjects together for a degree. I had felt so divided that I'd decided to study them both.

Manchester was to reveal another England,

so unimaginably different, especially at that time, from our beautiful, mainly rural, south-east corner. After the war, farming subsidies and all the new machinery would transform even our little patch; already we had begun to see the reaper-binders pulled by machines rather than horses. I knew there were many poor people in parts of our county, especially in the bigger towns, and in the Medway area and of course in London's East End, where the terrible bomb damage had destroyed so many slums, yet I had never seen anything like the poorer parts of the North, grimy from industry, and with such damp, bitterly cold weather. I had been lucky to live at Pettiwell. It was only one of many beautiful houses, like those I had seen when I went on that holiday with my father, and which I was to see more of as I got to know more of my own country.

But Pettiwell did not belong to me, though I had belonged to it. Soon I'd have to find my own way in the world. It was the end of my childhood for me, I suppose. Caro had already become 'grown up', and once Sally had left school all three of us would be launching out.

6

Dear Sally

I thought of you back at school this evening and decided I would write to you as I had promised. I am always so busy once I get back to Manchester — which will be next week. Don't worry about replying to this — I know Queen E's keeps you busy! It was a lovely Christmas, wasn't it? but the snow should have come earlier. This morning, Mother asked me to go to the village, and as it was so cold I wore your present of red gloves and walked back the Secret Lane way, and then up to the farm in the snow to get some more exercise. It was absolutely gorgeous, a bright-blue sky and the sun sparkling on the snow. The ruts on the field path were all frozen — it all made me want to write a poem. So far I only have the first lines. It starts:

'Like diamond fires
That pierce and heat my heart,
These frozen ruts and runnels,
These shards of crystal ice,
Lodge in my memory . . . '

I can just hear Miss Jarrett saying, 'How can frozen ice heat your heart and if a shard lodges in your memory it will probably kill you!'

I know it doesn't make ordinary sense. I have the rhymes 'mire' and 'part' somewhere in my head. I can't seem to get any further with it, but I shall go on trying. I'm sure Dylan Thomas, my favourite modern poet at present, could make a wonderful poem with these words. I just want to describe the beauty of the whole scene — sun and frost and ice. Perhaps one can never express all one feels. My tutor here says poetry is not about feelings but about words. Well, I wish I had the right words to describe the stars last night pricked out as sharp and silver as I have ever seen them.

I keep remembering your chilblains — it's a crime against humanity to let people get chilblains at school. I'm sure Caro would agree, but she has gone with your Aunt Clare and Lily to Paris for a few days' holiday. Your mother is hoping your aunt and uncle will sort out where they are all going to live, and settle their differences. Caro doesn't seem to mind, but I think Lily does. Her school starts next week and she is even more miserable about that. I promised your mother I'd help Jim with his holiday prep before I went back north, so I'd better go and find him.

Good luck with the hockey team this term!

Lots of love
Jennie.

3 Park Place
20 May 1950

Dear Pa

Our exams will finish in three weeks so I shall come to France as soon as poss. Expect me on Thursday 8 June. I have an interview at the shop on the rue Napoléon on the 12th. I expect they will only want me for running errands to and from the atelier but I might see a bit of what is going on in their world. As you say, the world of high fashion and the couturiers might possibly be approached sideways from the 'lower ranks'. I'd really like to make clothes

135

that were both beautiful and not too dear — to create my own fashion! I think that big Dutch department store, the one that sells clothes in England, or even a London workroom, might take me on after Paris. Thank you for sending the money order. Ma says you are not to bother about me as I can look after myself perfectly well. Thank you for sending the reference for me to the foyer d'étudiantes. It will be nice not to have to bother about meals at first. They wrote to say they had a room from 19 June for five months till November. By then I'm sure I shall have found a room of my own for myself. I hope all goes well in the world of Franco — British culture?

Love from Caro.

It was extraordinary how remote she felt from him at present, thought Caroline Fitzpatrick, as she finished this letter to her father. Lily was to stay with him in July and the two were going to Brittany on holiday. She had been invited too but had declined. She probably did need a holiday, but she was determined to start work — whatever kind it might turn out to be — as soon as she arrived in Paris. She guessed her mother felt her enterprise was fated to fail, but then her mother was a confirmed pessimist. Clare was still working for the publisher in Bedford Square and busy in the evenings writing something mysterious. Lily thought it might be her memories of the war. Perhaps it was the autobiography of a failed woman artist, thought her other daughter unsympathetically.

★   ★   ★

There was an optimistic spirit in the air, in spite of the continuance of rationing — the meat ration was especially tiny — and the fact that the King looked ill. The Conservatives had won the election in October, and Sir Jack, who, like his in-laws had been dismayed when Churchill had lost to Labour after the end of the war, said that people might have been very ungrateful, but they had now come to their senses and realized he was their best bet. There was a new foreign secretary's signature on passports, and the newspapers were full of Princess Elizabeth, who was on a visit to Canada and the United States. De Valera was once again Prime Minister of Eire, Perón had become leader in Argentina, the British had withdrawn from the Canal Zone, and the stolen Coronation Stone had been rediscovered in Forfar. The popular press used up more pages on the last-named event than on the other three put together. Not much of what was in the papers interested Sally, but Caroline raved over the newly released photographs of Dior dresses in his spring and summer collection, especially a dress called *Cachottier*. Dior had over a thousand workers and had made of *haute couture* an art form as perhaps never before. But her favourite was still Madame Chanel!

The number of road accidents increased as more people began to own cars, and it took only eight hours to fly to America now. Only the rich were able to afford the flight, and most still went on the big Atlantic liners. Some people — not many — had purchased television sets, but most relied on the wireless. Sir Jack had cheered up for a time when the Morris Oxford he had ordered was delivered.

Caroline had worked hard in her last year at Wimbledon Art School, where she had concentrated on commercial art, learning how to delineate trends in mainly feminine fashions. For relaxation she used to go to London cinemas, for there had recently been some amusing English films. They said that even England would soon have 'X-rated' films! Later, if she had a free evening in Paris, she began to savour the French cinema, so different from Hollywood offerings or from the sturdy or vaguely salacious British films, and a form of art in itself. France was another world, but she was still not sure in which world she belonged.

Sally was still doggedly trying to master Pitman's shorthand, as well as being groomed to be the perfect secretary. She almost gave it up for a *cordon bleu* course but forced herself to continue at the secretarial college in Hampstead.

Jennie did read the newspapers but preferred fiction. She had read *The Catcher in the Rye*, wondering if such a book could ever be written, never mind published, in England. She wished *she* might write it. What a sheltered life I have had, she thought. She had fallen in love several times but kept it all to herself. Girls — even friends of hers — were marrying in their early twenties, many of them straight out of college. Her friend Joan now had a boyfriend, met at university. Most young women's preferred option was early marriage, followed by three or four children, but Jennie was sure this would not be the life for her.

Her degree course lasted four years, unlike that of most of her friends, and she felt she was being given a bonus, more time to make her mind up what sort of life she wanted. The possibilities were not endless. Teaching of one sort or another, librarianship and secretarial or social work exhausted the options — except of course for that other 'career' of marriage.

The Wilsons went to see Humphrey Bogart in *The African Queen* and sat through a long newsreel about fat King Farouk of Egypt. Sir Jack took his wife to see *Kiss Me Kate*, and Jennie hummed 'So in Love'. Sally preferred '*Wunderbar*' and 'Some Enchanted Evening' and sang them out of tune. Lily winced but retaliated with 'My resistance is low'. The previous year, Caroline, who had had a passionate flutter with a young man in the new graphics department at college, had decided she was *gonna wash that man right out of my hair*. Nobody, not even her father, knew whether she had found a French replacement.

Life had gone on much the same at Pettiwell. Sometimes Ruth wondered if the war was really over. Her mother had been right, she thought. Nothing had gone back to what it had been like before the war. Then she remembered she had had her forty-third birthday and existence might never again be so pleasant as in her youth and early married life. The women's magazines she read at the dentist's and hairdresser's appeared to consider her middle-aged. Life just went by so quickly and they had all been held up by the war — or perhaps paradoxically made to feel older.

For some time the government had laid plans for a Festival of Britain and these came to fruition in the summer of 1951. The whole Page family, including James, now thirteen, went to contemplate the Skylon and the Royal Festival Hall. James eventually discovered the Battersea funfair, which was more to his taste.

Lily had already sat the new 'Ordinary level', as it was now called and had two more years at school. She spent some of her holidays with her mother in London but much preferred life at Pettiwell. When Lily was in London Clare did her best to interest her in museums and exhibitions, but her younger daughter was not very interested. Her chief talent was for music, especially for singing. The Pages took Lily to the South Bank when they visited it a second time, and on this trip she made friends with the eighteen-year-old brother of one of James's school-friends, Nigel, who came from a rich family. He was distantly related to the old Cozens couple who had come back to live at Stair Court, part of which had been used by a government office during the war, probably something highly secret, or at least that was what the villagers had believed. In the war Mr and Mrs Cozens had evacuated themselves to Scotland.

Lily knew that her Aunt Ruth was easier to hoodwink than her mother, whose attitude towards the young men who might want to be more than 'just friends' with Lily was surprisingly less liberal than that of her sister, the Country Mouse. Lily tended to rely on Sally for advice and was less confident than her mother might think. In looks Lily resembled her father as far as her facial features were concerned, but she hadn't got the Irish blue eyes and dark curly hair. It was Sally who had the black curls! Lily had early on declared she was not artistic like her father or her mother. But she might have inherited her mother's analytical mind, if not her cynical nature. This talent she was showing for singing amazed both her parents.

Jennie had not yet visited the festival but had seen its evidences from the train. She was more concerned with the problems of the world than those of renascent England. The Iron Curtain had already descended, and the terrible war in Korea was still going on. She had seen a film about it that summer, showing refugees stumbling through snow that impeded their cruel flight back home, a place they would never see again. The cruelty of wars and the generalized cruelty of the 'civilized' world depressed her. Some of her friends from school were doing their National Service in Korea; others had been in Malaya. Boys had a much harder time than girls, she thought. Why should the accident of gender endanger the young lives of the Western half of the human race? Why should young men actually lose their lives in what she felt sure were pointless wars? It was all so horribly unjust, but what on earth could you do about it? All wars were senseless, and the last one had led to the nuclear bomb, settling something but not solving anything.

She talked about these things to her father. 'People say: 'Oh, would you have let Hitler carry on as he wanted?' — and I know we had to bomb Germany, but did we have to bomb Dresden the way we did?'

She was forced to come to the unhappy conclusion that perhaps some wars had just had to be fought, but surely not all these new wars springing up, so far away?

William Wilson agreed with her. His war had been the 'war to end all wars'. 'Some hope of that,' he said.

Jennie was glad she had only been a child when war broke out. Would she have had the guts to be a pacifist if she had been called up at eighteen instead of starting a new life at university? She might have been sent down the mines as a Bevin Boy — but perhaps that was not quite so bad. She considered joining the Commonwealth Party, whose founder thought nuclear weapons were immoral, but realized that she was not the sort of person who could believe in one political party. Most of her strong feelings were defensive, and she did not know what she believed in. During her Christmas vacation in Pettiwell at the end of 1950 she had been both amazed and horrified to find that Sally, sweet kind Sally, was considering joining one of the women's services! Caroline, home to see Lily on a flying visit, had listened to Jennie's opinions, taken no sides in the argument which she could see Jennie did not want to have with Sally, but had then told her that her father was still seeing wounded young French soldiers in Paris who had been out fighting in Indo-China.

'Young French conscripts have had a ghastly time out there for years,' reported Caroline.

'How long will all these struggles go on?' cried Jennie.

Caroline was not quite so prickly as she had once been towards the 'housekeeper's daughter', but replied ironically that some uniforms were very chic.

'Well, I wish you'd tell Sally it is not at all chic to fight,' replied Jennie.

'I'm sure you'd have more influence than I would with her,' replied Caroline. 'Is it that you don't like the idea of *women* fighting?' she asked curiously.

'No, it's not that. I just don't believe that *any* young men or women should fight old men's wars,' replied Jennie.

'Then you'd agree with Papa. He says they're always having demonstrations and processions against something in Paris — most of the young students over there are Marxists. Personally, I've never understood politics.'

She was surprised that Jennie, whom she had marked down as an academic in an ivory tower, should worry about war. French intellectuals did, as she knew from her father, but she had thought the English had had enough of wars. Why, they had even given away India, to the great sorrow of Sally's grandparents before they died.

'Pa says there will be worse trouble in Algeria one day,' Caroline continued, in a rather complacent way. Jennie had no time to ask her for more details. Caro never stayed long at Pettiwell and was off again to finish some cartoon sketches she was about to try and sell to a commercial gallery.

Instead, Jennie talked to her father. She was only just beginning to realize how awfully people had suffered in the war; could not recollect reading in the paper, or hearing on the wireless, or from grown-ups in the family any account of what must have been happening between 1941 and 1943.

'We tried to spare children the truth,' her father said. 'Unless they were in a place where it was happening, what was the good of frightening children to death? Especially if a child was in any case over-imaginative.'

'I feel I ought to have known!' she cried. 'Now it's like when we suddenly found out about concentration camps.'

'Well, we didn't know much about them', he replied, 'And you were only a little girl in the war, Jen, before the doodlebugs, anyway.'

'I was twelve in 1943 — that was not so young. And now I've been reading about the continual and continuous bombing going on then. I knew about the bombs on St Paul's Cathedral, but I read the other day that a boys' school in Sussex was bombed in 1942. Did you know about that?'

'We did know in 1940 about the fifty-seven nights of London's aerial bombardment. From people who'd been there — not from the wireless,' replied her father. 'There was hardly anywhere in London that escaped — or anywhere on the south coast. In those years the announcer would say day after day there'd been bombs on 'waste ground in southern England'. Southern England meant London! We all knew that by then, and Londoners told us later that 'waste ground' was code for Hyde Park!'

'Daylight raids must have worried you and Mother.'

'Yes. I remember one in Sussex — there was a woman pegging out clothes in her garden when she was machine-gunned. I heard that from an ARP warden.'

'It says in my book that forty little girls were killed in a South London school playground in January 1943,' Jennie went on. 'That's only one of the hundreds of incidents. It doesn't bear thinking about.'

'No, there was hardly a place in London that escaped — windows blown out, shops destroyed, restaurants hit, air raid shelters wrecked — and once in Bethnal Green a panic rush to get into shelter in a tube station that cost nearly two hundred lives.'

'Sally told me her father wanted to evacuate her mother and James in 1944 but Lady Page refused.'

'She'd have gone if they'd been living in

London! Those doodlebugs! A million Londoners left the place — and just when we were beginning to win the war!'

'You all knew about most of these things — and I've only just found out. We must never go to war again, Father!'

'Well, think of the nuclear bomb — that put an end to it, didn't it?' Her father always said that.

'We mustn't let it be used again!' she cried.

'People aren't always asked their opinion, love,' said her father.

★   ★   ★

In 1950 Caroline's final portfolio from Wimbledon was placed for the time being in the Pettiwell attic, next to her father's abandoned paints and easels, left there by Polly Wilson after her mammoth post-war cleaning. Caroline didn't need it at present but it would come in useful when — if? — she returned to England. Jennie had not thought Caro would live in England once she could choose. She did not quite comprehend how anybody could be as keen on fashion as Caro was, but you had to try and understand people who were different from yourself, didn't you?

She rather liked the new Caro, a tall,

fashionable young woman. Jennie also mildly envied her figure, never having bothered her head too much about clothes, certainly not enough to want to become fashionable herself. Some of Caro's ideas for clothes were rather odd. She preferred simple skirts and jumpers herself, but Caro interested her. She had become less astringent towards other people, perhaps more confident of her own taste. She was not a simple person.

Sally, however, had not changed. A kind, jolly, pretty girl she was clearly popular, but she admitted to Jennie that she disliked London life.

'The army would be an escape from that,' she'd said.

A nice open-air life, thought Jennie ironically. Sally's brother James, becoming a gangly adolescent, adored his sister, and told her sternly that women should not join the armed forces.

Whenever her vacations landed her at Pettiwell Jennie would spend hours in her old bedroom in the Wilson quarters revising for one of her many exams.

'Jennie's exams' seemed to Ruth Page to happen very frequently. She liked to talk to Polly's daughter who was so different from Caro or Sally, and reminded her just a little of her sister Clare before she went to France in her twenties. Lily liked talking to Jennie too, and Lily often happened to be living at Pettiwell.

Jennie herself felt dislocated, as if they were all marking time.

It seemed to her that she was waiting for Real Life to begin. Were all of them waiting for that?

★ ★ ★

2 Jan 1951

Dear Caro
Thanks so much for your card — I am glad you are really enjoying Paris and your work. We missed you at Christmas.

Jennie was here swotting for more exams. She says she thrives on them as they keep her mind too busy to think. I can't quite see what she means but I expect you can. I am off back to London to the dreaded secretarial course in a few days. Actually, I quite like the typing but the Pitman's is still really difficult. However, I am working at it. The other girls are all nice. I try not to find London too depressing. It will lead to a good job, I hope. I'd like to help my parents by getting a decent job, but you

150

just can't save money in London! Can you in Paris?

The sister of one of the girls here has a bed-sitting-room that costs one third of her entire salary! — and she has quite a good job.

A very happy New Year, Caro. Mummy joins me in this, as does James who is practising something or other in the yard. His friend Brian is here for a few days. They are very noisy and eat a lot but seem to enjoy life. Father sends his love — he has a lot of pain in his joints. Lily came here for Christmas as I expect you heard. She is such fun and very popular with everyone round here. I think she ought to go on studying her music — she sings so beautifully. She sang in church on Christmas Eve and Mummy said it was quite angelic! I thought your mother was very enterprising, going to Spain for some sun. I wish Mummy would go out and see her for a little holiday, she never seems to stop working. Well, I must stop and go and pack for London.

Lots of love — hope to see you in the summer — Sally

London Sunday 11 Feb 1951

Dear Jennie

Just to say I can come up to Manchester
next weekend — am looking forward to it.
I am OK. I was a bit depressed at the
beginning of term after getting flu but am
much better now. I passed my last typing
test! Hurrah! See you Friday evening
— (16th) — have booked my ticket from
Euston and can stay till Monday morning if
you can put me up and put up with me till
then —

Lots of love,
your Sal

May 1951

Dear Caro,

Thanks a million for enquiring on my
behalf at your little foyer off the Boulevard
Montparnasse where you stayed last year
— sorry I shan't see you when I arrive in
July, but congratulations on the fashion
cartoon you got into the gallery — your
father will be so pleased. I hear from my
mother that yours is back from Spain and
visited Pettiwell the other day. I must write

to Lily to wish her luck for her final exams. I shall be glad to see the last of mine next year, though Dieu sait what I shall do next. Perhaps I too shall come to Paris? Let's all meet this summer at Pettiwell — I hear you may come back to Dear Old Blighty next autumn?

Mille remerciements
Jennie

Rue Monsieur le Prince
Paris 5
21 6 51

Dear Lily,
Silly old thing — of course you can tell Ma he'd be pleased to see her. I just don't know the exact state of play between them but he adores you, so why not both come and stay in Paris for a bit after your exams? Don't worry about the work — you're nearly grown up now and can concentrate on your singing as I do on my drawing and design. I feel seriously adult, my dear, and know I must now specialize, try to get experience in London and then perhaps return here after that if they will have me in a top atelier and train me up as a humble

seamstress. *It takes simply years getting good at it you know. Like singing.*

You know you're Pa's favourite person on earth so please come. I don't mind a bit about that — he's been very nice to me and helped me out with cash, so now it's your turn, ma petite. Tell Sally to cheer up — and good luck with your music exam —

Grosses bises de ta soeur
Caro.

Part Three

SISTERS, FRIENDS AND COUSINS

1952–1955

7

In the year that the King died and his daughter succeeded him, before the new queen's solemn coronation the following year, there began to be talk of a New Elizabethan age. It was also the year Jennie Wilson left Manchester University with a first class honours degree in English and French.

She was still not sure what career to follow, or whether one even existed in which she would be capable of succeeding at the same time as enjoying her work. Her supervisors told her she was quite scholarly enough to study for a post-graduate degree, even a doctorate, if she wanted to become an academic. She'd need to transform her state scholarship into a studentship and she felt a bit guilty about receiving more money from the state. She had received a grant for four years, so unless she definitely decided to carry on with post-graduate work she would have to find a job.

She supposed that if she remained uncertain, she might teach, whilst beginning some research. Teaching abroad would give her a small salary, but if she stayed away too long from academic life her grant might not be renewed. Fortunately, there was a scheme for English graduate *asssistantes* in French schools, and faculties had been reestablished, so a compromise would be to begin upon a subject of research in France, and in the meantime teach English. If that failed, she could always teach French in an English school, but this was a prospect she did not find very alluring. French was such a very unpopular subject with most English children!

Jennie's chief supervisor in Manchester suggested that as she was still only twenty-two, she might stay for at least a year in Paris, working as an *assistante*. She could offer English conversation lessons to French students in a *lycée* not far from the Sorbonne, and perhaps take classes also at the Sorbonne itself. She might also apply to use the Sorbonne library whilst she considered a thesis in French literature.

'I've never known whether to concentrate my energies on French or English,' she said to Joan, who was teaching in a small grammar school in Surrey. 'I love the literatures of both. They're so very different, but they complement each other — just as England and France do. When you've had enough of one you can switch to the other.'

'I suppose poetry is poetry and novels are novels whatever language they are written in,' suggested sensible Joan, who was now officially engaged to be married, though the date would be some time in the future.

During the vacation Jennie wrote for more advice to a friend in Manchester, Aidan Welsh, a scholarly young man who had been in her seminar group. He was now a post-graduate student.

'I seem to find myself in between two worlds — trying to make links between them', she wrote.

It made her wonder whether the reason for this was her childhood bridging of the gap between her parents and the Page family, so that she belonged to both, but perhaps not completely to either. Always 'in between'.

Aidan was severe in his reply.

'I do not see you as a pure scholar,' he wrote. 'Go to France and do a bit of teaching whilst you make up your mind. I see you as a good teacher,' he added, which surprised her. She didn't want to teach English as a foreign language in France for the rest of her life, any more than the other way round in England. University teaching was different but also very specialized.

She replied to Aidan: 'I'll give myself at least one academic year to read round and try

159

to discover my ideal subject, whilst at the same time I'm being of some use to pupils or students.'

Already the idea of *la vie de bohème* in the nineteenth century, as it concerned both French and English novelists, had presented itself. English writers who did not conform to society had often migrated to France. Even Charles Dickens had had his hideout in Boulogne, had written much of *Bleak House* there. But *he* had wanted to have his cake and eat it.

There was a kind of unconventionality in London too, later on, in the years before the Great War. What were all those Bloomsbury writers but rich Bohemians? Did you have to be poor to be a *real* one? Jennie began to envisage a book rather than a thesis. The trouble was, one day soon she would have to earn her living. Nobody went on paying you to spin books and ideas unless you were attached to a university, or were a successful journalist.

The idea of living in France was tempting, although she was wary of committing herself for too long, expecting too much from it, knowing the traps into which her optimistic idealism might lead her.

She made up her mind: a job in Paris for a year. See how it went. Surely she was old enough to know what she was doing.

160

★ ★ ★

Jennie set off in October 1952 to spend at least one year in Paris. She looked into the spume and spray in the wake of the Newhaven to Dieppe boat, thinking her usual thoughts. If only she were more creative . . . Only last night Caro had shown them all some more of her sketches. After the five years at art school in England, followed by the year in Paris, she had decided not to return for the time being but to come back to England. She did not explain why. Caro, Jennie acknowledged, was a truly creative person, if not in the way she would dearly wish to be herself.

A week later Jennie was writing to her friend Aidan.

'I just have a feeling for words, and I have read a lot of books,' she scribbled. 'That doesn't make me an academic or a real writer.' Writing to Aidan was more to set her own thoughts in order, than with any conviction that her correspondent might be interested. She was sitting at a table before the window of her small study bedroom on the first floor of an old house in the *sixième*, now a hostel for students, which Caro had told her about, having stayed there during the winter of her own time in Paris. The house had a courtyard behind high walls, a *porte cochère*, and a garden with an old well in the centre. Delightful. Where could you find such a place in London? It was not quite as convenient for the Sorbonne as it was for the school where she was to give her English conversation lessons, but it was near enough to walk there.

The first visit Jennie had ever made to Paris had been the usual sight-seeing one with school. They had been taken round La Sainte Chapelle, a kind of beautiful museum now, not a religious place. Notre Dame, the Louvre, the Opéra, the Champs Elysées, had followed. The English schoolgirls, even including Jennie, had been quite amazed, even shocked, to see people eating and drinking at little tables on the very pavements of a capital city! Nothing in London had prepared them for this. How ignorant they had all been.

Ever since then, Paris had gone on delighting her — and now she could stay for at least a year. There was so much to see and do here, a city so much more compact than London, or even Manchester. Seeing and doing and pottering was a pleasure. London sprawled for miles and was still battered from war-time bombing, with vast tracts of land for redevelopment. Paris had not suffered in this way, but emotional scars were buried deep in the sensitive, and especially in the politically minded, of whom there seemed to be many in Paris. The shame of the German occupation might not be visible on the surface, Jennie thought, but it was there among the older people, especially those who remembered the Great War.

The buildings in Paris looked much older than those in most of London, except for vestiges in Soho or in various London 'villages'. There was regularity to the plan of Paris, so it was not hard to find your way around. Little narrow streets could lead to out-of-the-way squares and cafés and small parks, or occasionally to *impasses* that ended in high walls. She did not frequent so much the *grands boulevards*. The *quartiers* of the southern bank of the Seine were what delighted her, so different from London's new South Bank. She would pass in the street the sort of people whose lives she would like to imagine, almost like characters in books: old men; down at heel but fierce-looking concierges; children coming out of school. She lingered by flower-stalls sprouting mimosa, and by little newspaper kiosks, admired elegant wrought-iron arches that descended to Métro stations that smelled of Gauloises and perfume and garlic, and observed equally elegant old ladies leading poodles. The *quartier* was also filled with loving couples. Not everyone else looked as happy as they did, but they looked interesting. Middle-aged men wore berets, young ones were hatless and often curly-haired. Many appeared to resemble her favourite film star, Gérard Philippe. She began to feel part of it all, glad to be alive.

The older university students were not yet back, but she practised various walks to the university, sometimes down the rue de Rennes, remembering Caro had lived there as a child, crossing the Boulevard Raspail to St Sulpice, and then into one end of the Luxembourg Gardens to walk through to the Boulevard St Michel. English lessons with the university students were to be held on the other side of the Boul' Mich' in an office across the rue Soufflot. The whole of the *quartier* was such a pleasure to stroll through that she would return a different way through another part of the gardens, or sometimes by the boulevards.

Other days, if she had time, she would go a little further to the Place Fürstenberg or down the rue Bonaparte or the rue de Seine or the rue Jacob where Samuel Johnson and Laurence Sterne had once stayed, not far from where Balzac, and before him Racine, had lived. It was not quite her own country but near enough. Other, more modern, writers were all of this magic part of Paris, only a meandering walk away.

Many of her favourite writers walked in her imagination by her side, ghosts of a literary past whose books she might have read. They never seemed far away, all those American expatriates, and Katherine Mansfield, her favourite woman writer, whose books she bought on the *quais* and whom she liked to think she saw coming out of her door on the rue de Tournon, down from the Luxembourg. This was the part of Paris she had discovered with college friends on her second visit to France, when they had stayed in a small hotel off the rue Madame.

Later, during the summer vacations when Parisians deserted their city, she had stayed at the large Foyer International, not far from where she was now teaching her students. This small old *foyer* was so much more friendly and comfortable; it already felt like home. Without Caro she would not have known about it.

She wrote her in her journal almost every day.

I am not at all lonely. The poetry of life pervades this part of Paris. I shall try to

165

describe my reactions to the place, find the right words and write something original. But I'm speaking French all the time, which makes it harder to find the right English words . . .

Paris was far too interesting for her to have time to describe it all! Perhaps she'd try writing in French. To her parents Jennie wrote dutifully every week. She was already envisaging the days of teaching which stretched ahead with a certain amount of optimism, and told her mother this. She hoped the optimism would not be displaced, for her parents wanted her to be a teacher; it was something they understood.

In small things I am optimistic, she wrote in her journal, *even if in all the big things I am a complete pessimist.* In the past, her friend Aidan had urged her to consider joining the Catholic Church, the place, he said, for pessimists who believed in original sin, but felt they could be saved. But Jennie's pessimism had no religious base, was more the result of a nature divided between scepticism and enthusiasm. She often thought about such things. One thing about the French was that they loved discussing these issues as much as they adored fashion.

Jennie knew her own limitations, and was

still not taken up with clothes, though she might imagine them on others. She still thought Caro very stylish, indeed the most stylish woman she knew, but it was no good wanting to be tall herself. Nature had decided that for her! She now favoured knitted waistcoats and berets, and hankered for a black Cossack hat. Here the students, both male and female, wore black polo-necked jumpers and trousers, a fashion Jennie found most agreeable.

★   ★   ★

Back now in London, the tall and elegant Caroline Fitzpatrick, who was slim even though she was large-boned, had features that had settled into what the French call *jolie laide*, in her case a full mouth belying the faintly cynical remarks that passed through her lips, a large straight nose and deep-set eyes. She wore her clothes with aplomb. After her five years at Wimbledon and the busy year in Paris trying to break into fashion journalism, Caroline's recrossing of the Channel and her return to England, which had surprised Ruth and her mother, was actually for practical reasons. Margrove's, a famous fashionable and rather expensive retailer, was to employ artists to sketch advertisements for the clothes they were going to sell. Rather than go to the agencies they preferred at the present to use their own artists. These sketches appeared every week in a superior Sunday newspaper whose readers would be likely to patronize the shop. It was better to be a big fish in a small pond, thought Caroline. There were far too many fashion journalists employed in Paris and, strangely enough, she had begun to prefer solid old London, and even solid young Englishmen, very recently one young Englishman in particular, a certain amazingly handsome Robert Cozens, whom she had met only once, at a friend's birthday party, but whom she could not seem to get out of her mind.

She was hoping that if she got a commission from the superior department store it might help her introduce some of her own ideas to London couturiers. She must then get experience in a workshop. The art school had not had a course for the actual making of clothes, and she had been only an observant dogsbody in Paris. There was no school of fashion in London but she heard of a trade school somewhere behind Selfridges where useful and innovative things were reportedly going on.

Caroline had learned quite a lot about

marketing in France. She wanted to earn a living from designing clothes and making them, not sketching them. One day she would acquire her own 'stockmen' — she had learned the term they used in the couture houses: separate dressmaker dummies with the exact measurements of each client, so that the clothes would be a perfect fit. But she must learn the procedures of simple couture, make her own *toiles*, learn to cut and sew, before the world of *haute couture* could be glimpsed on the far horizon, and, one day, her own designs!

Once she had learned all that, probably in Paris, she wanted to found her own house in London. Too many people were expert in Paris, where nobody thought the English had any ideas or techniques worth thinking about. Contact with the London retail trade might eventually help her to market creations of her own. She was full of hope, and practical enough to be sure she could exploit her talents one day if she was given a chance. The trouble was the usual one — money. Her mother did not appear to have much and she did not want to keep asking her father. Fashion was a risky business.

It would take a long time — might take years — to establish her own label, but she dreamed of the day when she had her own boutique above which was written CARO FITZPATRICK. Perhaps one day it might be written above a shop in Chelsea or on a street like South Molton Street, and over the door of her own workshop in the East End. On bad days she feared it would never happen, but she did not give up her dream. The only thing to do was to go on working hard and at the same time cast a sharp eye around for possibilities of acquiring some capital.

* * *

Sally had at last finished her secretarial course. She was just twenty. How she had hated her bed-sitting-room on the Finchley Road! Nevertheless, she had been determined not to give in and go to live with Aunt Clare, who had surprisingly offered her a room in the small flat she had in WC1. Sally suspected her aunt had only made the offer out of compunction.

If she were honest, it was living in London she loathed. Noisy and smelly, not a bit like the London of twenty-five years ago that her mother had told her about. Mother had, however, lived at home. The land on which her home had stood was being sold for development, now that after the bomb-damage one whole side of the square had

170

been demolished. The same thing was happening all over London. Her mother and Aunt Clare had once been quite rich, but her father could not now afford to give her a big allowance.

Sally wanted to get married, but the sort of men she met had so far not been her type at all. All she wanted whilst she waited for Mr Right was to help out at Pettiwell. Her mother was keeping the place going but the house was an even greater burden in the days of no servants and many shortages.

Sir Jack was now over sixty, his chief pleasure still his car. The problem of the house weighed on him. William Wilson was a great comfort. About the same age as Sir Jack, William looked younger than his old companion. Jack was ashamed that he could no longer pay the Wilsons a wage commensurate with their duties, but they had their quarters free from rent, William sold his vegetables and fruit locally, and they had saved carefully before and during the war. The new 'old age pension' might soon help the Wilsons too.

The Young Ogilvies, Laura and Andrew, had become older and greyer before they died, Laura six months after her husband, just at the time that Sally was living in London. Ruth had brought her mother back to Pettiwell from the little house they had bought in 1947 near Oxford, knowing she would be lonely after her husband's death, but she had swiftly declined both in spirits and health.

Sally made up her mind. She could type, and her shorthand was passable. She would look for work in the country, in an estate office or auctioneers'. One day, home for the weekend whilst she was supposed to be job-hunting in town, she saw a job advertised in the local paper. It was at the newly extended stables not far from Pettiwell, and they wanted someone to help run the riding-school, do the accounts and keep the records.

Opportunities might eventually exist for helping with riding, and running the recently re-established pony club. She knew she could cope with that kind of office-work — and at the same time help small girls to learn to ride. In addition, she'd be there at home to help her mother.

She got the job.

★   ★   ★

Clare Fitzpatrick was now settled in London. Her husband, who had been kept on for a time attached to the British Council in Paris, had been transferred to the British Institute, and was at present organizing exhibitions of British painting in Paris and Lyon. Francis had offered to re-establish their home in Paris, not in the flat that they had had to leave before the war, but in the same district. Clare had been reluctant, and had then definitely refused. London suited her now, and if Francis wished to join her, he could, but she was used to living on her own. Her attitude was scarcely enthusiastic.

If Francis wondered how long she had been really alone in the war it suited him not to ask. They had agreed to remain more or less separated for the time being. At present neither he nor she wished to divorce. Lily could live where she liked. Lily was known to want them to get back together, but where Lily liked best to be was Pettiwell. If she could not live with her father she felt she belonged with her Aunt Ruth more than with her mother. Fortunately, she had enough tact not to express this feeling.

If Clare was hurt she did not show it, insisting only that Lily kept a room in the flat. She knew she had no right to expect her daughter to want to live with her after all those years of separation in the war. Neither had she enquired too closely about what had happened during that war to her attractive husband. She, having long since abandoned painting, intimated that she was now writing her war memoirs, as well as doing some editing for a publisher. Wald & Epstein was one of the many new firms which had sprung up in London just after the war, founded by refugees from Hitler. Clare appeared content to have seventeen-year-old Lily to live with her during some of her holidays and go on visits to her father in Paris whenever she wanted. Otherwise she lived alone.

The war had marked Francis Fitzpatrick, who now looked as old as his years, though previously he had seemed eternally youthful. He had the fine features, aquiline nose and heavily lidded eyes of a seventeenth-century cavalier, and that slightly raffish look possessed by some Anglo-Irishmen, but his dark curly hair was now streaked with silver. His daughter Lily still had a look of him. Her hair had grown darker and her features even more like his in the last year or two. He felt he hardly knew her after all the years of war, and wished he saw more of her. It was sad that her French had almost disappeared. He knew she was always welcome at Pettiwell, as they all were, and until she was eighteen she could stay at her school in England, not Queen Eleanor's but a small boarding-school in Sussex. He did not worry quite so much about Caro, who appeared to be able to look after herself.

James Page was now fourteen and at his father's old school not far from Pettiwell. He was very spoilt in the holidays by his mother and his big sister Sally when she was at home. Sir Jack did not spoil him, only worried about his future, but then Sir Jack seemed to worry about everything, now that his Home Guard duties were long over, along with his active directorship of the old firm.

All Polly Wilson worried about was that Pettiwell would be sold and they would have to move into a council house. Jennie's future was, as far as her mother knew, secure. Her degree and her brains would see her settled in life.

★   ★   ★

The Lycée Durand, a large rectangular structure that began on the corner of the broad boulevard and stretched a good way along and behind it, stood back a little from the pavement. From the look of this main entrance, with its big black door, you would never have guessed that behind the building there stretched a large garden which adjoined the garden of a museum. The school had three principal floors and a floor above with mansard windows and narrower corridors.

Here, Jennie discovered, there dwelled the usually overworked and slightly unhappy *pensionnaires*, boarders from provincial cities, or girls belonging to families who moved around the world and needed a good education for their daughters. The school, which had begun as a convent, became secular sometime in the nineteenth century. It was well known and had grown extensively between the wars. Its front entrance looked over to an enormous church on the opposite side of the boulevard. This church always appeared to be having funerals, if one judged by the black velvet pall covering its vast door.

Jennie thought the school had hardly expected her. The bureaucracy appeared to be as vast as the building, so that it was some time before her credentials were recognized and she was given the go-ahead to teach English to small groups in a classroom on the third floor. She remembered Caro's account long ago of her school in France and the *tablier* she had worn, with her name embroidered on the front in loopy blue cotton.

On the day her English conversation lessons were to begin with *Classe Première B, 2*, Jennie toiled upstairs to the third floor and located *Salle 26*, a large empty room. She regarded the pristine blackboard, gazed through a window, which looked out at the back over what seemed to be a park, and wondered how to find her students. Now that she was here she itched to begin to do something useful. How could she find them? She waited for a few more minutes and then, hearing a shuffling outside the door, ventured back into the corridor. A row of about twelve girls was waiting outside. Perhaps she should have waited for them and then gone in with them. When would she ever learn her way around? The English teacher supposedly in charge of her had not made an appearance and there did not seem to be a staff-room like the one she remembered from her own school.

The girls looked at her curiously as she said in French:

'I think you are waiting for me? Do come in if you are looking for some English conversation!'

They trailed in and sat down.

One girl spoke up. She was about sixteen and had large spectacles. She replied in perfect English:

'We were waiting for you, Mademoiselle.'

'Well, here we are then,' said Jennie in her own language with a smile. One or two smiled back cautiously, but they appeared subdued. Jennie had heard enough tales of *chahuts* — riots — to be wary. English might not be the favourite school subject for most young people but perhaps it was less disliked than French was in England.

She sat at first on one of the desks at the front rather than on the chair on the raised teaching platform, and asked them all to sit a little nearer. There were several ways she might start them off. However, they might as well have their notebooks out to write down any English words of hers that they did not know or understand. This done, she brought out from her bag a book of songs and poems, a map of England and a few children's books which might get them going. They would know the stories. Then she launched into a description of herself — and spelled out her name, which necessitated a trip to the blackboard.

'Will you tell me your names one by one, so that I can get to know you all? Then I might give you each an English name,' she suggested.

She knew that French girls of this age were often addressed as 'mademoiselle' rather than by their first name, so she added: 'Tell me your surname as well as your first name — and if you would rather I called you miss, then I will!'

Some looked puzzled and a few looked shocked.

'Lemoine, Monique,' said the girl with the specs. So she was not English.

'Aren't we doing the programme?' asked one large girl seated on the front row next to Monique.

'There are various ways of attacking it,' said Jennie, feeling her acting powers returning. 'Your name?'

'Dujardin, Anne-Marie.'

'I shall consult you about your English requirements once we are better acquainted,' said Jennie magisterially. 'For the present, let's do it this way.'

Slowly she went round the group, writing down the names and trying to remember the first names rather than the surnames — Marie-France, Janine, Nicole, Joëlle, Françoise, Evelyne, Michèle, Josiane, Isabelle, Sylvie, Madeleine, Bernadette . . .

She began by asking each girl a question in English, remembering from her own school days, suddenly back in her head, that if you went round the class in order, the next girl prepared her answer, so she chose haphazardly. They had all dragged out a textbook from their bags so she asked if she might have a look at one of them at the end of the lesson. Nobody had thought to acquaint her with the 'programme'. Perhaps these conversation lessons were not taken very seriously by the powers that be? French children were usually required to do a good deal of written preparation and learning by heart!

'I shall see you learn the essentials,' she said. 'We may however do it in a slightly different way. I can teach you some English songs too and answer your questions about England.'

'Are we not having any *dictées*?' asked a fat girl with long blonde hair. She was Josiane.

'I shall give you all a list of topics and how we shall divide the hour we have together. I'll write that up on the blackboard.'

'I can do it for you,' said a solemn-looking girl.

'Are you a *pensionnaire* then?'

'Yes, Mademoiselle Wilson. I can write it up if there is nobody here before your lesson. I will do the register for you as well — that is my job,' she said in French.

Jennie remembered that the boarders usually took the register.

'I have done it for today,' added the helpful girl, one Madeleine.

She was thinking: there is so much I might teach them, if I can manage to hold their attention. They will not always be quite so amenable. This is their first lesson with me, and therefore a novelty. I want them to enjoy it — and to make them laugh too. She must find some *faux amis* — silly translations from one language to another. They might even get on to literature? There were only three classes for her to be responsible for at the school, this one in the first year of the Bac, and another in the second year of the Bac, along with one class of younger children. They needed oral practice. Apart from being tested in English conversation they were also examined orally in many other subjects which in England would have been written exams.

'I shall read you a story in English now — and then ask you questions,' she said, 'You will know it — it was written by a Frenchman.'

She launched into *Cinderella* and they began to smile.

Jennie devised questions that needed new vocabulary and correct tense construction. They wrote down 'pumpkin' and 'ugly' and 'fairy godmother' and then she asked them to tell her the rest of the story in English, making certain every person had had her say.

'I don't know if I am really supposed to give you any *devoir*?'

They groaned. Jennie smiled. 'Just write down a question in your best English which you'd like to ask me about England before the next lesson. That will be on Thursday, I believe.'

181

'Will you answer anything we ask you?' enquired a cheeky-looking girl. Marie-France, thought Jennie.

'I shall try,' she answered. 'Within reason.'

'Homework,' muttered Monique. She was writing it in her notebook.

Groans went up whenever Monique spoke.

Oh dear, thought Jennie, what if she had been confronted by a whole class of girls called Caroline? She had no idea of their prowess in written English but they seemed quite intelligent, if also extremely varied in their abilities. One or two of them might have lived abroad or perhaps had an English mother. Their English was certainly better than the French of the average grammar-school pupil in England.

She decided they had understood that she did speak quite passable French, but thought she must emphasize that in future — unless there were no other way of making them understand — only English would be spoken.

'You can correct my mistakes if I speak French by mistake,' she said as the bell for the end of the class sounded through the school. The hour was up. The girls looked surprised at her remark but laughed.

Jennie was amazed how much she had relished the hour. Had she always been meant to be a teacher? There was so much she could devise for these classes of hers, though there would probably never be enough time to carry it all out. There did not appear to be any half-measures if you were to communicate your enthusiasms. For a few minutes after this first class she felt both exalted and exhausted. As she followed her pupils down the stairs she was thinking that one day she would read to them from the kind of English novel she had delighted in at their age. Or even from an English children's story. There would be sure to be something down on the *quais*, in the many second hand bookstalls, the *bouquinistes*. She had already found Katherine Mansfield there. Jennie had discovered these stalls on an earlier visit to Paris and often browsed there. If only she had more money

As she strode back down the boulevard du Montparnasse in the late autumn sunshine, turning left further down to take a lingering look round the big department store on the rue de Sèvres, she felt free and happy. The world was good, and life was good.

★ ★ ★

The war had liberated Clare Fitzpatrick. She could not imagine what she might have been

183

doing if the war had never happened, if she had never left Paris, if she had stayed there looking after her husband and children, doing the marketing, trying to cook delicious dishes, accompanying Caro to school and Lily to the Luxembourg Gardens. Oh, there would have been the occasional *vernissage* to visit and there might have been the occasional flirtation, but she did not think she would have cheated on her attractive husband, for whom she had especial feelings of gratitude. The trouble was that she had never been in love with him, and he was well aware of that. Her sister Ruth might possibly have some idea of her past life but Ruth did not know the half of it. Clare felt removed from all that, from those pre-war days of responsibility and worry, and from the desire to draw and paint, or, rather, be an artist. The war had catapulted both her and Francis into a completely different way of life, as it had done so many couples.

Long before that, the birth of her daughter Caroline had altered her own priorities and led for a time at least to the obliteration of her ambitions. Perhaps it had made her realize in time that she would never be as good a painter as she had once hoped. What had been the point after that of living in Paris, except for the fact that Francis could earn a better living there than in London? She had not married him however for mainly financial reasons. She had known that he had loved her, but she had guessed that the war had moved him away from her and her from him. There had always been Pettiwell waiting in the wings for their two girls, and she had often felt since, that it had all been meant to happen and that the children had returned 'home' to England. Francis, whose parental home had been burned down in 1921, could never feel the same as she did. Pettiwell was not strictly her own home but she knew London well. After she married, Ruth had written to her, saying: *You will always be welcome here, Clare.*

In the war there had been a job for her to do, sometimes a very dangerous job, and there had been danger and excitement and success for Francis too on his secret missions. However, even before all that, he had had to confine his own painting to any vacation he could take from his work for art dealers, who appreciated his expertise. For them he had worked ever since the birth of Lily. You could not live on air, and long before England had been plunged once more into armed conflict, her grandparents, who had helped her out a lot in the past, had begun to find London life too expensive, though they had carried on their London lives until they died. Her mother and father, Laura and Andrew, had been no help at all to her and her sister when they were growing up. She and Ruth had fended for themselves, Ruth landing on her feet, she supposed, when Sir Jack had proposed to her all those years ago.

Now here she was, still in London, scene of her ambulance work and her VIP-driving, and there was Francis nicely settled in a pleasant Parisian niche, working for the British Institute, a much larger concern than his pre-war art dealers, putting all his vast knowledge of painting to the advantage of the fledgling post-war art scene.

Clare reflected that if it had not been for Ruth and Sir Jack at Pettiwell she would never have managed to work in the war, and might very well have returned to France after it. The reality of her work in the war had made her see she that she might have other gifts that could be exploited, and had set her on a different path. Not that it had anything to do with the blitz, except that she had grown in self-confidence. What could be more different from driving ambulances than working in a publisher's office? For four days a week she was a conscientious copy-editor and proof-reader and had recently been given more editorial work.

On the fifth day she toiled at writing an account of her wartime years, reconstructing her life in a pattern. At present however she seemed to have come to a full stop with this account. It had become more personal, surprising her, and making her think she might not be in control of the pattern. If she was to make sense of her life there were matters she had never revealed to anyone, which she must confront, or at least try to analyse. Otherwise she could not bring the book to a satisfactory conclusion. Then she might try her hand at the biography of a woman artist.

Ought she to go back to Francis? She did not think he wanted her back. *Ought* she to take up the burden of *mère de famille*, a little late in the day? She had never really felt maternal; it had been forced upon her, an irksome task for which she knew she was not suited. Lily liked staying with her sister . . . And Caro? What about Caro, in whose presence, aroused by past memories, she felt both guilt and pride.

She did not want to dwell upon her future — it would be up to Caro herself. She would be all right; she felt sure she would succeed one day, for she was a talented young woman, more talented, although in a slightly different direction, than her mother?

Perhaps harder-headed? She hoped so. Caroline, after sharing a flat with two women friends from college at the Earl's Court end of Kensington, had moved into a basement bed-sitting-room in Pimlico and was busy with her fashion sketches for Margrove's. They had taken her on for an initial six months. She had also made mention of this new 'trade school', but her mother was not sure if she had enrolled there.

Sitting musing in her small flat, an electric fire turned on, now that the days were drawing in, Clare felt those pangs of self-reproach that were so useless and unproductive. She got up to make a cup of coffee in the minuscule kitchen and turned back to the pages spread out on her little table next to her portable typewriter. Except for wartime, she had never had a regular job, had not had to 'go out to work', (as they used to say before the war) for years. Francis had spared her that; there was no need to feel guilty about it. She was sure her sister Ruth did not feel guilty about her title and her life in that lovely house — even if it was now becoming too much for her to manage.

No, she must concentrate upon the task in hand. Tomorrow she'd be back at the office. She was quite a good copy-editor. The firm was not quite well enough established to pay anyone else to do this so she with her sharp eyes and quick brain read the proofs of their entire small list and corrected them.

The others were all right, she thought, as she put her mind back to that day in 1941 when she had nearly gone up in flames with a house that had taken an incendiary bomb . . . She turned her thoughts to her husband. Francis was in his element, earning a decent salary, introducing exhibitions of British paintings, landscapes and portraits and genre paintings to French museums and galleries, and working also in a sellers' market with some of his old dealers who had eventually reappeared a few years after the end of the war.

As for Ruth, her sister's home life in Pettiwell was predictable if too busy. Sally, according to her sister, was already blissfully busy taking little children out on leading reins and typing up accounts; Sir Jack, according to the same source, might be tired and dispirited but he had had a good innings; the Wilsons were being as usual indispensable; James Page was probably enduring trig and logarithms; Lily was in her last year at school singing solos in the school choir and hoping to start at the Royal College of Music next year. And that little girl, the Wilson daughter, the clever one, doubtless now learning to speak even better French and wearing her eyes out reading.

Ah well, thought Clare Fitzpatrick, I do much the same myself! She bent to concentrate on the matter in hand.

★ ★ ★

Caroline Fitzpatrick was actually neither at home nor at work that evening: she had been invited to a party in Maida Vale where she hoped she might see Robert Cozens, the young man who was often in her mind. He was about her own age, but seemed older, and he was so handsome! Caroline had always responded to beauty and he was a beautiful young man in both face and figure.

She knew that her vow never to let love get in the way of success might one day be compromised if she allowed herself to give full rein to her feelings for a man, a vow which up till now had been less powerful than her ambition. Usually so cool and collected, and never yet a victim of passion, Caroline set off for the party with butterflies in her stomach. Perhaps he wouldn't be there? It was just that it was exciting to think he *might* be.

At Pettiwell Sally Page had already glimpsed Robert once or twice in the village where he had been staying for the weekend with his grandparents at Stair Court. She had first of all got to know his sister Nadine at the stables, for whenever Nadine was staying at Stair Court she would go to the stables and ride for hours. Sally asked her mother how well she knew the Cozens family.

'I did hear that Edward Cozens had two children,' replied Ruth, 'I thought it must be his daughter you'd met. I've never met either of the children. I believe he married an Honourable Susan or Janet somebody — your father would know more than I do about it.'

'We don't know many young people in the village,' said Sally, who was a sociable girl. 'I'd like to know them better.'

'The older Cozens were more your grandmother Page's friends than ours,' said her mother, 'They must be in their late seventies now — they used to come over for bridge before the last war when your Ogilvie granny and grandpa were staying with us. Your father and his family knew the elder son better, I think, but he was killed in the Great War.'

'How sad — that must have been Nadine's uncle, then?'

Ruth was remembering Mrs Gibbs, who had occasionally come to help them with the spring-cleaning, since none of the former maids or gardeners had returned to Pettiwell. Mrs Gibbs had 'done' for the Cozens at one time and told her how the old couple doted on their grandchildren. Ruth remembered Edward Cozens, but nursed an instinctive suspicion of the Cozens tribe, which only her politeness and her efforts to entertain her own parents when they visited Pettiwell had allowed her to hide. Maurice and Beatrice Cozens loved bridge and conversation, but Ruth always found them a trifle 'flashy'. In Jack's mother's opinion, years ago, having lost their elder son on the Somme, the couple had spoiled their younger son. She and Clare had both met Ted Cozens, the surviving son, at different times in London, before she was married, before she had even visited Pettiwell, and since then he had made a successful career in the City, and made a lot of money in some stockbroking business or other. He must have had an eye to the main chance and also been quite clever, and he had married a rich wife.

She said to Sally: 'I believe your friend Nadine's father was very successful — it must be over twenty-five years ago that he was around the town.'

'You actually *knew* him then?'

'Not well — he wasn't my type,' answered her mother. 'And he did what they call 'marry money'.'

She spoke rather slightingly of him, thought Sally, but Ruth added: 'I believe lots of young women liked him. Do have his daughter over to Pettiwell if you get on with her.'

Sally however was not thinking so much of the blonde and good-natured Nadine, who rode a grey mare in a rather stately way, but of her wildly attractive brother, whom she had once glimpsed in the distance.

8

Jennie was busy, but not yet too busy to forgo Paris and all it had to offer. She still enjoyed meandering round her *quartier*, but would now take pleasurable strolls further afield, after taking the métro to more central parts of the city, or even to the more northerly and easterly districts. She was now addicted to the smell of the métro, that heady mixture of essence of Paris. She had visited museums and galleries, bookshops and department stores, and had already been twice to the Comédie Française. She had taken the little green bus down to the river, or further south in the opposite direction, beyond the railway station of Montparnasse, whence families left for holidays in Normandy or Brittany.

She had always wanted to live in Paris as worker rather than tourist. Once, as a student, she had tried very hard to find a job selling perfume at the store Aux Trois Quartiers. Employment laws however had been rigid: you required a work permit, and this Jennie had never been able to acquire. Now she was an accepted salary earner — for a time at least — even if the salary was hardly munificent. Part of her contentment was that she was earning her small living and was accepted as a grown-up citizen, with the right to conduct her life independently.

After her university class she would walk down the Boul' Mich', not a street she liked very much apart from its bookshops, and go across to the île St Louis. After her lessons at the school she would walk in quite a different *ambiance*, in the more expensive *septième arrondissement*, to the Champ de Mars where some of the *lycée* girls did their *gymnastique*, or played games, lessons that, like religious instruction, were not obligatory. She still preferred what she regarded as her home ground, the *sixième*, faithful to the old rue Vaugirard, the church of St Sulpice, and the boulevard St Germain, where those famous philosophers were said still to sit and talk, though she did not think she had ever seen any there. Above all she liked to wander in the Luxembourg Gardens under the trees at one end, or stare at the goldfish in the Fontaine de Marie de Médicis at the other.

The Sorbonne classes she was teaching took place twice weekly. Up to now, six weeks after her arrival in Paris, she had spoken no English except to her two sets of students, and these classes often included people older than herself. They were individuals from all over the world, who for some reason or other needed to improve their English. There were French students as well, of course, mostly female, but several Latin-Americans, and perpetual students from Iraq, Albania and Indo-China. A few of the older ones might even have been caught in Paris in 1940 and forced to stay throughout the German occupation. What they were studying was usually a mystery to Jennie. She concluded they must possess private incomes. Others, men and a small scattering of women in their mid to late twenties, were post-graduates who had jumped through the many hoops placed for those who wished to achieve the *agrégation*, or a doctorate.

Any official syllabus for these university conversation classes of hers was apparently non-existent, and as the students were all at different stages of understanding and speaking English, it was hard to know where to begin. At first she had decided to spend twenty minutes reading them items from the English newspapers she bought and brought with her, to initiate discussion and through questioning see whether they had understood what she had read before she asked them to read it aloud themselves. They had to make an effort to understand spoken English, and this led to her systematically teaching them vocabulary and idioms. She was not sure how much they were learning, and it worried her. They all needed a text and she had had no guidance about what to use. Two weeks previously, however, one of the women, Françoise, had produced a little book with selections from English writers and questions to answer orally.

'We are all expected to buy this,' she stated. She was a neat brunette who wore crisp creamy blouses, no black polo neck jumpers for her, and she had attended the class the previous year. Jennie discovered the following week that she had prevailed upon most of the others to buy second-hand copies of this book. She felt relieved but annoyed. How could she be expected to know what to tell them to buy if nobody ever told *her*?

She purchased one for herself, a pristine copy, not one of the many tattered ones sold off cheaply to students every year. Yet she didn't want to be restricted to this one book. The French were so prescriptive. She'd decided they could all spend a few moments at the beginning of the class discussing any matter raised by the students themselves.

'There are plenty of English books down on the *quais*. You must read for pleasure!' she kept urging them.

They looked faintly astonished. Sometimes, she would bring a book she'd found interesting and proceed to tell them about it. This also amused them. She was younger than many of them, but they did not appear to have read very much. Most of them had certainly heard of 'Grim Grin', if of no other English writer apart from Shakespeare, and Graham Greene, along with Waugh, might amuse them, if at the same time convincing them, as far as the latter was concerned, that the English were quite mad. American writers, yes, they had read some of *them* or at least knew of Hemingway and Mailer but seemed vague about the connection between Britain and America.

After last week's lesson she had feared they might have stopped being interested in her offerings but she found she was wrong. She had brought along a newspaper and some novels, and urged them to use the British Institute library. They were intelligent people, some of whom must have read widely in their own languages, and she might learn as much from them as she hoped they might from her. She had been amazed that many of the students who had not yet done their licence — and even some of those who had — often received their intellectual sustenance from cyclostyled copies of lectures. Some of them appeared to learn these grubby summaries by heart. The system was so impersonal, the lecture theatres overcrowded, and the courses took so long. Half of the students failed their first examinations. She began to think that English universities were superior. Of course anyone in France could start a course provided they had their sacred *Bac*.

Her classes were held in a dark cramped room round a long table and Jennie had not at first been sure if she was in the right place or even that the students were the ones she ought to be teaching. Some of them turned up to both her Tuesday and Thursday classes, but on the other hand she had been given the names of students who had not yet put in an appearance. She hadn't yet received a salary cheque either, and went every week to the office on the rue Soufflot to make enquiries about it. The *lycée* had by now actually paid her a salary, so she was able to manage for the time being.

Today she had in her bag some copies of well-known English poems, made on an ancient cyclostyler at the school. She would read these aloud to the students and see how they went down. It would be a change from talking about novels, or the news, or the British Constitution.

Jennie did not despise a blackboard for

teaching vocabulary and English idioms, and the women copied down assiduously every-thing she said. It was however usually the men who spoke up, especially if politics were being discussed. There was one man, Miguel López, who was equally voluble whatever the subject was. He enjoyed sparring with her and she rather relished that. His English was excellent, with a slight American intonation, and she wondered why he bothered to attend. At the beginning she had gone round the table asking them what they were studying, and Miguel, a tall rangy man who looked about twenty-eight, had said he was at the *Sciences Po* — the Institute of Political Science, studying international law.

'Then you can teach us all something,' she said.

'Oh, the necessary *vocabulary* for all that is much the same — mostly English or American,' he replied. 'Maybe some people in this class are not very interested in what is happening in other parts of the world?' Several of the others looked wary.

'We may be ignorant, but not uninterested,' said Jennie. 'If there is ever anything you would like to draw our attention to in the newspaper . . . ?'

He smiled. She was thinking, I wish I could stick to talking about literature and language.

I wonder if he is a Marxist. Señor López came from somewhere in Central America, but did not look like her idea of a student revolutionary. He had mobile features, high cheekbones, a lively look in his eye and a finely modelled mouth. For a man who must descend from a Spaniard he was tall. There might perhaps be a tiny admixture of American Indian in the biscuit-coloured tone of his skin.

Señor López was a polite young man, even if he liked to disagree with everybody including Jennie. He seemed very much at home in France.

'I need to know better the English of the English,' he said to her. 'Not American. I must also study the European point of view. This Cold War is cold for you — and for the French too. At home we were always very much influenced by France,' he added.

It was clear that he was also a literary young man and Jennie felt sure he would need no encouragement to talk about literature. She ought to concentrate more on the two silent scientists, and the quiet young women, never mind Françoise, who was an expert grammarian.

This Tuesday morning Jennie had an as yet unanswered invitation from Francis Fitz-patrick — the man she always thought of as

'FF' or Mr Fitz — in her pocket as she reached the door to her classroom. She was thinking of Caro, whom she had missed seeing in the summer. For a change, she had gone to Catalonia in July with her old friend Joan, and a new friend, Eileen, who was studying at Manchester with her, to enjoy the sea and the sun and the sherry. Caro must have told her father that she was now in Paris.

Miguel López arrived just before Jennie. He bowed and held the door open. Some of the other students were already waiting. Today, having noticed they often got it wrong, she must correct their use of the English past tense in conversation. They had asked her why you could say: 'Did you have a good day yesterday?' but not 'Have you had a good day yesterday?' You could say both, 'Have you had a good day today?' or 'Did you have a good day today?'

It was difficult explaining about time. She ought to have had some training in all this but the thought of spending her life teaching such things did not enthrall her.

She began: 'Well, you could say 'When did your cat die?' but not 'When has your cat died?' On the other hand you might say 'Did you have a good time?' or 'Have you had a good time?' They have a slightly different emphasis according to how far away the events are. The only way of getting them right is to listen to English people. I believe Americans have a slightly different way of expressing time.'

'They write dates differently as well,' said a scientist who did not usually add to the discussion.

Françoise looked up, and addressed Jennie. 'You would not say, 'Have you had a good time on Thursday?' '

'No — but I might say after — er — watching some children play a game together: 'Have you had a good game?' It's more immediate. You never stop to think about English tenses until you are asked to teach them,' she added with a groan.

It was the ubiquitous use of *did* that was the saviour of learners of English. English grammar was quite easy, they all said, because *did* and *got* got you everywhere.

It was not like her teaching at the school. Most of these older people could after all make themselves perfectly well understood.

She'd much prefer to introduce them to Keats.

Miguel López was looking at her ironically this morning as she unpacked her books. His long, olive-skinned face always had a quizzical expression.

What nice wavy brown hair he had . . .

'What have you brought for our delectation today?' he asked. One of the women tittered.

'Some grammar — and then a poem. There's no point learning English just to write conference papers or chat. I want you to realize what a lovely language it is,' replied Jennie.

Françoise Vernier was thinking, Mademoiselle Wilson is so *English* in her enthusiasms. She liked her, and these classes were not easy to manage — last year the German *assistante* had left in tears. Mademoiselle Jennie, in spite of her youth, was made of sterner stuff. Stamina they called it in English. She had a nice voice too — Mlle Vernier did not find the English accent easy.

'May I make a statement?' said one of the scientists, when they had all commented upon last week's problems of various past tenses and written down a few examples. Now Jennie had distributed copies of *Ode to Autumn* round the class.

'Yes, of course.' It was Serge Locatelli. Was he Italian, Russian or neither?

'I do not think we need to know about your literature — we are busy with much work in *chimie* and mathematic and so need the scientific language, not the poetry.'

Jennie considered. 'Mathematics is a universal language,' she offered. 'Poetry can be in any language — and indeed,' she aimed wildly, 'Pushkin — or Leopardi — *I* should like to study them. Here I teach English and you cannot fully understand a nation unless you have read a little of its literature. Our Romantic poets were part of what made modern English.'

Miguel smiled and raised an eyebrow and one of the women, a blonde Dutch girl said, 'Hear hear!'

'I cannot offer expertise on scientific English,' said Jennie 'I think we must just try to cover as many different areas as possible. I am happy to translate anything from English that you need help with.'

Serge subsided but closed his eyes and took no further part in the proceedings.

Jennie said, 'I don't mean to analyse this poem — you will probably have studied it at school. I want you to hear the cadences of English through this language of Keats.'

Was she being pretentious? She explained a few of the more unusual words and read aloud the first eight lines — she knew them by heart — before asking others to continue. When they had all read a few lines, Janine, a round girl with round glasses and a snub nose, ventured:

'It is very different from French verse.'

'We must read some Shakespeare,' suggested Miguel López.

'Not very useful for the *oral*,' said a thin girl with frizzy hair, called Nicole.

This reminded Jennie that she must find a copy of the requirements of the English oral for those students who had to pass it as part of their next examination. Those who had their *licence* and were proceeding towards the next hurdle and an eventual master's degree — as she was herself — still had oral examinations. They were how she imagined an Oxford viva.

She takes it so seriously, thought Señor López.

Jennie was hoping they enjoyed their hour with her, but had been told the great trap for a teacher was to want to be liked. Ah well, would she ever rid herself of her need to be liked? It was about time she grew up. She often castigated herself in this way. Still, she thought she would know if she was unpopular. As the class ended she went up to the aggrieved scientist.

'Have you read the life of Madame Curie?' she asked him in French. He seemed surprised to be addressed.

'No.'

'I think you could read it in English — it will have some vocabulary that might be useful. It is in the *bibliothèque* — I saw it there. I don't want to bore you with poetry — you could read the biography of an English scientist,' she added. 'Isaac Newton — or Faraday — I don't know . . . '

He laughed. 'I won't come if I am too bored, mademoiselle!'

Well, she supposed not.

As she went out: 'Keats is all very well,' said Miguel. 'Come for a cup of coffee in this season of mists and I shall recite you some Spanish poetry.'

'Thank you — I will.'

It was the first time any student had spoken to her after the class, never mind offered her a drink. They walked down the street to the big café at the corner and once she had sat down and put her bag of books on an empty chair, he said:

'You can't please everybody — you do very well. I had to tutor a young boy from Mexico last year in English myself.'

'You don't need my classes, Señor López!' she exclaimed.

'Oh, I don't want to get — how do you say? — 'rusty'? I have studied in the States — or shall I say 'I did study there'?' He was looking crafty and she realized he was giving her a counter example. He went on: 'Believe me the standard there — apart from the best

— is pretty abysmal. And please call me Miguel.'

'You should come to London then,' said Jennie.

'I had to come here to perfect my French,' he replied. 'Not however to forget my English — never mind my own language.'

He said something in Spanish.

'That's one of our Romantic poets: Vallé-Inclan — you'd like him.'

'I don't know any Spanish, I'm afraid.'

'Then you must start to learn some at once — it's not a difficult language. Quite phonetic.'

'I went to Catalonia last summer but they all spoke Catalan — that would be a hard language to learn, I thought.'

'I once learned an English poem off by heart, you know, when I was learning English — before I went to the States. It was Kipling's *If*. Do you think I ought to have learned your *Ode to Autumn* instead?'

'Yes, certainly!' They both laughed.

Jennie decided he might call her by her first name, and said so now.

'Jennie,' he said pronouncing it in the Spanish way — it sounded like 'Hennee'.

She smiled. The English 'J' was also a problem for most of the French.

Having drunk their coffee they shook

hands on parting. Really, he was very nice, she thought, but you could see he might be dismissive of those less intelligent than himself.

It was only on the way back to her hostel, as she walked through the Luxembourg, followed by the occasional 'Ss-ss' from young men who were ever on the look-out for young women, that she remembered the letter in her pocket. She waited until she was in her little room at Accueil before opening it.

Mr Fitz, as she still thought of him, was inviting her to a party, a sort of reception some British and French officials were giving on the rue de la Sorbonne. He enclosed a large gold-embossed invitation and a hand-written note:

Dear Jennie
Caro tells me you are here for a year and that you are staying at her old 'foyer'. I am sorry not to have seen you yet but hope we can remedy that next week. I trust your teaching is going well? Do come — no need to dress up.
Yours ever — Francis Fitzpatrick.

Well, yes, she would love to go to a posh do, but what on earth should she wear? It was all very well his saying she need not dress up.

He probably meant not wear her tiara, she thought gloomily. She did reply however, accepting with pleasure.

* * *

She glimpsed Miguel López several times during the next ten days — at the restaurant Jean, a cheap lively place on an alleyway off the boulevard St Germain, where students went for their midday meal, served at long tables in an open courtyard if the weather were fine; and also in a bookshop on the Boul' Mich'. The first time he came up to her in the restaurant he sat down and chatted away, saying: 'I must profit in my free time from your English accent.' Jennie had become used to his arguing with some of her more political remarks and did not mind his disagreement, was indeed quite grateful that he took her seriously. She had earlier decided that the English did not really take politics seriously, and Miguel López was certainly a very well-informed man.

She had the impression too that he was probably from a very rich family. You usually found that the most radical people had had extremely comfortable backgrounds. One day she might tax him with this. Most rich people of course — possibly most — never gave a thought to making the world a better place. The battle of ideas took place in fact between one lot of the middle class and the other. Where did this leave the proletariat? She was reading some French writers who were very outspoken in their defence of the common people but she did not believe they understood them. As time went on she began to express these kinds of thoughts once or twice to Miguel. After all, she had not so far met anyone else in Paris to whom she could talk seriously.

Miguel asked her about the war.

'I have never been ... conscripted? ... myself.'

Sometimes the war seemed like a dream she did not deserve to have survived. She had been only fourteen when it ended, so what could she have done? As she and the others had only been children in the war they had lived through it without really experiencing it. Unless you were bombed out or lost a relative you'd either lived the war as a sort of adventure or seen it at second hand — like a play you were not really involved in. She said:

'I suppose if I had lost a relative or friend, or seen a person killed by a bomb — or been just a few years older — my memories would be utterly different. I was just too young to take part in it or be of any use in the war effort. People only a few years older than me and my friends really took part in it all.'

She was remembering something her father had said, about the people who remembered the Great War mostly being dead in twenty years or so and that it was up to those who were still alive to bear witness on their behalf and testify to events. Her father and mother had been the unluckiest generation, suffering a war twice in their grown-up lives.

'You look thoughtful,' Miguel said.

'I was thinking, one day my generation will be the only one that remembers the war.'

'That won't be for a long time, I hope, Hennee,' he replied.

'I wonder how long memories last? The war is already mixed up in my memory with my childhood. All we did was listen to grown-ups and believe what they told us — and knit squares and learn how to bandage arms and legs — and later on towards the end of it all wait for the news on the wireless. We got used to the blackout and the rationing and never being warm enough — it was our parents who were worked to death — 'digging for victory' and 'making do'. My father fought in the first war. Of course there were the V-1s and -2s — they were really nasty and I was frightened of them. If I'd been only three years older — and a boy — I suppose I'd have had to go into the services at the end of the war. Boys my age were all called up three or four years ago. They still are.'

'Called up? What is that?'

She explained: 'You said 'conscripted'. I meant for National Service — we say 'called up'.'

'Ah, the draft,' he said.

'Yes — called up,' she said.

'How you English love your prepositions!' he teased.

'My parents' employers,' she said, 'were all terrified their house would be commandeered for a hospital. It was — is — a big house but all we did was take in people bombed out from nearby villages when their homes had flying bombs — doodlebugs — or rockets descend on them.'

He said, 'Even so, if you live through a war, though you're only a child, it must make a difference to your sense of security?'

'It would if I'd been in London, I suppose. I think I worried about my parents but they never for one moment thought we might not win it! I expect the Germans felt the same — but I am only just finding out what we did to Hamburg in 1943 — terrible beyond words!'

She thought, and then Hiroshima. Who can be confident about humanity?

'I think the English had an irrational confidence — years of not being invaded strengthens one's psychological make-up,' he said.

'We could not have won the war without the Russians,' said Jennie.

Another day they talked about English food ('It is nursery nutrition!') and the English class system, which, like the food seemed to intrigue him. She explained the term 'landed gentry' and how it no longer necessarily meant you were rich, or even had any land left.

'I have read in a book the term 'shabby genteel' said Miguel. 'Explain please.'

That might be Sally in future, she thought, if they lost more money. Caro would never be shabby and I have never been genteel. You might think Mother would like to be!

'People who were once quite well-off who have fallen on hard times and now have to make do. Mostly now the people who used to have tons of servants have none — or only one or two. The people I know best lost their money before the war. It was the war that really changed everything for most of the English upper classes. They are still mad about animals, especially large dogs and horses.'

'They liked tigers too,' said Miguel, 'if they were dead.'

'I had a small tiger — a cat,' said Jennie.

He had been amusing, and her conversations with him had always stimulated her and made her think more about her own place in the world. Where did she belong? At the moment she was happy to live in France but suspected that at the bottom of her heart she was English. A mixture of the two nations would be ideal. She was very happy here in Paris; life seemed more vivid and she even felt more appreciated. As she had guessed, she discovered that Miguel came from a well-to-do family of professional politicians and lawyers. He did not elaborate except to say his grandfather had once been president of his country.

The day of Mr Fitz's reception was looming nearer and she had still not decided what to wear. The day before it was to take place she went to the Samaritaine and bought a straight dark-blue slipper-satiny looking ankle-length skirt that was reduced in price. She could team it with her best blue blouse, the one with the ruffles, worn only once for the 'Leavers' Ball'. She had almost not brought it with her, fearing Frenchwomen — so much more chic — would think it an 'English' colour. So it was, but it suited her and she could always draw attention to her eyes and face with long dangly earrings. Jennie's best features were her eyes. She knew she could never be fashionable, and still did not spend too much time bothering about clothes, though here in Paris you were more aware of how you dressed. She liked strong colours and had a skin dark enough to get away with them. She did not think she looked very English.

What would Caro say about her choice? Probably smile with slight condescension. Caro however was not going to be there and she felt confident she would not be the worse dressed woman guest. The sort of English girls who might be doing courses in Paris as an adjunct to Cordon Bleu or 'coming out' were not known for their fashion sense, and it was never any use competing with the older more sophisticated or eccentric ones. She had hopes of being one of those by the time she was thirty-five.

* * *

Francis Fitzpatrick thought, 'How fresh and bright she looks,' when Jennie came into the big room which was already lit with a central chandelier. Already some academic dignitaries, various English students of indeterminate age and some others from the British Institute were standing around.

I ought to have entertained her before, he thought, as he detached himself from a group of men and went up to shake hands with her. He could see she was not shy although her manners were not brash or forward.

'*Soyez la bienvenue!*' he said, and smiled into her eyes. 'Tell me how you are getting on — and then you must meet some nice young men,' he went on in English.

'Oh, I'm kept quite busy,' she replied. 'It's very kind of you to invite me here. Are they all painters?' she asked, looking round with interest.

He laughed. 'No! I'm afraid not — hardly any of them. Most of my work here is in administration — we're a rather popular part of the university, you know, so my job is easy. I also arrange exhibitions all over France. How do you like the Sorbonne? Caro told me you were staying at good old Accueil! Just about everyone does at some point.'

He was very easy to talk to, full of charm. She thought, he is not at all like the others at Pettiwell. It must be because he's Irish. They chatted away and then he took her up to a group of young Frenchmen saying:

'You'd better meet some new people or I shall not have done my duty.'

217

He was sorry to have to release her to the others and decided to go back and talk to her once the party was in full swing.

'You know our artistic director then?' one of the horn-rimned-spectacled men asked her.

'Oh, he is a family friend from home,' she replied. What would be his reaction if she had said: As a matter of fact my mother helped to bring up his wife — she was maid to his wife's family, and also a sort of nursemaid?

Jennie was enjoying herself though she knew nobody and did not find the stilted conversations very interesting.

A waiter poured her a glass of champagne and she stood a little irresolutely as she let the deliciously cold nectar irradiate her.

'Well, if it isn't Miss Wilson!' said a voice and there was Miguel López, also glass in hand. *He* was not English! How did he get to be invited?

'Hello.' As far as she could recall she had not mentioned to Miguel that she was invited to this party.

Her manner could not help showing him how pleased she was to see him.

'Are you to be one of the English regulars then?' he said. 'This is their 'At Home', I am told.'

'No, I know one of the directors who works

for the Institute. He arranges the art exhibitions — Francis Fitzpatrick.'

'He's quite famous, I think,' said Miguel.

'Really? I didn't know that. He is the father of one of my friends and this is my first visit here.'

She waited for him to tell her how or why he had been invited, and he went on:

'My father was a diplomat and so his old friends often ask me to things. I don't usually bother to accept.'

Her first real Paris party! And Miguel had probably been to dozens and despised them.

'I like it here,' she said, 'though I haven't spoken to anybody much yet.'

They were walking round the room now. Miguel was always in transit somewhere. She would introduce him to Mr Fitz as a 'real pupil' of hers — show him she already knew people.

As if by magic Francis came up just as they were looking out of the long window, sipping their second glasses. Turning to the older man she said to him:

'May I introduce Señor López?'

'Francis Fitzpatrick,' said Francis with a slight bow.

'Señor López is one of my students,' said Jennie. 'Probably my *best* student!'

'I went to your little Constable show last

year,' said Miguel.

They exchanged small pieces of information about themselves. Miguel looked as though he was very much used to this type of conversation.

'Miss Wilson is a very hard-working teacher,' he said at one point.

For some reason Jennie hoped Francis Fitzpatrick would not say: *I have known her since she was a little girl,* or tell him about her parents. He did not, but instead asked Miguel which part of the Americas he came from. Jennie had never been sure but now heard he was from Colombia. How handsome he looked tonight. He was always elusive, a bit mysterious, but in a strange way she trusted him. Francis Fitzpatrick was being extremely attentive to them both.

How lucky she was, she thought, as the second glass of champagne lifted her spirits up to the chandelier and swung her around. Two glasses were enough, she thought, wishing that the feeling you had after two glasses — large ones it must be admitted — would stay with you for hours . . . but either they were dissipated, or you had a third drink and spoiled it all getting too talkative.

The three of them sat down on a gold-green sofa and waiters came up in an English way with small hors d'oeuvres.

'You'd get a proper supper with the Americans,' said Francis.

'Oh, I like this best, I can never eat and talk,' said Jennie.

'And American food is terrible,' said Miguel. 'Plentiful but not nice.'

'Well, in Paris it must be nice, surely?' said Jennie.

'You have lived in the States?' asked Francis of Miguel.

'Yes, three years, just after the war. Yale.'

No wonder his English was good. Francis began to speak of Ireland and his childhood. She had never heard him talk about it before, and he seemed youthful as he did so. She knew he had been very brave in the war. He must be about forty-seven, almost fifty perhaps? He must have married very young. Did he regret that? He hardly seemed connected here to his wife, Sally's Aunt Clare, to be Caro and Lily's father. Jennie began to ask him about Lily and they talked about Lily's music before he got up reluctantly and said he had better see to his other guests.

'A nice man,' said Miguel when he had gone.

'He has always been nice to me,' Jennie said.

Mr Fitz had always treated her well, as a

person rather than as the housekeeper's daughter.

'I can see he likes you!' said Miguel.

'Really?'

'Of course! My dear Hennee, I can always tell!' he said teasingly.

She felt a little sad, wishing Miguel would add that *he* liked her too. She liked him very much indeed.

After the party they walked to the river and looked at Notre-Dame in the moonlight, a very romantic backdrop. Miguel was rather quiet whilst piloting her across the road but then he suggested a cup of coffee. They walked to St Germain des Prés. In the café he asked what she really wanted to do with her life. He himself wanted to bring about political change, but explained that that would be a job for the whole of the next century. Jennie felt that all her ambitions were rather squalid and petty as she listened to his extremely lively and impassioned explanations of the vile situation most of the inhabitants of the world lived in. He obviously took it for granted he was the member of an élite caste — the only people who could pioneer change.

'Intellectuals unite!' he said. He was self-mocking. She was pleased to think he might consider her an intellectual and told him as they walked back by St Sulpice that she was not from a rich caste herself.

'In Western Europe people find their own level,' was all he said.

When they parted he kissed her forehead, and took her hand, saying, 'I have enjoyed your company — thank you.'

How very much she had enjoyed *his*.

The little kiss on the forehead was something she had never had bestowed upon her before.

9

Caroline Fitzpatrick was amazed at herself. With looks like his, could he really be the solid sensible Englishman she thought he was only pretending to be? Could she really be having these strange sensations? She had had one or two short and unsatisfactory affairs with men in the past five years but she had been drawn to this man ever since seeing him at that party in Maida Vale. She *was* amazed at herself; hope struggled with disbelief. About half an hour after she had arrived he had come into the room and she, usually so cool and collected, had felt the phenomenon of a glance across a crowded room. Was it just wishful thinking?

He had recognized her; he was crossing the room; he was at her side; he was smiling. She felt dizzy.

He said: 'Hello — we met at Geraldine's, didn't we? I'm Robert Cozens.'

As if she did not know his name, having asked it from her hostess before she left that last party.

He was so extremely good-looking. Caroline always appreciated the look of an object, or of a place, or of a human being, and knew she had a weakness, the overvaluing of a man for his appearance, and that she must always discount this. Was it simply a fancying? It felt more like a revelation! She wished she could paint him. Was it her mind or her body responding in this way, or some other obscure part of herself? She must act sensibly and appear ordinary, knowing very well that nothing could put a man off so much as an over-eager girl.

'I'm Caroline — Caroline Fitzpatrick,' she said. 'People usually call me Caro.'

'Can I get you another drink?'

He went off but whilst he was away she decided she did not want to drink too much tonight. Drink could so easily spoil the kind of feelings she was having.

'And what do you do, Caro? Isn't that what we are always meant to ask?' He smiled.

'I attend a trade school,' she began with a certain grim relish. If he was a snob that would put him off! He looked puzzled.

'I sketch clothes too — and design them as well. I'm just back from Paris.'

Paris! Nothing interested young Englishmen more than the idea of Gay Paree. She had not lost her wits.

'What exactly were you doing there?'

'Being a dogsbody. What about you? What do you do?'

'I'm in pupillage at the Bar.' He looked both guilty and resigned.

'Was the law always your great ambition? What sort of business?'

'No. I just thought it might be more interesting than the Stock Exchange. I did work in the City for six months. Really, though, I'd like to live in the country and be a farmer. After National Service I almost stayed in the army.'

Was this what he confessed to everyone?

'You could be a country solicitor. I was brought up in the country,' she said.

'You don't *look* like a country girl!' he replied.

He was thinking, she doesn't look English either. Too smart. Yet, did she say Fitzpatrick? She might be Irish? She doesn't look Irish either.

'No, well, I lived in Paris till I was eleven — and then the war came and we were sort of refugees at my aunt's house in Kent.'

Why was she telling him all this? Was it nerves?

'Whereabouts? My grandparents have a house in Kent and I go there from time to time.'

'I lived in a house called Pettiwell — near a

village of the same name.

'Really? How extraordinary!' He looked astonished. 'My grandparents live in Pettiwell village — at Stair Court. Do you know it?'

'I've heard of it.'

'What did you say was the name of your aunt?'

'I didn't. My mother's sister is Lady Page . . . '

She wasn't sure now that she wanted all this ordinary domestic detail to spoil their getting to know each other.

'I believe you must know Sally Page then — my sister Nadine has often talked about her. Nadine's mad on riding, and at the weekend she goes to the stables where Sally Page works.'

'Of course I know Sally — she's my cousin. I've never seen you around the village. Not that I'm there so often now — too busy.'

'I haven't met Sally yet. Nadine stays more often with our grandmother than I do at the moment. Too busy swotting for my Bar exam.' He was thinking, what a sophisticated-looking girl. Nadine has never mentioned her. He smiled at her. He was quite a straightforward young man who usually got on well with girls. This one looked a bit terrifying. He didn't want to talk about himself to her.

'Which do you like best, designing super clothes or wearing them?' he asked her, looking at her tight-waisted, swirly skirt. He could not tell if it was dark green or black — the lighting was not too good.

He appeared to have taken in what she had said.

'Oh, I never design for myself,' she replied.

'Do you design for men too? I always think we have to wear such ridiculous things.'

Caroline cast an eye on his discreet grey waistcoat. Rather conventional, really. It suited him, though a tweedy jacket might have suited him even better.

'I don't at present, but I might learn one day. There's not much scope for women designers at present in men's fashion — men's tailors have nobbled that market. A green velvet waistcoat might suit you!' she added.

'Oh, Lord, I'd really rather muck around in old trousers and chunky jumpers,' he said. 'I told you I was a country boy. Would you like to dance?'

Some couples were already dancing to an old big band record at the other end of the large high-ceilinged room.

'Reminds me of the war,' she said, and took the arm he proffered.

He was not a bad dancer. Once, years ago,

she had learned the quick-step and the foxtrot, but she preferred the easy continental way of dancing where you either jigged up and down or smooched along in a haze of Gauloises. He and she were almost the same height, since she was wearing very high heels. Perhaps he'd like her to take off her shoes? No, why should she? She had the feeling she'd be willing to do whatever he asked her.

Robert seemed a little abstracted as they danced a slow waltz.

Then, 'Do you know many people here?' he asked, conventionally enough.

'Just a few. Some are friends of friends — it's usually that, isn't it?' There was no one from Wimbledon, or from work, or from Pettiwell, apart from this young man.

'I know the Mathewsons — they're friends of my dad,' he said, 'John M. is in the City.'

She saw a middle-aged couple. This was a 'respectable' party.

When the music stopped for a time they leaned against the wall near french windows which appeared to look out over a canal, and sipped more wine.

'So your people still live in Pettiwell?' he asked.

'Oh no! My father works in Paris. He did something rather dangerous in the war over there and stayed. He was a painter. My mother's in London though. What about yours?'

Really, however would she get a proper conversation going? She realized that this beautiful young man was neither an intellectual nor an artist, the sort of man she usually met. It was refreshing in a way, as she need not make much effort. Would he ever find her attractive? He was a pleasant but dull conversationalist, and had clearly been to a good school. She was aware that she might not be an easy person to talk to, since her general manner (so she had been told by another young man whom she had not much liked) was too cynical and sarcastic. Well, she had no wish to be sarcastic to Robert Cozens.

A few other people came up to them then, a small chattering woman apparently named Maidie, who was concentrating on a slightly *outré* conversation she was having with a disreputable-looking older man, and a couple who were obviously married and had not much to say to anyone or to each other. These respectable parties were all alike, she thought. She wished she could show Robert that she was not a boring girl.

The disreputable man now concentrated on talking to Caro herself, to the clear disapprobation of the small woman, with whom Robert started a teasing conversation that seemed not to amuse her. Up came another girl, tall and auburn-haired and very beautiful. Robert turned to her and was trying his best to bring her into the general conversation but *she* was looking for someone else. In Caroline's experience, people always were.

'I say,' said Robert, turning back to her and looking rather relieved, 'Are you doing anything next Saturday? I've just remembered: an old school friend of mine — like me he's eating his dinners for the bar and swotting up for the exam — invited me to a little dinner party next week.'

As a matter of fact he'd almost decided not to go to Lewis Jardine's dinner party. He hoped this did not sound like awful cheek but she looked the kind of girl who might go down well there. He wanted to go and see his grandparents in Pettiwell for a weekend soon but there'd be plenty of time later.

Caro wondered if he had been asked to bring along a woman.

'Well, I was thinking of going over to my aunt's either next week or the week after myself,' she replied. 'That can wait.'

'Then you will come? That's nice.'

They had another dance, then: 'I think I shall have to go soon,' he said, looking at his watch. 'I promised my pa to look in at the family home and stay over.'

Caroline, secure in an invitation for the following week, was quite happy to leave with him. He accompanied her in a taxi and dropped her off at her new digs in Pimlico to continue his own journey into Mayfair. Whilst they were sitting together on the back seat he made no move to kiss her. She wrote her address and phone number on a piece of graph paper she found in her pocket and he took out a small diary, tore a page out, scrawled his own telephone number, and added the address of his friend Lewis. He said: 'I'll ring you. I think he wants people about eight. We might go to the flicks before Saturday — or next week?'

She would leave it to him.

Had she made a conquest or not? It had been rather a sedate party, not what she had expected. He didn't seem to be the kind of man who moved in circles where nothing was thought of inviting a woman you'd just met to a party. He'd probably been quite daring!

*　*　*

The visit to the cinema and then the dinner party went well. Caroline hoped she'd made a good impression. Robert, who had asked her to call him Rob, had kissed her goodbye after the dinner, which had been in a smart little mews, and had hinted at the possibility of their having a weekend away. Did he mean at Pettiwell? It sounded a bit vaguer than what she was used to from young men but he'd said it quite straight-forwardly and she had found that rather refreshing.

The following week she had a letter from Lily, who wrote to her from time to time. Lily had spent her February half-term holiday mostly at Pettiwell. The great news was that she had been provisionally accepted at the Royal College of Music to train as a mezzo-soprano, provided she passed the rest of her academic and further music exams. You had to study a musical instrument as well for a year, and Lily had already chosen the oboe. One might think that enough breath was to be expended on the voice but apparently the other instrument was never to be more than a side-line and would help in expanding the chest.

Sally is enjoying her job, she wrote. *She has made friends with a girl called Nadine who comes at the weekends and rides as much as she can from Sally's HQ. How are you? How do you like the new place — is it a sort of technical college? Are you still* 'toiling at your toiles'? I shall be so glad to leave school, you can't imagine. I do wish Mum and Dad would get together again. Do you think there is any chance? Mum could go and live in Paris and then we could stop worrying about her. She always says she is fine — she certainly seems very busy. I stayed the night and she'd been working very hard on this book of hers. Sorry I didn't see you — I had to dash across to Victoria — thought I might have an hour or two to visit but you'd have been at work.

Hurry up, spring! I don't want a cold for our next concert.

Lots of love — Lil.

She'd changed, the little Lily, thought Caroline. She was growing up. She'd never called their mother Mum before, and as for *worrying* about her, Caroline had never worried about her mother once the war had ended. She'd grudged her all that time she'd worked away at being a heroine during the war, and now her mother was once more doing what she wanted.

As for getting back with Pa, well, why should she? *He* was all right. It was true that once upon a time she had wished her own parents were more like Sally's, with their settled family life. She had been uncomfort-ably aware in her childhood that Sally had always loved both her parents equally and it had made her feel a little guilty that she could not love her mother in the way Sally loved hers. The sisters were so unalike, she thought now. Aunt Ruth was hardly a challenge. Lily loved their own parents equally too. It was herself who was different.

As she sat taking down notes at a lecture on fashion — an unusual occurrence at Barratt Street — Caroline found her mind wandering back to the handsome Robert. This would never do. She never let her mind wander when she was actually working — planning or measuring, cutting or sewing. Now she spent a bit more time thinking about Sally's new friend Nadine. Perhaps Rob would go down to Pettiwell soon and then they could meet for more than an evening.

★   ★   ★

Sally Page was a talented young woman in her own way, which was not the way of either her cousins Lily and Caroline or her old friend Jennie. Nadine Cozens genuinely admired her: Sally was brave, she was kind, and she worked hard. Everybody liked Sally and she had never yet been known to quarrel with anyone. Nadine realized that Sally could also be stubborn, which was a jolly good thing for a horsewoman, provided it was combined with know-how and a true love of the equine quadrupeds. This Sally had, and unlike some people, who loved animals but were not keen on the human race, her new friend did like most people.

Sally really must meet her brother Robert — they had a lot in common, she thought. Robert was an amiable person, and he was always expressing a desire to leave his studies at the Bar and take up farming or some physically taxing but healthier way of life. His sister could not help being a little sceptical about this; he ought to have more experience of country life to be certain. And what would their parents think if he did?

Edward Cozens was an immensely successful businessman who had taken up his London life again after a war spent fire-watching in the City, and trying to keep his firm going. His present business was still something to do with steel, a protected industry in wartime. Nadine was vague about it. Robert perhaps felt he would never match up to such a father, who had made a good deal of money in the thirties when others were not doing so well.

Nadine herself had a secretarial job, which she did not take too seriously. She'd prefer something more adventurous. She liked village life and would be happy to settle down one day in a place like Pettiwell, but not yet. She was a heavily built young woman with straight, very fair hair, combined with velvety-brown eyes. She did not resemble her handsome brother in any of her facial features and was more admired by women than by men, who found her directness a little disconcerting. Sally had introduced her to Lily the last time she had stayed in Pettiwell and Lily had approved of her.

Like Nadine, Lily was no shrinking violet and had plenty of opinions. Sally thought no one in her own family had yet taken Lily seriously enough. Caro was so much older and experienced but Lily was just as talented and might also need encouragement. Sally knew little about music and on this subject Nadine too had kept quiet.

'Rob is much more musical than me — he's a great jazz fan,' Nadine told her.

★　★　★

Three weeks after Caroline had met the physically godlike Robert he broached the idea of going to Pettiwell for a long weekend.

Nothing more definite had yet been said about the other projected weekend, except for his murmuring that the *Spread Eagle* at Thame was said to be a jolly nice place and they must go as soon as the weather improved.

Why would the weather matter? Caroline asked herself. She longed for Rob to make love to her, and a weekend of passion did not need warmth or sunshine. She found him so attractive, had really fallen for him in a big way, but however much she wanted him, she'd have to accept for the present his own more leisurely approach to an affair. Perhaps he was shyer than he appeared. That was an added attraction.

Caroline had been indignant when Annie, a woman acquaintance who also sketched for Margrove's, and had been introduced to Robert one evening in Oxford Street when he met Caroline after work to go to the cinema, asked if he were, you know, 'queer'?

Why ever would Annie think that? How could anybody think that!

'No, of course not,' replied Caroline, stung. 'Do you think I'm that naïve?'

'Oh, well, you know, men as good-looking as that often are,' opined Annie.

Caroline had realized that Robert was in fact shy and moreover loathed his work, and was frightened of failing the Bar exams which were the sort of exams you had to cram for. So much she had gathered from the friends of his who were already qualified barristers in chambers, some of whom she had met the evening he had invited her to that dinner.

Well aware of her own passion for good-looking men, she had been determined not to let Rob's handsome features influence her judgement of him as a person. Yet she smiled at herself over the sheer impossibility of her possessing such impartiality as far as he was concerned. She was also strangely convinced that in spite of the sexual longing she could not seem to help having for Rob Cozens, her strongest feelings for him were what people called 'romantic'. This had never happened to her before. Was she perhaps returning to adolescence?

She must be stern with herself if he invited her to go away with him. One Wednesday evening, after they had been to see an Italian film at the Academy cinema, Caroline feeling he should be introduced to continental films, he had said:

'I thought of going down to stay with my grandparents next weekend — Nadine's been on at me. Could you be there too at your aunt's? Or do you have to give her notice? If she can't put you up I could ask Grandmamma — they don't do so much entertaining now . . .'

Caroline's' heart gave a little lurch.

'I'm always welcome at Pettiwell House,' she said. 'I'll give Sally a ring. Is your sister going too?'

'Oh, *she* spends all her weekends down at Pettiwell now. I meant to go before but I was too busy. Do come. It'd be nice to relax and go for a walk and see the folks, though I expect Nadine just wants me to compliment her on her riding skills.'

Before Caroline took her 24 bus back to her digs they went for a quick drink. She had the feeling that if she asked Rob whether he wanted to introduce her to his family it would sound silly — he must surely have taken girlfriends there before? Was she in any case, his girlfriend? She wished she could throw caution to the winds and ask him whether he'd like to go back home with her that night. Women could never do that — and the urgency of the need had never happened to her before. Usually it had been the other way round, when some man keen on her would have jumped at the chance. Rob was different.

She was glad he was different, even if it was to be a matter of a formal visit to Kent. She would not risk enlarging on the opportunity presented by their being together late at night. She must not try to inveigle him. Anyway, her digs were not all that comfortable, even if she'd been lucky to find an unfurnished basement for rent. Most students or young workers of her acquaintance inhabited bed-sits. She wasn't all that tidy either. The only things she was meticulous about were her drawings and portfolios and work. Did Rob notice his surroundings?

In her sitting room she had thrown around a few brightly coloured shawls and cushions, put up some paintings and installed one or two pieces of furniture her mother had given her, but he had never yet visited her there. The bed was narrow; the kitchen primitive and there was only cold water in the pipes. Was a Pimlico basement the sort of place you wanted for the backdrop of what you thought could be an important new stage of your life?

All she said was: 'Did you like the film?'

'What I could understand of it!' he said.

★　★　★

Sally was delighted when Caroline telephoned to ask if she might come to stay for the weekend. Nadine spoke to her later that very afternoon from her office to say she'd be

241

coming Friday night and was bringing her brother with her. Caro had not mentioned she might be travelling with Nadine's brother.

They all met on Biddwell station. Caroline emerged from the train with Rob, followed by Nadine who had arrived at the last minute on the train at Charing Cross. She had seen her brother waving at the window and hurled herself into his carriage just as the guard waved his green flag.

Introduced to Caroline she'd smiled, saying, 'Sally's told me all about you.'

Caroline thought she had looked a little surprised, that she had not expected to see her brother and Caroline Fitzpatrick so obviously together in the train. Rob couldn't have told her, then. She was interested to see how the brother and sister got on; Rob had sketched an easy relationship. Caroline could not help wondering if Rob had said anything at all to his sister about her.

Sally was waiting on the station, with her father's car outside ready to take Caro to Pettiwell. The others were soon fitted into the roomy Morris Oxford and put down half-way along the village street, where a lane led off to Stair Court.

'You know Nadine's brother, then?' asked Sally the minute the others had departed, arrangements having been made for meeting

242

at the Stables the next morning.

'Didn't I tell you? I thought I had. I met him at a party not long after I came back and then about a month ago we met at another. I've never seen his sister before, though I've heard a lot about her. How's the job?'

'Lovely. I really enjoy it, you know, Caro. What about you?'

'It's OK. I'm getting practice, I suppose, and I've found a sort of trade school for fashion that's just been started up — a pity it didn't exist when I went to Wimbledon. Still, all that was useful, I suppose. Margrove's seem to like what I do for them, but I want to *make* these clothes, not just *draw* them!'

She'd tried to explain that to Rob who had looked mystified.

'What a pity Lily can't be here — she's met Nadine. Mother says she and Daddy used to know the Cozens family years ago. I think it was Nadine and Robert's father they knew — and his parents once upon a time,' said Sally as she garaged the car in the stables at the back of the house.

'Wasn't it odd — when I told Rob I'd lived in the country all through the war, it turned out it was in the very same place as his grandparents!'

'Nadine and Rob were evacuated to the States,' said Sally.

'Oh?' Rob had never mentioned that.

'Come on in — Mrs Wilson has cooked us a nice pie. She heard from Jennie the other day.'

'Pa wrote to say he'd invited her to some do or other last term and she's still busy teaching.'

Ruth Page was waiting to welcome them when they went round to the front entrance of the house and entered the hall. Caroline breathed in the familiar mingled fragrance of Polly Wilson's often-applied beeswax and Ruth's pot-pourri. The March spring was cold but there was a fire in the breakfast room. She asked herself why she didn't visit Pettiwell more often, but she knew why. She had never felt it was truly her home; since she had become an adult she had always sensed a certain constraint on the part of her aunt. It was easier to be independent alone in London or Paris. Now that she had a good reason for coming to the village she might feel differently about it!

'I always go to bed before eleven on Friday nights,' said Sally as they sat sipping coffee after supper. 'I have to work Saturday mornings, but I've got tomorrow afternoon off.'

Sir Jack had already retired. Caroline thought how much older he looked. She slept soundly. They were all to meet at Sally's stables the next morning where Nadine had her lessons or did a bit of hacking. Ruth had invited them all back to Pettiwell for lunch. What would the Cozens grandparents be like? Would Rob want to introduce her to them? They wouldn't want to be bothered getting meals for young people, so it was kind of Aunt Ruth.

The stables were about a mile or two away and Sir Jack deposited her there on his way to the shops in town. Sally had already left at eight in her own little second-hand Morris Minor. Caroline had forgotten that Sally had learned to drive three or four years ago. That was something else she'd better do herself: pass the driving test; somehow she'd never yet found the time.

Would Rob be waiting at the stables? Perhaps he had already deposited his sister there. She said a breezy thank you and goodbye to Sir Jack and went in search of the riding-stables office. The Pretty Vale stables — what a silly name! — consisted of a long low building that looked as if it had been a prefab just after the war.

Nobody about. She went round from the building to a paved courtyard where there were several loose boxes behind three-quarter doors but no sound or smell of horses. On the other side of the gate were fields. They must all be out riding. Sally had intimated that Saturday was a frantically busy day.

She went into the building and rang the squat bell sitting on a table at the back of the room. Looking out of the window she saw Rob coming down the path. She waited a moment but nobody came in answer to the bell so she went out to meet him.

'Hello!' he said. 'Nadine went off early. Shall we go and find them?'

She would have preferred a little chat before they saw the others, but acquiesced.

'You're coming to Pettiwell for lunch aren't you?' she asked as they crossed the yard to the gate.

'It's kind of your aunt — thanks.'

'How do you find this neck of the woods then? I expect they were pleased to see you!'

'Oh, yes! I love it here — apart from needing a change. I feel almost human again.'

They had skirted the field and reached a hedge and gate and then on the other side was another much larger field you could not see from the yard. It was dotted with many little girls on ponies. Sally was holding a leading rein for a toddler who did not look more than eighteen months old. Caroline shut the gate carefully; it would never do to be negligent. Sally was stern about gates.

She felt slightly awkward seeing him against such a different background.

'Do you ride?' she asked him politely, never having felt any desire to do so herself.

'I used to. I think I'd like to take it up again. If I lived here I would. Rotten Row is quite pricey — Dad would rather I spent my money on Bar dinners.'

Was he so much under the thumb of his parent?

He was dressed in an old sports jacket and cavalry twill trousers. Before, she had seen him only in a dark working-suit. The country colours matched his fair hair and he looked happier than she had ever seen him. Funny she hadn't noticed before that he'd been looking less than joyful.

'Nadine will have gone hacking over in the Wellham direction,' he said. 'She said she'd see us about half past eleven.'

Good! They had an hour to themselves.

He smiled, and said: 'Shall we go for a walk? I find London life makes me tired but as soon as I'm down here I feel full of energy!'

'Rejuvenated?'

He laughed. 'You don't look tired.'

'No. I like London, even if I'm kept very busy.'

'I thought you must like it. Being busy, I mean?'

'Yes.'

They were walking along by the edge of the field where the grass was cropped bright green. The sun had gone in and the breeze was slightly chill. Caroline thought, I do wish it were warmer.

She said: 'I love France — and the sun — but I've got used to England. I didn't like it at first. It's fine so long as you don't expect good weather or good food very often.'

'Where do you like best to go for holidays?'

'Southern France. A Mediterranean climate, anyway. I'd like to get to know Italy better — especially Florence. How did you like living in America? Sally told me you and your sister were evacuated over there in the war.'

'We were sent to my mother's sister — she married a Yank. I liked where we were at first. It was a bit like England — Vermont — very quiet. Then they moved to the Mid-West. Nadine and I were there only there for a year or so. She liked it but I was glad to go home. I was nearly fifteen and had a lot of work to make up at school.'

He seemed different here, smiling, just as handsome, chatty, but in a curious way more remote. Just then they heard the sound of hoofs and suddenly there was Nadine in the next field. She waved, pulled her mount up quickly, and came up to them on the other side of the hedge.

'I thought you were on a long hack?' her brother shouted.

'The ground was so muddy poor old Centaur couldn't cope,' she said, patting the horse's neck. 'It's better here. I shall just give him his head over in the next field. See how fast he can go in circles!'

She was off again, blond hair tucked under her hat, eyes bright. Caroline thought she looked very much at home.

She turned back to Rob. Perhaps if she herself had ridden up all glowing he would have found her enticing. Here at Pettiwell she must look like a young woman who really belonged in town, which was true.

'My sister met yours,' she said. 'She came over at Christmas — I was in Paris.'

'Is that the musical Lily?'

'Have I mentioned her before? Yes. Your granny probably heard her sing at Christmas, if she goes to the village church.'

'You must meet my grandparents before we go back to London. Do you play bridge?'

'I'm afraid not. I have no social graces. Do you? I know you can dance.'

He laughed. 'Very badly. I play bridge and

chess about as well as I dance!'

They walked back to the courtyard and now there were several mothers and daughters, the latter waiting for their mounts and shouting merrily to friends. A girl in jodhpurs came up from the back of the building leading a pony, and another came out of a door marked OFFICE that Caroline had not noticed before. She sat down on a bench with Robert and the sun came out. Nadine arrived shortly afterwards leading her horse, a fine chestnut. She waved to them.

'Someone else wants Centaur. I'll be with you soon — I've to take him to the stables. Sally said she'd be ready in about twenty minutes.'

She disappeared at the back of the building where there was obviously more stabling. There was a pervasive smell of horse. Caroline supposed it would be Sally's job to rub the horses down or whatever you did to them — feed them? get them ready for the next customer? She was vague about equine ways. All she knew was that they were herbivores.

Rob stretched out his legs and shut his eyes. She felt an urge to take his hand, say something important, but was not quite sure what. She knew she had to resist these feelings and let him make the running.

Maybe he had no idea how attracted she was to him. It had never happened before to her like this. Usually it had been she who had been playing slightly hard to get, but she was sure Rob was not playing any sort of game.

Nadine came up again as Caroline was still wondering if she should suggest a walk after lunch, and then Sally followed from the field soon afterwards, her riding hat removed. She was brushing her hair from her forehead, as introductions were made.

'It must be tiring being in charge,' Caroline said.

'Oh, I'm used to it.'

Sally had barely glanced at Rob. Caroline knew she was shy of new people but was determined they should like each other. Nadine had apparently borrowed her grandparents' old car and so Rob and Caroline climbed into it to return to Pettiwell House, followed by Sally in hers.

Ruth Page welcomed them all as they piled through the Pettiwell side door. Nadine and Sally took off their dirty riding-boots. Nadine appeared quite at home.

'This is my big brother,' she said to Lady Page. Rob shook hands with her and then with Sir Jack who appeared from the morning-room, rubbing his hands.

'Well, it's a long time since we saw your

grandparents. How are they? Your great-grandfather used to come round here, you know.'

Rob was suitably polite and pleasant in reply and they all sipped dry sherry before sitting down to what Ruth called a scratch lunch.

'Mrs Wilson has made us her Pettiwell tomato soup and there's bread and cheese and fruit.'

Out of the corner of her eye Caroline saw Ruth looking surreptitiously at Rob. She ought to say something about having met him in London and then discovering his sister was a friend of Sally's, for she was feeling almost *de trop* in all this Pettiwell *bonhomie*. No, it should be Rob who told their hosts that.

Then Rob indeed said, looking at her: 'Isn't it a small world? I met Caro in London, and it turned out she used to live here!'

She smiled at Rob, feeling grateful to be acknowledged and included. Rob had perfect manners: a discussion about the smallness of the world was just what Sir Jack liked, but Ruth looked up sharply. Her husband made enquiries about Rob's parents, Edward and Janet Cozens. Perhaps he had never bothered to ask Nadine any of this, or was just being polite himself.

Ruth was looking at him rather disapprovingly now. She knew his reminiscences would continue if she did not put a stop to them, and she adroitly changed the subject to Rob's career.

Caroline said, hoping she did not sound proprietorial: 'Rob is working very hard to pass his Bar exams, aren't you, Rob?'

'Alas,' said Rob. 'Pa wanted me to do something different from him, but I don't think I'm really cut out for the law.'

'Of course your father is still in business?' asked Sir Jack.

Caroline thought, they all know his father's very rich. Sir Jack probably envies him.

Now Rob said: 'I do like country life better.'

Ruth looked interested and said: 'It's hard work, though. Sally's the same — didn't like London at all.'

Rob perked up at this, probably thinking he had said too much about his reluctant role as a pupil barrister.

Sally, who up till now had said little, looked up, saying: 'I think people should do what they like best. It's hard to earn a living on the land though.'

'And how's the world of fashion'? asked Sir Jack, turning towards Caroline kindly.

'Oh, fine . . . '

'She works hard too,' said Rob.

'I enjoy my work,' said Caroline.

She offered to take the plates into the kitchen and bring in the coffee. She'd like to see Polly Wilson and find out how Jennie was enjoying Paris.

As she went out through the little door at the side of the room that connected with the back corridor, she heard Sir Jack telling Rob that he must meet their son James.

'Now he wants to go into business y'know.'

It had perhaps been a mistake to introduce Rob to what was in effect her family in this way. They were taking him over. And anyway, what was there yet to tell them about her and him? That she was in love with this handsome young man? She hoped she had not allowed that to be obvious to anyone, even for a moment.

'If it isn't Caro!' exclaimed Polly Wilson. She had never called her Miss Caroline or Miss Caro, even when talking about her to others. 'We haven't seen you for quite some time, have we? Lady Page said you came last night. Jennie will be glad to have news of you when I next write. I guess you're as busy as ever?'

'Yes. I'm 'at school' again now, as well as selling sketches to Margrove's. Did Jennie tell you about that? How is she?'

'She wrote last week — very busy herself — but your father invited her to a do at their embassy or institute or something. She had a lovely time — she likes Paris!'

'Who wouldn't! I must write to Pa,' said Caroline. 'Can I take the coffee in for you?'

How she had changed. Just grown up, perhaps? Polly thought. And what about that young man, Nadine's brother, whom she'd glimpsed on his arrival, She well remembered their father years and years ago, in London. Miss Ruth had been in love with Sir Jack and had taken no notice of Edward Cozens. She probably didn't remember him very well.

'Tell Jennie I hope to come to Paris in June, will you. And that I hope Pa gave her a good time.'

'How's your little sister? And your mother — Miss Clare?'

'As far as I know, Ma is, as usual, preoccupied and Lily is longing to leave school, so nothing has changed!'

She took up the tray and Polly thanked her again.

Seeing Caroline and the other young people made her miss her own daughter. Jennie was fine though, doing well, wrote to her and William every week or so. When Polly next wrote she'd tell her that Caroline had, in her opinion, improved. She'd always been a good-looking girl but had given an impression of slight heartlessness. Now she looked more ... she searched for the word ... Jennie would know what she meant. Softer, perhaps? More sensitive? A word came to her Jennie had once used to describe a girl at school: *vulnerable*.

Ruth Page said she'd like a short walk too so they all, except Sir Jack, set off to walk down the lane to the pond and the farm and then beyond by the little wood.

Caroline was happy to walk along with Rob to point out some of the paths and lanes she had known as a child. He obviously did not know the place as well as she did.

'Usually when we stay with the grandparents they like us to stay indoors and chat to them — or play bridge. Grandmother Cozens has arthritis so she can't walk very far. Till recently she was taken out in the car by Grandpapa but his sight is none too good now.'

'I always think how terrible it must be to grow old,' said Caro. 'I expect they've had a good innings. How old are they?'

'Oh, I think Grandpapa is about seventy-eight and Grandma a bit younger — they're not absolutely ancient, but Nadine thinks they'd be better off being looked after properly. They do so love their house and garden.'

'I've always liked the look of that house myself, though I've only seen it from the lane. It looks so modern for a house about . . . what? Seventy years old?'

'Spot on. It's a gem. Early work of some famous architect, I believe. I wouldn't mind living there myself if they ever did go elsewhere. They wouldn't sell it to just anybody. I expect Father might buy it from them. Mother likes Somerset better — wild horses wouldn't drag her to live here, even just for weekends!'

'You ought to visit more often if you like it so much — you could drive them around a bit,' said Caro, thinking: here I am saying something against my own best interests. I love London weekends and I don't want to spend them all in the country like some typical débutante. She said none of this.

'I drove them into the town a few times last year but I haven't been at all since last autumn. Nadine enjoys the change and the riding, and she doesn't mind the bridge, but I've been so holed up in London, I'm afraid I've neglected them.'

'When you qualify, will you have to be on hand just in case there's a brief for you to handle? Even at weekends?'

'Yes, even some Saturdays. You take your work home with you. There usually isn't much at first for beginners unless you know how to make your mark — you have to look keen. The clerk is the one who finds you the briefs. I'm really fed up with it all. Coming here just makes me want to leave the whole bang shoot and find another job!'

Caroline felt she must sympathize but at the same time caution him against a too impetuous decision.

Ruth came up to them both and they trooped one by one through a gate on the far side of the home farm. The sun had come out and Sally was talking about primroses.

She must not monopolize Rob. Ruth would want to talk to him. Her aunt seemed to get on well with Nadine but gave the impression of being rather oddly outspoken with Rob — or perhaps towards her — when she said to him as they closed the gate:

'You like the country better than Caro does!'

'Oh, I love it here,' replied Rob. 'And Caro likes the change, don't you, Caro? She works so hard,' he said again, turning to Lady Page.

'We haven't seen much of Caro in the last year,' said Ruth. Looking at her niece she added, 'I don't think you really like country life, do you?'

Before Caroline could make some excuse for suddenly descending upon Pettiwell

— Ruth obviously suspected she'd had an ulterior motive for her visit, probably Rob, her aunt added:

'You're like your mother — a town person.'

'Well, I suppose if I had to choose . . . ' Caroline was beginning but just then Sally came up.

'Look — windflowers!' she said. 'Nadine's looking for primroses in the hedge bottom. Do you remember, Caro, we used to have competitions every year to see who could find the first meadow flowers.'

'It was usually you,' replied Caroline. 'I liked the bluebells in the woods over there best. I suppose it's a bit early for them now.'

'Yes, they usually appear in May,' replied Ruth.

Caroline thought she had better let Rob go ahead now with Sally. She'd see if she could find some wretched flower or other herself.

Nadine came up to walk at her side, and said: 'This will do Rob a lot of good — he ought to come more often. Mother's worried he's been looking what her old Nanny called 'peaky'!' She laughed.

Caroline wished she could get Rob to herself. Families were all very well but they did monopolize one's time. She heard Ruth saying to Sally:

'You should get up to London a bit more, dear!'

259

'No, I'm a country mouse,' Sally said.

She was looking very pretty, Caroline thought, her dark curls tousled and her cheeks glowing with health. She must have a very open-air life most of the time, and riding would be good for her. She'd been so miserable in London. Strange how different people were. She supposed her mother and Aunt Ruth had been very different the one from the other.

Tomorrow she was invited to meet Grandpa and Grandmamma Cozens. Would they expect her to be smart and London-wise? She had travelled in a grey flannel costume, her most respectable item of clothing. She hated suits, but her usual garb of long skirts and floppy blouses would probably be too bohemian for the Cozens. Did she really care what impression she made on them?

Rob and Sally were discussing racing. Strange, he'd never mentioned to her that he dabbled in this and she was surprised at Sally, until she realized that Sally's knowledge was not employed in practice. It was apparently Sir Jack who liked a flutter. Had he ever won much?

They tramped back for tea at Pettiwell and then Rob and his sister said they had promised to spend the evening with their grandparents but they would call for the others tomorrow. With a shock Caroline realized that she was not to be the only guest. Well, she supposed they could hardly leave out Sally who was after all Nadine's friend.

After tea, and then supper, and a desultory game of Scrabble with Sally and her mother, it had suddenly started to rain.

Caroline thought she had better go up to bed. She was just about to take her sketch pad up to her old room when Sir Jack indicated he'd like a chat. This usually meant that he would talk most of the time, reminiscing pleasantly about the old pre-war days, and she need make very little effort.

'Nice chap, that Cozens boy. D'ye know him well?' he began.

'Yes, he is. Did you know the older generation of the family well?' Caroline neatly circumvented his curiosity.

'My parents knew his grandparents. Ruth and I knew the lad's father a bit. Seems a long time ago. We lost touch. Ah, well.'

He soon went up to bed himself. Sally declared she felt sleepy so Caroline went into the small-sitting room where there was a table among the nineteen thirties' leather arm-chairs with their fringes and gold studs. She gave a sigh of relief to be at last by herself and spent half an hour sketching from memory.

First the horses, which she did not find easy, and then some windflowers, which would make a nice repeated pattern of white against pale green. You might call the material 'Milkmaid'? She ended with a couple of drawings of Rob Cozens. She'd tried to draw him before — unknown to him — and now she found herself longing for him to appear before her suddenly, saying: Come on. Let's go out for a drink!

She sighed. Perhaps next week she could see him in London alone. She could at last ask him round to her digs. He'd seemed different here. Not displaced so much as . . . what was it? At home? Yes, more contented.

She shut her sketch book and went up to bed, leaving it on the sitting-room table.

Caroline woke to a morning of showers and sunshine more like April than March. She was never hungry at that time of the morning and went downstairs hoping just for a drink of Nescafé and a few pieces of toast. It appeared that breakfast at Pettiwell was now no longer the substantial one she remembered.

Sally was already at the table eating cornflakes.

'Goodness you're up early!'

Sally looked a little embarrassed. She knew

262

Caro had not been a regular churchgoer for years.

'Did you go to early communion?'

'Yes, I got into the habit of it when I came back from London.'

Caroline nibbled her toast and poured herself a cup of the coffee Sally had made.

Sir Jack came down and was presented with bacon and eggs and the Sunday paper by his wife who came through from the kitchen. Previously, it had always been the domain of Polly Wilson, but it was clear that things were changing.

Caroline finished her coffee and went to fetch her sketch book from the sitting-room. She might do some sketches of Stair Court. The book was now on the sofa — maybe Sally had been having a look at it. On returning to the breakfast room, and her cousin, who was now piling a tray with plates and cups, she said:

'You must sit for me, Sal. I don't get much time nowadays to draw from life.'

'Let's see what you've been doing,' said Sally. So it wasn't she who had been curious.

Sir Jack had gone up to dress and her aunt looked up from her paper. She seemed to Caroline to be staring at her in a rather peculiar way.

'Your horse drawings aren't at all bad. Look, there's old Centaur!' said Sally.

'I'm no good really at drawing horses. I'd rather draw people. I don't want to stop sketching men and women just because I spend a lot of time thinking about dressing them!' said Caroline.

Sally turned the page and saw the sketches of Rob.

'He's a good subject,' was all she said.

'I've never actually drawn him from life.'

She felt quite nervous.

Ruth said: 'I suppose you see a lot of young men in London?'

'Fishing' was most unlike her aunt. She must have noticed her interest in Rob. Heavens above, thought Caroline, I'm not doing anything very unusual. Am I not allowed to have a serious boyfriend? Then she thought, he didn't talk to *me* any differently from the way he spoke to the others yesterday. Perhaps I'm just deluding myself. She was certain her aunt had guessed her own feelings.

'I believe your mother used to know the family too, years ago,' said Ruth. 'You must ask her.'

Mother had known the Cozens? Not that Caroline had ever mentioned Rob or any of her previous passions to her mother.

'Sir Jack said his family had known them years ago too.'

'Oh, did he? Well, of course they would, in the village, and the present lot at Stair Court used to come over here before the war to play bridge when my parents visited. We didn't keep up with them after my parents died.'

'Why don't you come along too today, then? Rob wants me — us — to meet his grandparents.'

'My dear, Jack and I aren't invited — it's just the young people they'll want to see. Sally of course knows Nadine Cozens quite well, don't you, Sal?'

'Yes, I was invited by her earlier, but it was one Sunday I was working. Nadine is great fun.'

Caroline sensed that her Aunt Ruth seemed less keen for *her* to visit the Cozens, or was at least discounting the fact that the invitation had come from Rob. She could hardly say that he had specially asked her to go over and that it was really nothing to do with Nadine or Sally, because that might not now be true. She could not quite explain it, just had a hunch that her aunt was not particularly fond of Rob's family.

★ ★ ★

265

This Sunday visit to Stair Court was to be a disconcerting one for Caroline. The Cozens had telephoned to say 'tea rather than lunch', if they didn't mind, some unforeseen problem at the butcher's yesterday. They were invited to come round for the afternoon instead. Ruth groaned at having to provide an unexpected lunch but Caroline offered to make omelettes for everyone if eggs were available, Polly Wilson not being expected to cook on a Sunday.

Ruth accepted her help, saying: 'That old couple are most unreliable!'

They arrived at Stair Court at half past three. Caroline found it was a very large house of three storeys with two giant triangular gables and tall chimneys, built on land at the end of a lane off the village street. She thought the land must once have been part of a large estate. Rob was nowhere to be seen. Then he was discovered round at the back of the house with a very wet dog.

'He needed a bath,' was all he said.

Old Mr Cozens was a tall, straight-backed, silver-haired old man who wore very large spectacles. His wife was narrow-faced, thin, with an absent-minded air.

Nadine had welcomed the arriving guests in a roomy oak-panelled porch, and now she did the introductions, leading them into a large room on one side of the entrance hall. The hall had a baronial feel to it.

Caroline looked round with interest. It was an enormous house for two old people, and the heating did not feel very powerful.

'You know Sally, Granny?'

'I believe we used to see her at Pettiwell years ago,' was all the old lady said, but she did attempt a slight smile.

'Is your mother well?' asked the old man. 'We used to play bridge up at your place.'

'My mother and father send their kind regards,' answered Sally.

It was Nadine rather than Rob who said, 'And this is Caroline — Caro.'

'You are Sally's cousin, I believe?'

Rob said then: 'Caro works in London, Gramps.'

'Ah.'

Desultory conversation followed, interrupted by the still-damp dog coming snuffling into the room.

Caroline said to herself, it is not that he is ignoring me — on the contrary it's Rob who has just introduced me to his family, so I am not a dark and dusty secret in his life. Perhaps I'd be more hopeful if I were. It's rather that he is making me feel — or giving others the impression — that I am just some friend from London who happens to have her family living near his. Not the young woman he might — or might one day — be in love with. She had better admit that to herself. Did he realize how deeply she had fallen for him? Was he utterly unaware? Had so many young women swooned before his looks that he was used to it?

For the first time Caroline admitted to herself that this might be true. She did not usually show her feelings to men, and this time, because she did feel so much for him, she had made a special effort not to show them.

Rob was not a vain man, but he must be used to being popular. He was friendly — and perfectly normal. He had probably kissed her once or twice as a matter of course, and she had thought it was a special — and mutual — attraction. He might have envisaged going away with her for a weekend at some unspecified date, and he had certainly gone to the trouble of introducing her to his barrister companions a few weeks ago, thus accepting her as a friend, but he was not in love with her. He could never have felt that immediate physical attraction, that dizziness of the senses she had felt for him.

Caroline was old enough to know that a sudden infatuation was one thing, and deep love quite different, but had hoped that the one could predate the other. It surely must do sometimes, for some people? She would accept either without the other. She felt a strong physical desire for him now as she watched him talking to Sally. At the same time she was convinced that she would be — would have been — capable one day of also feeling a steady affection for Rob Cozens.

She must stop thinking about it all. Maybe she was wrong and she had not been completely mistaken about him. Maybe he had felt — did feel — something for her.

What was the matter with her? She was usually so cool-headed.

Sally was saying something about 'Caro's sketch book'. Rob turned to this grand-mother, and said:

'Caro draws so beautifully.'

Caroline took her sketch book out of the large tapestry bag she carried around with her. She was so used to people wanting to see her drawings that it was almost an automatic action.

'Let's see what you've been doing,' said Rob, just as a maid came into the room with a teapot and crockery on a tray.

Caroline answered brightly: 'Oh, yesterday I mostly just sketched some horses.'

Nadine said: 'Let me look. Oh, there's two

of *you*, Rob! They're awfully good!'

'Let me have a look,' said old Mrs Cozens. After a minute, 'Very nice, dear,' she said with a sharp look at her. 'I'm afraid my husband can't see too well.'

Sally had another look at them. Caroline had the sudden feeling that Sally might have introduced the subject of her sketches so that Rob should see how the artist felt about him. Sally was perceptive; she had sensed how her cousin felt about Robert Cozens.

In an alcove of the large room the maid was spreading out an embroidered tablecloth over an Edwardian gate-legged table.

'We take tea in here on a Sunday,' said Mrs Cozens.

Once everyone had a plate there followed a sorting out and placing of a nest of small tables and then a ceremonial handing round of cups.

Caroline thought, I couldn't bear to live in this formal way. Rob must be used to it. He was clearly a favourite in this house; his grandmother kept giving him fond glances.

She drank her tea. There might still be a chance that he would reveal a blossoming of feelings for her, but a bit unlikely against the background of a large cold house and the presence of his sister, his sister's friend and two grandparents How she longed for him to say something affectionate to her. His comment on her sketches of him had elicited a 'Crikey! You've really got me there!'

After tea, Sally said: 'May we have a look at the gardens?'

Caroline would have preferred to look over the house, this architectural gem of the turn of the century, but Rob led the way with alacrity to the gardens. What she could see of the rest of the interior of the house as they went through to the back was much wood panelling and oak doors opening into large rooms. As the others went through a side door she lagged behind and peeped further into one of the rooms. It had, as she had seen from the outside, stone-mullioned windows, and the floor, like the floor of the room where they had taken tea, was of wood — unpolished this time. There was also an immense fireplace, and specially designed chairs carved to match a long medieval-looking table. Surely not just the two of them could eat here? Did they still entertain? The whole house had a sense of space and modernity along with a feel for someone's idea of the past. It did not seem to her to be the sort of place the Cozens would have chosen to live in. Perhaps they had inherited it themselves fifty years ago.

She caught up with Mr Cozens at the door.

'William Morris?' she said under her breath.

Mr Cozens heard her — his sight might be bad but his hearing must be acute.

He said: 'Nearly right dear. It's one of Voysey's houses.'

As they followed the others into the gardens at the back she saw long borders, which would be full of delphiniums and hollyhocks in summer, and a large rose garden on one side.

She realized also with a sudden stab of understanding that Sally, by whose side Rob was now walking, would share most of his tastes. He had not expounded to her on the subject of the famous architect of Stair Court. As if to echo this thought she heard him and Sally discussing neither the house nor the garden but the dog Caspar. Talking about the dog!

Rob was looking at Sally with an expression she had never seen on his face, one that she would recapture later in her sketch book. He had never looked at *her* like that.

He and she had walked, and talked, and kissed, and enjoyed each other's company; she had liked him and he had liked her, but she had never seen that look. It was a look that plainly betokened the word 'love', a word that might have been in her mind but never in his. She was sure Sally was completely unconscious of the effect she was having on Robert Cozens, although she would not be unaware for ever. Caroline had a sudden sharp intimation of a *coup de foudre* on Rob's part, and then she saw Nadine looking at the two of them, and felt suddenly sure that Nadine had realized her friend Sally would be exactly the right woman for her brother.

★   ★   ★

Caroline and Sally did not stay long after this at Stair Court. Caroline was to met Nadine and Rob on the station at eight o'clock to return to London together, and she was seen off by Ruth as well as Sally. The train was already in the station and the others were waiting on the platform, having already found an empty carriage.

'You must come again soon,' said Ruth Page. Caroline was uncertain to whom she was addressing this remark. Sally had appeared a little subdued after supper, saying only: 'It will seem very quiet when you've all gone.'

The three of them were quiet too in the train, drugged with country air.

Rob seemed to rouse himself as the train drew into Charing Cross, saying:

'We must go to that French film you were telling me about. What evening would you have free?'

She felt sure his heart was not in it, but she replied:

'Well — perhaps Thursday? If you can manage it? Give me a ring.' She was allowed by the lady who lived on the ground and first floors of the house to receive calls on the telephone in her hall, but not to telephone people herself. This concession was in exchange for small items of shopping she would bring for her on the way back from work.

That night she woke after an hour or two's deep sleep and could not get back to sleep again. Might it be that she had too active an imagination and was creating a problem where none existed? Her relationship with Rob, though slow to ignite after what she had considered mutual attraction, had been perfectly all right until the weekend!

No, she had been self-deceiving from the beginning and the thoughts she had entertained on Saturday came back to her . . . Rob was charming but Rob was not as attracted to her as she was to him. And this meant there was no possibility of reciprocal passionate love in the future. Sally, all unknowing, had revealed the truth and there was not a thing she could do about it. She was crazy about a nice, handsome, rather conventional man who, unless she was much mistaken had just fallen for her cousin. Maybe he didn't even know it himself yet, but he had.

She was sure that Sally had not intended anything. She would have heard about Rob from Nadine and probably wanted to meet him, but Sally was not a plotter. On the other hand, Aunt Ruth seemed not to have been too keen on her niece knowing him. Was it because she was thinking about him as a serious possibility one day for Sally? Why else should she be so against her niece having him for a boyfriend unless she wanted him for Sally?

Her aunt had not seemed very keen on Rob's family either! It was puzzling. His family was obviously very rich. I never thought of that, I was never bothered that he might be a good catch, thought Caroline. Did I think about anything more than a love affair? I hoped something would happen between us, and I can't deny I was confecting a sort of future, which I've never done before with a man. It was only in my secret self. I never flirted with him or acted as if I wanted to take him for granted. He'd be amazed if he knew my thoughts!

As there was nothing to be learned before Thursday, when she would see him again, she would close her mind firmly to idle supposition. With the aid of the very strong willpower people always said she had, she would concentrate on her work.

10

They met on the Thursday and decided not to go to the pictures but to have a meal out in Soho, Caroline's idea. She had heard her father speak of Leoni's, so there they would go. She had taken out some money from the bank which she could ill afford but was determined to pay her share.

The restaurant had what she thought of as an old world flavour. Loads of hovering waiters; ample helpings. Not that she had been up till now in very many London restaurants. Used to French food she found the Italian meal at least better than an English one.

Rob seemed utterly oblivious of any change in himself that might alert a girl who was in love with him. She introduced the subject of Pettiwell after they had ordered half a bottle of Burgundy.

'Yes, it was a very enjoyable weekend,' he said.

'I was interested in your grandparents' house,' she remarked. 'I was surprised they should be the sort of people who'd choose a house like that!'

'Oh, they didn't really!' he said. 'Someone who'd known and admired him left it to my uncle in the first war. My Uncle Robert — I was called after him — was killed on the Somme. This friend of his had inherited Stair Court and he left it to my uncle in his will. He was killed — before Uncle. I suppose Robert then left all he owned to my grandparents. He wasn't married — I don't know the exact details. Anyway, Gramps and Gran decided to live in it after the war because it was where Uncle Robert would have lived if he had survived. They knew the district — they had a family house in a village not far away. I think my grandmother couldn't bear to go on living there as it reminded her too much of the past. Robert was her favourite son — my father was quite a bit younger than his brother.'

'How sad and tragic. It's a lovely house.' Without thinking, she added: 'It needs a young family in it.'

'They're going to leave it to me,' he said. 'My mother has always been very firm about it, says she won't ever live there, and Father wants to buy a house in France for his retirement one day.'

Caroline digested this along with her plate of spaghetti. She said after a moment:

'Yes, I can see you living there.'

He sighed. 'I do want to live in the country,' he said.

After this he became rather quiet and Caroline decided to introduce the subject of the Pages and Pettiwell.

'How did you like Pettiwell?'

'Very fine. I expect it needs a good bit of upkeep.'

'I think Sir Jack finds it a bit much now. I'm quite fond of it but not as fond as Sally is.'

There, she had done it! Introduced her cousin's name in quite a natural way. She was determined to discover what effect it had on him. He looked bewildered, as if he was collecting his thoughts.

He said at last: 'She does belong in the country, doesn't she? Nadine so much admires her riding.'

'We are all very fond of Sal,' said Caroline. 'She hated living in London.'

Robert looked preoccupied as he chewed his fillet steak, and nothing more was said on the subject for the time being. He was, however, just as amiable as ever. At the end of the meal he reluctantly accepted her going Dutch.

As they put their coats on, he said: 'We must come here again,' but without much conviction. She was sure she had been right about Sally. He really seemed not to have noticed that she was well aware of his preoccupation.

She would give him the opportunity to be vague about a future meeting.

'Will you be awfully busy at work?'

'For the next week or two, alas,' was his reply.

Caroline answered: 'Oh dear, so shall I. I have a practical test in a few days.'

'May I give you a ring to arrange something? I just don't know when I'll next be able to get away early enough. I'm supposed to be swotting something up . . . '

If he had any *idea*, she thought, of how I felt — and feel — about him. He did not realize that she had any idea of the direction of *his* thoughts! Last week she would have felt in despair. Tonight she felt extremely sad. Was she going to resign herself?

Maybe she was mistaken and it all arose from her own imagination. There was nothing she could do but wait.

She refused a taxi so they walked to the bus stop for her 24 bus to Pimlico. Rob said he would walk home — the fresh air did him good.

When they parted this time Rob did not kiss Caro goodbye. Had he not done it on purpose, or were his thoughts so far away that he had forgotten their recent relationship? I thought we were close, she thought, but it was an illusion.

★ ★ ★

From a letter from Nadine Cozens to her friend Lily Fitzpatrick at Denehurst School.

... *Poor You — never mind you've only got another few months to put up with. I was thrilled to hear about your auditions. Sorry you won't be in Pettiwell for your exeat weekend but you should have a good time with your sister. I've had a super time at the stables with Sally. About a month ago your sister came to Pettiwell at the same time my brother and I were there for the weekend at our grandparents. It's to do with that that I wanted to ask you a favour.*

The thing is, there's nobody else I can mention this to. It's to do with Mr Heart-throb, my brother Rob, and this is absolutely secret — I'd die if anyone found this! I don't know you as well as I know Sally but I could see when I met you that you were the soul of discretion. It's this. Rob never stops talking about Sally and I can see he's smitten!

Now this is the problem. I probed a bit

with Sally about what she thought of him etc etc and the upshot is that Sally will not encourage him because she believes your sister is sweet on him! She thinks Caro is madly in love with my brother! Is she right? Has your sister said anything about it? Can you find out? Sally won't encourage Robert if she thinks Caro might be hurt. And I just know that Sally is the right person for Rob.

I wouldn't bother you if it was just a commonplace sort of thing but I've never seen him like this and the thing is that I'm sure Sally could feel the same about him but you know her well and she is a shy sort of person isn't she? The way he mentions her! — sort of accidentally on purpose if you get my meaning. He asks me about her and pretends he's interested in the stables and the horses but I know better.

Lady Page is a bit odd about it, I think. She could see from the pictures Caro had done that she must know him quite well, and she looked disapproving. As you know, your sister never gives much away in conversation. But I could see that she thought he was the cat's whiskers.

Can you sort of casually find out what she thinks about him? I never know with Rob. I think he gets into entanglements with girls because he's kind hearted and *after all he's a man. Honestly though, he's not vain about his looks. She thinks Caro may have had a passionate fling with him — she wouldn't tell you if she had, would she? — but you might guess?*

I know it's not my business but if I could tell Sally that Caro isn't serious about him it would help. If you stay with her next week on your way to your Ma's keep your eyes and ears skinned!

I am invited out next Saturday by Chris Fazackerly. He's probably not worth it but I'll give the riding a miss this weekend and accept. Please forgive my nosiness — if you think your sister and my brother are a couple, and then of course I'll keep mum . . .

When she received Nadine's letter Lily had thought — what cheek! — though she did not think it would hurt to find out more. She had been invited to stay the night in London with her sister on her way to her mother's flat the next day, so she would try to hint to Caro what Nadine had hinted to her about Rob.

Caro had been so much nicer to her since she had come back from Paris that she thought she might help her rather than Sally.

They were sitting by the gas fire in the Pimlico basement bed-sitting-room. Caroline had provided fish and chips from a café on Warwick Way — she was becoming quite English — and she had started talking about Jennie in Paris. Lily saw to it that they then moved on to Sally.

'Sally was saying how much she missed Jennie,' she said. 'She is so fond of her, even though they don't have much in common now, Jennie being so clever.'

Caroline said: 'Sally is clever in her own way, which is not Jennie's way or ours.' She seemed to want to talk. 'I used to envy her settled family life and the way she loved both her parents,' she went on.

'*I* love both of ours too!' said Lily, surprised. 'I mean, I didn't see much of either of them when I was little, but I get on well with both of them now. Perhaps better, since it was Aunt Ruth who really brought me up.'

'I really envied Sally for liking her mother as well as her father. I think I really only liked Pa,' mused Caroline.

'Sally likes most people,' said Lily, feeling slightly uncomfortable. It was unlike her sister to talk about her feelings.

'Well, she may like most people — and *love* all horses — but she still adores her parents.'

'I think she is fond of you too,' said Lily.

'Well, she is of you, but for a girl like Sally

284

her priorities will change when a man falls in love with her!'

'How do you mean?'

'Perhaps I'll be proved wrong, but I think she's a man's woman.'

'I've never known Sally fall in love,' said Lily tentatively, thinking she might be getting somewhere with all this.

'No, I didn't say when *she* falls in love, I said when a *man* falls in love with *her*.'

Sally would be amazed if a man did fall in love with her, thought Caroline, but her native good sense would tell her how to react. Aunt Ruth too, unlike her own mother, might as a young woman have been surprised by the way men carried on — especially if they fell in love with her. Aunt Ruth had got the man she wanted in the end, most likely the only one she'd ever been interested in. Luckily he'd wanted her. Caroline felt sure her own mother had not been quite so lucky.

'You look very thoughtful,' said Lily, interrupting her contemplation.

'You're probably too young,' began Caroline in a jokey voice, 'but you'll find some men can be very demanding. Sally will find that astonishing — but she'll believe them . . . '

'You mean they don't mean it — they say they love you and they don't really?'

'What I mean is that some men I've known would do anything to get you, and if you were flattered, they'd succeed. Then off they'd go — another conquest marked up. The one you wouldn't mind chasing you rarely does. It works so that if you are keen, they are not, and vice versa.'

'How depressing,' said Lily. 'Surely they're not all like that?'

'Well some are like that with one woman and not with another.'

'Doesn't love come into it?' asked Lily.

Caroline was silent.

'Some people say love is just sex attraction,' her sister went on tentatively. 'It must be partly that?'

'Yes, of course, but not just that. I just think you should be prepared. Sally will be like her mother — quite amazed at men's ways at first — but she'll adapt — '

'How do you know what Aunt Ruth was like?'

When Caroline did not reply to this, Lily added: 'You mean, men's lustful ways? Women can behave in the same way, can't they?'

'I see my little sister is beginning to learn,' said Caroline.

'Aren't *you* a man's woman, then?' asked Lily, not quite daring to ask if her sister had experienced love, lust, or whatever they were apparently discussing.

'No, do you know — in spite of what you mean about falling in love — I don't think I am.'

Lily thought she sounded as if she were consoling herself.

She countered with an innocent expression: 'I don't know anyone *Sally*'s in love with, but Nadine did say she thinks Sally rather likes Nadine's brother.'

Caroline tried not to show any reaction to this but could not help getting up in case one might give her away. She poured them each a cup of tea.

'How do *you* like him? Nadine says you were all together at Pettiwell during the weekend not long ago.'

Lily took the proffered tea.

'Oh, I know him quite well,' said Caroline airily.

'Nadine calls him Mr Heart-throb!'

'Does she now? Yes, he is certainly very extremely good-looking. What else did she say about him?'

'Oh, nothing about *him*,' lied Lily. 'Just that she didn't think Sally would encourage him . . . '

'Why should she — does Nadine think he is attracted to her?'

Lily thought she had better stop and think. She took a sip of tea, and then said:

'I think Nadine is a matchmaker. What does she know about men? One may have a brother but brothers don't talk to sisters like that, do they?'

'I've no idea,' said Caroline.

Lily realized she had the knowledge she had fished for. Adroitly, she put the subject on to a slightly different tack.

'Nadine thought Aunt Ruth was not very welcoming to her brother, though she's always been nice to *her*. She thinks the Pages are not keen on the family at Stair Court.'

'We visited it,' said Caroline. 'Aunt Ruth probably thinks they are too well off for their own good.'

Well, at least, thought Nadine, I haven't hinted that Robert Cozens has never stopped talking about Sally. Ought she to tell Caro that? Or the *way* he talks about her? Not that Nadine might be all that reliable as a witness. No, better not.

Caroline changed the subject when they took the dirty plates and cups into the minuscule kitchen to do the washing-up.

'Will you go to Pettiwell when you break up in the summer? Or to Paris?'

'I haven't decided about that yet, but I thought of going to Pettiwell for a few days at half-term before I start final revision for A levels. I've got another audition too. We're allowed a weekend away.'

'How's the oboe?'

'I'm not much good,' said Lily modestly. 'I shall give it up soon — but it's expanded my lungs!'

They went on to talk of Jennie and no more was said of either Robert Cozens or his sister.

★ ★ ★

At the beginning of May, not long after this conversation took place, an epidemic of chickenpox among some of the younger girls at Lily's school allowed her to visit Pettiwell earlier than she had expected. The sanatorium was full and those girls in the sixth form who had already had the illness were allowed home for a few days. Lily did not think that either her mother or Caroline would welcome her when they were both so busy, so she telephoned her aunt, who said of course she must come.

Sally was delighted to see her. Lily had not yet replied to Nadine, thinking she would rather find out how Sally felt before saying anything whatever on the subject of Rob. She arrived on the Friday and it turned out that

Nadine had telephoned Pettiwell that very afternoon. She and her brother were both to be at Stair Court on Saturday!

Sally was surprised. She had expected Nadine, who often came over at the weekend for her riding lesson, but not Rob.

'Will they be coming over here?' Lily asked. She wanted Sally to herself, for she must test the water with her cousin before meeting the famous Robert.

'Nadine usually does,' answered Sally. The two were seated before a fire in the little sitting-room. The weather, as can so often happen in early May, was unseasonable. Lily felt rather annoyed, though she could not help noticing that Sally seemed a little agitated.

'What's he like then, this Rob?' she asked, taking the bull by the horns. 'Caro told me she had been over here a few weeks ago when he and his sister were visiting. She'd met him before in London, I think.' Lily was sure that the arrangement had been between her sister and the young man but she had played it down for Sally. Sally knew that.

'Oh, Lily, you can tell me then. Is Caro — was she — I mean, going out with him?'

'I think she met him at a party and they've

been out a few times. I don't know how recently . . . '

'He's written to me,' said Sally unhappily. 'He says he'd like to see me again. I didn't know what to reply. It's unusual, isn't it, for a man to write to you when he's only met you once? If he was — is — Caro's boy friend, I don't want to encourage him.'

This was just what Nadine had intimated. Lily thought she had better now come clean. If he had *written* to Sally, did Caro know? She hadn't spoken to her sister since returning to school and Caro was never a great letter-writer. Had there been some sort of rupture between them? What exactly had Rob wanted to express in his letter? She couldn't ask even Sally that. She said:

'I expect Caro can look after herself.'

'Is she keen on him?'

'I think she was. I don't know how things are at present.'

'Oh dear!'

'Look, Sally you don't have to encourage him if you don't want. Or if you don't like him. *Do* you like him?'

Sally bit her lip.

'Well, I hardly know him — that was what was so odd about getting a letter from him.' After a pause she added under her breath: 'Yes, I do like him, but I shan't encourage

291

him if he's Caro's friend.'

Lily now understood. She asked: 'Is he the sort of man to flirt?'

'No, not really. I don't think so.'

Well, not with you, thought Lily.

'No, not at all!' Sally added. 'I'm so glad you are here and then you can tell me what you think about him!'

★ ★ ★

Next morning Lily was surprised to find her Aunt Ruth returned from the town shops in a great pother of purchases for lunch.

'I've asked the two over from Stair Court,' she explained. 'Mrs Wilson hadn't known they were to come — it was a sudden invitation on our part.'

'Oh, I'll help her,' said Lily, who enjoyed cooking.

She was very surprised. Caro had said that Aunt Ruth had seemed not to approve of Robert Cozens, and here she was fussing over his lunch. She was to be even more surprised when her aunt positively enthused over the visitors to Mrs Wilson in the kitchen where Lily was making pastry. When they arrived after the riding lesson, she welcomed them most enthusiastically. Lily looked at Rob covertly. He was certainly good-looking, but not her type — as far as she yet knew what that was.

'This is Caro's sister Lily,' Nadine said composedly.

Rob, thought Lily, looked a little discomfited.

'Caro's not here this weekend,' she said. (As if he didn't know.) 'She's very involved with her course at the fashion place and with her work for Margrove's.'

'Caroline has always been a hard worker,' said Ruth.

Rob said nothing.

'So is Rob,' said Nadine. 'I thought he needed a change — he hasn't been anywhere for ages.' Lily thought Nadine looked a little conspiratorially at her but refused to respond.

Over the lunch, which was cutlets and new potatoes and spinach, followed by the apple pie she had helped to make, Lily was busy thinking. Sally was acting quite normally but she saw the young man steal a glance or two at her when he thought nobody was looking. In her judgement the man was clearly smitten. She would have to tell her sister. As for Aunt Ruth, she suddenly had an ignoble thought. Was it just that she had not wanted to encourage *Caro* but was not displeased for Rob to pay attention to *Sally*? That might explain things. If this were true, was it because he was very rich? Lily had never considered Ruth in this light.

Sir Jack was being as genial as usual and actually said to her that it was a pity her sister could not have joined them. Lily bit back her reply: that she might not exactly have been welcomed.

After lunch they went for a walk, Rob walking by Sally's side and the other two following behind. Lily guessed that Nadine was about to say something like: Don't they look good together! so she gave her no chance, quickened her step and joined the other two.

'Er, how *is* Caroline?' Rob enquired. 'We've both been so very busy . . . '

'I saw her about three weeks ago,' said Lily. 'She's fine.'

★   ★   ★

Lily was not looking forward to telling her sister any of this. It was clear that Rob had fallen in love, or lust, or something, with her cousin Sally and that he was feeling a bit guilty about Caro. Sally had been her usual friendly self to him and certainly not demonstrated either encouragement or discouragement. As far as Lily knew he had said nothing to Sally on the Saturday, and on

Sunday she had accompanied her cousin to church. She did not feel it was any more of her business to ask for details. If Sally wanted to tell her something, she would.

All that had happened before she was taken back to school by Sir Jack on the Monday morning, a cross-country journey, was that Sally had asked her on Sunday afternoon what she thought about Rob.

'Very nice,' had been her non-committal reply.

Sally had just nodded and gone off to the stables, where a little girl who had missed her lesson the day before had been promised an hour of her time.

Rob and Nadine were returning to London that afternoon. It was plain that Sally would not respond to her swain until she knew more about Caroline's situation, but Lily felt sure she was just as smitten as he was. She remembered from childhood how when Sally was agitated her forehead went pale and her freckles came up. They had been there on Saturday afternoon. Yet it was almost as if Sally needed permission from Caroline to make up her mind about him — or rather do what she wanted to do.

★ ★ ★

The examinations were looming and still Lily had neither spoken nor written to her sister. She could not easily telephone her. Caro's landlady was not keen on her using the phone for long conversations. She decided she'd better write to her, but before she set pen to paper, rather dreading what she would have to tell her, a letter arrived from her sister.

Lily scanned it quickly after breakfast at school.

> *Believe it or not, I've had a letter from Sal! I gather you were there at the weekend. She says will I please speak to Robert! What can she want him to tell me? She must have written to him herself. She also hinted that Aunt Ruth had the impression I knew him well. Really! Otherwise, she doesn't give anything away. Well, then he phoned to ask if he could come round here next Tuesday so I said yes.*
>
> *Just thought I would let you know. Glad you met him. Good luck with the audition in Manchester, and for all the exams. I am trying to keep myself busy.*

Lily knew her sister well enough to realize that all this banter was covering her true feelings. There was nothing she could do but it was nice of Caro to tell her the latest news.

Aunt Ruth had appeared very nosy about Caro, and she might ask her mother about that next time she saw her. She was also tempted to tell Caro to confide in their father if she were really miserable.

Or even ask their mother? No, she would not do that, thought Lily. Even in childhood she never remembered her sister confiding in Clare. Well, not once they came to live in England. Lily often wondered though about the seven years that separated them in age. Hadn't there been a time, when she was about four, before they came to Pettiwell, when she had been a little jealous of her big sister who seemed so close to their mother. She on the other hand had been her father's favourite. All that seemed a long time ago.

★ ★ ★

Caroline thought how silly it was that Rob had never visited her digs before and now here he was coming to see her just at the point when she imagined he was about to ditch her.

When Rob arrived, however, it was raining. She heard a taxi stop outside in the square and her bell was rung a few minutes later.

He said: 'Hello! Long time no see!' and

looked round for somewhere to park his umbrella.

His manner appeared unchanged. They might just have met for a meal or a visit to the Academy Cinema. She must not appear awkward herself so took his umbrella and offered him a cup of tea. As he looked round she began to realize that his feelings, like hers, had not changed. It was just that his had never been romantically involved! She had been a friend, a good friend, and had come because Sally had asked him to. She looked at him a little more closely as he parked his long body in her only armchair. He looked thinner — was that what love had done to him? She was not going to disclose her old feelings, would treat him as the friend he obviously imagined her to have been.

She made the tea and sat on her bed, which was respectably covered in a folk-weave bedspread, to give the impression of a sofa. She was not going to help him but waited for him to speak.

'How's the fashion industry?' he asked.

'As you can imagine, I've been kept busy. I was lucky, I got a commission to sketch suits for another store — one in competition with Margrove's. So I accepted and tried a completely different style. They'll never know!'

He laughed.

'Clever Caro!' He frowned slightly so she offered him a biscuit.

'How's the Bar?' she asked.

'I intend to leave. I've made up my mind. My father might find me a job for a bit in the City.'

'I'm not really surprised.'

He seemed young, but determined. She changed the subject.

'I hear you were at Pettiwell the other weekend — Lily told me.' At least she had given him an opening. 'How were they all? Did you ride this time?'

'No, though Sally says she'll get me on a saddle one day. Why is it girls are always so keen on horses and we aren't? Some chaps are but I never was.'

'Not all girls — I never was myself. Sally was always a rider.'

'You must have known her well as a child.'

Oh, Lord, he wanted to talk about Sally. She mustered her forces.

'Of course. Since I was eleven and we came to England. I didn't like Pettiwell at first.'

'Sally's mother — Lady Page — is your mother's sister?'

'That's right. They are very different kinds of people.'

'She's very nice, your aunt. Grandma says

she remembers her when she came out!'

'That must be a good quarter of a century ago. My mother was a bit older.'

'I'm so glad I've met your family. Fancy my grandparents living so close! Lady Page told me they used to go over to Pettiwell to play bridge with your grandparents.'

'Did your mother and father not visit as well?'

'No, I don't think so, though I suspect — from something my mother once said — that my dad was once sweet on your aunt!'

'Good heavens, really?'

That might be why Aunt Ruth had been a bit reluctant to entertain him at first. But why? She had clearly come round since.

'It's aeons ago. They've probably forgotten. Sally didn't know anything about it.'

'We don't know much about our parents before we were born,' she answered sententiously, knowing he wanted to go on but not wanting him to. She wished they could talk about something else.

He said then, quite simply, putting his cup down carefully on the carpet:

'I think Sally is the most marvellous girl!'

Telling *her* of all people! Had he told anyone else? He must be very serious about Sally.

She looked enquiringly at him, a sort of

why are you telling me all this? look.

'I thought I ought to tell you — since we were — sort of going out a bit — you know, and Sally said I ought to . . . '

In case I was in love with you? she wondered. No, she did not believe that had ever occurred to him. He just wanted to get things straight between them.

Very old-fashioned. Honourable really.

What could she say? *I don't mind. I'm glad you've fallen in love with Sally. She's much more the type for you.*

She said aloud, thinking, well he's been open so I'll be slightly rude myself.

'How does Sally feel?'

'Sally knows how *I* feel. Now we have to get to know each other better!'

'Well, faint heart never won fair lady,' she said rather wildly.

'I knew you'd understand . . . '

She swallowed.

'It's nice that your sister is such friends with her.'

'We might not have met for years if Nadine hadn't met her!'

You might have met through me, she was thinking.

'Horses have their uses,' was what she said.

He smiled.

'Has it stopped raining — have you eaten?

We might go out for a meal.'

'Oh, I'm sorry, Rob I have a portfolio of sketches to finish, but I've got a bottle of sherry with a little left in it. Let's drink to Sally!'

The sooner he left, the better. She had been going to tell him to do what his heart dictated but her advice was not needed. Now it was all up to him. Months of courtship, she supposed, with a wedding at the end of it.

When he had gone she did not feel hungry. She had not eaten and the sherry was making her feel preternaturally lucid. Thank God he had not realized. Sally had, though. She would try to forget him, as everyone was advised when they were jilted. Yet he had not exactly jilted her. She had been caught up in her own desires . . . it seemed she had been completely wrong about him.

She lay on the bed, tears dripping down her face. But then she got up and took her sketchbook and drew his face from memory, a face transfigured as he had talked about Sally. She hoped to goodness he was as steadfast as she could have been, and that Sally would never have her heart broken in the way she was sure hers was.

★ ★ ★

A few days later Caroline had to see her mother about a signature necessary on an insurance policy that Clare had bought on behalf of her elder daughter years ago. This policy, Clare wrote, was to come to maturity when Caroline was twenty-five, which would be towards the end of the year. The amount could be recouped, or might serve as the basis for a new arrangement that could be drawn up when the other ended.

Her mother very much wanted her to make arrangements to buy a new policy, but Caroline had argued — justifiably, in her opinion — that even with the small allowance from her father, she was as yet earning only just enough to make ends meet. It was not the time to be investing in her financial future; the money from the policy would come in useful at the end of the year.

Clare invited her over for lunch one Saturday at her flat in WC1. Caroline was aware that once she had signed the document, her mother would continue to try to persuade her to continue with the insurance policy. She could not remember her mother ever having mentioned it before. Perhaps she had only just remembered it herself. It seemed somehow not like her to have opened a policy twenty-five years ago on her behalf. Perhaps her own grandparents had suggested it? She ought to feel grateful.

Caroline did not often pay Clare a visit and felt a little guilty about this but on the day of the lunch she was also feeling low-spirited. She had managed not to think about Rob by immersing herself in a punishing schedule of work. All her effort had not so far led to her earning enough to live in any financial ease. She was still sure that one day she would, and that eventually she would be successful. It was only a matter of making ends meet for the next year or so — and using whatever money came her way before she burst upon the world with her ideas.

She tried to explain this to Clare, thinking as she did that perhaps there was no reason why her mother should believe implicitly in her talents.

'I'm sure you will succeed,' said Clare, in a manner that sounded more soothing than her usual way of talking to her elder daughter. 'And anyway, although one can never count on anything, you will probably marry and be able to afford to do what you want! Make your own creations . . . '

'I don't think I shall ever marry. Is that why *you* did?' asked Caroline rather cheekily. She was well aware how difficult it always had been, still was, for a woman to be solvent without a man in the background. After all, where would she be without the £200 per annum her father put into her bank account?

Clare looked a little uneasy, but after a pause answered her. 'Well, Caro, Francis could earn more than I could — and then I found I didn't possess enough of the talent I'd counted on.'

For the first time in her life Caroline found she was feeling rather sorry for her female parent.

'That must have been a blow — but it was having children that made you change, wasn't it?'

'Partly.'

'And you are successful now — I don't mean painting — but working, with a good job. Being paid for what you want to do.' Not needing a husband, she did not add. She sounded to herself a bit like a cheer-leader. Her mother would not appreciate this tone of voice. Clare however seemed more concerned with finances.

'Do think over the policy — you never know,' said her mother, 'pay the minimum, and once you are making a bit more you can up the amount. Don't cash it in at the end of the year, will you?'

Caroline realized that maybe her mother could no longer really afford to be paying this out for her. After all, she was of age. She had not wanted much to be made of her twenty-first.

Clare went on: 'When you're young you just don't think of things like insurance policies. It's only when you are responsible for someone else that it occurs to you. I hope you *will* marry one day — for love, not for pecuniary reasons!'

She actually smiled.

Clare was not the sort of mother who had ever been curious about a daughter's love life. When her next remark was:

'You must meet lots of young men?' Caroline wondered if Lily had been saying anything about Robert Cozens. Lily was closer to their mother than she was herself, in spite of being away at school most of the time and staying so often at Pettiwell.

'Oh, I meet scores!' Then she added, inadvertently surprising herself, 'Knowing lots of what people might consider suitable young men — even liking a man — doesn't always mean he'll find you attractive. Men often appear not to like independent women, don't they?'

'That's true,' said Clare meditatively. 'And I would never never say marry because it's expected of you. Some women just seem lucky in love!'

'Well, *you* were!'

'You think so?'

Caroline did not reply to this; it was her mother's business if she didn't want to return to Paris to live with her husband.

'And Aunt Ruth, she got the man she wanted didn't she?'

Now why had she said that? She had wanted to change the subject but might now be embroiling herself.

'Ruth only ever wanted Jack Page. I don't think she even noticed other men — and she was very pretty as a girl.'

'Like Sally?'

'I think prettier than Sally, though Sally is a pretty girl.'

'The sort to marry young, do you think?'

'Sally? I don't know . . .'

So Lily had not said anything.

'How well did Aunt Ruth know the Cozens tribe — that family at Stair Court?'

'The Cozens? I believe she met the younger son.'

'The other was killed in the war, wasn't he?'

Clare nodded. 'Have you met them, then?'

'Yes, I was over in Pettiwell the other weekend. Sally teaches their granddaughter to ride — Nadine Cozens. Lily knows her, and her brother came over with her. Apparently the family is very well off.'

It all sounded plausible, but she hoped she was not blushing, or growing pale. She did not want to confide completely in her mother. She went on:

'Why I asked, was that Aunt Ruth seemed not at all keen at first on Rob — Nadine's brother. I think she suspected he might be keen on *me*. Lily was there again the other weekend — she may have mentioned it. It was because the school had chickenpox, and they gave them a few days' leave. Anyway, Lily says Aunt Ruth seemed quite keen on Sally knowing him.'

Had she said too much? Her mother could be astute and she was looking interested.

'She didn't seem to like him much when I was there but Lily thinks he's fallen for Sally!'

'And does your cousin reciprocate?'

'I think so. I wondered whether Aunt Ruth — not Sally — had suddenly realized how rich he might be!'

'Somehow I don't think my sister — in spite of Pettiwell and the title and all that — is the sort to put money first.'

'She might on behalf of her daughter, though, mightn't she? Like Mrs Bennet in Jane Austen. You were just talking to me yourself about money and marriage.'

Clare had now guessed what might be eating her daughter Caro.

'It all depends on what people really want. I don't imagine that the Bennet girls were quite as concerned with wealthy husbands as their mother was — or the novelist herself!'

'No, of course not. I didn't mean Sally was. Just that it might have occurred to Aunt Ruth . . . '

To put her daughter first, and encourage the young man, thought Clare. Well, it might, but there are possibly other reasons for her not encouraging *my* daughter. She changed the subject, asked Caroline whether she had heard from Jennie Wilson in Paris.

'Lily told me that Papa invited her to a reception at the British Institute.'

Caroline noted that her husband had not informed his wife of this. Perhaps they didn't write to each other much. Now she felt she would like to be able to say, I wish you and Papa would sort things out between you, but she did not utter such a personal remark. She didn't want any probing questions about Rob Cozens, had already said too much, so she'd better not sound as if she were prying into her mother's and father's lives.

'Jennie will be enjoying herself,' she said.

After she had gone Clare sat for a time, mulling over old tensions, past lives.

The next day she wrote a very simple note to her sister:

I have nothing against Ted Cozens's son going out with my daughter.

She wondered whether Sally was encouraging Robert Cozens. She did not doubt that young Cozens himself would soon tell her, if he had not done so already, that he had recently seen her cousin Caroline and revealed his feelings. Sally was a loyal child and fond of her cousin Caro.

She drew the line at mentally wishing little Sally luck in love. Sally *would* fall in love with him, she felt quite sure about that, even felt it in her bones, if that were possible. Lily too might already have told Sally not to worry about Caro, who might have said she 'understood.' Maybe sister Nadine was already writing to her friend with more details of her brother's new infatuation. She tried to imagine what Rob and Sally would talk about. From what she had been told by Caro he was obviously in love with her, and love did not always need long conversations. But it would be a new experience for little Sally Page.

11

It was a Saturday morning, and Jennie
Wilson's *lycée* class had just finished. She was
in a café reading a letter from Lily Fitzpatrick
which had arrived that morning. After a few
allusions to her exams, and school, and her
plans for the summer holidays, she had gone
on to say what was clearly the point of the
letter:

> . . . *a man called Robert Cozens — Rob
> — you remember the Cozens family at
> Stair Court? — has fallen in love with
> Sally!! Caro knew him first and was rather
> keen on him. If she suddenly descends on
> Dad for sympathy you will know the
> background. Personally, I can't understand
> what they both see in him except that he is
> frightfully handsome. I don't know if you
> see my father now and again but don't say
> anything to him about it unless he asks
> you. Caro thought Aunt Ruth did not like
> him but apparently Auntie doesn't mind
> his taking notice of Sally! He is rich, I
> think, but Caro was not concerned with
> that . . .* '

It sounded as if Lily wanted her to understand she was deliberately understating the situation, thought Jennie, folding the letter and putting it into her bag. She had to get used to the idea of Lily as a grown-up person; to her she was still the bouncy little girl singing in a loud voice all over the place. Obviously she had changed. She was, of course, still singing.

Mother would know all about it, thought Jennie. She always did. It sounded unlike Lady Page who was always welcoming. If she was in love with this Cozens man, Caro might have been hypersensitive. She'd be jealous, though she might not show it. She had always envied Sally.

Maybe she would hear from Caro herself, though she couldn't imagine Caro wanting to confide in her.

Jennie was thinking of Miguel, of whom she had seen a good deal recently. He could be elusive, so she was careful not to make any effort to contact him except after the class, when he might issue an invitation to sit at one of the boul' Mich' cafés, or stroll in the Luxembourg. She had never liked a man so much.

She was seeing him that very afternoon. One day she had mentioned the Closerie des Lilas on the boulevard du Montparnasse, in connection with a novel she was reading. In this café, in the early years of the century, the characters in the story, a collection of painters and writers, had conducted fascinating conversations about life, and it had made her want to see it. She was still discovering new places in Paris she had read about in books or seen in paintings. Miguel informed her it had once been a popular haunt of Hemingway, and all those 'Americans in Paris' after the Great War.

'We'll go and drink a Dubonnet there if you like.'

She was to meet him at three o'clock. Cafés nearer the Sorbonne on Saturday afternoons were crowded with students relaxing after lectures and canteen meals. She preferred Montparnasse. Already 'out of date', it had a past connected with so many of the writers and artists she loved. Bohemian life might have changed its character but had a great attraction for Jennie. She supposed that too was 'out of date'. The very name Closerie des Lilas was magical. If it had been called Closerie des Escargots she would not have thought twice about going there. She often argued with Miguel about such things. He said she was a romantic and that art was not made up of names or affinities, but of forms. She knew that, but words in themselves did carry magic, not only because of their associations but also on account of their sounds and every single person's past history.

'Then a poem would not mean the same to you as to me?' he asked. She thought about this and reluctantly but ruefully agreed that she supposed that was true.

'Yet Shakespeare, whom you so much want your pupils to read, conveys the same excitement to people — even in translation.'

'Well, he invented much of our language,' she answered, knowing that was not much of an argument. She puzzled about translation. The longer you lived in a country the less you 'translated' thoughts into your own language. And great writers did seem to alter people's ideas of the world. Your own language was something special, since you had learned about the world through it. They discussed being bilingual, which Jennie knew she would never be, however much she now thought — and even dreamed — in French.

Their conversations continued to stimulate her mind. At the same time, she knew how easy it would be to fall in love with this man. She had always loved intelligent people. Was she already in love with him? It was not what most people meant by the phrase.

★ ★ ★

This afternoon they decided to sit inside the Closerie des Lilas since a soft rain was falling outside on the pavement. Miguel began to talk about music. Jennie knew she was an ignoramus: liked what she knew and knew what she liked.

'You must listen to more music from before the romantics,' he was saying.

'Tell me some composers' names.'

'The Spanish composer Soler — early eighteenth century. Ah, you would love his Fandango in D minor. He studied with Domenico Scarlatti, another composer you must listen to, although it would take you a lifetime since he wrote over five hundred sonatas!'

'I must begin soon then!'

Miguel was going on enthusiastically: 'Corelli too — an Italian of an earlier time — he was popular in England; concerti grossi, trio sonatas — you may have heard some of his music.'

'I have heard of Corelli,' said Jennie faintly.

Why did men always know more about classical music than most girls did? Her education had been neglected; there was so much to enjoy. They were interested in the same kinds of things — music and poetry and painting even if they did not admire the same writers or painters or composers. Miguel knew more than she did about almost everything. She would never catch him up, and even if she did he wouldn't love her for that. Was that what she wanted?

He had already warned her about easy infatuation. *I am your friend*, was what he always said. Alas, she thought, understanding that he meant he didn't want her as a girlfriend.

They sipped their Dubonnet, a drink Jennie loved, and Miguel was happy to drink with her. She had asked him if he did not perhaps prefer beer, or even whisky.

'A Scotch is all very well in a cold climate or in Manhattan,' he'd answered her, 'but I am not a Yankee and it is not very cold here. If I ever come to Scotland or Ireland I shall drink it there!'

Today was mild and rainy, the kind of afternoon that was always slightly depressing at home. Why was it not depressing in Paris? If she had lived here all her life and was not sitting talking to an intelligent man, would she feel depressed? European music had led to her declaring she had always been fascinated by the idea of Europe, especially by Paris and southern France, and Italy, and Spain too, in spite of the result of their civil war. She could easily become interested in Latin America.

'I used to say the word 'Bellagio' to myself when I was about eighteen — there was a perfume called that — so to me the word meant the scent of carnations and silk suits and cigars,' she said. 'Like lilac being such an evocative word — not poetry in itself but giving you some of the same feelings.'

'I told you that you were a romantic — it came from your reading, Jennie!'

'I suppose so — lilacs in a dead land? Were you ever drawn to a place and time that you had just missed? I have an idea of the nineteen thirties in London even although I was alive then as a child! I don't want politics to be part of it — or depressions, and wars. I know it was a dishonest decade.'

She was thinking, that poem: *all of London littered with remembered kisses* — yet MacNeice was in the swim of it all, on the left, like most writers then . . .

'One day in the future you will have the same feeling for your country childhood and a past shared with your friends,' he said. '*De petites vignettes de désir*,' he added in French.

'You understand me very well.'

'Well, romantic idealists are always nostalgic for something either in the past or in their childhood. It's very English!'

'Nostalgic even for someone else's past?'

'Sure. And it is good for your teaching — to convey enthusiasm.'

He thinks I shall go on being a dreary teacher, she thought.

'I'm not so well up in criticism. So much of teaching literature is to do with criticizing it. I'm not so certain about my tastes, either in music or painting. You have to know so much before you can judge. Who am I to do that? I mean for example, Francis Fitzpatrick is sure of his artistic tastes because he knows a lot.'

'Certainty must always arise from knowledge and I believe he is very knowledgeable.'

'I expect he knows everything about English painters — especially the modern ones: Hitchens, John Piper. *I* like those painters too — '

'Romantics all of them, what the English have liked for the last two hundred years: gentle landscapes, the water colourists of life. Fitzgerald is Anglo-Irish I believe? — now that is almost more English than the English!'

'You are being very unfair!' she protested. 'Turner is not gentle, and the Anglo-Irish lost their homes and land after 1921.

'Other, more vulgar Anglo-Saxons liked the decorative in art.' Was there nothing he did not know about?

'Yes, I am insufferable, dear Hennee. I have lived a little longer than you, that is all!'

Jennie recognized that the feelings she had for this man arose partly because he was interested in the same things as she was, and yet was more knowledgeable, and surely more intelligent. She found him extremely physically attractive on top of all this, and it was hard to separate these two elements in her feelings for him. A sort of melancholy joy would suffuse her, for she did not expect her desire would ever be reciprocated. Also, he often said he might have to return home for family reasons in the summer, though a date had not yet been fixed.

This time however, when they parted upon leaving the café, Miguel invited her to a concert the following week, and she felt more cheerful on return to her small student *foyer*. It was only a walk down the boulevard as far as the ugly rue de Rennes, in left by the post office, across to the rue de Vaugirard and then she was back in the much older street where the hostel was hidden behind its high walls.

She would not think about Miguel leaving, would concentrate on her work and enjoy Paris in his company — and enjoy it too when she was alone. You were on your mettle in Paris; people, not just men, stared at you so you felt you must dress slightly more fashionably than at home. In a way Jennie resented the French obsession with the look of clothes and people, yet she knew she ought to make more of an effort. Women here spent their money on one perfect handbag, one perfect blouse. Clothes cost more and the general effect had to be classical chic. She ought to talk about it with Caro one day.

As she walked along now a middle-aged man murmured '*jolie!*' as she passed, which she presumed ought to be regarded as a morale booster.

After supper she remembered Lily's letter and reread it in her room. She sympathized with Caro, if it was true she had lost a boy friend to Sally, but you never knew how Caro would react to things. As far as she knew there were no other women whom Miguel took out or to whom he talked in the way he talked to her. She'd feel cross and jealous if there were.

It might be rather nice to have Caro visit Paris for a few days, and see how they got on now. She could not deny, either, that she'd rather like to show her how well she could speak French. Caro had always appeared to know what she wanted. She'd be what the newspapers called a 'career girl'. Sally was the opposite; she'd always seen Sally as a wife and mother. Which would she be herself? Could you be both? If a man like Miguel — well, Miguel himself if she were honest

— wanted to marry her, she knew she would be more than tempted to throw away her chance of fame and fortune, or even of a successful academic job.

What would she not be prepared to sacrifice for love? Her inner life, her reading, her thinking, her independence? Maybe all of them. She'd never been tested in the fires of a man's passion. Could she be an outsider, strong and independent? Perhaps not, but she could see the creative Caroline as one, a true artist, even if it was in a world she herself did not understand or even sympathize with. In a way Caro was to be envied.

The following Monday she found another invitation waiting for her in an envelope on the *foyer* breakfast table. The students got up much earlier than comparable students in England, but Jennie had become used to rising earlier and looked forward to the fresh new bread, pale unsalted butter, and greengage jam which they all dunked in their large bowls of milky coffee. She had enrolled as an occasional student at the Alliance Française on the boulevard Raspail and there was a *cours* on Monday morning at ten. They were reading *Madame Bovary*, or rather not just reading it but using it for what she thought must be the favourite occupation of French teachers, the *explication de textes*, comparable perhaps with the solving of crossword puzzles, which preoccupied many English intellectuals of her acquaintance.

It was good for her to be forced to analyse in this formal way, which was so different from that of most teachers in England. On the whole she enjoyed French methods of learning and teaching, if not quite so much as she enjoyed French food.

The note was from Francis Fitzgerald and invited her to lunch on Wednesday at Webers, a restaurant on the Right Bank. She remembered its being mentioned in some biography of Proust. Well, that would be very agreeable, she felt sure, but she wished he would invite Miguel along as well. Had it occurred to him to do so?

She had not yet tried to send a *pneu*, which would have been quicker, so she would write and accept that very evening. The lesson lasted an hour, after which she went for a walk by herself in the Luxembourg, used by now to the ogling of young men, and ignoring it.

The weather was becoming milder — spring had arrived. The flower-beds had been filled for some time with regimented primulas that in their tidiness reminded her of French teaching methods, but soon they would give way to summer borders. In the afternoon she had a lesson to take at the *lycée* with the older girls. They must think her ways of teaching undisciplined — but after all she was there to teach them English and that included the English way of doing things, didn't it?

* * *

She was eating a delicious sole, and Francis Fitzpatrick was obviously enjoying his food as much as she was. They had already mentioned Caroline and Lily and Sally, and the others at Pettiwell, but she had been careful not to say anything about his wife, or Caro's affairs, unless he introduced the subject first. It felt odd to be talking English again — her tongue felt heavy — and she kept breaking into French, which amused Francis.

He complimented her on her accent.

'After all these years they think I'm American, not English!' he stated.

She wondered whether the Germans in the war had known he was not French. This was a time of his life he never spoke about.

They had somehow got on to the subject of work, which had arisen from her telling him about the classes she took at the *lycée*.

'Caroline is very keen on her work too,' he said.

Well, so is her mother she thought.

'Is it as important for women as men?' he asked as he poured her another glass of deliciously cold Loire wine.

'I don't see why not — if men helped to bring up children,' she replied boldly.

'You are a feminist?' he enquired.

'Oh, I have always been a feminist!' she answered airily. She had had a similar discussion with Miguel not long ago. It was true that not many of her women friends were interested in feminism and were surprised that *she* was, as they regarded her in so many other ways as very feminine.

'Most men would say that looks were more important than work for women,' ventured Francis.

'Well, they are important for men too,' she replied, looking at his handsome face, which was handsome in a different way from Miguel's. He was almost flirting with her, so she might show him she could flirt too.

'It is such a waste for some women,' she went on, 'if they want to study, or write — ' (She nearly said 'paint' but stopped herself just in time) 'and have to spend all their time caring for others.'

'Somebody has to; many women appear to

enjoy it. Not so many people want to study,' he replied. 'Men or women.'

She was thinking of *A Room of One's Own*.

He was looking at her very seriously. At least he *did* take her seriously.

'What about love?' he asked.

'Doesn't that apply to men too?'

'Men can't have babies,' he said.

'No. It seems unfair — some men would be very good with babies. Children 'end-stop' their mothers' lives as they don't their fathers.' It was Caro who had once said that to her. She must be careful what she said, for she had had the impression from Caro that Clare Fitzpatrick blamed babies for getting in the way of her life's work. If only women could choose to be pregnant or not! Contraception was not foolproof. Some sort of simple medicine ought to be invented so you only had babies when you wanted them. If they did succumb to men, most young unmarried women spent their lives worrying that they might become pregnant. It made the expression of love so risky. She had better not say any of this to Mr Fitz. He was a very nice man, and what did she know about babies?

Miguel too had once, to her surprise, warned her against sexual infatuation.

'It is hard for enthusiastic women,' had been his words.

'You believe young people realize the sacrifices their mothers made for them?' Francis asked.

'I am very grateful to mine,' she replied.

'I remember you and your parents well,' he said.

'They would have liked me to have had a brother or sister,' she said, as a delicious chocolaty confection melted inside her mouth. 'Sally was like a sister to me, you know, when I was very little. I believe I was rather possessive about her.'

It was odd talking to this man who had known her and the others when they were only young children. She hoped she was not boring him. She well remembered how aggrieved she'd felt when Caroline had usurped her position as 'elder sister' to Sally. After that, Caro had been just as possessive about Sally as she had been herself. Caro did not appear to be so any longer, but if it were true that her young man now preferred Sally, well that was quite different, and she must be feeling terribly jealous. Did her father know anything about it? Whatever he knew or did not know about this, Francis kept his counsel. She couldn't easily imagine Caro confiding in him, though she knew she was fond of her 'Pa'.

It was inexplicable that Caro had been so snobbish; that had disappeared after she went to art school, she remembered. She couldn't have got it from her father when she was a child, for he was the least snobbish of men. He even went to the trouble of taking a servant's daughter out for a meal! Perhaps his wife had been a snob.

'You had a happy childhood,' he remarked. Not as a question but as if he took it for granted.

'I suppose I did. Yes, I did.' He must have been thinking about Caro too, for he said: 'Caro didn't, I don't think . . . '

'Well, it was the war — and she didn't want to go to England in any case and didn't like it there. She hated her old governesses, as well as that boarding-school. She once told me she wished she could go to my school.'

Jennie had thought *with all the little oiks!* — being well aware what some of the gentry thought of villagers and their children. That was all past history now, as far as she was concerned.

She added: 'And you were away — and her mother, whereas I had both my parents at home, which is nice when you are little. I suppose later I might have found it a bit too much of a good thing, but they *wanted* me to study. They never said they minded that I wanted to go away.'

'My sister-in-law could not have managed without your mother and father,' he said. 'We were all very grateful — they need not have done all they did.'

'I suppose everyone made sacrifices. It's true you don't realize when you are a child. What would it have been like if we hadn't had a war?'

'I think *we* might have gone to live in England — in London, in any case,' he replied. 'My wife really wanted to go back home.'

She was surprised. Clare Fitzgerald had always appeared to be a typical Francophile. She certainly did not dress or even talk in an English way.

He said, looking very serious: 'One day Caro will realize all that her mother did for her.'

Jennie was puzzled, but then he changed the subject and they talked about painting, which was a relief, in spite of her not wanting to say much about her artistic preferences, since according to Miguel she was an incurable romantic, and so was he. She told Francis an edited version of what he had said.

'According to Miguel, I (she did not add

328

Francis too) only like landscapes and flowers and genre paintings and watercolours! It isn't true!'

He laughed.

'Oh I am a romantic too!' he replied, 'but I had to learn about other kinds of painting, and one's taste can change as one grows older. Have you been to the Louvre?'

Yes, of course, though she preferred the Jeu de Paume and the Impressionists, and told him so. He told her about the Irish painters he liked. One was the brother of Jennie's latest favourite poet, Yeats. He was an old man now but he had just painted an astonishing picture of a blue horse! Did Francis talk to his daughters about paintings?

She wanted to ask him if he himself still painted, remembering the easels and paints and brushes in the Pettiwell attic, but did not dare. Instead she asked him whether you inherited a talent for painting. So often, musical people had musical children, yet Lily seemed to have got her talent from nowhere. It was not like a general intelligence thing, might or might not go with what people called one's IQ.

'Caro must have got her visual sense from you,' she suggested.

'No, not from me; I think from her

329

mother,' he replied. 'Clare is very gifted, in all kinds of ways.'

'And Lily too, in a different way. That must be a gift from the gods.'

'The Italians call a good voice a gift from heaven — a little touch of God's finger. I used to sing myself.'

'Did you really?'

'Choir boy at St Patrick's in Dublin!' he said. 'I never sing now — if you don't practise, it goes away. Lily knows that.'

She had plenty to think over when they left the restaurant.

Francis clasped her hand and kissed her cheek in the French way when they parted, saying:

'We must do this again. I've really enjoyed talking to you, Jennie.'

He sounded as if he meant it.

★ ★ ★

Jennie found Miguel López waiting outside the *lycée* when she came out about three o' clock one afternoon the following week. It was not one of the days for her university class; he had never met her before, and she was not sure she had ever mentioned the name of the school to him, but she must have done.

'A surprise!' he said. 'Classes over for today? Did you have lunch earlier at your convent?'

He persisted in calling her student hostel a convent since it was run by nuns.

'Yes, I always go back there for lunch on teaching days — it's too good to miss. I only had the hour's lesson this afternoon.'

'Then let me offer you a coffee. I have something to tell you.'

They walked along the boulevard together in the sunshine until he stopped before a café, next to the métro station Duroc.

'Will this do?'

'Fine.' Whatever had he to tell her? When they were seated, and the two cups of black coffee they had ordered were before them, with the oblong pieces of sugar in their pack, he looked serious.

'I only came to a decision the other day. I am to leave earlier than I'd planned. My father is ill — my mother wrote last week. It appears urgent, so I have booked a flight, rather than returning via Cherbourg to the States.'

'You mean go back for good?' She knew he was to return home later that summer after his two years in Paris, and had put off thinking about it. If only she had come here earlier she'd have known him for two academic years, not just one!

'I'm afraid so. I wanted to reassure myself that I had decided, and so I thought I must tell someone and you were the person I called to mind.'

She supposed it was a compliment that he should think of her. Did it mean that he was sorry to be leaving her as well as Paris?

'I am worried about my father, but disappointed I must leave so soon. It will be for good, as far as anything in this world is, 'for good'. If I join our diplomatic service I might be sent back to Europe one day.'

She noticed he did not say 'try for a post' but 'join' — obviously a job would be easily lined up for him.

'What date will you leave?'

He mentioned a date just over a week ahead. 'There are only six weeks more of term in any case.'

'Only' six weeks — a lifetime of talking to Miguel and looking forward to seeing him. All French academic terms ended before 14 July, the *lycées* not to start again until October and the university not before November.

She felt terribly sad and a lump came in her throat. She managed to say:

'Oh I am sorry — I *shall* miss you!'

How much would *he* miss *her*?

'And I shall be sorry to leave you, Hennee.'

They were both silent for a time, drinking their coffee. She knew that if he was as fond of her as she already was of him he would say: Come back with me! He did not say that but he looked sad. He had come especially to tell her, so perhaps she did count for something.

He put his hand across the little table to hers and squeezed it. It was the first time there had been that kind of contact between them and it made her realize how she had longed for it. Then he tapped his spoon against his saucer, and sighed.

'Would you write to me?' she asked.

'You'd like that?'

'Very much — but men are not so keen on writing letters as women.'

'It will do my English good to write to you now and then! And I *should* like to hear from you. You know Latin and French, Jennie, so learn some Spanish too! It is not a difficult language and for someone like you, Spanish will slip down the throat as easily as an oyster! Soon you would be able to write to me in my language.'

'I do want to understand the world you are going to,' she said, thinking mournfully: *the world you are leaving me for.*

'I think you will easily learn to read my language, and as I have told you we have many good poets, so your time would not in any case be wasted!'

'Will you copy out one of your favourite poems for me? I promise I'll soon learn enough to translate it!' She meant it.

'I promise to find one for you!' he replied, looking up at her. 'It will be a modern poem!'

She was pleased. More than anything of a closer nature that she had dared to hope might grow up between them she knew they were close in interests. For her, at twenty-three, closer than anyone else she had ever met. She had known him such a short time but it seemed much longer. Since he had first begun to talk to her after the Sorbonne class they had got to know each other very well on this level: that of conversation about books and paintings and music and politics and the problems of the world.

As far as anything more intimate went, he had been very careful to keep her at a slight metaphorical distance. He might even be married? No, she did not think so. As far as she was concerned his slight wariness had not influenced her own way of being with him. She knew she could be impulsively intimate — what could one lose? She was aware that he knew she liked him and could feel more than that for him if he would let her — and even if he did not.

All that was to be nipped in the bud. Now

Miguel had his life's work to go on carving out. He had only had to make it clear if he hadn't wanted to see her but he *had* wanted to see her and *her conduct has been reasonably circumspect this term*, as she remembered a teacher once writing of her in another context. All he had done was to warn her not to become too easily infatuated — and he had meant that for the future too.

'Before I can leave I have to pack and check tickets and connections and book some international phone calls, so I'll only have one more class with you,' he said now. 'We'll go for a walk after that, shall we?'

'I *am* sorry Miguel. Is your father very ill?'

'Mama thinks he will not recover. She has asked all his children to return.'

He stood up. 'Now we must part. I shall write out those verses for you when I get back and I shall give them to you next Tuesday.'

★   ★   ★

How did she ever get through that Tuesday class? She had woken feeling slightly sick, partly with the anticipation of seeing him again — the *longing* to see him again, even if it were to be for the last time — and the desperate knowledge that so long as she had not yet seen him again she could still look forward to it. After today it would be over. She was to lose a friend, yes, but since he had told her of his forced early departure, during the two or three days following he had, in her mind and imagination, become more than a friend, had become a person — a fascinating man whom she felt she could truly love. She was never going to be given the chance to tell him or show him.

She comforted herself with the notion that he would return to Europe in the not too distant future; indeed it was quite possible that he would. By then though she would have left Paris, and he would have changed. The one thing that was sure was that you could not capture the present and keep it unchanged for ever.

He was going to give her the poem after the class, so she too would copy out one for him, to read after they parted. She thought a long time over which poem to give him, not wanting to sound pathetic, or bathetic. He had said she was a romantic so she would write out a romantic poem that expressed a little of what she was feeling so sincerely and desperately.

Jennie knew much romantic verse by heart, so did not need to go to the library to look it up. She sat in her room the evening before her class, writing out Shelley's *Desire of the*

Moth for the Star, a short and beautiful poem that had always been one of her favourites since she had discovered it on the shelves of the library at Pettiwell. It was not a conventional love poem but it spoke of the yearning that was part of all romantic souls, and she felt sure he would understand.

Miguel was one of the last to come into the classroom and when he sat down, she said to the others:

'Señor López has been recalled home before the end of term, so today will be his last lesson with us.'

One or two of the women looked up with a slight expression of interest on their tired faces — the women always looked tired, just as many of her *lycée* pupils did. One of the scientists said 'Good luck, old boy!' in English. Jennie began to ask them questions on a paragraph in English, which she had prepared by translating it from French and of which she had given them copies the week before. Only last week! It seemed an age since she'd been here with her class, before she knew one of them was leaving. Most of them had prepared the task carefully. She was relieved that this morning was not a morning for the discussion of anything more lyrical or emotive, for she scarcely trusted herself not to burst into tears.

The subject was Kent, the 'Eden' of London, seen from the point of view of a French writer. He did not hesitate to say that it was over these beautiful little towns and villages that bombers had passed not so very long ago to attack London. After this the students were asked to discuss 'commuting' and 'the charm of English villages'.

The lesson went surprisingly well, and she read them the French original in case anyone had still not understood all the English text. Miguel, with whom soon she would be walking in the Jardin du Luxembourg, took an active part, and she summoned up all her professionalism to concentrate on the matter before them. It was all too quickly over.

As they were getting to pack their bags, Miguel rose and said:

'I would like to thank Miss Wilson for a very stimulating course!'

She said 'Thank you,' in a quiet voice but really she was surprised. He went out but was waiting at the door when she reached it herself.

'Let's have a drink first. I'm sure you need it after all that talking!' he said.

'It was nice of you to say what you said,' she said weakly.

'I meant it. What we were discussing was interesting — it gave the real flavour of England.'

338

'It's my part of the country. It made me quite nostalgic.'

By this time they were seated at their usual table at the corner of the rue Soufflot. Miguel ordered two coffees. The sun was beaming across the road over the green gardens. He looked across at it.

'I shall miss Paris,' he said, looking at her, and she felt a lump in her throat.

He took out an envelope. 'I've written it out for you. Don't read it till I've gone!'

'And here's one for you,' she countered, handing him a similar envelope. They both smiled.

'Have you put your address in England?' he asked. 'I know you won't be here for ever. I've put mine at home.'

'I will write,' she promised. He told her when he was leaving and when he would be home but she did not want to think about it. It was somehow worse that he was leaving rather than that she was. She'd be here in all the places they'd been and he would not. Nothing at his home would remind him of her.

She put his envelope in her bag and he put hers in his breast pocket.

'I just can't imagine your life so far away,' she said.

'What matters is one's inner life,' he said seriously. 'I'm sure you would agree with that, Hennee?'

'It doesn't seem the utterance of a diplomat!' she said shakily.

Then they got up and crossed the road and went into the gardens. They walked to the central *bassin* in silence and then back. Somehow it seemed that the best place to sit would be by the fountain, or rather, large pool — which went by the name of La Fontaine de Marie de Médicis, where orange fish darted or sulked. They sat there in silence for several minutes.

How she loathed farewells. Echoing her thought he took her hand, saying:

'I wish I were not going — but you will be one of my best memories, Hennee.'

She had tears in her eyes. In English, she said:

'I shan't forget you, Miguel.'

'I have to go to the embassy this afternoon,' he said. 'I shall get up in a minute and walk away through the big gates over there. You will stroll back to the *bassin* and I shall think of you walking down through the far gate, down rue Fleurus and on to Raspail and your lunch! Keep up your spirits — learn some Spanish from my poem!'

He leaned over and kissed her on the forehead. She squeezed his hand and kissed his cheek.

Then he got up and walked away, turning once to wave.

She read the poem as soon as she got back and could sit alone in her room. Miguel had thoughtfully appended a rough translation that she read over and over again as she read the Spanish, feeling she had already begun to understand the language. Much of it was easily comprehensible. She could feel it was a beautiful poem through the veil of the language:

> Me gustas cuando callas porque estás
>   como ausente,
> Y me oyes desde lejos, y mi voz no te
>   toca . . .

> I like you when you are silent — it's as
>   if you were absent,
> hearing me from afar, my voice not
>   touching you . . .

There were five verses in all, and the words *melancolía* and *distante* and *dolorosa* sounded like a knell in her head.

12

Back in London, Ruth had replied to her sister's letter, sounding in a great flap. Maybe, though, things had moved on so quickly since then that her own note had been superfluous?

Clare heaved a deep sigh. It was up to her to put her right, and thereby calm her, but she had not yet done so. She dreaded meeting her sister, which had to happen sometime in the not too distant future. She decided to consider matters further, one way of putting things off. Perhaps she would write to Francis. Caro might go to see him and he had better be prepared. More than any business with her sister, she dreaded a confrontation with her own elder daughter.

Meanwhile, she'd have Lily round and pump her for more details. Before this could happen, as Lily was still revising or writing her exams, she had another letter from Ruth:

It doesn't matter any more. I'm sorry I wrote as I did. I gather that young Rob has got it together with Sally.

Panic over, then, thought Clare sardonically. And *doesn't matter!* — when her own daughter had clearly been ditched! Couldn't Ruth trust her to speak the truth? She had never told her any lies. She put a fresh piece of paper in her typewriter and typed a quick letter to Francis in Paris.

She'd see Lily at the end of the month after she had stayed in Pettiwell. Then Lily was going to some intensive 'summer academy'. The girl did work hard, but loved her music so much it would obviously not seem like work to her.

Lily would tell her how the land lay at Pettiwell.

★ ★ ★

'Caro was really keen on him I think,' said Lily. She was sprawled in an armchair and had been eating scones. Clare always bought scones for Lily and had a special pot of strawberry jam for her. Lily was always hungry. Her mother supposed singers needed a solid amount of food to provide ballast for their diaphragms or whatever part of the body was involved in song. Lily might one day grow fat, she thought, like most opera singers, but that day had not yet arrived. Butter was still on the ration, and the English were still

343

not back to eating as much as they had before the war. Lily loved fish and chips, whereas for Caro, on her infrequent sojourns with her, she cooked omelettes and provided plenty of salad.

'I can't believe I've left school at last,' said Lily.

'When will you know about the Royal College scholarship?'

'They say mid August — keep your fingers crossed. I might go over to see Dad before that but Ann wants me to stay with her in Norfolk first.'

'Have you seen Caro recently?' Clare tried to sound casual but Lily was not deceived.

'She didn't come to Pettiwell. There were only the two love-birds. Even Nadine wasn't there at the weekend. I think she's going to the South of France with her parents but her grandmother's been ill and the family plans were held up.'

'And your sister?'

'I'm seeing Caro before I go to Norfolk. She's been awfully busy doing something rather technical — I think actually making the same sort of patterns as for *haute couture* — it's not like working 'in house', she says, but the school lets them make their own designs. Caro wants to produce dresses from these designs of hers for a competition.'

'She's not stopped working then. I was afraid that all this business with the young man might make her . . . depressed.'

'Oh, Caro won't have a breakdown!' said Lily cheerfully. 'I mean she was really keen about Rob and must have been awfully cut up, though she hasn't said much to me.'

'And Sally?'

'You saw Caro a few weeks ago, didn't you? Well, Caro told me to tell Sal not to worry about her but just follow her real feelings. Rob Cozens is crazy about Sally! It was noble of Caro, wasn't it? And the priceless thing is, that Sally told me that Rob told *her* he thought his father was once sweet on Aunt Ruth!'

'Really? History repeating itself, do you mean?'

'Do *you* remember that? Sally says her mother has never mentioned it to *her*.'

'I do remember that my sister, many, many years ago, had eyes for nobody but Jack Page, so history in this case has not repeated itself. Did Sally tell her mother what he'd said?'

'No idea. I shouldn't think so. Aunt Ruth seems to like him though. Personally,' said Lily, wiping a crumb from her perfect mouth, 'I don't think he'd have been good enough for Caro!'

'You look so like your father when you say

that,' said Clare meditatively. 'I suppose Sally reciprocates his affection?'

'I think she does — not as madly as he does, but I feel he's the one she'll settle for. I'm sure Caro was very fond of him. At first, Sally was really upset — she asked me ages ago if I thought Caro would mind. I said it depended on Rob, not on Caro, which was true. Caro told me to say that. I guess she minded a lot.'

'Yes,' replied her mother. 'Caro knows that unfortunately you can't make people fall in love with you.'

'He had seemed keen on going out with her, so it was a blow when he fell for Sal — so awfully unfair . . . '

'Love is unfair. Caro will know that too by now. Do you think she'd like me to talk to her?'

Clare was thinking: I must talk to her. And to my sister too.

She murmured aloud: 'Thank you for keeping me up to date, Lil, and when you see Caro tell her she's very welcome to stay here.'

'I think she said she might go to France when she'd finished the competition work.'

'So she'll stay with her father?'

'I suppose so — she hasn't made any plans yet. I telephoned her and she hadn't heard again from Jennie. I don't know if Jennie's

346

coming home for the summer. Mrs Wilson would like her to, but she knows she'll always be busy over there with her work.'

'Term will have ended in Paris,' said Clare.

After her daughter had gone, she sat down and wrote impulsively to her husband.

R. wrote to me in a great flap some time ago. I told her I'd nothing against Ted Cozens's son going out with Caro. Since then Lily has informed me that history is repeating itself! I know I ought to see R. to settle things, yet I have the feeling she will soon come over herself to see me. What will you say to Caro if she comes over to France?

What a pain it all was, having things out. It was imperative to see her elder daughter soon.

Term had indeed ended for Jennie in Paris and she was missing Miguel terribly. It had been even worse just after he left. Such was her sorrow that she experienced a real dislike, even a physical nausea, at the sight of the young men who crowded the Latin Quarter, or strolled in the Luxembourg Gardens, or idled away in the cafés. Not one of them was Miguel and she hated them. Miguel López was the only man she wanted to see, and she would probably never see him again.

For a few days she haunted the music machines on the boul 'Mich' listening over and over again to songs in Spanish. The tango La Paloma was her favourite. She had already begun to learn Spanish, with the help of a small French-Spanish vocabulary book, and an elementary grammar. It was easier to learn this new language by way of French, and she had already managed to understand all the Spanish words in Miguel's gift of Neruda's poem, without referring to his translation. This, and the words of the melancholy tango, seemed to represent her feelings exactly.

She supposed that love poems were usually written by men about women. For a woman writing of love she would have to return to her favourite English women writers. She spent some time at the *bouquinistes* and in the second-hand shops of the boulevard searching for anything she could find about romantic love, for it seemed to her that this was what she was suffering. She found her favourite Stendhal, and then a book in Spanish *On Love*, which she determined to read with the help of a dictionary. She might even find an English translation to come to her aid. She saw a certain absurdity in finding comfort in such literature, but it helped.

She kept herself as busy as possible as long

as the academic term was not over. Something impersonal like marking *devoirs* or preparing vocabulary was best. After Miguel's departure the class had been muted, weary. She knew it was her job to enthuse them and she had done what she could, but with a heavy heart. Did the others know how much she missed him? She didn't think she had let her feelings show. At the *lycée*, where the term was longer, she had been able to forget him occasionally for a few minutes, but most of the time it was as if she had a sore place, a bruise that would not fade. She did not want it to fade away because then she might forget him.

She confronted herself with the truth: he had not been in love with her, and she had scarcely been aware until the end how miserable his absence would make her. This did not appear to help. Absence certainly did make the heart grow fonder. He had *liked* her: about that she was sure — and for such a man to like you was indeed heart-warming.

He had not been, what she was sure Sally would have called him, her 'Latin lover'. Neither a lover nor very Latin. In fact an extremely modern and clever young man if truth be told.

Why could she not be as men were supposed to be: people who could like a person without falling in love with them? It was not exactly the first time it had happened to her. Before, in England, she'd realized she was susceptible to the sadness of unrequited love, and the absence of loved ones, and had always — eventually — got over it.

One warm evening she decided to begin a letter to him, guessing that he would not write straight away himself. It mattered more to her, so she would write first. She left the start of her letter in her room the next morning and went down to breakfast. It had been hard to find the right tone of words, for she did not wish to appear silly or sentimental. Sitting in a denuded dining-room, as so many of the students had departed home, on the morning of the same day that Clare and Lily were to mention her name in conversation, Jennie found on her plate another invitation from Francis Fitzgerald.

She was surprised that he was still in Paris. Those professional men who could, left town at the first possible minute for the Côte d'Azur or the countryside, and stayed away until September at least.

Francis wrote to the point. He was still here in Paris and would love to see her if she too had not yet left on holiday.

'Give me a ring if you can come round tomorrow.'

No mention of either of his daughters. Jennie was mystified. What could Francis want with her? She had enjoyed his company, and he would not make her feel sad, since he was not a young man to be compared with Miguel. She might even be able to talk about Miguel to him. Yes, she'd telephone and accept.

Francis Fitzpatrick lived in a first-floor flat on the boulevard, a little to the east of the rue de Seine, and he invited Jennie to meet him there. She wondered if this was where Caro and Lily had once lived. It did not seem likely from what she had heard. This flat most likely went with his work.

A lift deposited her on a red-carpeted landing and when she got out she found a door at each end of the landing, with number 2 on the left. She rang the brass bell in the centre of the mahogany door. Francis did not take long to open it and welcome her in with a smile. She thought he looked a little tired and strained, but his affability sounded sincere when he said:

'Hello, Jennie. How nice of you to come! I thought we might have a drink here, and then if you like I can take you to lunch in one of the restaurants on the boulevard?'

He took her though an inner door into a large room, with three long windows.

She knew that the famous 'Existentialists' had often hung about in cafés on the boulevard. Most of them appeared to have gone now.

'That would be lovely,' she replied.

'I must go and open a bottle,' he said, and disappeared into what was presumably a kitchen. 'Amuse yourself looking at my pictures.'

There were several landscapes that she thought looked English, a tiny oil of a woman looking out of a window, and, hanging over a Pembroke table, the portrait of a boy. She moved over to look at it, glancing down at the table which was covered in envelopes and papers — he was not very tidy. An opened letter on the top of the pile caught her attention. She tried not to look at it but could not help seeing that it was written in a very English hand and was the last page of something for it was signed *Clare*, and she saw the name Caro quite unmistakeably in the middle of the page.

She looked back up at the painting. Surely this was of Francis himself when young? She could hear a tap running in the kitchen and then a pop and the sound of crystal glasses. She firmly refused to let her glance fall on the letter again and walked away to look at a picture of a bowl of lilac.

Francis came back in, bearing a tray with an opened bottle of champagne and two brimming glasses. He put it on another little side table, offered her one of the glasses, and took the other himself.

'I know I should have poured it here,' he said apologetically, 'but it isn't my carpet — it's rather valuable and as I am very clumsy I might have spilled the champagne.'

She laughed. He sounded so comically worried. When he sat down opposite her on a velvet-covered chair by one of the long windows that led out on to the balcony, and overlooked the boulevard itself, she did wish it was Miguel who was sitting there.

The chilled champagne was delicious.

'To your health — à ta santé!' he said and clinked the no doubt precious crystal glasses. Then he asked her how she was getting on. She forbore for the time being to say that Miguel had gone back home and that she was feeling a little lonely. It would not be quite true anyway. It was not loneliness that was affecting her. Being alone, with the time to think about Miguel, did not bring about only feelings of sadness, but rather a sensation of being bereft in a sort of timelessness.

'Fine!' she said.

He continued: 'You might advise me . . . '

She waited.

'I heard from . . . Lily,' he said. 'She seemed worried about her sister. I wondered if you had heard from either of them?'

So he only wanted advice? She was a little disappointed, but replied:

'I did hear from Lily. Caro doesn't write often. I gathered that a man Caro . . . rather liked . . . had fallen in love with Sally.'

'Do you think Caro is OK? She might have taken it hard. Particularly because it was Sally . . . '

Had he realized that his elder daughter had once been as possessive about Sally as she had? But that was when they were children!

'Oh, I think she'll get over it,' said Jennie. Perhaps it was worse for Caro than for herself. If Miguel had clearly preferred another young woman to her, she'd have been unhappy, but she would have tried not to let it show. Nowadays, Caro betrayed her feelings even less than she herself did. Jennie decided it would be safer to try to steer the conversation to talking about childhood. After all, Pettiwell was the reason she was here drinking champagne with Mr Fitzpatrick today.

'Lily seemed to think she'd be all right — at least that was the impression she gave me,' she said. 'Caro was always fairly self-sufficient.'

She wanted to ask whether perhaps Caro's mother might help, or at least tell her husband if she was worried, but it might look as if she had been reading his letters. She had considered the couple estranged but supposed people got together to deal with their children's problems.

'Do you often think of Pettiwell?' he asked her suddenly. Good, they could talk about that!

'Yes, quite often. I was very happy there as a child. Of course it wasn't the same for your children, since they'd been snatched away from France . . .'

'No, Caroline didn't like it at first, I'm afraid, but it was good for her to have girls about her own age to play with. There were seven years between her and Lily and Lily seemed to accept the change.'

'Lily is a different kettle of fish,' agreed Jennie. 'I loved that house, even though I didn't really belong there.'

'Of course you belonged there! Who more than you and your family? You know, I remember you very well as a child.'

'When I was little I liked to think of how the place and the house had once been. Did you ever see it before? I mean, before Sir

Jack's parents died.'

'No. When my wife and I came over for the first time to Pettiwell I was told things had changed a good deal from what they had been before the Great War. Sir Jack had closed up half the house after his parents' deaths, and sold off a lot of stuff to pay death duties and just keep going. He was in great financial difficulties long before the war, I believe. My sister-in-law used to tell us what he had told her the place had once been like. I think she was really quite relieved not to have to keep up the old ways. Of course her husband hated change and was quite ashamed of what the place had become.'

'It is a lovely place!' exclaimed Jennie. 'And even if they were relatively poor they weren't *really* poor! In many ways they kept up their way of life. Closing off the attics only made it more romantic to me!'

'And also some of the second floor in the older part of the house was closed off. Page sold a good deal of the silver. His sister did once tell us about the way of life she and her brother had lived as children before the first war. Now, of course after the second, almost everybody in England is having to pull in his or her belt! Did you know that hundreds of houses have either been pulled down, or allowed to become ruins? And a lot more will be pulled down soon. That's progress: you can't live in the old way without scores of servants.'

She was thinking that as a child she had never thought to ask Sir Jack what the house had been like long before! It was her mother who had answered her questions. Sir Jack must have known the place better than anyone, having lived there longer than anyone else.

'Was it like your own house in Ireland?' she asked him now.

'Architecturally, yes, not very different. My life as a child didn't last all that long there. Walks with a nanny, and nursery tea before you were washed and dressed and sent down to the grown-ups for an hour in the drawing-room . . . that sort of thing. Even so, in Ireland we were probably not quite so formal as over in England. We had a cook — she wasn't a very good cook! and a butler in livery for a short time, and much Georgian silver, good furniture and porcelain — *and* a well-stocked library. Lovely gardens and flowers too — plenty of rain for them in Ireland! Some people have never stopped regretting our passing but I was glad when I was fifteen that I needn't live like that any more.'

'Old houses are so romantic, though,' said

Jennie. 'I used to haunt all the old corridors and back stairs in both parts of the house, especially the top corridor with the door at the end that led to the original part — Sally's part. Mother stopped me; she said it was dusty and she just couldn't see to it all. She had enough to do polishing the rosewood furniture in the best rooms.'

'I should think she had! Your mother did the work of six!' He was thinking: *probably for a pittance* but did not voice this last observation.

Jennie said: 'Mother went to Pettiwell as a sort of lady's maid to Lady Page — you knew she'd known her as a child? Well, of course you knew, as she'd helped to bring up your wife too!'

'She ended up as housekeeper,' said Francis.

'And the old servants' hall became Mother's sitting-room! I wonder if that happened to any other families? Tell me about your family house in Ireland.'

'Oh, after the Troubles there were more or less over — though not as far as the Northern Irish and the English were concerned — we were out for good as landowners. Not even a sitting-room left. One reason I came to France to study was to get away from the English and Anglo-Irish class system!'

We are being very talkative today, thought Jennie. As if we were nervous.

'Do you love Ireland?' she asked him.

'Naturally,' he went on. 'I loved the part of Ireland we lived in — and Dublin — and I wouldn't mind living in that part of the country again one day when I'm an old man, if they'll let us. 'Behind the golden curtain' we call it now . . . but I expect I had much the same childhood as your Sir Jack. Read all the same books: *Treasure Island* and *Alice* . . . well, we *were* English really!'

'Caro always seemed so un-English — at first, anyway,' said Jennie. She was thinking again that it was Caro who had been the snobbish one, reminding her that her parents were servants, though she wasn't going to tell Caro's father that. She was sure it hadn't come from him.

'Did she? I expect your environment and school-friends make as much of an impression on you as a child as your parents do. Once you go to school anyway. After all, you adapt to your school-mates' language and their habits as far as you can so as not to be an outsider.' He had such a lovely Irish voice, she thought.

'Caro spoke French when she was little — but she spoke English at home, didn't she?'

'Yes, of course.'

'Well, I spoke reasonable English with my parents. Mother had learned to 'speak nicely' in London, though she always had her country accent not the Pettiwell one. I talked in a much more common way with the children at school — to mix in with the others, as you said. I was between two stools more than most, I suppose, but it must have been harder for Caro to adapt.'

She remembered that Caro used to mock her accent. One of her reasons for learning French had been to get her own back!

'You were always adaptable, Jennie — and hard-working, like your parents.'

'I knew my face would not be my fortune!' she said ruefully.

'Really, Jennie, you are a very pretty girl!' he said.

She stared at him. He was looking at her the way she wished Miguel had looked at her. The thought of Miguel stopped her in her tracks. It was all very well talking about the past, but she wanted to live the here and now, and Francis Fitzgerald, for all his charm, was not the right person to be looking at her like that.

He seemed to recollect himself, for he got up, saying:

'It is true what I have just said! And now

we must go out for lunch. So long as you don't think there's anything I can do about Caroline. She may come over soon, I think, for a change.'

Over the lunch, in a brasserie that she felt sure had often been patronized in the past, if not now, by Juliette Greco and the philosophers, Jennie felt emboldened enough after a second glass of wine to ask him if his *wife* was worried about their daughter.

'I think she might be . . . but there are — complications . . . '

He did not elaborate. After this they talked about work. He said that Freud had once stated that Work and Love were the two most important things in life. Francis capitalized the two words in his speech, and Jennie, after thinking about it, agreed.

She added: 'Work lasts longer!'

'You are too cynical for a young lady!' he replied, but with a slight smile, looking rather searchingly at her.

'No! I'm not at all cynical,' she replied, quite honestly. He was such a nice man — and he did appear to enjoy her company.

'I didn't really mean it,' he said after a pause. 'I know you are very straightforward. Dear Jennie. Of course it depends what you mean by 'love'.'

She realized that he had been flirting with

her but also from the look in his eyes that something more serious underlay all he said to her.

★ ★ ★

A few days later Jennie was sitting in the park trying to make up her mind whether to go back home for a week or two, stay in Paris and work, or go to Spain with her friend from Manchester who had written to say she might go to Catalonia again in August if she could afford it. Would Jennie like to come too? A group of mutual friends and acquaintances was off to camp near a place called Rosas, or one called Cadaqués, on what was — they had been told — a completely unspoilt coastline. Jennie felt she needed a change: to go to a place where the shadow of Miguel did not loom, but she had no desire to go camping. Perhaps, though, she could learn Spanish. Then she remembered that they would speak Catalan there, and in any case what would be the good of fleeing Miguel only to miss him more if his language were spoken around her?

Money was also a problem. Once she had paid her fare home she could stay at Pettiwell and do some work there, some writing, without needing to pay for her keep. Her parents would actually be insulted if she offered to pay for a short visit home, and would be only too delighted for her to spend some time with them. She might learn Spanish just as well from a book to begin with, and there might be classes in London.

But ought she to stay here and get on with some research in the libraries? Yes, but that need not be for the whole summer. Most of the faculty students had left the *foyer* already for three or four months, giving place to student tourists who came for those months when Paris was emptied of Parisians. Families as well as students and teachers nearly always departed for the sea or some ancestral family village.

She had decided that she would go home for a time, when she saw a familiar figure ambling in her direction. Francis Fitzpatrick must be walking to his office through the gardens. He must surely go away on holiday himself soon. She felt a little reluctant to wave to him but he had evidently seen her, for he quickened his pace, and came up and sat down next to her on one of the spindly iron chairs.

'What a bonus to see you, Jennie, on such a lovely summer morning! You know, I was hoping I might!'

She did not want to associate the

Luxembourg Gardens with anyone but Miguel, so she said:

'I was just about to leave. I've decided to go home for a few weeks.' It sounded rude, so she added: 'I often come here just to think, make decisions.' It sounded odd but she was looking directly at him as she spoke. What she saw in his eyes was a mixture of surprise — seeing her so suddenly here where he had not really expected to see her, even if he had been hoping he might — and a look of what she could only describe as longing.

He said: 'I have been thinking about you so much, Jennie!'

She was astonished, continued to look at him enquiringly.

'May I kiss you?' he said suddenly, but quietly. 'I think I might just be falling in love with you. Fate has clearly brought us together this morning.'

It was true that she had realized since their last meeting that he had been flirting quite outrageously with her, and also that as (she supposed) a married man, a serious man, he might even mean what he said. He was a well-known person, a scholar, and a war hero even. What on earth would a man like that want with her?

Then he went on: 'You are so young — it's like the breath of youth. Extraordinary!' and took her hand. She knew quite certainly that if it had not been for Miguel — if only he had said such things to her! — she might have succumbed. She could tell that Francis was not playing an amorous game for she was sure that he truly desired her. It was frightening, but also exhilarating. Frightening, not because she was shocked or afraid of sex, but because she understood that he evidently did mean what he said, that he was serious. What she wanted — needed — was experience of a man: of sex, to be blunt, and here was probably the person best equipped to give it her, a man she had known in some way almost all her life. He's 'family', she thought — although this was not strictly true — and he's *old* — he must be nearly fifty. He's more like an uncle, though he's not *my* uncle! And I don't want anyone but Miguel to fall in love with me, even if they want me. Above all he is Caro's father.

She would not deceive herself. She was quite attracted to him, but she certainly did not love him, and could never love him. She believed what he had said, and she would have leapt into bed with Miguel, love or not, if Miguel *had* asked her. This, though, would be wrong, however much excitement it might bring in its train, because Francis had spoken of love and she did not want *love* from him.

She did like him, though; it was flattering, and made her see herself differently.

All these thoughts hurtled through her head. She looked away.

'Now I have upset you,' he said. 'I do mean it Jennie, please believe me.'

She let her hand lie in his as she said: 'I believe you, but you are my friend's father, and it would be . . . ' she searched for the right words — not wrong — certainly not incestuous but . . . bad taste.'

He gave a genuine laugh. 'You don't worry about my wife — only about Caroline.'

She was startled to realize that, no she didn't worry about his being married, about his wife Clare. Why?

She said: 'You see I am still missing Miguel. I was in love with him and I will be for some time, so you must not fall in love with me — you must *not*!'

'If your heart was free — or if I was not the father of a friend of yours — you would have no objection?'

She thought, if she had never known Miguel, and if Francis Fitzpatrick had belonged in no way to her childhood, she might have had no objection to having some sort of affair with him one day. But she didn't want his love. Her heart was still filled with Miguel, and love was too much of responsibility.

'I told you — you are Caro's father. I like you so much, and I know you mean it, but I don't want to — to do anything on the rebound, you know, because I am so missing Miguel. You would probably be very good for me, Francis, I know that,' she added humbly.

'You are such a delightful mixture,' he said. 'We can forget what I said. It is still a great pleasure to be with you and I shall have the satisfaction of knowing that in other circumstances you would have let me kiss you!'

They both got up and Francis took up his briefcase.

'And this will seem like a dream one day!' he said softly. Then, 'Caroline is most likely coming to see me — she is to confirm whether it will be Friday. She'll perhaps stay for a while. Will you come and see me — us?'

Jennie said: 'I shall probably go home next week. Let me know when you'd like me to come and see you, and I will. Write to me, Francis,' she added impulsively.

Somehow she would like to have a letter from him. It was true what he had murmured: it would seem like a dream to them both.

He said: 'Before you go . . . ' and took her hand and kissed it.

Then he quickly walked away.

13

In England, other matters had been preoccupying Clare and her sister, and their daughters.

Lily wrote to Caro:

Sally says that Rob told her his father had once, long ago, been sweet on her mother! She asked her mother whether it was true. Lady P. looked really surprised and said, 'Oh, he might have been, a bit,' — but she seemed very vague about it, and she certainly denied ever having been 'sweet' on him. She said, if anyone, it had been our mother who had been 'fond' of Edward Cozens. Sally told Rob this and he said his Dad had never mentioned Mother, but he'd certainly got the impression that his father had once thought that Ruth Ogilvie was the cat's whiskers! Fancy Lady P 'hardly remembering'! What do you make of all this? Shall we ask Mother?!

I probably won't see you before you go if you decide to go to Paris in July. I've been asked to attend a summer school in Westmorland next week and later Evelyn has asked me to stay with her family in Cornwall. I leapt at both chances. I might come over to France later, in September, after I get my results. Tell Dad when you see him.

Love Lil.

Caroline thought, perhaps Sally's mother did to mine what Sally has done to me? Yet Ma told me that her sister only ever wanted Jack Page and was always a 'one man woman'. A puzzle. And it really wasn't Sally's fault that Rob Cozens had fallen in love with her.

Caro had somehow got used to this outcome, though it still caused her sorrow. She had not seen Rob again but knew she eventually must, if she were to go on seeing people at Pettiwell. If it were true that her own mother had been 'fond' of Rob's father, had he left her for her sister when he became 'sweet' on Aunt Ruth? She considered the language: *the cat's whiskers* . . . *sweet on:* people used these expressions to cover long-ago anguish. Well, you had never been able to make people fall in love with you, and that had not changed. If history did repeat itself there was nothing you could do about it.

I must ask Ma one day though, she

thought, I really must. I didn't tell her much about Rob, and by now she may have heard from her sister, if Sally and Rob have become what they call 'serious'. Lily will have kept her posted too. Lily likes these intrigues — perhaps she thinks they are milder versions of the operas she goes to, whose arias she will sing . . .

Caroline kept putting off seeing Clare. It was all rather embarrassing — and she was busy.

★ ★ ★

Clare Fitzpatrick was holding two letters in her left hand. She had been reading them both over breakfast, which in her case consisted only of a cup of coffee and a slice of toast. She put the letters down on the table, poured herself a second cup and considered. One letter was from her husband and the other from her sister.

She must reply to them both, and then she must speak to Caro, have a long talk with her. Francis was right: *You really* ought *to see her now, Clare*,' he had written.

Ruth had been less prescriptive but had agreed to meet her sister in London when she next came up.

Clare had obviously been trying to sound

casual, thought Ruth. *Don't come specially,* she had written, *I know you'll have to get back, and it's a long way so shall we meet in Bloomsbury? I'm at work in the morning but I have the afternoon off on Wednesdays. I'll be around Bedford Square at lunch time if you'd like to meet for lunch or a drink.*

She knew her sister did not like London and always scurried back home with the excuse she must get supper for husband.

This was actually what had been in Clare's mind when she wrote. In small matters the sisters knew each other well. As though Sally couldn't rustle him something up in the evening, Clare had said to herself, and then: Should I have her round here? She was so anxious not to appear inhospitable that she telephoned the day before their meeting to make sure that Ruth might not prefer to go back to her flat with her on the Wednesday afternoon.

'Oh no,' replied Ruth. 'That's fine by me. I'd like to see where you work, and I have to get back to get Jack's supper. It's Mrs Wilson's day off.'

⋆　⋆　⋆

Ruth admired Clare's place of work, a beautiful old house on the square, now

371

publishers' offices, and they walked to the next square, where there was a large hotel nearby with a lounge for coffee and sandwiches next to the bar. They both felt constrained by all they knew had never been said.

Clare bought them each a Martini Vermouth, as she knew this was her sister's favourite tipple, and let Ruth plunge into conversation. Ruth had no need to feel nervous, she knew. It was she herself who should feel nervous. She had not yet decided all she was going to say.

Ruth said: 'I'm sorry if I was unkind to Caro — I imagined — '

'I know what you imagined,' said Clare. 'It isn't true. You must believe me. Not that it matters now.'

'I do believe you.'

'Thank you.'

'He does appear to be besotted with Sally,' said Ruth after a moment, unable to avoid entirely a slight tone of satisfaction, and perhaps maternal pride.

'What's he like?'

'Terribly handsome. Was Caro really in love with him?'

'I imagine so,' said her mother drily. 'Not that she has ever unburdened herself completely to me — after all, she might have preferred to tell *you*. Those years when she was a child at Pettiwell, it was mostly you who were there.'

'She never regarded me — or treated me — as her actual mother,' said Ruth. 'Had it — the — er — relationship — gone . . . very far?'

'As far as I know it had scarcely begun!' said Clare. 'She just knew he was the man for her, according to Lily, but it turned out she was wrong.'

'I'm sorry.'

'Don't be silly, you did nothing wrong. It just appeared to Caro that you were keener on his falling for Sally than for her. She and young Cozens had after all travelled to Pettiwell together! What happened afterwards was probably inevitable. What's his sister like? I get the impression from Lily that she was very keen on her brother meeting Sally.'

'Nadine? She's a great friend of Sal — '

'Well, there you are!'

'But, Clare — I swear I was only thinking of her. I'd no idea he would fall head over heels with my daughter!'

'Well, as I have said many times, history has a habit of repeating itself.'

'But — his father — Edward Cozens . . . '

'As far as Ogilvies went he only ever had eyes for you.'

'For me?' Ruth looked stricken, amazed.

Clare said to her sister: 'Can't you trust me to speak the truth? It *was* you he loved.'

'I remember he had a bit of a thing for me — I think it was just after I came out — but it wasn't serious! I never encouraged him.'

It was clear that she had almost forgotten the man.

'Ruth, you were so keen on Jack — even before you really knew him at all — that you just didn't realize Edward was in love with you! As his son is now in love with Sally.'

'When I try to remember, I think I found his attentions faintly annoying! It can't be true — that Ted Cozens was ever in love with me! It was you he — '

'You ignored him, having a heart reserved for Jack Page.'

'Was that very wrong?'

'No. It's just that some people can be so — impercipient. Like Caro's ex-boyfriend. All that wasted emotion — and then you completely forget! I expect Ted has too. I don't think Caro will forget Rob quite so easily, though.'

'Nothing had . . . happened! I mean, to me then. Or with Caro.'

'No, I know it hadn't with you, and I don't believe it had with her.'

They were quiet for a moment, both

reflecting upon the past.

Clare said: 'I think he only had an affair with me later because he couldn't get anywhere with you.'

She spoke quite calmly. Ruth stared at her.

'*You* only had eyes for Jack. *I* was in love with Ted!' said Clare, 'For ages I couldn't forgive you because it was you he really wanted.'

'I just don't believe it! I mean, I guessed about you and him, but it didn't seem to have any connection with *me*.'

'You are a good woman, Ruth. I find that hard to forgive, too.'

'Well, you trusted me enough to ask me to look after the girls in the war. We were very grateful for the money, you know that.'

'Yes, and I'm still grateful for what you did. Pettiwell was the best place for them.'

'You never could bear to live in the country.'

They had both withdrawn for the time being from recriminations.

'No, I couldn't — especially not at Pettiwell.'

'I don't think Mother or Father had the slightest idea that the son of their old bridge-player friends had ever known me; he wasn't the sort of man to tell his parents things, although he apparently told Sally he was once sweet on me!'

'Well, the Cozenses certainly didn't know anything about him and me,' said Clare briskly. 'Nobody has anything to worry about on that score, though I don't particularly want to see him again.'

Ruth said: 'If you come over to Pettiwell you're bound to see Rob.'

'I'd be interested to meet the Hon Janet's offspring,' said Clare.

Ruth poured them each another cup of coffee, and Clare went on: 'The war brought me — and Francis — to life again. I decided to be selfish and do my own thing — like a man does. I can't say I regret it.'

'How *is* Francis?'

'Enjoying his work, I expect, and probably enjoying all the pretty young students around him. I'm still grateful to him, you know.'

'Francis isn't a — a skirt-chaser?'

'No, just a middle-aged man. I don't think he minds that I don't want to live with him any longer, and I'd rather live here than in Paris. We haven't quarrelled.'

'The girls would like you to get together again, I'm sure,' said Ruth.

'Doubtless. Perhaps we will one day. There's nobody else. I'm busy with my work and my book. At forty-nine it appears I don't feel the need for a man, though Francis is a good husband. I miss that side of it a bit, though it's a long time since we had a peaceful domestic life together. Perhaps I'll feel different if he ever really needs me.'

Ruth began: 'I've never asked you this but — '

Clare cut her short. 'Well, don't ask.'

'Does Francis know — '

'Don't let's start all that up again. No. It's between me and my maker.'

'And your daughter!'

Clare looked uncomfortable. It was her turn to say: 'I'm sorry — I know I lack moral courage.'

Ruth was silent.

'Let's have a sandwich,' said Clare. 'They do quite good ham sandwiches here.'

'Yes, that would be nice,' said Ruth. They gestured over to the waiter, a man with a walrus moustache.

'He looks like a character from Dickens,' said Ruth when he had departed with the order.

'A lot round here reminds me of Dickens — Doughty Street's not far away.'

Ruth looked at her watch. 'I can get a train at half past three.'

'Haven't you any shopping?'

'No, I've done the Army and Navy and Robinson and Cleaver — I came up with the commuters.'

When they parted, each felt a sense of relief, although Ruth was still curious and Clare was not looking forward to seeing her elder daughter.

There was a lot of unfinished business.

★ ★ ★

Caroline had been working very hard. At first it had not stopped her feeling bitterly jealous of Sally, but as the month of May ended and June arrived, and then her sister's letter, she thought about Sally less. On the other hand she began to have bad dreams, which would wake her up suddenly in the middle of the night. She could never properly recall these nightmares when she woke up, knowing only that she felt angry about something, a feeling that stayed with her for part of the day. Perhaps she had been overdoing things — she had completed a great many designs for her college course and for the shop.

The dreams were not about Rob, she was sure. She thought they might be something to do with what Lily had written about their mother, which had led her to wonder if what Lady Page had done to her mother was the same as what Sally had done to her. She had pushed these questions away, and not reread the letter.

Not being able to remember what exactly Lily had written, to refresh her memory she had to dig down for the letter, which was buried under a pile of sketches and samples of material. She ought to have answered it, ought to have gone to see her mother too. The school had a break in July, and the department store did not need anything further sketched before August, when they would begin to gear up for winter, so she decided she would go for a week or two to Paris, perhaps get some new ideas, see her father anyway. She reread the letter.

. . . If anyone, it had been our mother who had been fond of him. Sally told Rob this and he said his dad had never mentioned Mother . . .

If Lily had by now asked their mother about the past she would certainly have told her about it. She had obviously had better things to do. Well, if Rob's father had never mentioned Clare to Rob, perhaps there was nothing to mention. Or perhaps there was *too much*. Otherwise, why should Aunt Ruth say her sister had been 'fond' of Mr Cozens? In Aunt Ruth's parlance 'fond' meant 'in love with'. Caroline was very sure about that. Why should Rob's father mention Aunt Ruth to his son? Because Ruth was Sally's mother and it was safe to mention *her*, that was why.

Caroline badly needed to talk to her mother. She felt the letter was connected in some strange way with the bad dreams. Whenever she had had bad dreams as a child at Pettiwell it had been Aunt Ruth who had comforted her, but maybe she had had nightmares when she was a very small child. Long before Lily was born.

For a day or two she decided to try to stop thinking about it, and booked a train and boat ticket to Paris which could be used at any time the following week. The old Newhaven-Dieppe crossing had just gone up from the eight pounds ten shillings it had cost for ages, but she had enough cash to buy a ticket with the money Margrove's had just paid her. She had just made up her mind to do this when a letter arrived from her mother. This was sufficiently unusual for her to read it carefully.

Dearest Caro,
I feel I have neglected you since we last spoke. I hope that you are 'getting over' Rob Cozens, if that is the right phrase. I do know how you feel. I have just seen your Aunt Ruth and heard about the young man

— and Sally — from the horse's mouth, so to speak. I have also heard from Pa who will be in Paris till the end of July and hopes you will see him before then. He thinks it would be a good idea for me to see you soon, before you go to France.

Could you come round here on Saturday and stay the night? Do give me a ring.

With love from your
Ma

Well! Her father thought it would be a good idea for her mother to see her, did he? This was the first time Caroline could remember her mother obeying such an implied directive from him. She had been putting it off for ages herself, and she really had better go and see her. Her mother did sound more sympathetic than usual. Had she perhaps come to the conclusion that she ought to have stayed with her daughters in the war and was going to ask their forgiveness? Unlikely. Had she decided to divorce Pa? Or he her? It must be that. Perhaps Ma needed comfort.

Seeing her mother from this unusual angle was a new experience for Caroline. She telephoned her at work that very afternoon, to say she would come and stay with her for a night the following Saturday. Clare, who never said much over the telephone, sounded both pleased and anxious.

That night Caroline had another most peculiar dream. It began with her feeling terribly happy and comfortable, with her mother kissing and stroking her. Then everything suddenly changed and she heard herself shouting: 'Go away! Go away!' shocking herself into wakefulness.

★   ★   ★

They had finished their lunch at the table in Clare's kitchen and moved into her small sitting-room to drink their coffee. So far nothing intimate had been said, both of them unsure how to begin. Then Caroline swallowed her tiny cup of coffee in one, put it down and plunged.

'Lily told me that you were once fond of Rob's father. Is it true?'

'Fond doesn't sound like one of your sister's words,' Clare replied drily.

'Well, Sally told Lil that her mother told her you were 'fond' of him!'

Clare was silent, drinking her own coffee slowly, peering down at it between sips.

Caroline went on: 'Did it happen to you

382

too? Ruth took him away from you — just like Sally has taken Rob from me?'

'Good heavens, no!' said her mother, looking startled. 'It wasn't Ruth who took him away — and anyway all that with her was before I got to know him. Men usually know what they want, and his feelings were the ones that counted. He was 'in love' with your aunt long before she married, but she was too busy chasing Jack Page to notice.'

'So you came on the scene afterwards?'

'I knew him slightly, and then got to know him better a few months later. He didn't love me; I thought he did. I certainly loved him. It was the year Ruth came out that he fell for her — I believed he was still hankering after her when I knew him.'

'In one way we are similar. Sally didn't really take Rob away from me, though in my case I knew him before she did. It was just that I was . . . mistaken about him.'

'You will get over it, I promise. However far things had gone between you and him. Just take care not to dash into another affair out of despair.'

'No!' said Caroline surprised. 'Then, if Ruth really had nothing to do with him — she knew *you*'d loved him — why was she so odd when she saw that *I* knew him? She didn't mind him getting all hot and bothered about Sally!'

'I got to know Ted Cozens in early 1927, and — '

Caroline suddenly cut her short:

'Was he my father? Did Pa marry you to save your reputation?'

'No, it wasn't like that at all!'

'That *was* the reason. She thought Rob and I might be related?'

'Precisely. Your aunt *imagined* he might be your father.'

'She thought you'd committed adultery?'

Clare did not reply to that, but said firmly, 'Ted Cozens was *not* your father. Your Aunt Ruth thought he might be. You are in no way related to Rob — who, I now hear, wants to marry your cousin. There was no secret reason why you and he shouldn't have loved each other. My sister now knows that.'

'Oh, he'll marry Sally,' said Caroline, thinking on her own lines. She looked pale.

'How are you really, Caro? When are you going over to France? Pa does want to see you ... ' Clare hesitated, seemed about to add something but did not.

'Next week. I shall get my results for advanced pattern-cutting from the trade school on Monday and whilst I'm over there I shall try to get a semi-permanent placement doing something lowly again with a big house. One of the tutors at the school knows someone at Dior. I can at least try, now that I can cut my own *toiles*!'

'You'll have to come back to settle all your stuff though, won't you? When would you like to start over there?'

'If I can get a job, I'll go whenever they want. I'd prefer autumn, to give me a break, but I can still go on sketching things for Margrove's — not at the French collections yet, but just putting down my ideas of what's in the air. I'm not going to stay over there for ever, Ma. I just want to be able to say I've worked for a good house as a seamstress and then I shall start making stuff for my own shop one day in London.'

Her enthusiasm belied her facial expression. She looked tired, and Clare was still worried. However little her affair with the Cozens boy had progressed, Caroline must have been feeling fairly wretched but was too proud to say so.

'I'll give you ten years to be famous!' said her mother. 'Promise you'll come and see me before you go back in autumn — you must get some roses in your cheeks. We could go and take a little break together somewhere if you like. Have you not been sleeping well?'

'I keep getting bad dreams,' said her daughter. 'Did I dream a lot when I was very young, Ma? I can't remember what my dreams are about, but I know I feel very angry with someone. They are more like nightmares.'

'Is it me you are angry with, do you think?'

'I don't know!'

'You used to get very angry with me,' said Clare. 'When you were a toddler — but all toddlers hate their mothers at times!'

They went to the cinema later that afternoon and both enjoyed a new Italian film. It was a long time since Caroline had felt so close to her mother. On Sunday morning when they had breakfasted and she had gone out for the paper, and enjoyed some more coffee, she found she was quite sorry to leave.

'I'll see you again in a week or two, I promise,' she said when she left.

Clare sat staring before her when her daughter had gone. She had still not found the moral courage to do what Francis had begged her to do. He would find out that she hadn't and she knew he would then deal with it himself.

★   ★   ★

Caro enjoyed her train-and-boat odyssey to Dieppe. However many times she made the

386

journey she always found it a sort of odyssey. You noticed so many different kinds of people and it was amusing to guess their nationality from their dress. It was comforting to find the big train waiting in Dieppe, always on time and, like all French trains, higher and harder to get on from the platform than the trains of England's Southern Region that looked like little green caterpillars. Through Normandy now and eventually the Seine-et-Oise department — and finally Paris St Lazare. She asked herself, as she always did on arrival in the land of fresh bread and delicious coffee and formal manners, why she had chosen to live in England. Because she had a feeling there would be less competition in the field of fashion in London than in Paris was the reason. No Chanel across the Channel! She smiled at her own pun.

Her father knew she would arrive some time that evening and had said he had a room with a bed for her: no need to go anywhere else. In Paris she decided to take a taxi to the *sixième* to her father's flat on boulevard St Germain, but first she would sit down at the station and have a coffee and brioche and acclimatize herself.

★　★　★

Jennie had decided to go home to Pettiwell for two or three weeks' holiday. She had asked Francis to write to her and he had done so, a letter she might one day treasure. He also asked her if she would come to say goodbye before she went back. She did not want to do that; her asking him to write had been a way of putting an end to this thing he apparently had for her, but she thought she might as well call in to see him for an hour or so. She wrote to tell him she would be there at about five o'clock the following afternoon. That would give him time to telephone her if it was inconvenient, which she half-hoped it was. He did not telephone next morning so she spent the afternoon walking around the quarter.

She walked to the Odeon from the Place St-Sulpice. First she went to the church, trying to locate a Delacroix painting. It was supposed to be there but she could not find it; it must have been in one of the side chapels she had not explored. It was time to go. She'd have to come back after her holiday.

Just as she arrived on the pavement in front of the house in which was Francis's apartment, the outer door of the building opened and out rushed Caroline Fitzpatrick.

'Caro!'

Caroline stopped in her headlong rush.

'What are *you* doing here?' she cried. 'I've had enough!'

'Come to say goodbye to your father. When did you arrive?'

'Yesterday night.' She looked distraught, as if she had decided to leave in a hurry.

'What's the matter?'

'I want some fags, but I had to get out — I can't tell you . . . '

She stopped and the door that had shut behind her opened again. There stood her father, apparently out of breath.

He took in Jennie's presence immediately, said 'Hello Jennie,' and then: 'Both of you go back in. I'll get you some cigarettes, Caro. Calm down. Go on up. Jennie's here now. Caro — go back, please.'

What on earth was the matter with them both? Caroline looked suddenly limp. Jennie took charge.

'We can go up in the lift. Come on, I'll make you a cup of tea.'

What a silly thing to say! She knew Caro didn't like tea. And when had she arrived in Paris? Had Francis not got her letter? He wouldn't want *her* there with Caro!

She took her friend by the arm but Caro shrugged her off.

'All right, I'll go back in. I've had a shock,' she muttered to Jennie, but followed her meekly. The lift came down; they went up in it, got out, and went through the door of the flat, which Francis had uncharacteristically left open.

Caro said: 'Have you been seeing a lot of him?'

Jennie had dreaded Caro discovering her father's feelings for her and instinctively made light of it.

'He took me for a nice lunch and I just came round to say goodbye; I'm going home the day after tomorrow. Let's sit down, Caro.' She looked more closely at her. She had been crying, you could tell — her face, usually so well made-up, was tear-streaked. She must have suffered more than Lily had let on over that boyfriend of hers.

She offered her a cigarette, which Caroline took, lit shakily then inhaled greedily.

Then Caroline looked at her and said:

'Don't fool me — I know you've been having an affair with him. Sally's taken Rob away from me and now you've probably taken Pa!'

Tears began to roll down her cheeks though she was still trying to smoke through her distress.

Jennie, alarmed, said: 'Caro, I am not having an affair with your father! I know about Sally — Lily wrote — and I'm sorry, but for God's sake tell me what I can do for you.'

'Nobody can do anything. *He*'ll tell you when he comes back — it's awful, terrible!' She became calmer when Jennie gave her a handkerchief.

'Where is the kitchen?' asked Jennie.

'You can't make tea, he doesn't have a kettle. They don't have such things in Paris — didn't you know!' She began to laugh in a silly way. Was she about to become hysterical? Well, if Jennie had forgotten where the kitchen was, it didn't look as if she knew her way around a lover's flat, and that was a relief.

Jennie said: 'A few weeks ago I said goodbye to a man I was mad about — truly — so you're not the only one . . . '

Caroline looked at her, said nothing at first and then said in a very small voice:

'It's much worse than that.'

Was she pregnant? They heard the door being opened and Francis came in, tossed his daughter a pack of Gitanes, took out another new pack, offered it to Jennie, who refused one, took one for himself and then sat down in another chair. He appeared to be

391

contemplating them both. They sat in silence. Jennie broke it saying:

'I only came to say *au revoir*. I'm off home the day after tomorrow . . . '

Whatever this was all about, they didn't need her.

'No, Jennie — stay,' said Caroline. 'He'll make us a cup of coffee.'

To her father she said: 'I do want to talk about it. She might as well be the first to know — outside the family I mean!'

Jennie said: 'Let me make you both one.'

Francis did not answer at first but got up, and went into what she now remembered was the kitchen.

'I have a *cafetière* ready,' he said, 'If you don't mind my boiling it up?'

Whilst he was in the kitchen Caroline turned to Jennie and said, as if she was remarking about vagaries of the weather:

'He's not my father, you know. Pa is not my father, not my dad as they say in England.' She bent her head. Jennie's eyes widened. She did not usually like to register surprise especially if people wanted her to do so but this was not like that. She was stunned, said stupidly:

'What do you mean?'

'What I say. He's not my — what do you say — biological father. He married Ma and brought me up — and everything — but he's not my father.'

Jennie thought for a moment before saying: 'If he brought you up and loved you he *is* your father!'

'No. He's Lily's father but not mine!'

Francis came out of the kitchen with a tray, a *cafetière* and three square white cups. He set it on a small table and carefully poured out three cups of coffee, but Jennie noticed that his hand was trembling slightly. Then he sat down, and handed a cup to each young woman.

'I'm glad you're here, Jennie,' he said. 'Caro's had a shock.'

'I know.'

Francis went on: 'Her mother told her some of it — that she wasn't the child of a man called Ted Cozens.'

Jennie started at hearing that name.

'She didn't tell her that I married her two and a half years after little Caro was born.'

He took Caro's hand. 'Of course you are my daughter — in every way that matters,' he said softly. He turned to Jennie and said:

'Her mother found herself unable to tell her. She knew she ought to have done so before. Caro is a grown woman now and she had to know.'

'He won't tell me who my father is!' Addressing herself to Jennie, Caroline sounded about three years old.

Francis looked extremely sad, dropped her hand and said:

'That is for your mother to say.' Jennie thought, perhaps he doesn't know!

'You've had to do the dirty work. Poor Pa!' said Caroline.

Jennie wondered how long the two had been talking before Caroline had rushed out. When exactly had he told her all this? Poor man indeed.

'How would you feel, Jennie Wilson, if your father told you he wasn't your father at all?' asked Caroline.

Jennie said: 'As a matter of fact, when I was a little girl I used to imagine that my real father was an aristocrat — some earl or duke who'd been staying where my mother was working. I wasn't really serious, I suppose, but if I now discovered that that was true I hope it wouldn't make me feel any differently about the dear man who brought me up! I would naturally be very upset.'

'It's a wise child,' said Caroline weakly. Then, turning to Francis: 'Couldn't you have told me in a letter — or through a solicitor or something?'

'That would have been cowardly,' said Francis.

'Well, Ma was a coward anyway — leaving it all to you.'

Jennie thought, so if he isn't Caro's father, need I have been so worried he might seduce me? If only she could escape all this and find Miguel waiting for her down on the boulevard.

But he had gone away.

They were having to grow up, she and Caro.

When Francis went out for a moment after this, Caro said, as though it all needed further explanation:

'When I arrived Pa asked, had I seen my mother? And when I said yes, he said, what did she tell you? I told him — that Rob's father was certainly not mine. Then Pa asked me if she'd said anything else and I answered: No. Why? And he said: 'I'm not your father either, darling!' ' Her voice broke on those words. Then she rallied and went on: 'I know he fancies *you*, Jennie! I can tell *that*, whether he's my father or not!'

'Why do you think that?' Jennie asked, fearing that if she ever admitted that Francis had been even a tiny bit attracted to her, Caro would have cause to feel more jealousy and start crying again.

'He *loves* you Caro. You aren't a victim,' she said earnestly. 'It was — is — your mother's problem. Nobody is going to abandon you!'

She was sure of that.

'Ma insisted I came to see Pa. She said he wanted to speak to me. I'd asked her if Rob's father was the same as mine — I told you that — but it was why Aunt Ruth was so funny about him. She thought we might be brother and sister! We aren't. Then who is my father? I've got to know!'

'Are you going back to England to ask her? — It must have been awkward for him too — awful, really. Will you tell Lily?'

'No, he will. It won't make any difference to *her*. You know, Jennie, your mother practically brought mine up, didn't she? Do you think *she* knows? Pa says nobody knows. Do you think it really was Rob's dad — and Ma's lying to us all? I just feel disgusted.'

Jennie was looking out of the window. The evening was golden. How she loved Paris. She said:

'Caro, did you hear about your exam results — at that fashion school?'

'Yes. I passed highest,' said Caroline sounding unconcerned.

'Have you told your father?' Jennie stressed the last word.

'Yes. He's thrilled!'

'Then he must take you on holiday — give you a treat. You've had a rotten time, but you're going to be a great designer. I just *know* that.'

'At the moment I just feel like rushing off and having a mad affair — like *she* probably had. You know, I bet Pa fancies you!' she added.

'Don't be silly, Caro . . .'

The last thing *she* could have done after the man she loved went away would have been to be interested in another man. But maybe you got used to sex. She guessed that if the Cozens man was not Caro's father there must have been someone her mother had turned to? Why? Because the Cozens man had rejected her? Perhaps Clare was not so different from her daughter. Had it just been bad luck that she'd become pregnant?

'Caro,' she said, 'does it matter who your father was? It's just a good thing *you* were born!'

Caro gave a watery smile and replied:

'I was telling Pa that I shall go straight back to London — have it out with Ma — and then come back here and try to find a job at Dorinel's or somewhere!'

'Well, have you an interview lined up? I always find work is the only thing to do if

I'm upset.' She sounded to herself like a grandma — not that she'd ever known either of her grandmothers. 'Sorry to be sententious,' she said now. 'I can wait a day or two and we could go back together. My ticket has no reservation. Would that suit you?'

Francis came in as she was speaking.

'I telephoned your friend who knows the couturier,' he said to Caroline. 'They'll see you tomorrow. Better get it all over!'

★ ★ ★

Caroline did have her interview the following day, expedited by Francis. She scarcely knew what she was saying but showed them the samples of her work which she'd packed at the bottom of her suitcase.

Yes, they would take her on in the autumn!

She and Jennie returned two days later to England, Jennie to Pettiwell, Caroline to her mother.

On the boat, Jennie said:

'What you said about your Pa. If you thought he had a thing for me, you wouldn't mention it to anyone else, would you? With the parents I have, they'd be terribly worried if they thought I had been having an affair with *anyone*, even if it isn't true. And even if

398

it had been with Miguel — the man I told you about. I just have to be careful. I shall one day of course . . . I mean . . . have a love affair. But I don't want to hurt them. Don't mention it to Lily either . . .'

'No. She's a gossip. But I trust you, Jen. As my mother has said many times: *You can't help falling in love with the wrong person*, so you can't help who falls in love with you. Pa is so handsome and clever and nice. He'll find another woman if Ma doesn't want him. Did she make a mess of her life, do you think?'

'You told me she's working — writing. And Francis is enjoying his work in Paris. You know, Caro, I think I'm going to give up the challenge for a time!'

'What challenge?'

'The challenge of romantic idealism: those were my friend Miguel's words. Now I know about your father I don't feel so bad about the fact that he was attracted to me — I didn't respond, but I wouldn't like to shatter my mother's idea of a real gent!'

'You are the apple of your parents' eye,' said Caroline.

'I'm obliged to them both,' said Jennie. 'I just don't want to act like 'a guilty thing surprised' if someone mentions the name of Francis Fitzgerald or anyone else in future.'

'I'll keep your counsel,' said her friend, 'if you'll keep mine.'

'And you'll get on even better with Francis and your mother now,' said Jennie. They were in the bar of the Canterbury packet drinking blanc de blancs.

'It must be the wine,' she said, 'making me feel so optimistic!'

* * *

'I've got to see Ma straight away — I'm dreading it,' Caroline said, when they got off the boat train at Victoria. Jennie was preparing to cross the station to get a more local train.

'Get it over, Caro, and then have a holiday. Why not come to Pettiwell?' she suggested.

'I don't think I could bear seeing the lovebirds at present. You can report to me. Tell me what you think of him, Jennie. I'll probably be back in France before you . . . '

'Well, we'll both be there by September.'

'Thank you for being there,' said Caroline. 'I'll never forget that afternoon.'

She turned, waved goodbye and was off to the Underground.

She was putting a brave face on it, thought Jennie. She was a brave person, but it would take a long time to get over the shock that the father of your childhood was not your father, and to adapt to that fact. Jennie herself felt bruised, and didn't envy her friend's forthcoming confrontation with her mother. Now she understood one or two of the more mysterious pronouncements of Francis Fitzpatrick. She sympathized too with his wife. Who would not avoid telling a daughter that sort of truth? Yet she should have told Caro when she was a little girl, let her grow up with the idea, and then she would just have taken it for granted. And even now Caro did not know who her real father was!

As Jennie got on the train to go home — though 'home' would not for ever be Pettiwell — she half-looked forward to being welcomed joyfully by her mother. She would not mention Miguel to either of her parents. She had told Caro, but that was to comfort her as a sort of fellow sufferer. Miguel would be something she would keep to herself.

14

As he had promised Caroline, Francis telephoned his wife to tell her he had spoken to her daughter. He had always thought of Caro as his daughter, too. Her knowing now that, strictly speaking, she was not, changed nothing for him. It would be bound to change something for her, but he hoped it would all work itself out so that things could be, if not the same, not too different from formerly. He had a fairly sanguine temperament, which had stood him in good stead in the war and had been a calming influence on Clare in the past, but he admitted to himself that his daughter's shock had been hard to bear. He had so much wanted to see Jennie again that day; his unflappability did not extend as far as love, but he knew that he had been self-indulgent and must desist from any further attempts to capture her.

Caroline went straight to her mother's flat. There would be time for packing up and sorting out other aspects of her existence later. She was self-conscious enough to ask how she was going to play this scene with her female parent.

In the event Clare was at the door as soon as Caroline rang the bell of her flat. This was unlike her, and she looked nervous. Caroline had decided to play it cool, as the Yanks were wont to say. When she actually stood there, holding her suitcase in the tiny hall, nothing seemed at first to have changed since their pleasant Sunday morning together ten days ago.

'Come along in. I was just going to make tea,' said Clare. 'Pa rang to tell me what time you'd be here. I'll pay your taxi.'

'I took a tube and then a bus,' said Caroline, putting down the case and going into the kitchen. Should she have burst into the flat demanding the name of her father?

'He told me your wonderful test — and term — results. I'm thrilled,' said her mother.

'Has Lily got hers yet?'

'Not till the middle of next month — I had a card from the Lakes.'

It was not till they were both sitting at the table with tea and a plate of scones, for which Caroline found she had quite an appetite, not having had much to eat on the way, that she said:

'Well then, Ma, who is — was — my Dad?' Trying to sound as light-hearted as possible.

'He's dead. He was a man called Peter Cross — he was killed by a bomb in the war.'

'Peter Cross?'

'Yes. He was a friend of Ted Cozens. Not a close friend. It was Ted who introduced me to him.' *Passed me on to him*, she thought.

'Was he a painter?'

'No. He thought he wanted to be for a time but he ended up as an accountant.'

'So any artistic talents I might have don't come from my father but from you?'

Caroline did not ask: why did you not tell me all this before, and Clare did not tell her that she had never been in love with this man, that it was an accident, that he had speedily departed from her life the minute she told him she might be expecting his child. She'd have to say something, though. Cross had meant nothing to her. It was Edward Cozens she had still loved. How jealous she had been of poor Ruth, who had no idea of her feelings. Did Caro feel the same about Sally? It wasn't Ruth's daughter's fault either.

'He was about three years older than me. Like Ted Cozens, he'd just missed being in the war by a year or two.'

'Was it on the rebound for you?'

A bounder on the rebound, indeed, thought her mother.

'Yes. It was in early February 1928, in Paris, and I was lonely, I suppose.'

Let her daughter think she'd loved Peter Cross.

'I went back to England to have you, and we . . . lost touch, but I found out later that he'd gone back to England eventually and disappeared in London. By that time I had decided to go back to Paris.'

Their paths in London had never crossed except once. She had never seen him again. Most of that early time with the little baby she had been helped by Polly Hicks. She hoped she had succeeded in softening the stark details of her rather sordid affair with, or rather seduction by, Peter Cross. She had not exactly excused herself, nor introduced mitigating evidence. That would have been dishonest; she had just tried to give the impression of a headstrong young woman who had been let down by one man she loved, and perhaps exploited by another. Which was true. Caroline must draw her own conclusions. She could not tell her daughter that Peter Cross had meant nothing more to her than the partner in a short lustful episode.

'So then you met Pa in Paris?'

'Yes. He'd been at the Beaux Arts, and I'd known him a bit before, but not well. Then, when I went back there I found I couldn't go on painting. My grandmother had given me an allowance . . . '

'To stay away?'

'No, not really. It paid for me to go on painting if I wanted and for help with looking after a baby. It was mainly that she felt I'd be less bothered by silly questions if I stayed away a bit. Of course, after I got married I could have come back and everyone would have thought you were Francis's baby anyway. I didn't marry him till you were nearly three. I was too proud. I thought he was just being noble. He was very quixotic. I had a lot of help looking after you from a young Russian woman my grandmother, Christina Ogilvie, found for me. Ludmilla came every day, but at night it was just you and me.'

'Poor Ma!'

Clare ought to have told her all this long ago, Caroline thought. Her mother had shown physical courage, in the war for example, but had perhaps not had enough moral courage.

'How much do you remember from before you were three? They say children don't remember much from that time but you were an early talker, so perhaps you do?'

'I think I do remember being very cross — perhaps that was like the dreams I've been having — feeling angry. I told you . . . '

'It was when Francis began to come round a lot that you were angry. You'd had me all to yourself after my nursemaid had had to emigrate to the States with her parents. You were very angry with Francis — you once bit him! Really, you were angry with me, I suppose, for 'betraying' you with him. You and I had been very close.'

'In the dreams, at first, I was on your lap and you were stroking me and I was kissing you and feeling very happy. Then I was screaming.'

I never imagined, she thought, till Pa told me, that Ma had not been married when I was born. I bet Jennie would have suspected and done some research.

'I suppose if I'd looked up your marriage certificate I'd have found out the truth,' she said.

'Yes — you were born at the end of November in 1928 when I was twenty-five. I married Francis in the autumn of 1931. I took a bit of persuading, didn't want it to look as if I'd been 'saved' — or for him to think that!'

Had she ever been in love with Francis? Caroline wondered. Ma had never known her own mother as a child, so maybe that was why she fell in love with one man who didn't love her, had an affair with another who certainly didn't, and married the one who did! Pa *did* 'save' her — why can't she go back to him now? She likes being alone, she thought . . . and whatever he says, and even if he has infatuations for young women, Pa would be quite happy if she moved back to Paris with him.

'How did you come to know he'd been killed in the last war?'

'That was extraordinary. I was driving ambulances — it was in '43, and there'd been a direct hit on an office in the City. The nameplate was blown on to the pavement, still intact. Nobody was injured — they were all killed, so the ambulance wasn't needed. They'd dig out the bodies later. It was a firm of accountants and I looked at it and one of the names was his. I looked up the death later to see if he had been working there, and it was true. He had been killed.'

My seducer, she thought. I didn't even like him. I love Caro though.

'What a life you've had, Ma!' Then another thought occurred to Caroline. Had she brothers and sisters she'd never seen? She would not say anything to her mother about that idea.

'I never told anyone, not even Francis, who your father was, I thought that best. I wanted to start afresh.' And Peter Cross wouldn't

408

have wanted to know, would probably have denied it.

Let Caro think she'd loved him, but he'd been a cad.

All Caroline said after this long talk was, 'Thank you for telling me.'

★   ★   ★

Clare was anxious lest Caroline might have some sort of a nervous breakdown, but she was apparently made of sterner stuff and did not collapse. After the revelations, Caroline admired her putative father Francis Fitzgerald even more and did her best — tactfully — to persuade her mother to rejoin him. The hints fell on deaf ears but Caroline did not give up hope.

Clare rented a cottage for two weeks in Suffolk and wanted her daughter to stay with her for a rest. One day she might, said Caro, but not yet. It was a truce, but not an armed one. Caroline realized that she was not going to be told anything further; bits of her mother's past might slowly reassemble themselves for her. Her mother had implied that if she wished to pursue her real father's family it was up to her.

Caroline did not. What she intended to do was pack up her belongings soon and move for the time being to Paris. Clare had to resign herself to this. After all, her daughter was a grown woman; there had been no quarrel after she had put her cards on the table, but it would take some time for their relationship to reach a new level. She hoped it would improve and one day she would know that Caro had forgiven her, without the need to say so.

Caroline said that Lily might have the Pimlico bed-sit for the time being, for Lily was to live in London, having been offered a definite place to study at the Royal College of Music. She had received distinctions in all her music A levels, both for theory and practice, and both her mother and father were delighted.

★ ★ ★

It was August and Jennie was still in Pettiwell. From all the fields around the harvest would soon be gathered in, after an averagely mediocre summer. For once Jennie did not hanker after the warm south.

Caroline wrote telling her she now 'knew all there was to know' about her real — or rather, she added, 'unreal' — father, and that he had died in the war. She did not go into any details, and most of the rest of her letter

410

was about her new hobby, photography. 'It's useful for anyone who wants to be big one day in fashion to know how to photograph their own stuff and to find the right background.' She sounded enthusiastic.

She added: 'By the way, I know nothing happened but I have kept counsel over Pa!'

He had apparently mentioned Jennie in the letter she had just received from him. I wish he wouldn't mention me, thought Jennie. She was bound to see him again when she returned to Paris and was determined to keep it all on a purely friendly footing, or be obliged to refuse his invitations. She realized that Caro and her mother probably thought that like many middle-aged men he had a weakness for young women. It hadn't been quite like that. She had seen something else in his eyes, but she kept her own counsel.

Caroline had also very much wanted to know what Jennie thought of Rob Cozens, and Jennie considered this carefully before she replied. She had indeed observed Rob Cozens and Sally. Sally's 'young man', as her mother called him, stayed over at his grandparents every weekend, departing to London late on Sunday night. He had bought a sports car — Jennie wondered where the money came from — and spent as much time with Sally as he could, driving to the stables every Saturday morning. After she had finished her job there he took her out to lunch at a pub or hotel in one of the many picturesque villages around Pettiwell.

He was indeed a fine figure of a man and extremely good-looking: tall, with regular features, a straight nose, blue eyes, full mouth, thick light-brown wavy hair. She could understand what Caroline had seen in him superficially. After all, Caro herself was tall and slim and what you might call striking. He was pleasant and friendly, intelligent, but no intellectual. Jennie had been introduced to him on the evening of her first Saturday back at home, when the talk had at first been of buying farms and land and she had realized that Sally's swain wanted to leave London and settle down as a farmer in Kent.

They had eventually got round to discussing something other than pasture and acreage and horses when the conversation had turned to what was on at the local cinema. A few people had bought a television set but most people still went weekly to the cinema. There was still no television set at Pettiwell.

Jennie mentioned one or two old films she'd recently seen in Paris.

'I did see that Italian one,' he had said. 'Couldn't make much of it — no plot, really.'

She was convinced that Caro had taken

him to see that particular film in London. Caro might not be an intellectual but she had taste, and she was cleverer than this man, who Jennie decided was a bit of a Philistine. She supposed he had what her parents had called 'It', and what people had begun to call sex appeal. Not that she found him attractive in that way herself, but then she never liked the men most women did. Francis Fitz certainly had sex appeal, and for her Miguel had had it too, as well as much more. She must write back tactfully to Caroline. She knew better than to cast aspersions that might reflect on a friend's taste, even if it were for an ex, a man who had let her down.

She was enjoying the slower pace of life here after the dash and rush of Paris, and even relished sitting in the back courtyard wearing an old apron of her mother's and shelling peas. Polly would be sixty-five next summer but was still as active as ever. Her father, a little younger, had slowed down a bit but spent a lot of time that summer driving Sir Jack around. Sir Jack, though only just over sixty, had more problems with his eyesight. Young James Page, now in the sixth form of his public school was home on holiday and got on well with Rob Cozens. He was soon to go off on a school trip, walking and climbing in Scotland.

For the time being Jennie was glad to stay and potter, as long as she had plenty to read. Her more scholarly research could wait a week or two; by September she might be impatient to get on with it.

She went for solitary walks. Her friend Joan was away and would be getting married next year. Having asked permission from Lady Page, Jennie went up one afternoon to the old attics and explored the top corridor of the main part of the house. She found it all less magical than in the past, but discovered a room behind the 'secret door' which she had never before entered. It was stacked with old paintings — still lifes and watercolour landscapes, some signed 'FF', some 'CO'. He must have had them all sent from Paris just before the war. Had their owners forgotten they were there? How long had the paintings been in the attic? Fifteen years? It was a lifetime, more like fifty years than fifteen, thought Jennie.

She remembered a book she had read in Paris. Your feelings about the duration of time were relative sometimes to your age, or to the intensity of your experiences. Childhood lasted for ever for everyone Her time with Miguel in Paris now seemed extensive, and yet she had known him only a few months. What she longed for were feelings and experiences that were intense — but also 'for ever'. You got a glimpse of them occasionally when you were not looking for them, but up here in the attics life seemed sad; the direction of so many lives had changed.

Change *was* necessary, she supposed, especially if you were young. Mother had said only the other day how she hated change. Maybe only the young were really able to look forward to it and savour it. Looking out from a rather smeary small window at the top of the house Jennie thought, I have always been a bit nostalgic. I hope people don't think I'm old for my age. Francis hadn't, and Miguel had teased her about her youth. Men seemed to like you young!

A new future was implicit in Sally and Rob Cozens, Jennie felt sure of that. Having seen them together she knew Sally had found the right man for her. Oh dear, she must reply soon to Caroline.

The night after her foray into the past of the old attics, she was woken by light from the full moon shining into her little bedroom which overlooked the back of the house, and then over fields and trees to the old pond. She crept to the window, drew the curtains right back, and looked at her watch in the moonlight. The light was almost supernatural in its power.

Three o'clock — the time they said most people died. Jennie had seen harvest moons before, low on the horizon of the sky like a sun, dark orange, almost menacing, but the moon tonight was different. It was low in the sky and it looked *too big*. Everything was silent with an unearthly stillness, and over everything silver was poured, over the earth, from an enormous orb, casting an eerie sheen on the trees and the fields. The silence, the silver, the stillness of this satellite that looked as large as any sun and was even in the part of the sky where the familiar sun usually set, was awesome! The moonlight itself was so splendid, so unexpected, truly an unearthly vision, bright as a prolonged camera flash. She thought she had never seen anything so beautiful that was also a little frightening. It would disappear, and change, and she wanted it to stay for ever. If only she had a camera in her hand to catch it. If only she could paint. Words were useless to convey what gave the weirdest impression of being the 'light that never was on land or sea'. This would be a good backdrop for one of Caro's creations — a gold ball-dress in the silver moonlight? Or perhaps one of midnight blue.

No lights were on; not a soul but she was awake. This scene was a personal consolation for waking in the night with thoughts of

Miguel in her head, and it was the same moon — worn poetic thought — that lit Miguel far away. Nonetheless, the moon one day would not only change, but be consumed, as would our earth if the scientists were right. She shivered, drew the curtains again, went back to bed and turned on her side to search for sleep.

... Robert is as you said a very good-looking man and I can see why you loved him. I think though that he wants the sort of girl who doesn't want a career, even if she would help him with his own job — as well as running a household, of course. That's just my impression. Do I mean Sally might become a sort of secretary to him in legal or City work? NO! The latest news is that he wants to leave London, settle in the country and buy a farm! (with horses I expect). My father says that all the new farmers will be business-men; agriculture had subsidies in the war but Dad feels sure this is about to change and that the land will become a business. My father is usually right. Rob seems to me the sort of man who would be good at a medium-sized business. There is the question of capital, you will say, being harder-headed than me in these things but

*I suspect that Cozens père has plenty of
that — or his mother has . . .*

She wanted to say, you have made a lucky
escape, but thought better of it. Caro would
come to her own conclusions. She was more
and more convinced that Rob would not have
been the right man for Caro. She'd add in her
letter that he was intelligent and pleasant and
kind, without overdoing his qualities in case
Caroline regretted them too much. It was
clear that Rob and Sally were seriously
courting and that an engagement would
obviously soon come to pass. How could she
palliate that fact? Perhaps Caro had never
thought of marriage but of a great love affair.
Rob Cozens was the marrying kind, and had
found his future wife.
She went on:

*I was — am — very fond of Sally, as you
know, and she is really good at her own
job. She and Rob have a lot in common.
They both adore country life.*

Actually Sally looked radiant and was
dreaming of her wedding. She herself, and
Caro, would not have it so easy; the kind of
marriage that would be right for Sally would
not suit either of them. If she, or Caro, ever

418

did marry it would be after a lot more experience of men!

She had done her best. She posted off her letter. Caro would soon be back in France.

The following week there was great excitement. Rob *had* proposed and Sally *had* accepted. Jennie congratulated Sally very sincerely, and Sally hugged her impulsively and said how glad she was that her old friend was there to share her happiness. Sally did not mention Caroline, so neither did Jennie. She guessed Ruth had telephoned her sister with the news.

The engagement ring was to be a bought one! Rather disappointing. Jennie had imagined some family heirloom would change hands. Rob's parents and grandparents had been told the good news — the former had only met Sally once on a flying visit to London by the young couple. Sir Jack and his wife were to entertain them all for drinks on the Sunday when they would come over from Stair Court. Jennie knew her mother's help would doubtless be needed but the Wilsons would not be guests at this essentially private meeting, quite apart from old Mrs Cozens's firm conviction that staff, though useful, were not to be indulged with familiarity. Sally had asked her, but not her parents, to come and have a drink with them but Jennie had declined.

'It's just the two families,' she said.

'Is it because of Caro?' Sally asked, mentioning their friend at last and looking genuinely upset.

'No, of course not, Sal. I hope you'll invite all of us to your wedding!'

Sally had looked perhaps a little relieved. It was strain enough being polite to her mother-in-law-to-be, the Hon Janet.

The day before, Jennie had helped polish the silver in the housekeeper's room, and helped to bring out the best crystal from the one-time butler's cupboards. She would keep well out of the way.

On Sunday morning she observed the guests' arrival from her bedroom window. An unfamiliar car drew up by the stables, followed by Rob's little red sports car. She peered at Rob's parents: a tall, silver-haired man with an equally tall, athletic-looking wife. Nadine, dressed in a brocade coat, and wearing high heels and a pillbox hat in the latest style on her blonde head, got out of her brother's car. She looked almost unrecognizable. Jennie thought, Caro would not have got on with these people. She would hear about it all later from her mother who was to serve the drinks and hand round the tiny vol-au-vents she had cooked herself. Jennie knew that

Lady Page was extremely grateful to her. Would Edward Cozens remember Ruth's chaperone from all those years and years ago? What would he say to Ruth Page, whom, according to Caro, he had once worshipped? When would the Great Day be? She had the impression that the future groom was very impatient to get the wedding over. Sally on the other hand was, as she confided later to Jennie, determined to make the most of it all and planned it for June of the following year.

Jennie felt glad she was not Sally and found she was looking forward to returning to Paris at least until Christmas. Then she might return to Manchester and continue her research.

★ ★ ★

The engagement party seemed to have loosened her mother's tongue. Everyone, according to Ruth Page, had complimented her on her 'cook'; Mr Cozens senior had looked very frail; Rob's father was very handsome, his mother a bit frosty, but it had gone off well and they had been invited to a reception at Stair Court next month. The wedding would probably be here at Pettiwell next summer, once Rob had been bought a farm by his parents as wedding present.

Jennie had sometimes wondered what families were for. They were needed when you were very young, and when you were very old. What about in between? It now seemed they presided over love-matches.

'Gracious me,' she said one afternoon later that week over a cup of tea in the housekeeper's room, 'why can't Rob and Sally just dash off to the register office, tie the knot and buy a little house with a paddock for a horse?'

'They're not all like you and your father,' said Polly. 'They're very family-minded.'

'Well, I like *my* family,' replied her daughter, 'but I would not like all this fuss!'

'In-laws are in-laws,' said her mother. 'That's what families are for, making a fuss of their children and seeing them settled — if they're lucky.'

'You wouldn't want me to settle down yet Mother, surely?'

'Well, you're different — got to make your way. I wish there was more we could do for you. I shall always be your mother and I ask myself, am I needed, or am I superfluous? What can I do for you — except be there as a support?'

'You've done so much for me, Mother — it's your turn now! I'm grown up. I want your life to be easier.'

'It's true you've never been a worry to me, but a mother should always be a refuge. Miss Clare and Miss Ruth's mother was never that. I learned I ought to act better than that. Miss Ruth — Lady Page — is doing her best now for Sally.'

'Don't you ever stop worrying, and feeling responsible? Does the same apply to fathers?'

'Not in my experience! However good your dad was — is — to you. It's women who keep families together. Don't your books teach you that?'

'I know, Christmases and birthdays and meals and bringing you up. Sally will carry all that on! I don't think Caro would have wanted to bother with it all . . . '

Her mother looked at her sharply.

'Has she written to you? Is she upset?'

'She'll get over it with her work — she's so talented, you know.'

'Very like her own mother,' said Polly.

'She told me a bit about . . . her mother . . . and what happened to her.'

'I wondered how much you knew.'

'You always knew more about their past than anyone,' Jennie said. 'Even things Mrs Fitzpatrick and Lady Page didn't know about each other?'

'Miss Ruth only ever had eyes for Sir Jack. I don't think she ever realized how much that other man wanted her. She was only about eighteen when he fell for her, during her first season in the summer of 1926. I was asked by her grandmother to act as a kind of chaperone and I saw the way he looked at her. She was young for her age, not much more than a schoolgirl, but she'd already made up her mind for Sir Jack! It took Sir Jack a bit of time to realize — things were difficult at Pettiwell, I suppose, with the money and all. Once it was plain to Mr Edward Cozens that Miss Ruth wasn't interested in him, he realized it was hopeless, and as soon as he could, he made a beeline for Miss Clare. He knew *she* was potty about him, and I think he just wanted to punish someone.

'She'd been sweet on him as soon as she clapped eyes on him. I don't know when he told her it was really her sister he'd loved, I suppose much later, after he'd got what he wanted from her. That was cruel. It wasn't Miss Ruth's fault. Nothing to do with her at all, but Miss Clare must have taken it badly. She was only human and her sister was going to get Sir Jack and be happy ever after, even if the engagement was a long one. And the man *she* loved didn't want her!'

Jennie was surprised to hear all this and to perceive what a realist her mother was. Polly

Hicks would have been furious with her own daughter if she'd behaved in that way. She thought: the upper classes don't have a monopoly over falling in love . . . and how strange it was that just as Clare's beloved had preferred her sister Ruth, Caro's had preferred Sally. They had both had to deal with jealousy.

'Was Caro's mother with . . . Mr Cozens for long, then?'

'I think it lasted about a year; she was in Paris some of the time. Miss Ruth only heard about it later and jumped to the wrong conclusion — that it had been he who'd got her sister into trouble. I knew it wasn't! Miss Clare came back after he dropped her and I knew it was over. I knew for certain that they'd parted before Christmas, and she went back to Paris in the New Year of 1928, to that 'Boze Arts' place — to get over him, so I never believed he was the baby's father. Mr Cozens had begun going out with someone else — that lady we saw on Sunday — and she knew. I think she must have got to know that other fellow through him, though.

'I never saw the baby's father at all, not once. It all happened in France, what they call 'on the rebound', but I had the feeling from something she once said that he was English and that he'd been a friend of Mr

425

Cozens. She was very unlucky. Whoever it was, abandoned her as soon as she told him what was going to happen. With all his faults I don't believe Mr Cozens would have done that. When she came back again next summer it was obvious she was expecting.'

Jennie was thinking, I wonder if Caro's mother ever thought of not having the baby? It was perhaps a shocking thing to come into her head but Clare Ogilvie had never given her the impression of being a very maternal woman. I wouldn't have blamed her, she thought. There were people now who wanted to make abortion legal so that women would not have to have babies if they didn't want them, but she couldn't believe the law would ever be changed. And then there wouldn't have been a Caroline!

Her mother having now begun was unstoppable. She must have wanted to discuss all this with another woman for a long time and there was nobody left to whom she could mention it. Jennie felt flattered that her mother now thought she was old enough to know such things.

'All my dear Mrs Ogilvie said was, 'At least she came home to have her wean!' She sometimes talked Scotch. Our Young Ogilvies were still out in India, so it was her grandmother, my mistress, Mrs Christina,

426

who came to her aid with money, as well as — what do you call it — moral support? You'd think that an old lady like that would be shocked and upset. I suppose she was, but she arranged for Miss Clare to stay with a friend of hers in Scotland and I was sworn to secrecy. I went up there and helped her. Miss Ruth knew what was going on but was spared the details.

'Anyway, at the time her sister came home pregnant Miss Ruth wasn't thinking about anything but Sir Jack. She must have jumped to the conclusion that Edward Cozens was the father of the baby and had deserted her sister. She didn't know all that much about Miss Clare's life. The sisters never spoke to each other about it even later — I'd have known if they had — but it wasn't my place to tell either of them about the other, and Miss Clare would never say who the father was. She should have told her sister who it was *not*, but I think she was too hurt to confess — they were never very close.

'Miss Ruth could have asked *me* if Mr Edward Cozens was the father — *I* knew he wasn't — but she didn't want to talk about it. I think she was shocked, and perhaps she thought that Sir Jack would not want to marry a young lady whose sister had 'fallen'. Miss Ruth wasn't the sort, though, to cast a stone at her sister. She and Sir Jack had such a long engagement — at one time his father thought of selling up here — they didn't marry till 1930. Miss Clare had determined to go back to Paris, and finish her studies — and she knew it would make it easier for the family if she went on living in France.'

'Who exactly did Mr Cozens marry?'

'The Honourable Janet Buck — daughter of some viscount or other. I saw it in a society magazine left lying around here. Their son was born in 1930 — same year as you. Nadine is Sally's age but Lily wasn't born till 1935. I always take note of dates.'

'So Clare Fitzpatrick knew all about Edward Cozens having once wanted her sister, which Lady Page had more or less forgotten, and Lady Page for years thought that the son of her husband's neighbours was Caroline's father!'

'Yes, she'd never visited here except to see Sir Jack and his family — she'd only met Ted Cozens in London.'

'It must have been a shock when she got married to find his parents living in this village if she thought he was the father of her sister's baby!'

'She'd fear a worse shock for her sister when she came over in the war — but Miss Clare never mentioned the Cozens family.

Why should she? She knew Ted had married and lived in London. It was only the war that brought Caro's mother and father back.'

Jennie forbore to contradict her mother. Francis had said Clare was restless and wanted to return to London. She wouldn't have minded if she had come across her old flame there. Like her sister she didn't connect him with Pettiwell. Not that it would have mattered.

'Sir Jack and our Lady Page — Miss Ruth — were always good to the Fitzpatricks, even giving them space in the war as you well know. Of course he paid for it, and our family did need the money.'

So really it was Francis Fitzpatrick's money that had paid some of her parents' wages, thought Jennie.

'I used to wonder how much Miss Clare had told her husband,' her mother added.

'Did the Young Ogilvies, as you call them, know about their daughter's baby being born out of wedlock?'

'They were told, but they wouldn't have had any idea that the father *might* have been the Cozens's son. They didn't come back to England till Miss Ruth's marriage, and when they saw Caro for the first time her mother was already with Mr Fitzpatrick in Paris. The little tot was about two or three years old. I don't believe Miss Clare ever told *anyone* who the father was, even Mr Fitzgerald. We were all right pleased when she got married! Her mother and father chose to believe Caroline was Mr Fitzpatrick's child.'

'Was Lady Page worried when Sally met the Cozens's granddaughter Nadine?'

'No, it was when Caroline met their grandson! — you can imagine she'd worry then! She was scared stiff that Caroline had fallen in love with her own brother!'

'Well, only half-brother — but I see what you mean.'

Polly sighed. 'I don't think young Mr Cozens — Mr Rob — would have been right for her even if he'd wanted to marry her. Caroline is a bit like her mother, not ordinary, and he's an ordinary sort, even with his handsome looks. Mind you, I don't think he'd realized what she felt about him; they hadn't known each other very long from what you say but it doesn't take long for a young girl to fall in love! I could see she thought he was wonderful that first time he came here. I was surprised; I'd always thought her a bit cold-hearted. But it's all turned out for the best.'

'Yes, I suppose so, though it seems a pity.'

Love hardly ever struck in a sensible way, and it would be a pity to miss the experience, however madly it made you act. She didn't say this to Polly. What had it to do with marriage? Very little.

'Do you expect Mr Edward Cozens knows whose daughter Caro is?'

'No, why should he? He's probably forgotten all about his own fling with Miss Clare by now! I expect he may be pleased his son's marrying the daughter of the woman he once really wanted! Folk remember the one they loved that they didn't get, more than the one they had a fling with however long it lasted!'

'So *you* don't know who Caro's father was?'

'No, and I don't care. I hope her mother has told her by now.'

'Yes, she has. She knows who it was, but he died in the war.'

'Poor Caroline!' said her mother. 'And now it's Lady Page's own daughter his son's going to marry!'

'I wonder if she thinks Rob is like his father.'

'Miss Clare is the one who could tell that. I hope you're not thinking of telling Sally any of this?'

'No, there's no need for anyone to tell her all this past history.'

'All water under the bridge now,' said Polly

comfortably. 'Do you think Caroline and her mother will want to come to the wedding?'

'I don't know. Caro would come, I think. Perhaps her mother won't want to.'

'I wonder what Rob's father thought of his old flame Lady Page after all these years,' mused Polly. 'He'll be pleased it's gone right in the next generation.'

Jennie was wondering if Caro's mother would want, at her niece's wedding, to see the lover who had let her down so long ago.

'Lady Page likes young Rob,' said her mother.

'Well, he's very likeable. I expect even Mrs Fitzpatrick would like him, though he's not her type.' Or mine, she thought. 'And his father is very rich!' she added.

'Yes,' said Polly primly. 'There is that.'

15

1955

In February of the year 1955 Caroline Fitzgerald, now living in a tiny *chambre de bonne* at the top of an old house in the Avenue de Clichy, wrote to Sally Page offering to design her wedding dress. Caro had thought long and hard about this idea. Maybe Aunt Ruth would not want her to. Well, if that were the case, Sally need only decline.

It would be a fine chance for her to put the seal on the Ted Cozens — Clare-and-Ruth Ogilvie relationship, and her own past feelings for Rob, for good and all, and at the same time show the assembled family what she could do. Rob and she had not yet met again, but if Sally accepted her offer they might. The discussion of all the detail involved in designing and making a dress would prevent any embarrassment. She would need to do only two intermediate fittings as she was by now very skilled, and she could either stay in London with her mother, which would please Clare, or Sally could come over to Paris. She knew there was an old cutting workroom at Dorinel's which employees and pupils could borrow for a small payment. The final fitting and any small alterations could be done at Pettiwell.

Sally, delighted, wrote and thanked her profusely.

'Mother is going round the bend with plans. We do want to marry in July and she thought we'd have to buy a dress since her old dressmaker has died, and really nice wedding dresses are *so* expensive. You are clever and I know you could make just what I need!'

They would confer together on the style.

Ruth really was, as she said herself, 'in a tizzy'. *Only* six months to prepare everything. Should they have caterers? Who would do the flowers, the photographs, and the cake? Whom should they invite? How should the invitation be worded?

Jack said: 'Let's give 'em a wonderful send off — have everybody we know. We only have one daughter!'

Polly Wilson drew her own conclusion at this remark, which meant that Sir Jack intended Pettiwell to go out in a blaze of glory. She had offered to bake and decorate the cake herself. Outside caterers could do the canapés. They surely were not going to

434

give a full wedding breakfast?

Yes, said Sir Jack, they were. The service was in the early afternoon so they could all sit down at five o' clock for a good old-fashioned meal, he supposed. Then, to crown it all, Polly's cake and the best champagne. His wife tried to dissuade him about the repast, as he had begun to call it, but he stood firm.

He added: 'In the marquee, on the lawn in front of the house.' Even if he had to sell the rest of the old silver to pay for the whole bang shoot, he decided privately. In all it might run to several thousand pounds.

★   ★   ★

The village church was already booked for the wedding ceremony. Lily had been asked if she would sing a solo, and had agreed. All these decisions and preparations were reported by her mother to Jennie in Paris. Jennie privately thought it rather a waste of money even if the setting could not be more romantic. At least they would save on the dress! Caroline had insisted on Sally paying only for the materials, not the design and sewing. Lily too would give her services free.

Jennie wondered what she could do for them herself. There was nothing that came to mind. She was no good at sewing, no good at baking, no good at singing . . .

Caroline told her she wanted to convey 'essence of Sally' and at the same time make a statement of style. Not an extreme one of course, but it must not be out of fashion in the sense of the wrong kind of 'old-fashioned'. The bride was slim and of medium height and would not be hard to sew for, or clothe in a wedding dress, except that her tastes ran to the fairly plain and functional.

Caro did not doubt her own powers of persuasion. They would come to a compromise. Sally did not favour frills and furbelows but *had* set her heart on cream satin. This, Caro knew, she could persuade her to change, for she had her own ideas about material and style, realized she'd have to curb a little of the 'fashionable chic', and anyway would never use Sally as an experiment. Lily would be a different matter if *she* ever had this kind of wedding!

'I don't like what's in fashion at present in England,' she told Jennie over a drink in a café near the Place de la Concorde, half-way between their respective present living-quarters. She wanted something simple, perfectly cut, and neither severe nor too romantic. She saw soft silk rather than stiff satin, silk which, with the addition of a little detachable gold-and-white brocade bolero would be perfect for an English summer day.

'A touch of Regency — Jane Austen period simplicity,' suggested Jennie.

'Exactly! With also a soupçon of the flowing line of an ancient Greek statue!' Caro sounded as if she were being carried away on wings of inspiration but Jennie knew she could actually produce what she envisaged.

'No heart-shaped necklines, no full skirt and definitely no tiara,' Caro went on. 'Shoes with tiny medium heels; to have them flat — as they would have been in *Pride and Prejudice* would be taking it too far!'

The jewellery must be tiny but genuine.

Hair in a gathered up in a cloud behind a band of silk. Sally's hair was curly in any case and looked good.

'General effect — artful naturalness,' suggested Jennie.

'You've got it! Thank you Jen. You've been very helpful!'

Caroline wrote all her ideas out for Sally, adding: *Skirt not too narrow — it must be comfortable*. Sally would approve of that. The bridesmaids, the two little girls, could perhaps be in pale yellow, she thought, with buttercup headbands.

She drew and drew and pored over old fashion plates. She decided she'd embroider a tiny CC in blue under the back of the hem for luck.

Clare discovered the single Ogilvie diamond on its slender chain that had belonged to Christina Ogilvie and offered to lend it to her niece, who had as much right to wear it as anyone.

* * *

Over the next few weeks Jennie found herself wondering about Caroline's motives for making this dress for Sally. As in most things they were probably mixed. She could understand that it would be seen as a kind, even noble, thing to do. She thought that Sally, being a kind woman, would see it as a peace offering. Possibly Rob might be a little embarrassed when he thought of his past friendship, if that was what it had been, with Caro, but he would not see anything symbolic in a dress, clothes being the responsibility of women and nothing to make a fuss about. Ruth Page, her mind full of chores and problems and the usual nervous strain that seemed the inevitable accompaniment to weddings, would be relieved.

Clare Fitzgerald would be more sceptical, would realize that this was her daughter's way of showing the way she wished to be seen, perhaps as cousin of the bride and old friend of the groom, but certainly also as an accomplished professional.

Did Caro herself realize her own reasons? Probably. Lily had shown solidarity too by agreeing to sing for Sally, but Jennie would wager that she had asked her sister's opinion first!

★ ★ ★

Jennie agreed to accept an invitation from Caro's father for dinner on the boulevard one night in early June.

'Caro is coming along too,' he had tactfully written. Jennie knew she had to see him sometime but it was odd seeing him and Caro together, when the last time had been so traumatic. Nothing was said about that, and nothing untoward happened. Caro had obviously decided to go on regarding Mr Fitz as her 'pa', and Jennie was relieved. All three had been very busy recently and so they talked about their work. Caro said they must wait and see the dress. She would say nothing more about how it was getting on. They would all be able to judge soon enough.

★ ★ ★

There had been weeks of travail, weeks of Ruth biting her nails and Polly advising and soothing, weeks of Caro's free time from work spent first measuring Sally, then making and cutting the toiles, adjusting them, pinning them, cutting the silk, hand-sewing, pinning, and fitting. Finally at the end of June whist Jennie was finishing marking the last term *devoirs* in Paris, and Lily was enjoying her summer term at the college, Caroline was fitting the completed confection in Pettiwell two weeks before what Jennie had named W-day.

All of them would be joining the rest of the guests at the church on Saturday afternoon, 16 July.

★　★　★

Jennie and her parents were sitting at the front of the village church on the left-hand side. If she turned her head slightly she could see most of the various guests arriving, and she registered the several partners who were sitting so respectably in their pews. Simply everyone was here: Edward Cozens and his wife the Hon Janet, a big-boned woman, on the groom's side; Francis Fitzpatrick, who, Jennie admitted to herself, did look extraordinarily distinguished — on the second row

440

with his wife and Lily, Lily sitting at the end since she was going to sing during the service; Caro not there yet because she was putting the finishing touches to the dress before Sally swept down the aisle. Sir Jack would come in a minute with his daughter on his arm. Ruth was already in her pew and did look exhausted.

So many people once connected, though not all of them knew it, thought Polly Wilson, wearing her best navy blue silk dress and a straw hat.

All those past conflicts, thought Jennie: Clare and her sister Ruth; Clare and Edward; more recently Clare and Francis; Clare and Caro; Caro and Francis and herself; Sally and Caro, never mind Caro and Rob. Clare looked wonderful and extremely fashionable, wearing a large and splendid hat and a well-cut grosgrain suit of dove grey. Jennie was impressed; her daughter had clearly advised Clare on her outfit. Lily was in a sort of canary-yellow dress and duster coat, which would draw attention to her when she sang.

Lily and Sir Jack would be the only ones not intricately involved, thought Jennie. She had noticed before when she had been introduced to Sally's future in-laws that Ted Cozens still had eyes for Ruth. Had he yet spoken to Clare? If not, it would be interesting to see what, if anything, happened when he did.

The bridesmaids were to be two little pupils of Sally, who had wisely elected not to have grown-up ones. She could hardly have asked her cousin Caroline.

The organ music pealed louder and Sally would soon be in the church. Caro, wearing a hat of trailing feathers and a silk slubbed suit of dark crimson, slipped into the pew next to her mother, tall and elegant and poised.

A moment afterwards the bridal chorus from *Lohengrin* pealed out on the organ and there she was!

In with Wagner, out with Mendelssohn, thought Jennie, having been told that the traditional marches would be played to please the traditionally minded. Lily was to sing something fairly popular too. It was unusual enough to have a soloist at a rural wedding.

All through the service, thoughts of the hidden web of the past, of the long-ago private lives of these adults flitted in and out of Jennie's head. Was she the only one to have them? Uncovering adult secrets was like hearing about the dangers that you had just escaped in the war, dangers which as a child you knew hardly anything, or even nothing, about. Jennie thought how many emotions would be swirling around. She hoped there was no unfinished business that might mar Sally's day. Francis, she prayed, would not say anything injudicious to her parents. It would not be a good thing if her usually knowledgeable mother ever knew who had been — or might have been — in love with her own daughter. Would other old buried feelings resurface too? Her own possessive feelings as a child for little Sally, now the radiant bride, her old conviction that Caro was the interloper, the outsider, who had both fascinated and annoyed her. Did Caro remember that? Did Sally remember the blood sisters' pact?

What silly matters to recall at a wedding! She could not help wondering what secrets might lie in the future. One day, would she criticize her own and her friends' present actions? Would her future change the truth of the present? As time went on, would she question the reasons for the decisions people made today when it all lay in the past?

These were not suitable thoughts for a wedding day, she thought, and turned her introspection to observation as Sally came in on Sir Jack's arm. There was a susurration in the church at her arrival, not quite a gasp, but more than the usual stir that always takes place when the bride enters. Those at the back were thinking that Sally looked quite extraordinarily pretty, and some of them had already realized that the dress was out of this world. Jennie craned her neck to see Caro's creation but had to be content for the moment with a view of the back. Whether Sally had been wearing a veil and was about to lift it Jennie could not discern.

She concentrated on following this service for the solemnization of matrimony from the old prayer book they all had before them on the ledge of their pews. She loved its deep rich language, the kind the chapel did not go in for, but a language she had first encountered at the village school from the erstwhile curate of this church. She remembered he had later been called up as an army parson and had become a prisoner of war. He it was who had adjured the children to 'renounce the pomp and vanity of this wicked world.' Jennie felt she could still go along with that, but the sinful lusts of the flesh were more complicated. She wondered what Rob Cozens, now standing by her old playmate Sally, and whose tall back she could see in morning dress — would be like as a lover. You could not help thinking about such things on such a day, but she felt a little guilty, so she bent her head once again to the prayer book.

Well, the banns had been called, so that was all right, and the rector was now talking

444

about the enterprise in hand which should be undertaken 'reverently, discreetly, advisedly and soberly'. He outlined the three reasons for Christian marriage — the procreation of children, as a remedy against sin — to avoid fornication — then, more cheerfully, for 'the mutual society, help, and comfort, that the one ought to have of the other both in prosperity and adversity'. The 'Jane Eyre' clause having been disposed of with no objection from Caro, whom Jennie could see clearly now on the right in front of her, they proceeded to the rector's intoning his questions to the bridegroom and then to his bride, questions almost everyone there would know by heart: would they keep themselves only unto each other as long as they lived?

Jennie was wondering if Clare and her husband had got married in church. Being Anglo-Irish, Francis would not be a Catholic, so the service would have been the same as this one. How did you say 'forsaking all other' in French?

Rob's 'I will' sounded firm and hearty and Sally's just audible.

Then it was up to Sir Jack to 'give this woman to this man', Robert Edward, to Sarah Charlotte, to be wedded husband and wife, 'for richer for poorer, in sickness and in health, to love and to cherish, till death us do part,' repeated by groom then bride. Only the bride promised to 'obey'. Jennie had always cavilled at this but Sally repeated it now in a calm, clear voice. Rob then gave her the ring.

Jennie read on, fascinated, noting that the ring was given 'upon the book' and that the 'accustomed duty' had used to be given to the priest at the same time. She wondered how much it had cost to get wed in this very church 300 years ago. Or would that have been under Cromwell in 1655?

'With all my worldly goods I thee endow,' pronounced Rob. Well, there would be plenty, thought Jennie irreverently.

The rector prayed for them both and then, 'that those whom God hath joined together let no man put asunder', and the two were finally pronounced man and wife.

It was never a very long service but what a punch it packed. How could anyone marry in this way without believing it all and meaning it all?

The part of the service that most people had been looking forward to followed a psalm, various further prayers and a reading. No celebration of Holy Communion. It did draw out the service and Jennie guessed Sally would celebrate it soon after her wedding. Perhaps Rob was not a communicant?

Everyone seemed to know to sit down to

hear a few words from the rector, which amounted to no more than his having known Sally for years and knowing what a happy day it was for her and for them all, what a lucky man Rob was, and how happy it made him to see so many parishioners and friends here today. Then the bridal pair and the witnesses — Sir Jack and the Hon Janet — went out to the vestry for the signing, and then the noticeable Lily in her triumphant yellow went up to the front, stood composedly before the congregation, who had remained seated in anticipation and, after a short introduction from the organ, launched into Handel's 'Where'er you walk'. She had wanted to sing 'Let the bright Seraphim', but unfortunately it needed a trumpet.

Caro had suggested something more in the folklore tradition, and Jennie something from Purcell or Blow, but Sally herself had said she didn't mind, Lily must please choose something she enjoyed singing, she would leave it to her.

Lily's powerful young voice rang out now, and soared superbly up to the ancient timbers. The congregation — you might now call it an audience — drew in its collective breath. Goodness, thought Jennie, she is meant for the stage of Covent Garden. She would have sung the seraphim song wonderfully!

There was a hush after Lily finished, people perhaps wondering if they should clap, but just as she sat down the party came back in from the vestry. The choir stood up to sing the favourite wedding hymn, 'Love Divine, all love excelling', sounding so different from Lily. But then the organ pealed out to strains even louder than Lily's and, to Mendelssohn's Wedding March, Sally and Rob, arm in arm, came slowly down the aisle.

Now she could see the dress, and Jennie saw that it was indeed stunning: simple, flowing, dazzling, in white and gold, silk and brocade. Classical, she thought, but also Romantic. Caro had designed and made it *all by herself*. She'd told Jennie that, in spite of the circumstances, she was not being noble but believed the dress would bring her luck.

The little bridesmaids, now seen for the first time by most people, did not need to worry about the train for it was short, sweeping high from the back to only just below the waist, with the now unnecessary veil lying lightly over it. What a clever woman Caro was!

Sally's face was shining, smiling, hair in a halo of dark curls with the gold band of flowers lifting the cloud back from her face.

Soon would be the time to observe everyone else, thought Jennie, as they made their way very slowly out of the church, through the churchyard and down the path. Would it be a time of reckoning, or would the religious mood carry them all on a wave of glory through the lych-gate and on to the road that led from the church at the edge of the village to Pettiwell House and its sweeping lawn. Some people were being taken by car, including Polly, who squeezed her daughter's hand.

'Grand!' she said, and Jennie knew she meant the dress. Her mother and father were off to help with the final arrangements for the wedding cake and the flowers. Jennie waited her turn to congratulate Sally and Rob and then walked back to the house with several other young guests. The close family was still in the porch or in front of the church, about to be photographed.

★　★　★

As she arrived on the lawn, hoping soon to find Caro there, Jennie found one group of guests already milling round the lawn and waiters coming out of the marquee with trays of glasses, circulating the champagne. She knew that more photographs were to be taken in the gardens and, on the lawn, one of all the massed guests. Her father had been up since dawn tidying and preparing it all. The tables inside the marquee were already heavy with his flowers, and some from the town florists, in crystal vases.

The afternoon sun was bright, but it was pleasantly warm, not hot. Caro suddenly appeared from the direction of the church holding the hands of the little bridesmaids, so her part in the photograph in the church porch must have been completed. The little girls skipped off to rejoin their fond parents, then Francis appeared with Clare, and went up to Caro. He gave her a big hug.

'It was magnificent,' he said. 'I have never seen such a beautiful dress! It will adorn your first catalogue one day because it is timeless!'

Clare kissed her daughter too and then Lily arrived and Jennie thought she had never seen their mother look so proud of her children. Maybe she had not wanted to come to a place where she would be forced to meet Edward Cozens and his wife, but her own daughters' triumph, with her own husband loyally accompanying her, as if they had never been separated, had clearly raised her spirits.

Would Edward Cozens recognize her? Jennie could not wait to see, but castigated herself for her old habit of eavesdropping. It would be all right for her to go up to the family now, so, as soon as she had been given a glass she walked towards them.

'Caro,' she said, and continued in French — somehow it seemed appropriate, '*La robe était si belle que je ne trouve pas de paroles pour te le dire!*' She added in English, 'What your father said — it's *timeless*!' and toasted her in champagne.

Caroline laughed and did a cheeky thumbs-up gesture. Francis had caught sight of Jennie, came up and kissed her hand. Lily was being congratulated too by various people and took it all in her stride. Must be used to it by now, thought Jennie. Some villagers had been invited and were staring at Lily's yellow dress, and at the hats worn by her mother and sister, as if the clothes belonged to royalty.

'Isn't my big sister clever!' Lily murmured to Jennie. Suddenly Jennie felt she belonged most here with the Fitzpatricks.

'I loved your singing,' she said 'I had no idea . . .'

Everyone was waiting now for the bride and groom, when even more congratulations of a different kind would follow. The lawn was filling up with scores and scores more guests, most of whom Jennie had never met before. Some of them were obviously relations and friends of the Cozens and Rob.

Then Sally arrived with a beaming Rob.

All Jennie could remember later, when she tried to assemble the rest of the day in her head were snatches of dialogue and little cameos of colourful groups, until, after what seemed hours they all found their places at the table in the marquee.

She met many people, and carried on many disjointed conversations, before she talked to Sir Jack and Ruth, and James who was seventeen now and growing very tall. She was introduced to Rob's parents as 'one of Sally's oldest friends'.

Edward Cozens was as tall as James, but silver-haired and immaculately dressed. She burbled the usual bland comments to him, which he listened to politely, but she found the Hon Janet difficult to engage in any kind of conversation. Then she found herself talking to the old Cozens pair, along with Francis, just as out of the corner of her eye she saw his wife Clare standing next to Ted Cozens with a slight smile on her lips.

Beatrice Cozens was uttering such gems of conversation as: 'Do you remember when dear old Bates was head gardener here?' as if Jennie had been alive when old Bates had died, just before the Great War. Dear me, did she look so old? But Beatrice was short-sighted. She embarked upon a long and complicated story about Sir Jack, whom she had known as a boy.

Francis raised his eyebrows to Jennie and winked at her. Everything was all right; he had known how to lighten the atmosphere between them for good. They could be friends. She did like him. They were the same kind of people, even if she had not the slightest intention of ever betraying his wife, even if the wife might not mind. Then Francis went off to rejoin that wife, and doubtless provide a lifebelt to Clare as she made what looked like polite conversation to the wife of the man who could have been her daughter's father but was not.

Jennie found Rob just as difficult to talk to as his mother. Whatever had Caro found to say to him? She saw his eyes keep returning to his bride. Such an uninteresting man, but he was clearly in love. Nadine bounced up to kiss her brother, then joined another young man with a boyish quiff of hair and trousers slightly too short for him. So many permutations, thought Jennie. She wondered if Nadine had wanted to be a bridesmaid and been cheated of her role.

She did have a proper conversation with

Caro, both of them slightly tipsy with champagne.

'I no longer belong here, I've just realized,' she stated, even as she was enjoying the beauty of the place and the wine and the splendour of it all. It had come to her that her own life was going to be very different; she would never forget Pettiwell, but she had her own way to make now. She would never, like Sally, have such a wedding, in the midst of the kind of people who were milling around now. Her parents belonged to the place in a different way, as FF had once insisted, but she neither belonged in that way nor in the way her friends did. 'Sally really belongs here and I suppose you and Lily could if you wanted . . . '

Caroline understood her meaning, smiled, and replied:

'I never did belong, but I'll tell you a secret: these people will provide my bread and butter!'

Jennie laughed. They too were similar.

Then they all went into the marquee to eat poussin and drink cold Chablis and listen to some — mercifully not too lengthy — speeches. The man with the quiff turned out to be the best man and also the best speaker. He must be a fully fledged barrister. Jennie was placed between Francis and the owner of

454

the stables. Sally must have thought she needed to be instructed about foals and fillies.

It had been a lovely wedding. Everyone said so. Nobody had quarrelled or been embarrassing or had burst into tears. Rob had even gone up to Caro to thank her for the wonderful outfit, and Lily had been given a pearl necklace. The two small bridesmaids were sporting silver bracelets.

Nadine caught the bouquet tossed into the farewell crowd by the bride, now elegant in a pale-pink and grey suit, and the couple went off in Rob's shining car on the first stage of their honeymoon in New England.

Part Four

ENVOI

TOWARDS A BRAVE
NEW WORLD

16

Her marriage begins a new life for Sally Cozens. Caroline Fitzpatrick and Jennie Wilson are also to advance towards new horizons, though for them the direction of their lives is not set out quite so early or so predictably.

After their wedding, Sally and Rob live at Pettiwell for a few months. A small farm of a hundred acres called Hazelmere, a mile from Pettiwell, is bought by his father for Rob to manage but not live in. The Cozens grandparents, however, decide at last to move into a smaller house, and Rob, to whom they have already left Stair Court under a family trust, begins to alter and refurbish it. Both grandparents die not long afterwards in their eighties.

Later the same year, to his family's great sorrow, Sir Jack dies suddenly at the age of sixty-seven. He lives long enough to see his first grandchild, a girl named Nicola Ruth, but is never to see his grandson and namesake, John. Heavy death duties are exacted on Pettiwell, and after much agonizing, Ruth decides to sell it to a syndicate of nursing homes. As soon as this is accomplished the Wilsons are happy to retire to a place of their own, a cottage in Fairfielde, the next village to Pettiwell.

After Nicola and John, Sally and Rob have two other children, Jane in 1961, and Edward in 1963. Sally is a very contented mother and wife. She still rides whenever she can find time from her motherly and housewifely duties, and Nicola is given a share in a pony from an early age. Ruth lives in a granny flat carved out of part of the ground floor of Stair Court, and is happily available to help with the care of Sally's children. She is only fifty-five when the last of her grandchildren is born, but Sally takes care not to ask too much of her. James embarks at eighteen upon business studies, goes in for a time with his brother-in-law the 'gentleman farmer', as agent, but finds he prefers the larger world of management. This surprises his family.

Jennie leaves Paris in 1956, returns to Manchester to finish her doctorate and do some teaching, and in 1959 publishes a biographical fiction, *A Woman of Bohemia*, based upon her thesis. She is very pleased when it is translated into French. She continues to teach at another provincial university and will publish more books.

Caro returns to England only in 1959, fully

trained and experienced, ready to launch herself into the world of fashion. It is not easy to start with. She sketches for Liberty and Jaeger whilst she awaits the chance to begin making and selling her own label, at first in a small way. By now, she and Clare have become closer and have even been on holiday together.

Caro and Jennie, who lead such different lives, have become good friends. Both have been in love 'romantically' in their early twenties, and neither has renounced the opposite sex. There is still much living and loving before them both. They have, as Jennie realized on Sally's wedding day, a lot in common: both like their independence, both have interesting work, and the origins of neither of them fits neatly into conventional English society. Perhaps both are outsiders. Yet society itself is changing, and is to change ever more fundamentally within a few years.

There have already been some changes in less important matters. Many young women want the glamorous job of air-hostess, especially when flights across the Atlantic become more frequent. Nadine Cozens is one with BOAC for a time, but leaves to become a secretary and amanuensis to a technological whiz-kid. She is hopeful of interesting James Page in his projects one day.

It is in about 1959 that many American innovations, such as paper handkerchiefs, begin to arrive from across the Atlantic. Nylon tights arrive a little later, most useful when the miniskirt comes in, stays for some time, disappears, and reappears many times in some form or other. Women's make-up and hairstyles change; eye shadow begins to be used in a big way. Cheap fashion has already begun, by the time of Sally's marriage, to exploit the new teenage market. Before the end of the 1960s, the fashion for eternal youth takes over.

Jennie, who still takes little interest in fashion, does possess a good imagination and loves colour. To her immense surprise, Caro reveals one day that her friend has given her an idea for an outfit. They have been talking about old photographs when Jennie exclaims:

'I love that art deco time, don't you? A dress in eau-de-Nil? Or you could have lime green and orange? With a dark nutty brown . . . '

Caroline looks interested when Jennie goes on dreamily: 'You could adapt those little hats in the oldest albums; I think they were around the mid 1860s.' She speaks also of the long thin skirts their mothers used to wear in the early 1930s.

In answer to this Caroline says:

'We can't get the 1930s back, but I might do a pastiche of some of the hats and skirts one day.'

Of course, longer skirts had been taken up when the New Look arrived in England in about 1947, and they stay on in the fifties, but the time has not yet come round for what Jennie has made her consider.

A few months after this conversation, Caro designs another, quite different garment and presents it to Jennie. It is a lovely little dress in midnight-blue slipper satin with a Peter Pan collar, cap sleeves, a fitted skirt skimming the knees, and a waist that is only just not too small for Jennie, who has never boasted an especially small waist, even though she is thin.

'I'd never be able to afford this!' she cries.

'To say thank you for your ideas,' says Caroline. 'This is a one-off, a present for you!'

Jennie has forgotten all about her art deco and 1860 ideas and cannot believe it when, much later, in 1970, Caro actually uses them.

'Their time has come,' she says.

The Cold War, first mentioned along with the New Look in 1947, has been a habitual part of world furniture for twenty years when in 1967 Caroline Fitzpatrick at last founds her boutique, *Chez Caro*. Her sister Lily is by then launched upon her opera career after a further period of study at the Paris Conservatoire.

By 1969 the *Chez Caro* label is expanding, branches sprouting not only in London but soon afterwards in the provinces on the high street. Her couture clothes are to be much prized also in the States. It is still Caro's dream to found a boutique in Paris where modern English clothes, apart from old names, are not yet exactly popular.

The blue dress Jennie is wearing when she meets her future husband is the very same one Caro had once given her, for she has gone on wearing it for years, until her waist expands to more than its original twenty-four inches.

Christopher Mann, a university lecturer in Latin-American studies marries Jennie in 1968, and their son William is born in 1969. Jennie keeps the blue dress in her wardrobe, sure that one day it will be like the first edition of a brilliant new novel, worth a fortune.

It is partly Caro who eventually persuades Clare to set up house again with Francis in Ireland after he retires from his job in Paris in 1970. He returns to his sketching, and landscape painting, and Clare's memoir of war-work goes into its fourth edition the year

Francis brings out a handsome monograph on Irish painters. Caro stays with them from time to time in the west of Ireland, and practices her photography skills there for relaxation. Lily may also have had something to do with her parents' decision to share their lives once more, after she marries her agent and manager, Paul Percy.

Jennie is busy with babyhood but keeps in touch with them all. The new feminism has just arrived from across the Atlantic. Some of the women, ten years younger than herself, whom she meets with their toddlers, are passionately involved with the women's movement. But I've always been a feminist, thinks Jennie, and does not attach herself to it. Sally thinks it's all a lot of nonsense, but Caro is busy designing dungarees.

★ ★ ★

Jennie is not in love with her past self, but is the sort of person who will always be in love with the past, feeling that something precious is attached to childhood, especially her own. She keeps her remembrance of the glamour Pettiwell exerted on her imagination long ago, and her memories of the house and grounds she once knew so well remain with her. That must have been how Sir Jack had felt about it, she thinks, not wanting to let it go. If in her memory Pettiwell is preserved unchanged, in real time everything has changed utterly, or disappeared.

Occasionally, if she enters a house a little like Pettiwell, or sees a certain picture in a gallery, or a landscape catches her eye as she is carried past it in a train, the original is recalled suddenly and involuntarily.

The past will recede ineluctably further and further from them all; some of their memories might go underground, but will be restored in dreams, where subterranean feelings resurface. Jennie's own struggle to recapture her vivid dreams often makes them evaporate. As powerful as dreams are the feelings evoked by smells: the scent of lavender and beeswax polish, or sweetpeas, the essence of her early years in the mid-twentieth century, stoppered in a glass bottle, like her favourite perfume bought for the first time in Paris. These involuntary memories speak more truly than any conscious attempt to remember. They are an integral part of her, though that 'self' is just a shape you give to the bits of your story you remember. Self-consciousness is perhaps a quality that Jennie's childhood has encouraged.

She still writes to Miguel López from time

to time, and in spite of his busy life, he always replies to her. She tells him that she wants to be lifted up above the here and now, even beyond the idea of time, to feel joined to eternity. She writes:

May I catch hold of time, and make it stop by writing of ancient feelings?

I understand your mystical longings, answers Miguel. *But there is nothing really to be done with the memories of most people. Because she has a certain sort of imagination, your friend Caro makes dresses she hopes will be lasting works of art, but most of us are just carried on in our children. People who have enough imagination may try to write about what their memories mean to them, and weave them into stories, hoping they will last for ever. But will these stories mean anything to others? I suppose you will be one of the people who will try to make them mean something!*

Jennie replies, telling Miguel of her fear of what the passage of time might do to her fleeting vision of truth.

One day, if I read what I have written, shall I come to see my work look more like a

467

mausoleum I have preserved than a beautiful statue?

Even beautiful statues are weathered and altered as the years pass, he replies. Carpe Diem, Jennie, as you often used to say to me! The impetus for writing about other people always comes in part from knowledge of yourself.

His words comfort her. At least Miguel López understands. She will be glad she has known him in his youth, for he is already becoming an influence for good at the United Nations in New York, and yet still finds time to read poetry and listen to music.

After the birth of her son William, Jennie realizes that, for the time being, looking after a child will have to take precedence over everything else. Living has to be more important than recording life. A child's life is now the most important thing in the world for her, and it is good that it is so. Children at least prevent too much introspection, she thinks. Christopher earns enough for a simple life for them both, if not a luxurious one, and Jennie is able to carry on domestic life and part-time teaching as well as her writing, until William goes to school.

As life goes on she discovers that adult human beings are still the people they were when they first became self-conscious in adolescence, or even in early childhood. Polly hears Jennie saying this, and tells her how *young*, at eighty, she still feels herself to be!

Once her son is at school Jennie is even busier. Sally remains a good friend, and will one day tend the Wilson graves in Pettiwell churchyard for her. Jennie and her family have a permanent invitation to stay at Stair Court. If Jennie wishes, she may walk over to Pettiwell House. She prefers not to do this very often, would rather remember it as it was, but she does take William there one day and they walk down the secret lane together.

Sally and Rob will sometimes leave the farm with their manager and take long-haul flights to exotic places, or go sailing or riding. Sally is happy. She has not changed.

Lily is having a brilliant career, singing in opera all over the world, and teaching from a base in Switzerland.

Caroline Fitzpatrick travels all over England and Europe checking up on her retail boutiques. If she goes up to Yorkshire she stays in Leeds with Jennie. Everyone has heard of *Chez Caro* fashions, for they regularly appear in colour supplements and fashion magazines. Caroline is also promoting her new sideline, 'Caro' perfumes, in distinctive pale-turquoise packages, enclosing bottles with her trademark star-shaped stickers.

When she has observed her old friend on one of her visits, Jennie ponders the mystery of character. Who is the real Caro? The child of ten as she was when she first saw her, the puzzled and angry young woman of twenty-six in Paris, or the now famous designer?

How does she see her own parents now? As they were in their forties when she was a child? The middle-aged couple they had been when she was away working in Paris? The old people they had grown into by the time they died?

From the very beginning, she reflects, our bodies and minds and, she dares to hope, our souls, are our own, and different from those of others; yet understanding ourselves is no easier than understanding others.

Nevertheless, does there not still remain something of the child in all of us, that 'dead' child who has apparently ceased to exist?

Her son William will grow up, and she is familiar enough with herself to know that one day she will be nostalgic for his childhood too. Yet, as time moves on, earlier selves may not be lost, only submerged, flowing along the subterranean river that bears with it all our old selves.

We do hope that you have enjoyed reading this large print book.

Did you know that all of our titles are available for purchase?

We publish a wide range of high quality large print books including:
**Romances, Mysteries, Classics
General Fiction
Non Fiction and Westerns**

Special interest titles available in large print are:
**The Little Oxford Dictionary
Music Book
Song Book
Hymn Book
Service Book**

Also available from us courtesy of Oxford University Press:
**Young Readers' Dictionary
(large print edition)
Young Readers' Thesaurus
(large print edition)**

For further information or a free brochure, please contact us at:
**Ulverscroft Large Print Books Ltd.,
The Green, Bradgate Road, Anstey,
Leicester, LE7 7FU, England.
Tel:** (00 44) 0116 236 4325
Fax: (00 44) 0116 234 0205

Other titles published by
The House of Ulverscroft:

THE WAYS OF LOVE

June Barraclough

Without a mother since she was a baby, Mary Settle of Cliff House adores her nursemaid, Jemima Green. The girl leaves Mary when she gets married and it is up to Aunt Clara Demaine to bring up the child in France. When she is eighteen, Mary is attracted to a young Englishman in Biarritz. Eventually she marries, but is it to the wrong man? What happens then is strangely connected to Mary's earliest days.